UNFINISHED BUSINESS

"Diana . . ." was all Kane said, all he had to say, as his hand came up to frame her face. She saw the kiss coming, but rather than pull away, she met him halfway, lips parted.

When he gripped her shoulders and pulled her to him, the pressure of his mouth increased. But there was more than passion in his kiss. There was a gentleness, a tenderness that took away the tension and melted down her fears.

Oh, God, she needed this. She needed his hands pressing the small of her back, needed his mouth roaming over her face. It had been so long. . . .

Slowly, reluctantly, she drew back. "Zack will be home soon."

He nodded. Then he hooked a finger under her chin, forcing her to look at him. Her eyes had turned that smoky, sexy green again, and her cheeks were flushed.

"We're not finished, you know." His thumb brushed against her lower lip. "Not by a long shot."

She knew he was right. She knew it had only just begun. But she was afraid to think where it would end . . . in the arms of a man she did not really know, in a maze of menace where nothing was as it seemed. . . .

SILVER LINING

Christiane Heggan

AN ONYX BOOK

ONYX
Published by the Penguin Group
Penguin Books USA Inc., 375 Hudson Street,
New York, New York 10014, U.S.A.
Penguin Books Ltd, 27 Wrights Lane,
London W8 5TZ, England
Penguin Books Australia Ltd, Ringwood,
Victoria, Australia
Penguin Books Canada Ltd, 10 Alcorn Avenue,
Toronto, Ontario, Canada M4V 3B2
Penguin Books (N.Z.) Ltd, 182–190 Wairau Road,
Auckland 10, New Zealand

Penguin Books Ltd, Registered Offices:
Harmondsworth, Middlesex, England

First published by Onyx, an imprint of Dutton Signet,
a division of Penguin Books USA Inc.

First Printing, May, 1995
10   9   8   7   6   5   4   3   2   1

Printed in the United States of America

PUBLISHER'S NOTE
This is a work of fiction. Names, characters, places, and incidents
either are the product of the author's imagination or are used fictitiously,
and any resemblance to actual persons, living or dead, events, or
locales is entirely coincidental.

BOOKS ARE AVAILABLE AT QUANTITY DISCOUNTS WHEN USED TO PROMOTE
PRODUCTS OR SERVICES. FOR INFORMATION PLEASE WRITE TO PREMIUM
MARKETING DIVISION, PENGUIN BOOKS USA INC., 375 HUDSON STREET, NEW
YORK, NEW YORK 10014.

This book is dedicated to Lavone Broyles,
Trudy Pipkin, and Emily Baldwin—
three incredible women whose
friendship I treasure.

And a special thanks to Meryl Sawyer,
Beth Henderson, Yvonne Harris, and
Catherine Rieger for always
being there for me.

Was I deceived, or did a sable cloud
Turn forth her silver lining on the night?

—John Milton, *Comus*, 1634

Prologue

In her son's empty, dimly lit bedroom, Diana moved quickly. Her skin was damp with perspiration, and her hands shook as she yanked Zack's clothes at random and stuffed them into the suitcase that lay open on the lower bunk bed. There was no time to be tidy or selective. She would take only what she and Zack would need to get by for a few days. The rest she'd buy later.

As she started to open another drawer, her gaze fell on Zack's collection of Jurassic Park puzzles. For an instant, she considered taking them with her, then thought better of it. It would only add to the weight of the suitcase, slow her down. She would buy him a new set later.

A bitter laugh escaped from her lips. Buy a new set later. With what? She had only thirty-eight hundred dollars. Less than four thousand dollars with which to start a new life, buy a new identity, rent a house, furniture . . .

The thought that she would soon become a fugitive filled her with fear and remorse. Yet, she didn't slow down. And she didn't waver.

In the living room the grandfather clock bonged softly. Seven o'clock. In a few minutes the cab she had called to take Zack and her to the airport would be

here. She hoped he wouldn't honk his horn, otherwise
nosy Mrs. Carmichael across the street would see her
leave and wonder where she was going. She might
even call the police.

When the suitcase was full, she zipped it shut, carried it to the foyer, and set it next to a matching carry-
on bag on top of which lay two passports.

Coats. She opened the closet, pulled out a black
woolen cape for herself and a hooded blue anorak for
Zack. She lay them on top of the suitcase, then, clamp-
ing her teeth over her bottom lip, she stood under the
archway that led to the living room and ran through a
mental checklist.

Had she forgotten anything?

She didn't think so. She had packed all the warm
clothing she could fit into the single suitcase. She had
cash—whatever she had been able to lay her hands
on—and passports. The plane tickets were waiting for
her at San Francisco International Airport.

All she had left to do was pick up Zack at Kat's
house and they would be on their way.

As her gaze swept across the room, she let out a
small cry of alarm. On a console by the window, next
to the phone, was the slip of paper where she had
jotted down their flight information: United Air Lines,
flight 90, 10 P.M.; arrive Boston, 6:28 A.M.; transfer to
Northwest Air Lines, 7:15; arrive Montreal 8:30.

Crumpling the paper, she stuffed it inside her pants
pocket. Then, as she started to turn away, the phone
rang, freezing her in place. At the fourth ring, the
answering machine clicked on, and Kane's worried
voice filled the room.

"Diana, where in God's name are you? I've been
trying to track you down for the last hour. Please call
me as soon as you get home." There was a short

pause, then, his voice softer, he added, "I'm worried sick about you."

Diana gripped the back of a chair as tears of anguish pricked her eyes. The thought of betraying the only man she had ever loved brought a chill to her heart. She remembered the short but magic time they had spent together, the unconditional support he had given her, the affection Zack had developed for him almost instantly.

He would understand, she thought, watching the red light on the machine blink on and off. And ultimately, he would forgive her.

Running away wasn't her style. All her life, she had prided herself on being a fighter, a survivor. It was that determination to rise above the odds, to come up fighting no matter what, that had kept her from running away sooner.

But today, fate had dealt her a staggering blow. One that left her no alternative but to run.

A sob caught in her throat, and she stifled it. She could not allow herself the luxury of a single tear. Later perhaps, she would cry. Much later.

A loud knock at the door jolted her out of her grim thoughts. The cab. Thank God. "Coming!"

She threw the two coats over one arm, picked up the carry-on bag, and opened the door. A stocky man stood under the yellow porch light. "I have only one suitcase . . ." she began, pointing behind her.

Another figure stepped out of the shadows and into the light. A man in uniform. *A police uniform.*

Her heart slammed in her chest.

With eyes that had suddenly gone wary, the heavy set man took in the passports in Diana's hand, the coats, the suitcase behind her. Reaching into his pocket, he produced a badge and held it open for her to see. "I'm Sergeant Kosak. Homicide. Are you Diana Wells?"

For a few irrational seconds Diana thought of saying no. Maybe she could make a run for it, drop her bag, the coats, and just run. Then, realizing she wouldn't be able to run far, she sagged against the door, holding it with both hands. "Yes . . ." The word came out sounding more like a strangled groan than an affirmative answer.

Sergeant Kosak slipped the badge back in his pocket. "You're under arrest for the murder of Travis Lindford."

1

San Francisco, October 1993

Standing in the bedroom of her Victorian home on Pacific Heights, Diana Wells clipped the second rhinestone earring to her earlobe and pulled back to study the effect in the full-length mirror inside her closet door.

The Donna Karan ivory, midcalf dress she had chosen for tonight's grand opening of her restaurant had been a good choice after all. Straight and dipping lightly at the waist, it was elegant without being too formal, and was the perfect foil for her dark auburn hair.

She had bought it on impulse as she had passed the window of Sonia's Boutique in Union Square last week. It had cost much more than she had intended to spend, but after trying it on, she hadn't been able to resist it. After all, it wasn't every day that a girl opened her first restaurant.

Her first restaurant. No matter how often she repeated those three words, they still gave her goose bumps. She had done it. After eleven years of hard work and sacrifices, after hundreds of nights spent lying awake wondering if she was just spinning a hopeless fairy tale, her dream of opening her own restaurant had finally come true.

Grinning at her reflection, she turned to check her backside, admiring the dress's smooth, clean line. "You'd better earn your price tag," she warned in a playful tone. "Or you go back in the morning." Then, with a soft chuckle, she picked up a small silk purse from the top of her vanity table and walked out of the room in her brisk stride, humming softly.

The scene that greeted her downstairs was quite different from the one she had just left. Strewn across the yellow carpet was an assortment of toys ranging from motorized trucks and rubber dinosaurs to the latest in electronic games. Paper cutouts of witches, ghosts, and bats swung from various corners of the room, reminding those not in the know that Halloween was only two weeks away.

Her son sat on the floor, his blond head bent over a Star Trek board game. Across from him, Marty, a sociology major who had watched Zack on and off for years, threw her hands up in the air in surrender as he once again overpowered the enemy of the SS *Enterprise.*

Zack, who had always been fiercely competitive, laughed with glee as he pounded a victorious fist through the air. Diana stopped at the bottom of the staircase and watched him for a moment, struck once again at his extraordinary resemblance to his father, Travis Lindford. It hadn't been apparent in the beginning. For the first two or three years of his life, Zack had looked like thousands of other blond, blue-eyed boys. But as he grew older, the baby features had matured, the eyes had seemed to grow bluer, the straw-colored hair a little darker, and the dimple in his chin deeper.

All he had inherited from his natural mother was Nadine's passion for animals and her gentle disposition.

As if to confirm that last observation, he reached into a cookie jar at his side, retrieved two pumpkin-shaped cookies with orange frosting, and handed one to Marty.

Diana smiled and stood watching him for a few seconds more. No matter what experts claimed about the bond that existed between a child and his biological mother, she couldn't have loved him more if he were her own flesh and blood.

"Hello, you two."

At the sound of Diana's voice, Marty, a pretty twenty-year-old Chinese-American with long, black hair and expressive dark eyes, looked up. Her mouth opened in awe. "Oh, Diana! You look fabulous. Like a movie star on her way to a Hollywood premiere. Doesn't she, Zack?"

Eight-year-old Zachary bit the frosted stem off the pumpkin and gave the dress a quick glance. "What's a Hollywood premiere?"

"The first showing of a movie where everyone comes dressed to the nines," Marty explained. "Something like what's happening this evening at your mother's restaurant."

He tilted his head to one side, looking puzzled. "Why would you want to get all dressed up just to go to work?"

Diana came to sit on the sofa. Bending toward him, she pushed a stubborn blond lock from his forehead only to see it fall forward again. "Because tonight is a special evening, and I wanted to look, well ... glamorous."

He gathered his cards and stacked them in their respective compartments. "Moms aren't supposed to look glamorous."

Diana's met Marty's amused gaze. "Oh? What should they look like?"

He shrugged, his handsome face serious. "You know . . . like moms."

Diana laughed. "Thank you, Zack. I'll take that as a compliment. I think."

An image on the television set tuned to Channel 4 caught her attention. "Have they rerun my segment yet?" she asked, referring to her interview with the Channel 4 news team yesterday.

Marty fitted the lid over the Star Trek game. "Not yet. But my mom saw it on the twelve o'clock news and taped it." She flashed Diana another smile. "You were great, Diana. Very natural. And you," she added, leaning toward Zack. "You were so cool, punching away at your Game Boy, like you didn't care if you were there or not."

"That's because that man kept asking me dumb questions."

Diana chuckled, remembering the reporter's insistence that Zack would add a homey touch to the segment. To his disappointment, Zack had barely said two words. "Well, I'm glad you were part of my moment of fame anyway."

He grinned, showing strong white teeth. "Me too. The kids at school say I'm a celebrity now."

As he stood up, she pulled him to her. "Did they also tell you that celebrities are not exempt from doing their homework?"

The blue eyes grew mischievous. "Nope."

"Now you know. Is it done?"

"I'll do it a little later. Marty said she'd help me."

"That's fine, as long as you remember the rule. *You* do the arithmetic, not Marty." She winked at the baby-sitter.

"Okay." Then, turning on the charm, he wrapped one arm around her shoulder. "Afterward, can I stay up and watch *Seinfeld*?"

"No, you may not. Didn't we agree that show was too adult for you?"

He edged around the question. "Billy Cramden's mother lets him watch it."

"Then I'm sure he'll tell you all about it in the morning." Before he could protest, she added, "I'll make a deal with you. You go to bed at nine o'clock as you're supposed to, and on Saturday I'll take you to the pumpkin festival in Half Moon Bay."

His disappointment vanished. "Cool. Can Billy come, too?"

"Sure. But he carries his own pumpkin."

Glancing at her watch, she held back a sigh and stood up. She hated to leave him. Until recently, the catering service she had run from her home had allowed her to adjust her schedule to his. It would be different now. Being the owner of a restaurant was a demanding business and would require more than one sacrifice. At least until she was established.

"I've got to go, darling." She gave him one last hug. "Wish me luck?"

Solemn blue eyes looked up at her. "Good luck, Mom. I hope you make zillions of dollars tonight."

"Me, too," echoed Marty.

Diana picked up the keys to the Cherokee from a clay dish in the shape of a seashell Zack had made for her in kindergarten. "Thanks, guys."

She was halfway to the door when Zack called her. One hand on the knob, she turned around.

"Marty's right." He gave her an impish grin. "You do look like a movie star."

A small knot formed in her throat. "Thank you," she said softly. Then, blowing him a kiss, she closed the door behind her.

Standing in Margaret Lindford's vast penthouse on

the twenty-sixth floor of the Lindford Hotel, Travis Lindford, who had been summoned back from a business trip in Mexico, nervously adjusted the knot in his tie and said a quick prayer.

From the time he was a small child, he had known he occupied a special place in his mother's heart. Over the years, she had tolerated his tantrums, accepted, if not condoned, his lifestyle, and forgiven his weaknesses. Unlike his sister, Francesca, who was five years younger, he had been able to get away with just about anything.

One look at his mother now, however, confirmed what he already knew. His luck had run out. Obviously, something foul had hit the fan, and the bitch of it was, he didn't have the foggiest idea what it was.

Margaret Lindford was on the phone, discussing an AIDS benefit she had been asked to host. As he walked toward her, she gave him a curt nod and motioned for him to sit down.

The lack of eye contact was not a good sign. But he smiled anyway, although his heart wasn't in it. As he waited for her to finish her phone call, he let his gaze drift around the room, admiring once again its understated elegance, the carved moldings she had brought back from England, the green Italian marble fireplace, the ceiling-high Tiffany windows, and the rich green brocade that covered the eighteenth-century sofas and chairs.

Margaret Lindford had supervised the decoration of the penthouse herself more than forty years before, adding her own brand of charm to the three-story apartment that had been Travis's first home. Years later, the Lindfords had bought a nine-acre ranch in Seacliff, one of San Francisco's ritziest ocean-front neighborhoods, but it was this place with all its familiar nooks and crannies that Travis called home.

It was a mild October evening, and Margaret sat in a wing chair beside an open French window that led to a stone balcony. Behind her the spectacular view of San Francisco Bay was wrapped in a blue-gray mist as dusk moved in slowly over the city.

At sixty-eight, she was still the same elegant, alluring woman she had been all her life. Her short, ebony black hair had long since turned white, and time had etched dozens of fine lines around her eyes and mouth; but her blue eyes were as clear and compelling as ever, and her mind as sharp as a finely edged blade. Not even the heart attack she had suffered after her husband's death two years before had lessened her sharpness or her keen sense of observation.

At last, she was finished with her call and hung up. Taking his cue, Travis flashed her a smile, stood up, and bent down to kiss her lightly blushed cheek. "How are you, Mother?"

"I've had better days."

No one had ever accused Margaret of not coming to the point quickly. Travis braced himself. "What happened?"

"Mrs. Barclay's ruby necklace was stolen yesterday— moments after she checked into the presidential suite."

"Damn." Evelyn Barclay, of Barclay Pharmaceuticals, was the second wealthiest woman in America, and one of the Lindfords' most valued customers. Unfortunately, whenever she traveled, a fortune in jewels traveled with her as well, a habit that sent shudders of anxiety up and down the spines of hotel managers all over the world. "Did you call the police?"

"Of course I called the police. For the better part of yesterday, this hotel was crawling with nothing *but* police. I don't need to tell you how much our guests appreciated that."

"Do they have any clues? Are they investigating?"

"The necklace was recovered this morning in Chinatown." As Margaret turned to look at him, Travis was hit with the full force of her cold, blue gaze. "One of our maids was caught trying to sell it to a jeweler there."

His mouth went dry.

"Would you hazard a guess as to *which* maid?"

Travis, who had already guessed, remained silent.

"It was a Polynesian girl by the name of Suzannah—a girl *you* hired, Travis, without checking with Regis, who's head of personnel, or with me, even though you know I like to be kept informed of every change in staff."

"I'm sorry. I just thought—"

Margaret raised an imperious hand. "You *never* think, Travis. That's always been your problem. And mine, too, I suppose, for allowing you to get that way. But this time, you went too far. Not only did you hire that girl for reasons I'd rather not discuss right now, but you also never bothered to check her references."

"She told me she had worked at the Hyatt—"

"She lied. Her only claim to fame is a series of arrests ranging from solicitation to burglary. Have you any idea what this sort of publicity will do for the hotel?"

"But the necklace was recovered!"

She gave him a scathing look. "But the loss of our clients' faith will never be recovered. We've already received more than a dozen cancellations."

"I'll schedule a press conference right away. I'll explain that the incident was an isolated case and will never happen again. And of course, I'll talk to Mrs. Barclay—"

Margaret's icy voice stopped him. "Don't bother. Francesca has already taken care of the press. She also contacted our advertising agency and made an appointment for you first thing tomorrow morning. I want to start an aggressive ad campaign in all the major publications, local newspapers, magazines, television, and radio. You'll have to come up with a hook, something we can offer our customers to draw them back. A special holiday package perhaps."

He held back a sigh of relief. He had expected a lot more than a slap on the wrist and a few instructions. "Of course."

"As for Mrs. Barclay, she left early this morning and swore she'd never come back. Pursuing her at this time would only irritate her more. So don't try it."

"Very well." He waited a beat, then took his mother's hand. "That must have been a harrowing experience for you," he said, his tone warm and regretful. "I wish I could have been here."

"But you weren't here, were you, Travis? In fact, you never seem to be around when we have a crisis, even though you *are* the general manager of this hotel."

"Mother, that's not fair. I was in Puerto Vallarta, making sure the construction of our new hotel was on schedule."

"Oh, stop it. I talked to my friend Carlotta earlier. She told me you and her son have been having a grand time partying and sampling the tequila night after night. How can you expect to conduct business with a hangover every morning?"

Denying the accusation would have been futile. His father had once claimed that Margaret's network of spies throughout the world was better than that of the C.I.A. It had been a mild exaggeration and had made for pleasant dinner conversation. But there was more truth in that remark than he had realized. "I'm sorry, Mother."

Margaret leaned back in her chair and surveyed her

handsome son. With his ash blond hair and pencil-thin mustache, he looked more like Charles every day. Only his eyes, iris blue like hers, identified him as a Benson.

She disliked arguing with Travis. He was her first born, the son on whom she had placed all her hopes, built all her dreams. He was also the one who had disappointed her the most.

When she had begun to realize his shortcomings, she had blamed them on the impetuousness of youth and told herself he would change. He never had. Yet, she had continued to be his strongest supporter, bailing him out of trouble time and time again, ignoring her husband's repeated warnings.

"You're making it too easy for him," Charles had told her often. "Let the kid fend for himself once in a while. It won't kill him."

She hadn't listened, and when Charles had died, Travis had been no more ready to take over his father's duties as chairman of the Lindford Hotel than he had been ten years earlier.

Unwilling to appoint her daughter as Charles's successor, even though she was a very capable young woman, Margaret had stepped into the position herself and named Travis co-chairman, hoping the gesture would inspire him to try harder. It had, to a certain degree—but not enough to make a notable difference.

Until now, his lack of total commitment hadn't mattered all that much. Thanks to Conrad, Travis's unflappable assistant, and Francesca, who was superb as director of sales and marketing, and of course, herself, the Lindford ran smoothly and was still considered one of the world's leading hotels.

But she felt the time had come for her to step down. As much as she hated to admit it, the many duties and daily responsibilities were beginning to weigh heavily on her shoulders. She yearned to spend more time at the ranch, puttering around her garden and playing bridge with her friends—although these days, most of them were too busy with their grandchildren to have much time on their hands.

Grandchildren. That, too, had become a sore subject. The mere thought of tiny feet echoing through this huge apartment made her tired old heart ache with longing. How different her life would be if she had a young child around again, someone to care for, to love, to pass on the Lindford dynasty . . .

For a while she had thought her daughter would fulfill that dream. But although Francesca and Randall had tried very hard to have a baby, she had been unable to get pregnant.

As for Travis, children were the last thing on his mind. He was having too much fun chasing women and jet-setting around the globe to worry about something as mundane as starting a family.

Well, she had ran out of patience. Favorite son or not, this nonsense had to stop. "I'm afraid being sorry isn't enough anymore, Travis," she said at last. "You're going to have to make a few changes."

Travis gave her a startled look. "Changes?"

"Yes. I'm tired of this irresponsible behavior of yours. I thought that by making you co-chairman when your father died, you would have realized the importance of taking on new responsibilities. I was wrong. Instead of learning from your mistakes, you keep making new ones. Two years ago it was the firing of our chief of security; six months later, there was the fiasco with that English earl; and now you've taken to hiring maids who moonlight as cat burglars. What will it be next time, Travis? I shudder at the possibilities."

He gave a firm shake of his head. "I swear it will never happen again."

"Exactly. Because *I* won't allow it to happen again." She paused, then in a calm voice, added, "As much as it pains me to say this, if things don't improve, I'll have no choice but to give my shares of the hotel to your sister."

Cold panic filled him. "Francesca? Chairman of the board? You can't be serious."

"Oh, but I am. The only reason I never considered it before was because I was reluctant to take away your birthright. Traditionally, the Lindford has always been passed from one Lindford male to the next. But traditions can change."

"You can't do that, Mother. You know how much the hotel means to me."

"Then show it."

"How?" he asked anxiously. "Just tell me what you want, and I'll do it. I'll give up my ski vacation. I'll put in more hours. I'll circulate more, be more visible . . ."

Margaret smiled. "I'm afraid that won't quite do it, dear."

"Then what?"

"I want you to start acting your age. And I want you to stop hopping from one bed to another. In other words . . ." She held his gaze. "I want you to settle down and get married."

2

A bomb exploding on Travis's lap couldn't have had a greater impact. Letting go of his mother's hand, he fell back against his chair. "You want me to do what?"

"You heard me. I want you to get married. Not to just anyone, mind you, but to someone I will approve of. Someone of whom I can be proud." She paused and leveled him with a cool gaze. "And after you're married, I want you to give me an heir."

This time, Travis turned pale. "An heir? You mean . . . you want me to have a *child*?"

"The request shouldn't come as a surprise, should it, Travis? Lord knows I have hinted often enough about wanting a grandchild, someone to carry on the Lindford name."

"Then why aren't you having this conversation with Francesca? She's already married."

"We're not talking about Francesca. We're talking about you. You are thirty-six years old, Travis. Don't you think it's high time you did something with your life other than chase women?" She gave him a pat on the hand. "A wife and child is exactly what you need to set you on a more productive course," she continued when he didn't reply. "The experience will mature you, and make you infinitely more valuable to me and to this hotel."

Still dazed from what he had just heard, Travis moistened his lips. "I intend to marry. Someday."

"You will marry sooner than that." Margaret's good humor had returned. "From now on, I'll make sure that you're invited to San Francisco's best soirées. As a matter of fact, my dear friend Harriet Dewitt is hosting a birthday party for her granddaughter next weekend. I'd like you to attend. You remember Dunbar, don't you?"

He remembered. And it took all his willpower not to groan.

Margaret smiled indulgently. "Dunbar's looks may not be as exotic as what you're accustomed to, but she is an attractive, well bred, intelligent young woman. She'll make an excellent wife."

"To someone else maybe."

"Give her a chance, Travis. That's all I ask. And if you should decide to marry her, then at the birth of your first child, I'll give you the controlling shares of the Lindford."

She rose, signalling the conversation was over. Still stunned, Travis stood up, and kissed the offered cheek in a stiff, automatic gesture. Then, without a word, he turned around and left.

Travis's own penthouse was on the same floor as his mother's. Although not as large, it was just as elegantly furnished with brown leather sofas and chairs, inlaid Chinese tables and desks, and Aubusson carpets, all of which blended exquisitely with his extensive collection of oriental art.

As soon as he had closed the door behind him, he strode directly to the well-stocked liquor cart by the window and poured himself a scotch.

A kid. Of all the demands his mother could have made on him, this was the last one he had expected.

Bringing the Waterford tumbler to his lips, he took a long swallow, waiting for the liquor to soothe his frayed nerves.

In all his thirty-six years, he had never doubted that someday the Lindford would be his. It had been promised to him. He had been groomed for it from the time he was a small boy, as his father had been, and his grandfather before that.

He knew he lacked the leadership qualities other Lindford men had possessed. And yes, he had made a few mistakes in his time; but was that a reason to take away his birthright? And give the hotel to a *woman?*

Francesca. He shook his head. His sister was a gifted strategist when it came to marketing, but she would never cut it as CEO. She was too conservative. And she had no vision. He, on the other hand, was loaded with vision. With him at the helm, the Lindford would become synonymous with power. He wouldn't content himself with a second Lindford in Puerto Vallarta, but would build other hotels in the world's most exciting capitals—Paris, London, Rome, and Hong Kong. His name would be added to those of other famous hotel magnates—men like Conrad Hilton and César Ritz. In time, he might even be able to fulfill his ultimate dream—that of buying the Ritz chain and attaching the Lindford name to it.

But to do that, he needed money—money that would only become available if the hotel went public. Unfortunately, the possibility of this ever happening under his mother's ownership, or Francesca's, were nil.

Well, he didn't have to wait any longer. He could have it all. Right now. Or at least within a year. All he had to do was give his mother a grandchild.

And that was the one thing he could not do. Not

because he didn't want to—but because it was a physical impossibility.

He took another sip of his drink, the memory of those few days in the summer of 1986 still vivid in his mind. *Painfully* vivid.

He had been vacationing on Aruba and indulging a little too indiscriminately in the pleasures of free sex. A few days before he was due to return to the states, he had developed an acute case of gonorrhea. Although he had had the dreaded disease treated immediately, he had come down with a secondary infection. Concerned it would spread to the joints and cause gonococcal arthritis, the local doctor had sent Travis to Caracas for further treatment. By the time Travis was ready to be discharged, his attending physician had pronounced him in good health, but informed him that the infection had left him permanently sterile. An examination conducted by a stateside doctor upon his return to San Francisco had confirmed the diagnosis.

The news had left him indifferent. He hated kids anyway. The thought of those grubby little hands touching his precious art collection always sent a chill down his spine.

How could he have known that seven years later, his mother, unaware of his condition, would present him with such an ultimatum?

Taking his drink to one of the chairs facing the television set, he sat down, picked up the remote control, and turned the set on.

Idly, he clicked through the various channels, his mind drifting back to his conversation with his mother. An adoption was out of the question. Margaret was a purist. She wanted a bloodline, an unblemished dynasty. Artificial insemination? That was a possibility. He could marry Dunbar, or whomever his mother chose for him, then he would convince his new bride to be artificially inseminated. They would select a donor with the same physical characteristics as him—blond hair, blue eyes, average frame . . .

He shook his head. Dunbar would never go for it. She, too, was proud of her heritage, of that famous blue blood that ran through her veins. And she was much too ethical to agree to such a ruse. Besides, something like that was bound to leak out, in which case Margaret would disown him for sure.

Expelling an exasperated sigh, he banged his glass on the table. "Shit."

As he leaned his head back, trying to think of another solution, the image of a young woman who looked vaguely familiar flashed on the television screen.

Curious, he reached for the remote control and turned up the sound. The woman sat in an attractive living room that was crammed with books, inexpensive art, and various mementos. Next to her on the blue-and-white striped sofa was a reporter, and on her right, a small blond boy played with some sort of electronic game.

The reporter, an Ivy League type in his late twenties, looked into the camera and smiled. "This afternoon we are talking to Diana Wells, who is preparing for the grand opening of her restaurant, Harbor View, in the Marina district. Miss Wells, a graduate of the California Cooking Institute, is well known to Bay Area residents. For the past eleven years she has owned and operated a popular catering service aptly named Private Affairs."

He turned to his guest. "So tell me, Diana. Are you ready for the big event? Any last-minute jitters?"

She laughed, showing perfect white teeth. "Jitters have been a part of my daily life for the last six months, ever since I realized that my dream was finally going to happen. And yes, every one at Harbor View is ready, and looking forward to this evening with great anticipation.''

Travis sat up, his problem momentarily forgotten. Diana Wells. Nadine Snyder's friend. He remembered her catering service very well. When he had dated Nadine, she had been working there on weekends to supplement her income as a budding journalist.

"Tell us a little about some of the specialties you'll be serving this evening, Diana. I understand you created most of them yourself."

While she talked, Travis's gaze kept drifting from Diana to the young boy standing next to her and then back to the woman. He wasn't aware she had married. Not that he had kept up with her after his breakup with Nadine. The truth was he had never liked Diana Wells. She was a pushy broad with a sharp tongue and a nasty temper.

Picking up his glass, he twirled the ice around. She had changed. She was prettier than he remembered. Sexy, in a rather subtle way. Her hair was still that same deep rich auburn, but he had forgotten how green her eyes were—as beautiful as the imperial jade pieces he collected.

As she continued to answer the interviewer's questions, Travis kept watching her—and the kid. He was about seven or eight, handsome enough, but quiet; he kept his eyes downcast. When the reporter asked how he felt about his mother opening up a restaurant, he shrugged and punched another key on his hand-held computer. "All right, I guess."

It wasn't until the end of the interview, when the boy finally looked up and smiled, that Travis understood what it was that kept pulling his gaze back.

The boy bore an amazing resemblance to him.

His eyes were a deep iris blue, the same blue as his and Margaret's eyes. And in the center of the small chin was a deep cleft, a trademark of the Lindford men.

It was like looking at a picture of himself as a boy.

Travis sat there for a full minute, then gave a shrug. So the kid had blond hair, blue eyes, and a dimpled chin. What was the big deal about that?

But he looks just like me.

Coincidence. Lots of people have look-alikes. That didn't mean they were related. And anyway, the kid couldn't be his. It was Nadine he had screwed, not Diana Wells. And when Nadine had come to him and announced she was pregnant, he had told her to get an abortion and had walked out of her life. He had never seen her again after that, but he was certain she had had the procedure done. She had been no more ready to be a mother than he had been to be a father.

He glanced at the screen again, but the interview was over, and the station had switched to a shampoo commercial. He glanced at his watch. Six fifteen. Which meant Harbor View's grand opening was about to get under way.

On impulse, he picked up the portable phone next to his glass and dialed the number of *The San Francisco Globe*, where an old friend of his father's ran the news desk.

When the veteran reporter came on the line, Travis didn't bother to waste time on civilities, coming straight to the point. "Pete, I wonder if you could do me a small favor."

"I'll do my best."

"I just watched an interview on Channel 4 about

that new restauranteur—Diana Wells? She own Harbor View."

Travis heard the old man puff on his pipe. "What do you want to know?"

"Personal stuff. Who did she marry and when? When was her child born? That sort of thing."

"That all?"

"For now, yes."

"I'll call you back."

Travis was pouring himself a fresh drink when the call from Pete Boyle came through. "You're in luck," the reporter said. "The *Globe* did a piece on Diana Wells when she catered a fund-raiser for the governor last year. Anyway, the lady is thirty-four years old, single—"

"You mean divorced."

"I mean she's never been married."

"But the child . . ."

"Adopted. One of Diana's friends, a Nadine Snyder, gave birth to the boy almost nine years ago. She died a year later, and since she didn't have any family—"

Travis sat up. "Did you say *died*?"

"In a boating accident in August of '85. I'm surprised you didn't hear about it. It happened right here, in San Francisco Bay. Her boat with two other girls on board collided with the Tiburon ferry."

He waited for some sort of emotion to hit him—pain, regrets, sadness. But he felt nothing. It had happened too long ago, and she hadn't meant that much to him anyway. "I was in Japan that summer . . ."

"The boy, eight months old at the time, was adopted by Diana Wells. His name is Zachary."

Travis sank deeper into his chair, digesting the news he had just heard. Nadine had had the baby after all.

"Anything more I can do for, Travis?"

Travis shook his head. "Not right now. Thanks a

lot, Pete. Come for dinner in our restaurant one night, will you? Bring the family. I owe you one."

"Thanks. I'll take you up on it."

Travis slowly hung up, his eyes lost in the distance. Zachary Wells was his son.

3

Diana couldn't have asked for a more successful grand opening. Even now, four hours after the first customer had walked through Harbor View's doors, the dining room was still packed. The rich aroma of espresso, as diners ordered one last cup of coffee, mingled with the lingering aroma of crêpes Suzette, which had been the hit dessert of the evening.

There had been a few minor disasters throughout the night, but, overall, things had gone well.

Diana had greeted each customer in person, taking time to exchange a few words with everyone. She had done the same as they departed, accepting their compliments with a smile and an invitation to return.

A woman she had recognized earlier as the famous soprano Muriel Cunningham, came to her, her hands extended. "Thank you for a perfectly glorious evening," the singer said in her rich, well-modulated voice. "If it weren't for an early rehearsal tomorrow, I would have stayed until closing."

Beaming, Diana squeezed the woman's hands, aware that her comment had been heard by several diners. "Then you must come back when you have more time."

"We will," she said as her husband helped her into a full-length mink coat. "Very soon. Meanwhile, I'll make sure to recommend Harbor View to all my friends and colleagues."

Watching her leave, Diana exhaled a sigh of relief, for the diva was known for her discriminating taste in food and her outspoken personality. Her compliment tonight couldn't have come at a better time.

"I think we're a hit," the bartender whispered in Diana's ear as he placed two espressos on the counter.

She grinned. "Looks that way, doesn't it? Elaine tells me we're booked solid every night for the next week."

"And after Muriel Cunningham has had a chance to pass the word around, you'll have customers lined up for blocks, dying for a chance to get in."

As Diana continued to gaze across the dining room, she was already making a few mental notes on how to improve the decor. The flower arrangements on the smaller tables were a trifle too large, making it difficult for two people sitting across from each other to carry on an intimate conversation. And the lighting above tables four and five was poorly angled, adding unwanted shadows on the people sitting there.

Otherwise, everything was perfect. The tables were laid with crisp pink linen from Ireland, glassware from France, and china from England.

Unlike some owners of waterfront restaurants in the Bay Area, she had resisted the temptation to decorate her establishment with fishnets, seashells, or other seafaring artifacts. Instead, she had hunted through local galleries and bought pastel landscapes from California artists, installed diffused lighting on the cream walls, and filled the alcove at the far end of the room with a huge flower arrangement she changed daily.

The cuisine she and her chef had chosen was eclectic—a mixture of California and Mediterranean dishes, many of which she had created during her eleven years as a caterer—fresh seafood, grilled meats, exotic salads, and mouth-watering desserts.

Circumstances rather than choice had dictated the path her career had taken. A native of San Francisco and the younger of two children, Diana's first love had been medicine. But when her widowed mother was diagnosed with lung cancer and forced to quit her job, Diana had turned down a scholarship to the University of Pennsylvania and enrolled at San Francisco State so she could stay home and take care of her mother.

As the bills began to accumulate, she had asked her brother to share some of the responsibilities, but Nick was too busy with his get-rich-quick schemes to burden himself with an ailing parent.

"Mom and I have never been close anyway," he told Diana. "So it's not as if she actually expects me to help out. Besides, I'm kind of strapped for money myself at the moment. I've put every cent I have in a new venture, and until it all comes together . . . Well, you understand."

She understood all right. He was washing his hands of his mother, which hadn't come as a total surprise. Even when he lived at home, Nick hadn't had much use for his family, except for what he could get out of them.

By the time Vivian Wells died two years later, the illness had drained her savings as well as the small inheritance she had planned to leave her children. Rather than give up college, Diana applied for a part-time job at Caterers, Inc. to help pay for her tuition.

Within a few months she had become one of the company's most valuable employees, and by the time she started her senior year, she was already envisioning a career in catering, but as her own boss rather than someone's employee.

One evening, as she and two of her college friends shared a pizza Diana had made from scratch, she told them of her plan. "Mrs. Collins says I'm a terrific cook," she explained as the other two coeds ate with great gusto. "And that I have a good head for business. So I thought ... why not start my own catering service?"

Nadine, who was a bit of a dreamer, was all for it. But levelheaded Kat didn't think much of the idea. "You're not ready," she told Diana with her usual frankness. "Stay where you are, learn and earn as much as you can. When you have enough money, enroll in one of those fancy cooking schools either here or abroad. Now, *that's* the kind of baggage that will get you places."

For impatient Diana who was eager to fly on her own, the advice was a disappointment. But deep down, she knew Kat was right. And so she had waited.

She had never regretted her decision. When Private Affairs was named as one of the four best catering services in the Bay Area only five years after its inception, she knew it was time to work toward her next goal—to own a restaurant.

It had taken another five years to save enough money to partly finance her dream, and more than three months to convince her banker to lend her the rest.

And now here she was—the proprietor of what would undoubtedly become one of the hottest restaurants in San Francisco—maybe, she thought with a grin, in the entire Bay Area.

"Hello, Diana."

Startled, for she hadn't heard anyone come up behind her, she turned around and caught her breath. Travis Lindford stood in front of her. Except for a couple of extra pounds around his midriff and the bags under his eyes, he looked the same as he had ten years ago—handsome, confident, arrogant.

Memories flooded back, reawakening all the animosity she had felt toward him at the time. If it hadn't been for the roomful of customers, she would have thrown him out. Instead, she chose to be courteous. "How are you, Travis?"

"Quite well, thank you." He glanced around the dining room, and from the expression on his face, she guessed he approved of what he saw. "This is very nice." Then, turning back to her, he added, "I caught your interview on the six o'clock news this evening and thought I'd stop by to wish you luck."

"Really."

"You sound surprised."

"I *am* surprised. If I recall, you and I never were very fond of each other."

He gave her an amused smile. It was the same charismatic smile that had won Nadine's heart. It hadn't won hers.

"I see that you're still as frank as ever."

"Did you think I wouldn't be?"

"I was hoping time would have mellowed you a little. After all, it's been nearly a decade since we first met. Don't you think we should put whatever differences we had aside? Bury the hatchet as they say?"

"Why should we?"

As a black-tuxedoed hostess passed by, Travis gave her his killer smile. "Because I need to talk to you about something, and I'd like our conversation to be conducted in a civilized manner."

A feeling of unease fluttered briefly in her stomach. "There is nothing we have to say to each other, Travis." Anxious to see him leave, she pulled away from the bar. "And even if there were, I don't have time to—"

He sidestepped, blocking her path. "*Make* time, Diana. This is important."

The congenial smile had faded, and something about the way he looked at her, with cold, dispassionate eyes, sent a frisson of alarm down her spine.

At a table for two, a young couple, who had obviously recognized Travis, was watching them. Diana cast a worried glance around the room. She couldn't talk to Travis here. He would attract too much attention, arouse unnecessary curiosity.

Reluctantly, she nodded toward a hallway in the back of the dining room. "We can talk in my office."

Travis followed her, admiring the supple lines of her body. She walked stiffly, perhaps more stiffly than she would have under normal circumstances. But he didn't need a sway of hips to tell him that there was a dynamite body under that silky white dress.

Perhaps, if he played his cards right, he might make this visit doubly rewarding.

He had debated a long time before coming here. After Pete's call he had sat for nearly an hour, absorbing all he had learned, thinking how he could make this extraordinary revelation work to his advantage.

Zachary Wells was the grandchild Margaret so badly wanted. Not just a grandchild, but a *grandson,* another male to continue her precious dynasty. She would be ecstatic. And all his problems would be solved.

All he had to do was bend the truth a little.

"You'll have to make it quick, Travis," Diana said, closing the door behind them. "I'm tired and I want to go home."

Pursing his lips slightly, Travis looked around, taking in the huge, cluttered desk, the textured stucco walls, the French doors overlooking a garden bathed in moonlight.

As he stepped deeper into the room, his gaze stopped on a photograph of Zachary propped on the desk. He picked it up, raised an eyebrow. "Your son?"

As his eyes bore into hers, Diana fought to control the nervous churning in her stomach. "That's right."

"I didn't know you had married."

The mocking gleam in his eyes told her he was playing with her. He already knew she had never married. "I didn't."

He saw the change in her. The casualness was gone from her voice, and her body had grown more rigid. His gestures deliberately slow, Travis put the photograph back. "Zachary is my son, isn't he?"

She let out a long, thin sigh. Now that the performance was over, she was almost relieved. Although she still didn't know why she was so worried. Zachary was legally adopted. Nothing Travis could do now would change that. "You helped conceive him. That doesn't make you his father—not in the true sense of the word."

"Why are you being so defensive, Diana? I didn't come here to fight with you. In fact, I'm very grateful for all you've done for my son. I'm sure that if you and I sit down like two adults and discuss the situation—"

"*Situation?* What situation? You have no claim here, Travis." She fought to keep her voice from growing shrill. "There is nothing to discuss."

"Not true. I'm Zachary's biological father. I should have been notified of Nadine's death, of the fact she and I had a child."

Diana's eyes grew wide with shock. *"What?"*

"She should have come to me," he repeated, summoning whatever acting ability he may have had. "I would have taken him. I would have given him a home, a name, the father he needed."

Contempt replaced shock. "What kind of sick game

are you playing? You know damn well why Nadine didn't come to you. You wanted nothing to do with the baby. You told her so. You handed her five hundred dollars for an abortion and then walked away as if she had never existed."

Although Travis had been prepared for her reaction, the fury in her eyes almost had him backing away. But he stood his ground, determined to win her over by doing what he did best. Charm. "I never did anything of the sort, so help me God. And I'm not the one who broke up the relationship. Nadine did."

"You're lying!"

"I'm not. We had an argument over a girl my mother forced me to escort to the symphony. Nadine read more into the arranged date than she should have, got upset with me, and threw me out of her apartment. I swear to you, Diana, I had no idea she was pregnant. If I had—"

Bewildered by what she was hearing, Diana shook her head. "I always knew you were a consummate liar, Travis, but I must say, you're outdoing yourself this time. A pity I'm not buying the act."

"It's not an act. I have an eight-year-old son who doesn't even know me. How do you think that makes me feel?"

"It's too late for regrets."

"No, it's not! I want to meet him, Diana." He allowed his voice to crack with emotion. "I want to see my son."

If the moment hadn't been so frightening, Diana would have laughed. In the last decade Travis Lindford had apparently become an actor—a good one. His voice held just the right trace of passion to convince anyone that he was speaking the truth. Anyone but her.

"I wouldn't let you within a hundred feet of him,"

she spat. "So do yourself a favor. Leave before I call the authorities and have you arrested for harassment."

Rather than allow the argument to escalate further, Travis decided not to push her. She needed time to digest what he had just told her, to adjust to his desire to be a part of his son's life. Once she had come to terms with that, they would talk again. There was no hurry.

He gave a short, conciliatory bow of his head. "I guess that was a lot to lay on you at one time. Why don't I give you a day or two to think things over?"

"There's nothing to think over."

"I'll call you soon."

As the door closed softly behind him, Diana sank into the nearest chair, her knees almost buckling under her. In her chest her heart pounded, powered by a fear she had never experienced before.

Could Travis actually have a claim on Zack? she thought as she clasped her hands and held them against her mouth. Could he, as the biological father, take him away from her?

It took her several minutes to calm down, and a couple more until she could stand up. Her legs were still shaky, but at least now, she could think rationally. No matter what Travis thought, Zack was hers. Nothing could change that.

Not even the Lindfords.

When Diana got home, it was almost midnight. Thanking Marty, she paid her and stood at the door until the girl was safely inside her car. Then, after gathering Zack's toys and setting them on the coffee table, she went upstairs to his bedroom.

He was curled up on his side, one arm wrapped around an old, battered teddy bear he hadn't yet had the courage to give up. That side of him, tender and tough at the same time, was one of his most endearing qualities.

Diana ran the back of her index finger along the smooth cheek, remembering the day he was born. She had been in the delivery room with Nadine, coaching her, encouraging her, wishing she could take some of the pain away from her.

Eight months later, Nadine was back in that same hospital, victim of a boating accident that had claimed two lives. She had been in a coma for three days, and when she had finally opened her eyes, the doctors' prognosis had been guarded. But Nadine hadn't needed a doctor to know she was dying.

"I want you to take care of my baby when I'm gone," she had whispered, her fingers gripping Diana's hand.

Diana had scolded her gently. "Shhh. You're going to be fine. A few days from now, you'll be back home, taking care of your baby yourself. Meanwhile, he's sending his mommy a big wet kiss."

Nadine's grip tightened, and the expression in her eyes grew more desperate. "No. It's only a matter of time before . . ." She closed her eyes, wincing against the pain in her chest where a propeller had gone right through her ribs, severely damaging both lungs. When she reopened her eyes, they burned with a determination so fierce Diana had to look away.

"You're the only one I can trust with my baby. He knows you as well as he knows me. He loves you. He feels safe with you."

"Nadine, I can't." Her voice broke as she took her friend's hand in hers. "I don't know anything about being a mother."

"Oh, Diana, you have great motherly instincts already."

Diana shook her head. "Babies are a full-time job,

Nadine. How can I give him the care and attention he needs when I'm working sixteen hours a day?"

"If you don't take him, who else can I turn to? My grandmother who's old and sick? Travis who never wanted anything to do with the baby? An orphanage where he'll be adopted by strangers?"

She remembered the day Nadine had introduced her to Travis, the way he had sized her up, with a quick, arrogant glance, not even bothering to get out of his Ferrari. She had disliked him on sight—not only because of his reputation as a philanderer, but also because of the way he had shouted insults at two neighborhood boys who were admiring the foreign car a little too closely.

The thought that Zack would have to depend on a man like that for love and support sent a tingle of fear up and down her spine.

"No," Diana whispered at last. "Not an orphanage. And not Travis."

"You." Nadine's voice was now a mere whisper. "I want *you* to adopt my baby. Right away, while I'm still alive. I already talked to an attorney. If I die before signing the papers, the courts could make it difficult for you because you're single. But if we act now, with my full consent, there won't be any problem."

As predicted, the adoption had moved quickly. Nadine had clung to life one more week after that, then, quietly, with a serene smile on her lips as she held Kat and Diana's hands, she had closed her eyes forever.

Diana's doubts about becoming a mother had evaporated long before the final papers were signed. Zack was an absolute joy, and except for a few tears as he called for his mother from time to time, he had adjusted quickly.

And now the peaceful life she had created for both her and her son was about to be shattered. No matter how often she told herself that Travis was in no position to make demands, his visit at Harbor View had left her shaky and frightened.

Pulling the bedspread with the racing car motif over the sleeping boy, she bent down to kiss his forehead. Then, without a sound, she tiptoed out of the room.

4

"Here. Drink this. You'll feel better."

Sitting in Kat's sunny living room in the Richmond section of San Francisco, Diana took the steaming cup of raspberry tea from her friend's hands and inhaled the soothing fragrance. "How did you know I needed that?"

Kat smiled. "Intuition." She was an attractive young woman with short, carrot-colored hair, round blue eyes, and a freckled nose that in her early childhood had earned her the nickname of Little Orphan Annie.

She removed a throw pillow from one of the deep, chintz-covered chairs and sat down, the pillow on her lap. "So, are you going to tell me what's wrong, or do I have to get the old crystal ball out of the attic?"

Diana, who hadn't told a soul about Travis's visit to Harbor View four days ago until she knew exactly what he was after, took a sip of her tea and gazed into her friend's eyes. "Travis Lindford came to see me the other day."

"Travis the Creep?" Kat exclaimed, using the nickname she and Diana had made up for him nine years ago. "You're kidding."

"I wish I were." Struggling to keep her voice on an even keel, Diana gave her a detailed account of her conversation with Travis. When she was finished, she looked at Kat again. "He wants Zack," she said in a toneless voice.

"What do you mean, he *wants* Zack?"

"He wants me to agree to joint custody, which means Zack would spend six months of the year with me and the other six with Travis."

"He can't be serious."

"He is. He called me the day after his visit to Harbor View, and said he wants to raise his son in the manner in which a Lindford ought to be raised."

"What did you tell him?"

"To piss off."

Kat smiled. Diplomacy had never been one of Diana's virtues. "Have you heard from him since then?"

"Yes. The last call was on Saturday morning after I dropped Zack off at soccer practice."

"That was two days ago. That's a good sign, isn't it? He probably figured he couldn't scare you and gave up."

Diana shook her head. "I don't think so, Kat. Just before I hung up, he told me he'd take the matter to court if he had to." She took a sip of tea, but the hot drink failed to dissolve the cold knot inside her stomach. "I think he meant it."

"He must be insane. What kind of case does he think he has?"

Diana pressed her head against the back of the sofa. "I don't know. What I *do* know is that the Lindfords are wealthy, influential people, with powerful connections."

"I don't care if they're connected to the pope, there's nothing they can do. You're Zachary's mother. You have the papers to prove it. And as his mother, *you* have the right to say who he will and will not see."

Diana smiled. "Spoken like a true lawyer's wife. Unfortunately these days, the courts seem to be favoring biological parents. Look what happened with Baby Jessica—"

"That was a different case. The child was never legally adopted. Zack is."

"Nevertheless, the court took her from the only family she knew and handed her over to strangers."

Kat remembered the case only too well. She and Mitch had been outraged at the outcome of the long, painful custody battle, as had millions of Americans across the country. "No court is going to take a well-adjusted eight-year-old from his mother and hand him over to a father who didn't want him in the first place."

"Travis vehemently denies that part. He claims Nadine made up that story because she didn't want him to know she was pregnant."

"That's a crock!"

Diana stared into her tea. "He's even suggested that she was heavily drugged during those ten days before she died and didn't know what she was doing."

Red spots of indignation colored Kat's cheeks. "She was as lucid as you and I!"

"I know. But he's fabricated quite a story, Kat. You can't imagine how convincing he sounded the day he came to see me and told me he knew nothing about the baby. If I feel that way, knowing what he's like, how do you think a judge will react?"

"We'll subpoena the doctor who attended Nadine. He'll blow Travis's theory right out the window." When Diana didn't answer, she added, "Have you talked to a lawyer?"

"Not yet." Too jittery to sit for long, Diana stood up and walked over to her friend's drawing table where the first two frames of the latest installment of Kat's popular comic strip, *Frisco Kid*, were nearly completed.

A talented cartoonist, Kat's career hadn't taken off until about a year ago when the strip, a big hit in the Bay Area, was syndicated to more than three hundred newspapers. "I was hoping Mitch could recommend someone."

"I'll ask him tonight—unless you want to talk to him yourself." She glanced at the clock on the wall. "He's coming home early, as a matter of fact. Why don't you go get Zack at school and bring him back here for dinner? I'm making his favorite, lasagna."

It sounded wonderful. After the traumatic last four days, Diana would have liked nothing more than to spend an evening with Kat and Mitch. "I can't. Zack has a soccer game, and after that I'll have to tell him about Travis before he hears it from someone else." She put her cup down and stood up. "But I'll call you later this evening, okay?"

A few moments later, Diana was at the wheel of her red Jeep Cherokee, heading toward Ridgeway Elementary School in Pacific Heights. She tried not to think of Travis's threats, but his last words just before he had hung up on Saturday kept echoing in her head, sounding more ominous each time.

"Zachary is my son, Diana. I don't intend to be shut out of his life any longer. You can count on that."

Diana's angry fist hit the steering wheel. How could a man who had been so adamant about not wanting a baby suddenly reappear into their lives and act as if he were running for Father of the Year? It didn't make sense.

Turning into the school parking lot, she pulled the Jeep into an empty slot, took a deep breath and got out.

A year before, when Diana felt Zack was old enough to understand, she had sat down with him and told him the truth about his birth—partly because she had vowed to keep Nadine's memory alive in his heart, and partly because she didn't want any secrets that might resurface later, to mar her relationship with her son.

It hadn't been easy. He had had questions, about his mother, but also about his father, and his reason for abandoning him.

"He was very young," she had told him, choosing to stretch the truth a little. "And the thought of raising a child frightened him. I guess running away was his way of dealing with that fear."

And now here she was again, faced with the equally difficult task of telling Zack that the father who had walked away from him years ago now wanted him back.

As the soccer match ended in a screaming victory for the Ridgeway team, Diana watched Zack run toward her, waving.

"Another win for the Falcons," he shouted as he slid to a stop in front of her. "That makes it 4 and 0."

Knowing he didn't like to be kissed in front of his friends, Diana contented herself with ruffling his hair. "Hi, short stuff. That was quite a play you made at the end."

"Yeah. Did you see how I faked that guard on the other team? I rolled the ball a little to the left, and when he made a move for it, I turned to the right and—pow—I rammed it into the net, right past the goalie." He kicked his foot to the side to demonstrate his technique.

Despite her low spirits, Diana smiled. "I saw. It was very impressive." When they were both inside the Jeep, she waited until he had buckled his seat belt, before backing out of the parking space. "How about an ice cream to celebrate?"

"Before dinner?"

"Let's live dangerously."

"And afterward, could we drive down Lombard Street? Real fast?"

Known as the crookedest street in San Francisco, steep and zigzagging Lombard Street was a favorite of many tourists as well as local youngsters. "Don't push it. One thrill at a time, okay?"

At nearby Huntington Park she bought two chocolate ice-cream cones from an outdoor vendor and led the way through the park as Zack went over his next game strategy in explicit details. When he was finished, she gave him a long, thoughtful look, then said, "There's something I need to talk to you about."

He stopped licking his ice cream. "Did I do something wrong?"

The question made her smile and eased some of the tension she felt. "Would I be buying you ice cream before dinner if you had?"

He laughed. "I guess not."

A nursemaid in uniform walked by, pushing a baby carriage, and smiled at them. Diana smiled back, remembering the not so distant past when she had pushed an identical carriage. "Do you remember last year when I told you about Nadine?" Calling Nadine by her name, rather than saying "your mother," had been less confusing for Zack.

He nodded. "She was my natural mother. But she died."

"Right. We also talked about your father."

His features tensed a little, but he nodded again. "I remember."

"He came to see me the other day."

He turned to look at her. "He's here? In San Francisco?"

She nodded.

"You told me he lived in Europe."

"Europe is where he went for a while after he left. But he returned at the end of that summer, although I never saw him again until this past Thursday."

A rivulet of melted ice cream slid down his cone, and Zack caught it with the tip of his tongue. "What did he want?"

She looked at the small, compact body, the scruffy soccer uniform, the huge, questioning blue eyes. She tried to determine what his feeling were, but for the moment, all she could see on his expressive face was curiosity. "You. He says he wants to meet you, start being a father to you. He also wants you to go and live with him part of the year."

She wasn't sure what came first, surprise or indignation. "Well, I don't want to live with him! I don't even know him." His eyes narrowed suspiciously. "You didn't tell him I would, did you?"

"Of course not. In fact, I was quite rude to him. I kicked him out of my office, and when he called a couple of days later, I hung up on him."

"Good." Then, more cautiously, he asked, "That's it, then, right? He won't bother you anymore?"

If only it were that simple. "I don't think Travis is going to give up just because I was rude to him. It's only a matter of time before I hear from him again. Which is why I had to tell you."

"I won't live with him," he repeated. "Kyle Patterson lives with his father during the summer and he hates it. I'd hate it, too."

Impulsively, Diana ran her hand over Zack's unruly blond hair. "Don't worry. I won't let that happen to you. The only reason I told you was because Travis comes from a wealthy San Francisco family, and this story is bound to get a lot of attention."

"You mean it'll be on television and stuff?"

"That's a possibility. And your friends will probably ask a lot of questions. That's why I wanted you to be prepared."

Zack finished his ice cream in silence as they continued walking. They had reached a fountain the locals called the Fountain of the Turtles, even though there were no turtles in it. Propping one foot on the low stone wall, he gazed into the water. "You said he was rich. What does he do?"

"His family owns a hotel right here in San Francisco. You've heard of it. The Lindford."

"Wow!"

His reaction didn't surprise her. The Nob Hill landmark hotel had as much clout as a famous monument. Zack had gone to see it once as part of a field trip with his first-grade class. He had come home overwhelmed by what he had seen, the huge lobby, its vaulted, frescoed ceiling, the gold marble columns, the crystal chandeliers, and the antique tapestries depicting scenes of famous European crusades.

The thought that such an establishment belonged to his father was bound to make an impression on a small boy—especially one who was accustomed to a middle-income lifestyle.

As if he sensed her concern, he slid his hand into hers. "I don't care how rich he is, Mom. I don't want to live with him. I can tell him myself if you want me to."

Diana smiled. She liked the fact that his first instinct had been to protect her. It showed that his resemblance to his father didn't extend beyond the physical similarities. "Thanks, darling. I'll let you know if I need your help." They headed back toward the Cherokee. "In the meantime, I don't want you to worry about anything, all right? No one is going to take you away from me—not even for a day."

*   *   *

Later that night, as Zack sat in front of the television set, watching an episode of *Evening Shade,* Diana went to the kitchen to call Kat.

"Kat, it's me. Did you talk to Mitch?"

"Yes. And he wants to talk to you. Hold on."

"Hi, Diana," Mitch said when he came on the line. "Look, I know you're worried about what that jerk is threatening to do, but I don't think he has a leg to stand on. However, since he's probably consulted with an attorney, or will soon, you should do the same. Our firm doesn't handle custody cases, but I have the name and number of a San Francisco lawyer who does. He's very good."

Diana pulled a thick notepad toward her. "Go ahead," she said, her pen poised over it.

"His name is John McKay." He gave her an office address on Bush Street and a telephone number. "Make an appointment with him right away, and tell his secretary you're a friend of mine."

"Thanks, Mitch."

"You're welcome. And please don't worry."

"I won't," she lied.

Travis couldn't remember the last time he had seen his mother show such emotion. As he told her the same story he had told Diana, she listened intently, her hands clasped and pressed against her chest.

"A son," she murmured when Travis was finished. "You have a son."

"Yes," Travis said with all the passion he could muster. "Oh, Mother, I can't begin to tell you how that makes me feel."

Margaret drew her head back, arching an eyebrow. "I thought you didn't want children."

Because he had been expecting the remark, he was

prepared for it. "I was talking about tiny babies, you know ... two o'clock feedings, diapers, colics. This is different, Mother. Zachary is a grown boy—a handsome, vital boy. I felt a connection to him right from the start, from the first moment I saw his face on the television screen."

Margaret's eyes bore into his. She knew him too well to believe he had suddenly turned into a proud, loving father. In all probability, his desire to have Zachary stemmed from the ultimatum she had given him a few days ago. But she felt certain that in time he would learn to love the boy. And if he didn't, she would be here, ready to give her grandson all the love and attention he needed—and an upbringing he'd be proud of.

God had given her a second chance, she thought with a tremor of excitement, another opportunity to raise a true Lindford man. And she wasn't about to let it slip through her fingers.

After a moment her gaze softened. "Does he really look like you?"

Without a word Travis stood up and walked over to a Louis XIV cabinet where he knew she kept the family photo albums. Selecting one labeled 1964 and 1965, he brought it back to the sofa. He leafed through the pages until he found a black-and-white photograph of himself taken on his eighth birthday.

"He looks just like this," he said, placing the album on his mother's lap and watching her smile broaden. "Except that his hair is longer."

Margaret took a long breath as she studied the photograph. What a proud, handsome boy Travis had been then. And so well-mannered.

Her fingers stroked the photograph.

This time she wouldn't make the same mistakes.

Closing the album, she handed it back to Travis.

"Where do you stand with this Diana Wells? When do you get to meet your son?"

Travis expelled a long, suffering sigh. "I'm afraid I don't stand anywhere. She won't listen to anything I have to say, hangs up when I call, and categorically refuses to let me see Zachary."

"What possible reason could she have to do that?"

"She claims I don't deserve him, that I walked away from him and his mother."

"But you didn't!"

"Diana doesn't believe me. She has her own scenario of what happened between Nadine and me."

"But that's so unfair. Doesn't she realize that you have a right to see the boy? To build a relationship with him? That he is a *Lindford?*"

The tremor in her voice as she uttered the beloved family name told him that he had done the right thing by coming to her. She might not have bought his motives entirely, but she wanted that boy as much as he did. Of that he was certain. "None of that matters to her, Mother. She's a cold, heartless bitch who doesn't know the meaning of the word 'compromise'."

"In that case, you must call Kane immediately."

"I already have," he said, glad that for once he had anticipated her wishes. "I left a message with his secretary. He should be calling me back shortly."

"Good. I'd rather not have to resort to a law suit, but we need Kane to advise us about our rights." Idly, she played with the pearls around her neck. "Meanwhile, I shall pay Miss Wells a little visit."

"Mother, are you sure that's wise?"

"It's more than wise, it's an absolute necessity. If there is any way to avoid an ugly, drawn-out court battle, we must explore the possibilities." Seeing the look of skepticism on her son's face, she patted his hand. "Just leave everything to me, darling."

5

John McKay was exactly the type of attorney Diana needed to boost her confidence. He was in his early sixties, with three decades of experience in family law, and he spoke in a gentle, reassuring tone.

While she briefed him on Travis, his visit at the restaurant, and his subsequent phone calls, John took notes, interrupting her occasionally to ask a pertinent question. At no time did his face show surprise or concern, a detail Diana found extremely comforting.

When she was finished, he dropped his pencil on the desk and leaned back in his chair. "All right. I'll give it to you straight. As the biological father, he has a case—a weak one, but a case nonetheless."

Diana felt the color drain from her cheeks. "Are you telling me he can take my son away from me?"

"Of course not. No judge in his right mind would agree to disrupt a child's life by ordering him to spend six months with a parent he's never seen before. From the moment you signed that adoption decree, Zachary became *your* child, as much as if he had been born to you. Nothing can change that. He can, however, decide to grant Travis visitation rights."

"What kind of visitation rights?"

"The usual—a weekend a month, holidays, summers."

She shook her head. "That's out of the question."

"He can make things difficult for you, Diana. Especially if he can prove Nadine kept her pregnancy from him—"

"She didn't."

"Can you substantiate your claim that he was the one who walked out on her and not vice versa? And that he knew about the baby? Did you overhear a conversation between them? An argument perhaps?"

She shook her head. "No. I only know what Nadine told me."

McKay rubbed his index finger across his lips in a thoughtful gesture. After a while he closed the file in front of him. "Well, as I said, being granted visitation rights is only a possibility. Influential or not, Travis Lindford's reputation as a playboy isn't something a judge can afford to overlook. No matter how much he denies knowing about the baby, his lifestyle will speak volumes. Yours, on the other hand, has been exemplary." He stood up and circled his desk. "So my advice for the moment is to sit tight and wait."

"What if he calls again?"

"Give him my name and number and tell him to speak to me. If he argues, hang up. Don't get into an argument with him or with members of his family, and don't enter any kind of verbal agreement without talking to me first."

By the time she came back to the restaurant, Diana felt as if a hundred-pound weight had been lifted from her shoulders.

"Right here is fine, Sam, thank you."

As the Lindfords' chauffeur brought the black Bentley to a stop in front of Diana's house, Margaret glanced out the window and gave it a quick but thorough appraisal.

Although not so grand as other Victorians on this

block, the two-story corner structure was nonetheless a study of late Victorian perfection, complete with a round tower on the upper floor, great bay windows, and a high front porch. The small, well-kept yard sloped gently toward the house, and a shiny blue bicycle lay on its side in the middle of the driveway.

She had found out Diana's address from the detective she had hired to check out the young woman's background. The brief report had also told her Diana Wells had no family except for a brother she hadn't seen in several years.

At last, Margaret stepped out of the Bentley and slowly made her way across the sidewalk, then up the half dozen steps, leaning against her cane a little more than she needed to, in case anyone was watching. When she reached the front door, she rang the bell.

"Who is it?" The voice from inside the house was clear and pleasant.

Margaret raised her chin. "Margaret Lindford."

After a short silence the door opened slowly.

The woman who stood in front of her was not at all what Margaret had expected. With her dark red hair in disarray and her face free of makeup, she looked more like a college girl than the hard-as-steel, polished career woman Travis had described.

Margaret quickly took in the baggy jeans, the yellow 49ers sweatshirt, the white sneakers, the dusting cloth casually draped over one shoulder. "Miss Wells?"

Diana remained still as a pair of piercing blue eyes measured her from head to toe. "If you've come to plead your son's case, you've wasted a trip, Mrs. Lindford. I've said everything I intend to say regarding Travis's ridiculous demands."

Margaret held the younger woman's gaze. "I haven't come here to plead my son's case, Miss Wells. I came to plead mine."

An eyebrow, the same color as Diana's hair, went up. "Is that supposed to make a difference?"

Margaret smiled. Years of dealing with difficult hotel guests had taught her that often diplomacy was one's best weapon. "I certainly hope so."

Diana hesitated. First Travis, now his mother. She didn't like it. It reeked of conspiracy. For a moment she considered slamming the door in the woman's face. After all, hadn't John McKay told her to stay away from the Lindfords?

But as she looked at the woman, at the parchment-like skin, the arthritic fingers gripping the cane, Diana felt herself weaken. Margaret Lindford was an old, fragile woman. What harm could it do to let her come in for a few minutes and hear what she had to say?

Moving to the side, she pulled the door open. "I can give you only a few minutes."

"That's all I'll need."

Margaret followed Diana into a large, breezy living room. In one quick glance she noticed the tasteful combination of contemporary and antique furniture, the wall-to-wall bookcase, the solid oak tables and chairs. A vacuum cleaner stood in the middle of the yellow carpet, and the windows were wide open, allowing the cool but refreshing breeze to blow through.

"You have a lovely house."

Diana didn't acknowledge the compliment. "You said you'd be brief." To offset her sharp tone, she pointed to a chair and took the one directly across from it. She didn't sit back, but stayed on the edge of it, crossed her legs, and clasped her hands around one knee.

"So I did." Margaret placed the cane in front of her and held it with both hands. "I took a gamble, Miss Wells. I gambled that in spite of your refusal to let Travis visit his son, you wouldn't turn an old woman away without granting her one small wish."

"And what's that?"

"I want to see my grandson. Surely that's not such an unreasonable request?"

"Maybe not in your eyes. But *I* find it unreasonable. And unacceptable."

"Why? What reason could you possibly have to keep me from meeting my first and only grandchild?"

"The same reason I have for keeping Travis away. You don't belong in my son's life."

"That's a rather harsh statement, don't you think? Considering we are his family?"

"*I* am his family, Mrs. Lindford. Travis had his chance to be a parent. He chose to walk away, therefore relinquishing all rights. Forever."

Anger flashed in Margaret's eyes. "But that's not how it happened at all! Why won't you believe him?"

"Because I know him, Mrs. Lindford. Apparently better than you do."

Margaret didn't miss the contempt in Diana's voice. By force of habit, she jumped to Travis's defense. "I'll admit my son has his faults, but he wouldn't lie about something like that." Bringing the cane a little closer to her, she said, "I understand that both your parents died several years ago, and that you have no family except for a brother you haven't seen in years."

At the thought that Margaret, or someone she had hired, had dug into her past, Diana tensed. "What are you getting at?"

"I'm simply trying to point out that it's not healthy for a child to grow up without a complete family. Wouldn't you want him to be surrounded by a grandmother who loves him, an aunt and uncle who are anxious to meet him? And spoil him?"

"He's managed just fine so far."

"I'm sure he has. But you must know that grandparents are a necessary and vital part of a child's upbringing. Why would you want to deprive Zachary of that?"

As Diana started to answer, she heard the front door slam shut.

"Mom, I'm home!"

Damn, Diana cursed silently. She had been so involved with her conversation with Margaret Lindford, she hadn't realized it was three o'clock.

Zack bounced in, his school bag slung over his shoulder, one blond strand over his forehead. When he saw Margaret, he stopped abruptly. "Oh, hi."

"Hi, yourself." Margaret glanced at Diana, and for a moment, their eyes locked.

Realizing it would be pointless not to introduce her to Zack, Diana lay a protective hand on her son's shoulder. "Zack, this is Mrs. Margaret Lindford. Travis's mother," she added, deliberately avoiding the words "father" and "grandmother."

Undaunted by the omission, Margaret stood up and came forward. "That makes me your grandmother." She extended her hand. "How are you, Zachary?"

After a quick over-the-shoulder glance at Diana, who nodded to him, Zack took the older woman's hand and shook it. "Fine."

"This is a great pleasure for me, Zachary. And I'm deeply grateful to your mother for allowing me to meet you."

Sitting down again, she drew him to her. In person, his resemblance to Travis was even more striking. "My son tells me you're eight years old. You must be in third grade."

"Fourth. I'll be nine on December twenty-second."

Margaret laughed. "My apologies. It's been a while since I've had a young boy around me. I'm a little out of practice."

Diana saw Zack relax. No wonder. In spite of her self-admitted lack of experience with children, Margaret Lindford spoke with effortless charm and knew exactly how to make Zack feel comfortable.

"Do you really own the Lindford Hotel?" Zack asked with his usual forthrightness."

"Indeed, I do. Are you familiar with it?"

"I came for a visit once with my first-grade class."

"Really? What did you see?"

"The lobby, the kitchen, the roof terrace, and the observation deck." He laughed. "Some of the kids were scared and wouldn't go near the edge."

"Were you scared?"

He shook his blond head. "Nah. I would have gone closer, but the teacher wouldn't let me."

He's got a bit of the daredevil in him, Margaret thought, swallowing the sudden knot in her throat. Just like Charles. "That was probably a wise decision."

He cocked his head to one side. "Is it true that Teddy Roosevelt slept at the Lindford?"

"He certainly did. He came for a visit during his last year in office in 1908."

"I learned all about him in school. They named the teddy bear after him because he saved the life of a bear cub one day when he was hunting."

"That's right."

"Did you know him?"

Margaret laughed and pressed a hand to her breast. "My, no. I'm not *that* old. But my husband's father knew him very well, and he told me some wonderful stories about that historic visit."

Realizing he was interested, she told him about the Lindfords' impressive family tree—an ancestor who had fought in the American Revolution, another who had made his fortune mining for gold, and a third who had founded the Central Pacific Railroad.

"And now there are only three Lindfords left," she added with a wistful sigh. "Your father, your Aunt Francesca and myself." She pushed the stubborn blond lock back. "And you of course."

"My name is Wells." He said it with a tilt of his chin and a hint of pride in his voice.

"That doesn't matter. Your bloodline is that of a Lindford." Ignoring Diana's hard stare, she added, "I would love to take you on a tour of the hotel someday and show you some of the things you missed during your first visit. Afterward, you could come to my ranch in Seacliff and see my horses. Do you like animals?"

Diana held back a groan. That witch couldn't have found a better way to get into Zack's affections if she had tried.

"I sure do," Zack replied, excitement bubbling out of his mouth.

"Well then . . ." She shot Diana a quick, inquisitive glance. "Maybe we could make a date right now. How does next Saturday sound?"

"I'm afraid that's out of the question," Diana interjected, trying hard not to snap at her. "Zack is very busy on weekends. Between sports and homework—"

He spun around. "I could do my homework on Friday afternoon, Mom. And the coach won't mind if I miss one game. Honest. Billy did."

"Billy had his appendix removed."

But Zack had already turned back to Margaret. "How many horses do you have?" he asked, breathless with curiosity.

"Six. All Arabians. I have them imported from Spain. Do you ride?"

Zack shook his head.

"Well, I'm sure my stable manager can teach you in no time at all." Her gaze skimmed the wiry, compact body. "It so happens that our youngest mare, Salomé, would be just about perfect for you."

Zack turned pleading eyes toward Diana.

"Oh, Mom, can I go? Please?" He took her hand in his and held it. "Please?" he repeated.

It took all of Diana's willpower to keep her irritation under control. "Why don't we talk about it later? Right now, Mrs. Lindford is leaving."

Taking her cue, Margaret rose. Her efforts to soften Diana had failed, but she had gained points with Zachary. For the moment, that was enough.

Opening her black alligator bag, she extracted a business card and laid it on the coffee table. "Any weekend would be fine with me." She walked past Diana. "Why don't you give me a call later in the week and let me know which day Zachary will be coming? My driver will pick him up. And bring him back, of course."

Stopping at Zack's side, she bent to kiss the top of his head. "Goodbye, my dear. I've enjoyed our short visit. And remember, the entire Lindford family is anxious and eager to meet you. So come and see us soon."

Diana walked Margaret to the door and waited to be out of earshot before hissing through clenched teeth, "That was a low blow, a despicable attempt on your part to worm yourself into his good graces."

"Nonsense. I was only—"

"I know exactly what you were doing, and it won't do you any good. Zack is too smart to fall for such low-handed tricks."

"I don't think he'll regard my offer as a trick. And neither should you. In fact, if you took the time to get to know me, you would realize that I'm a fair and rational woman."

Diana opened the door. "Goodbye, Mrs. Lindford."

Knowing when to retreat, Margaret gave her a curt nod. "I'll be seeing you soon, Miss Wells. I'm sure of that."

Then, her back straight, she walked slowly toward the waiting Bentley.

"You don't like her, do you, Mom?"

Startled, Diana turned around and met Zack's solemn gaze. "No, I don't." Her voice suddenly suspicious, she asked, "Why? Do you?"

Zack watched the slick car drive down the hill. "She's kind of neat."

Diana closed the door and walked back into the living room. "Because she has six horses?"

"Well . . . That's one reason."

No longer in the mood to clean the house, Diana unplugged the vacuum cleaner. "What's the other reason?"

Zack grinned. "She doesn't call me 'short stuff.' "

She arched a brow. "I thought you liked your nickname."

"I did, but . . . I'm a big kid now. I'd like to be called by my real name."

"Let's see, would that be 'Zachary,' " Diana mimicked in a perfect imitation of Margaret Lindford's finishing school accent. "Or 'dear?' "

Zack chuckled. "That's pretty good, Mom. You sound just like her."

It wasn't until the following morning as Diana was cooking Zack's oatmeal that he brought up the subject of Margaret's horses again.

"Do you think I could go for a short visit at Mrs. Lindford's ranch, Mom? I mean, it wouldn't hurt anything, would it?"

She spooned the oatmeal into a bowl and brought it to the kitchen table. "I think it's best if you forget about that," she said, sitting across from him.

"Why?"

"Because after that visit, she'll expect you to go for a second one and then a third. Before you know it, she'll want you there every weekend."

"No, she won't. She only wants to show me her horses."

"I'm sorry."

She started to reach for his hand, but he jerked it away. "That's not fair. I didn't do anything wrong, and you're punishing me."

"No, I'm not."

"Then why are you trying to keep me from having fun? From having my own horse?"

Startled by the hostility in Zack's voice, she almost snapped back, then stopped herself. She had lain awake half the night, wondering if her decision not to share Zack with the Lindfords was a reasonable one. Did she have the right to deny him his legacy? To deprive him of the wealth and security that was rightfully his?

She glanced at Zack, who was still sulking. He was so young, so vulnerable. What would happen to that sweet innocence, that candor, that loving nature if he were allowed to spend weeks at a time with a man like Travis?—a man with no morals and no compassion.

I'm doing the right thing, she thought, determined to trust her instincts. Whatever the consequences, I must protect him from Travis.

She stroked Zack's cheek with the back of her finger, half expecting him to jerk his head away. He didn't. "I'm not doing this to hurt you," she said gently. "I'm doing it to protect you. Trust me, darling. The less contact we have with the Lindfords, the better off we'll be."

He stared unhappily into his oatmeal. "I've always wanted to learn how to ride a horse."

"Really? You never told me that."

He shrugged. "What difference would it make? You're always too busy anyway."

The remark took her by surprise. Was that what he thought? That she wasn't making enough time for him? "I tell you what. If learning how to ride really means that much to you, I'll take you to the Haverford Stables next Sunday. How's that?"

He looked up, his gaze still suspicious. "Really?"

She nodded. "Really." This time when she took his hand, he didn't withdraw it. "Now hurry up with your breakfast, or you'll be late for school."

Moments later, as she watched the yellow school bus drive away, she wondered how she was going to fit one more activity into her already full schedule.

On Thursday afternoon Margaret was busy opening her mail when the phone rang. It was Diana Wells. This time the young woman's voice was calm, almost pleasant.

She's come to her senses, Margaret thought excitedly. She is going to let Zachary come for a visit. "How are you, my dear?"

"Fine. I hope I'm not catching you at a bad time."

"Not at all." Margaret paused briefly before adding, "Have you and Zachary discussed my proposition?"

"We have. And I'm afraid the answer is no. Zack won't be coming to your ranch. Or to your hotel. In fact, I don't want him to have any more contact with you. Of course, that goes for Travis as well. From now on, anything you or your son want to say to me will have to be said through my attorney."

Margaret's hopeful mood vanished. "Is that what Zachary wants?"

"It's what *I* want. And since I'm Zack's mother, it's the only decision that counts."

"You're making a very serious mistake, Miss Wells. You're denying that boy his birthright, his heritage. He'll resent you for it someday."

"I don't think so. But if that should happen, I'll deal with it when the time comes."

"You can't keep me away from Zachary! I'm the boy's grandmother."

Margaret heard the young woman sigh. "I have no desire to argue with you, Mrs. Lindford. To be perfectly honest, I wasn't even going to call. But after thinking it over, I decided I owed you the courtesy of—"

"You owe me much more than that, dammit!"

There was a soft click at the other end as Diana Wells hung up.

Margaret slammed the receiver down. Damn that woman! Travis had been right about her after all. She was nothing but a heartless bitch.

Well, she could be just as bitchy.

Margaret picked up the telephone and dialed her son's number. "Have you heard from Kane?" she asked in a clipped tone when he answered.

"Not yet. Why? What happened?"

"I want you to call him again, Travis. Try the winery, his house, the courthouse. Don't stop until you have found him."

"For God's sake, will you tell me—"

Margaret lifted a defiant chin. "We're suing Diana Wells for custody of Zachary—*full* custody."

6

"Good morning, Jackie. Any calls?"

As Kane Sanders stepped from the elevator and into the reception room of his law offices in San Francisco's financial district, his secretary, an attractive brunette with a bubbling personality, stood up and ran after him, memo pad in hand.

"Six," she said, trying to keep up with his fast stride as he walked down the long, gray-carpeted hallway. "Well, three actually, since the other three are from the same person."

Kane smiled. After seven years in his employ, five of which had been in New York, Jackie still possessed that same breathless, eager quality that had delighted him from the start. She hadn't had much legal experience then, but he had hired her anyway for nothing more than her enthusiasm. He had never regretted it. She kept his busy life in impeccable order, was loyal, and fiercely protective of him.

"The first call is from Judge Baxter. He wants to know if you'll join him at the country club this Saturday for a foursome. His brother is in town for the weekend, and he wants to beat him in a bad way. The second call is from Tony Santino, who, as you know, was arrested last week for extortion and drug dealing. So is the third call, the fourth, and the fifth."

Kane pushed open the door to his office and walked over to his desk. "What does he want?"

"A new lawyer."

"What happened to his legal staff? If I recall, he has about a dozen attorneys working for him."

"According to this morning's newspaper, he fired them all."

"Lucky me." Kane removed his brown herringbone jacket and tossed it on a chair. Underneath he wore a crisp, tan-striped shirt and a silk tie in a multicolor abstract design. "Who's the last call from?"

"Travis Lindford. He wants to meet you for lunch today at noon. He said it's urgent."

Kane shook his head. How typical of Travis to assume he could rearrange his schedule to suit his at a moment's notice.

"Call Judge Baxter for me, will you, Jackie? Tell him I'd be happy to make him look good on Saturday."

"What about Santino?"

"I'll call him myself."

Her eyes took on a worried expression. "What are you going to tell him?"

"The truth, that my schedule is full and I'm not free to take on another case." He gave her an amused look. "Don't worry. I'll be diplomatic. And courteous. I have no wish to end up on his list of people he uses for target practice."

"Don't joke about those things, boss. Santino is a dangerous man."

"I know, but he'll be behind bars soon enough." He put his briefcase on the desk and opened it. "Is there anything else on my agenda?"

"No, that's it for today." She made one last check mark on her pad, with a little flourish this time. "Did you remember to send flowers to your aunt?"

"Ahhh!" He hit his forehead with the palm of his

hand. Aunt Beckie's birthday. How could he have forgotten?

"I'll take care of it for you," Jackie promised. "Yellow roses, right?"

Kane nodded as he wrote Beckie's name on his desk calendar as a reminder to call her today. "Thanks, Jackie. What would I do without you?"

She rolled her eyes toward the ceiling. "God only knows." She closed her notebook. "Will you be needing me for anything else?"

"A couple of letters. But not until after lunch. I'll let you know."

She had barely closed the door behind her when the phone on his desk rang. He picked it up and lowered his six-foot one-inch frame into a brown swivel chair as he took Travis Lindford's call. "I was just about to call you, Travis. What's up?"

"I need to talk to you."

The absence of small chitchat and the urgency in Travis's voice took him by surprise. He sat up. "Is something wrong with Margaret?"

"No, she's fine." He paused. "It's me. I need advice about something. If noon isn't convenient—"

"No, that's fine. Tadich Grill all right with you? It's close to my office."

"Great. I'll see you there."

Kane hung up, a puzzled expression on his face. It wasn't like Travis to be so brief. A born charmer, he never missed an opportunity to dazzle whether on the phone or in person. It was a side of him many people found exasperating. Kane found it merely amusing.

They had met more than twenty-five years ago. Kane's father had been the Lindfords' comptroller at the time, and the two boys had struck a quick friendship. But there were too many differences between them to make it a strong and lasting one. Eventually, each had gone his separate way, only seeing each other occasionally.

It would be interesting to see what kind of trouble Travis had gotten himself into this time.

Ruled by time and bureaucratic protocol, San Francisco's financial district at the noon hour was a beehive of activity, with traffic clogging the downtown streets, horns blaring impatiently, and thousands of office workers storming out of their respective buildings at the same time.

Hands in his pockets, Kane strode down Battery Street, enjoying the frantic pace. After calling New York home for eighteen years, he had regarded his return to San Francisco two years before as an experiment, convinced he'd be back East before the last box was unpacked.

To his surprise, he had adjusted immediately. More than adjusted. He had fallen in love with the beautiful city by the bay all over again.

Although the pace here was similar to that of New York, San Francisco was different from any other city he knew, mainly because it had retained a certain mystique. Evidence of its rich past was everywhere—in the elegant Victorian houses that had survived the devastating 1906 earthquake, the famous cable cars as they plunged down the city's steep hills, the sound of a fog horn at dusk. Even the grim outline of Alcatraz couldn't be viewed without remembering the infamous men who had lived, and died, there.

As Kane reached the landmark restaurant on California Street, he pushed the door open and stood in the entrance, scanning the crowd. Then, spotting Travis at a booth, he waved and made his way toward him.

From his vantage seat in the back of the room,

Travis watched as Kane walked across the crowded restaurant.

As always when the attorney entered a room, female conversation stopped and lust-filled eyes stripped him from head to toe. Small wonder, Travis thought with a pinch of envy. At thirty-eight, Kane Sanders radiated confidence, success, and virility. He was tall, with brown hair and penetrating dark eyes, and moved with the understated grace of an athlete—which he was, time permitting.

It was no secret that Margaret adored him. He was the man she wished Travis had become—honest, self-reliant, and hard-working. Travis didn't begrudge the place Kane occupied in his mother's heart. As long as it didn't affect his standing where the Lindford Hotel was concerned, Margaret was free to love anyone she wished.

"Hello, Kane," Travis said, rising to shake his hand. "I appreciate your coming on such short notice."

"You caught me on a light day." Kane slid into the banquette and ordered the restaurant's famous swordfish and a Perrier. "How's Margaret?"

"Ornery as usual. She sends her love."

Kane settled back, studying Travis, who was sipping a scotch on the rocks. A preoccupied expression in the handsome blue eyes surprised him. Travis wasn't the worrying type. "What's the problem?"

Travis put his glass down. "I need your help, old boy."

Kane's mouth quirked into a smile. "Whom did you kill?"

"No one." Travis's expression soured. "Yet." He cast a quick glance around him as if to reassure himself they wouldn't be overheard. "I just found out that a girl I used to date years ago had a child—my child— and never told me about it."

The thought that Travis had fathered a child came as no surprise to Kane. With his lifestyle, it was a wonder he hadn't been served with a half-dozen paternity suits already. "Are you sure you're the father?"

"Yes. No one's denying that."

"Why didn't she tell you about the baby?"

He shrugged. "Maybe she thought I wouldn't make a good father. My guess is that she fell for someone else and wanted me out of the way."

"Is she putting pressure on you now?"

"No." Once again, Travis repeated his version of the story, his attempts to talk to Diana, and her decision to sever all contacts between the boy and the Lindford family.

While Travis talked, Kane watched him, listening to the inflections in the man's voice as they fluctuated, revealing anxiety one moment and anger the next. He found it odd that a man who had been rather passionate about avoiding commitment of any kind should suddenly be so fired up about a son he had never met.

He waited until the waiter had brought their lunch, then, casually, he said, "You surprise me, Travis. I never took you for the fatherly type."

"I wasn't." Travis speared a fried oyster with his fork. "Until I set eyes on that boy." He met Kane's inquisitive gaze without flinching. "Now that I know he's mine, I want to get to know him. I want to be part of his life, do things with him. You know . . . play ball, go fishing."

Kane held back a smile. Somehow, the picture of Travis hooking bait at the end of a fishing line was difficult to conjure. "Have you told the boy's mother how you feel?"

"Of course I told her. She doesn't give a damn. She's carrying this grudge over something that never happened.'' Chewing on the oyster, he added, "I want to sue that bitch for custody.''

"Not *full* custody.''

"Yes. Full custody. I tried to be accommodating, Kane, but she wants to play hardball. So we'll play hardball.''

Kane leaned his elbows on the table and steepled his fingers, talking over them. "Travis, listen to me. Custody cases are messy, emotionally draining for both parties, and devastating for the child.''

Travis waved his fork. "I know all that. What I'm asking is, do I have a case?''

"A few years ago, I would have said no. But things have changed. Last February the State of California even passed a law ruling that biological fathers would have as much rights as biological mothers. Therefore, yes, you could have a case.''

"What are my chances of winning?''

"Very slim.''

Travis put his fork down. "What do you mean, very slim? He's my son, dammit. My own flesh and blood. Not only was his birth kept from me, but he was given away to a stranger without my consent. Do you think that's fair?''

"No, but that's not how the courts are going to look at it.''

"Why not? What's the problem?''

"For one thing, this Diana Wells is his legal mother and the only parent Zachary has ever known. He loves her. He's emotionally attached to her. Second, you and Nadine were never married.''

"That doesn't make him any less my son!''

"That's true. Even so, you're going to have one hell of a time convincing a judge that Zachary would be better off with you.'' He took a bite of his swordfish.

"Why don't you take a simpler approach to the problem?"

"What's that?"

"Talk to Diana Wells again. Tell her all you want is to visit the boy from time to time. Enough time has passed. She might be in a more receptive mood."

Travis shook his head. "I told you, she doesn't want to talk to me. She's into slamming doors in my face and hanging up on me when I call. She even told my mother she'd get a restraining order if she had to. Can you beat that?"

"I'm sorry. I wish I could help you—"

"You can." Travis leaned forward. "I want you to represent me."

The request took Kane aback. "I'm a criminal attorney, Travis. I don't handle custody cases."

"I know. But Mother wants you."

"Margaret isn't suing. You are."

"And you're the one I want."

"That's nonsense. There are half a dozen lawyers in this state much more qualified than I could ever be in such matters."

"And not one of them has your courtroom experience. Judges respect you. And you are *eminently* qualified because you've been through a custody battle yourself—"

As Kane stiffened, Travis cursed under his breath. "Damn, Kane. I'm sorry. I shouldn't have brought that up."

No longer hungry, Kane slowly put his fork and knife down. He had come back to San Francisco to forget the past, but after two years it always seemed to catch up with him when he least expected it. Like now.

"I'm sorry," he heard Travis say again.

Through sheer willpower, Kane chased away the

memory Travis's remark had reawakened, and concentrated on the present. "It's all right."

"It's just that this boy means so much to me, Kane. And to Mother."

It would have been easy to turn Travis down. He had no ties to him personally. He didn't even like him. But he couldn't turn his back on Margaret. Not after all she had done for him and his mother.

"All right," he said after a while. "I'll do it." He pulled out a small appointment book from his breast pocket and leafed through it. "I won't be able to meet with you until the latter part of next week, but I'll have Jackie file the necessary papers."

Travis heaved a sigh of relief and leaned back in his seat. "I can't tell you how grateful I am."

"Don't be too optimistic. As I said, your chances of getting what you want are slim, and we have a lot of work ahead of us."

"I understand."

"One of the first things I want you to do is change your lifestyle. Diana Wells's lawyer is bound to bring it up at the hearing, so you'd better be prepared to show that you've turned a new leaf, that you're taking fatherhood seriously."

"I am, Kane. I swear I am."

Kane gave him a long, thoughtful look. "Good." Then, glancing at his watch, he stood up. "I've got to go." He started to reach for his wallet, but Travis stopped him.

"Let me. You can get the next one." Rising, he shook Kane's hand again. "Thanks, Kane. Thanks an awful lot."

"You're welcome." Kane's smile was skeptical. "I think."

7

Wrapped in an old, comfortable chenille robe, Diana sat in her bay window, sipping her morning coffee. Straight ahead, Lafayette Park was already bustling with activity—young mothers with their toddlers, joggers out for their mid-morning run and older men and women enjoying the warm autumn sun. Under an oak tree an old Chinese man dressed in black moved in slow, fluid motions, as he did his tai chi routine.

This was her favorite time of the year. The crowds were gone, the leaves throughout the city were turning brilliant shades of gold and russet, and the air was crisp and invigorating.

Diana felt at peace. More than a week had gone by since her phone call to Margaret Lindford. At first she had feared the worst—an army of lawyers storming her house, court summons, or at the very least, a succession of irate phone calls.

There had been nothing.

Her gaze followed a flock of brown pelicans as it headed south. Although it was too soon to draw an easy breath, her sixth sense told her what she had suspected all along. Travis's fatherly instincts were as fickle as the rest of him. No doubt he had found out what it would take to fight for his son, and simply given up.

As she took another sip of coffee, a gray car pulled up in front of her house. Curious, she watched as a short, nondescript man stepped out and headed toward the house.

Diana tensed. Had she been rejoicing too soon?

The doorbell rang.

Filled with a sense of impending doom, she tightened the robe's belt around her waist and went to open the door.

The man's face was expressionless. "Miss Diana Wells?"

"Yes."

Reaching into his breast pocket, he pulled out a folded sheet of paper and handed it to her. "This is for you, ma'am."

Her hands trembling, she unfolded the document and read it.

It was a summons to appear in San Francisco District Court on December 6.

Travis Lindford was suing her for custody of Zack.

Sitting in Margaret Lindford's drawing room, where the family had been summoned moments ago, Randall Atkins sat in stunned silence as his mother-in-law told them the incredible story of her miraculously found grandson. Next to him, his wife, Francesca, was equally silent.

Travis stood in front of the fireplace, one elbow resting on the mantel, his right hand twirling the ice in his glass. As the center of attention for the last several minutes, it was obvious he was making the most of the moment.

Randall took a sip of his drink, his eyes riveted to his brother-in-law. So, the favorite son had bailed himself out once again. Just when everyone thought he was drowning, he had found a life raft and pulled himself back to shore, alive and triumphant.

Two weeks ago, when Mrs. Barclay's necklace had been stolen from the Lindford presidential suite, Margaret had been ready to hang Travis by the balls and name Francesca as her successor.

Then, the impossible had happened. Faced with an ultimatum neither Randall nor Francesca thought Travis would tolerate, he had not only accepted his mother's terms, but also had miraculously produced the one thing she wanted more than anything in the world—a grandson.

"And so," Margaret continued as she let her gaze rest first on her daughter, then on Travis. "In accordance with an old Lindford tradition, I will turn over my shares of the Lindford to Travis not on the day of his first child's birth, since he already has a child, but on the day the court awards him custody of Zachary." She smiled. "Francesca, Randall, I hope you'll both join me in congratulating Travis."

As no one made a sound, she looked at her daughter, raising an eyebrow. "Francesca?"

Randall turned to look at his wife, his gaze skimming her lovely features, the thick black hair held back with a designer scarf, the serious dark eyes, the generous mouth. Although there was an unusual pallor to her cheeks, no one could have guessed the depth of her disappointment. Except him.

"Francesca? Did you hear me, dear?"

Francesca squared her shoulders. She knew what she was expected to say. *Congratulations, Travis. I'm thrilled for you. Let me know if I can be of any help.* But how could she when she knew that this omen, this "divine intervention" as her mother had so dramatically put it, meant that the Lindford was lost to her forever?

She deserved the hotel, dammit. At thirty-one, she had spent more than half her life preparing herself for the day when she would become the Lindford's first female CEO. She had worked hard to achieve that goal, surprising everyone, even her parents, with her commitment, her innovative ideas, and her guts.

She had almost made it. But now, with this startling announcement, the dream had ended. Travis had won. Not fair and square. But he had won.

Because she was a Lindford, and because in spite of everything, she loved her brother, she let go of her husband's hand, stood up, and walked over to the fireplace.

"Congratulations, Travis," she said, her voice trembling with a mixture of emotions. "A child is an extraordinary blessing." She smiled. "I can't wait to meet my new nephew."

That much was true. She adored children. The thought of having a small boy brighten those much too serious Sunday dinners at her mother's ranch almost made her forget how miserable she felt.

"Thanks, Sis." Travis kissed her cheek, then wrapped an arm around her waist. "What about you, old boy?" he asked with a taunting smile in Randall's direction. "Are you happy for me?"

Francesca saw the imperceptible tightening of Randall's handsome features. Behind the steel-rimmed glasses, the amber eyes, usually so warm, hardened as he skewered his brother-in-law with a hard stare.

Anxious to avoid a confrontation between the two men, she flashed her husband a dazzling smile. "Perhaps a more appropriate question would be 'Are you up to playing uncle?' "

For Francesca's sake, Randall forced a smile. "Of course. And you have my heartfelt congratulations, too, Travis." He turned his gaze toward Margaret. "Although I must say I'm a little surprised that Kane agreed to take the case. I didn't think criminal attorneys—"

"This is a family matter, Randall," Margaret cut in. "And I have always considered Kane a member of this family."

Later that night, as Randall and Francesca sat in their Telegraph Hill apartment, sipping white wine, Randall took his wife's hand and held it. She hadn't said a word in the car as they drove back from the Lindford, and he had respected her silence, her need to think things through on her own.

"I'm sorry about tonight," he said at last. "I know how badly you wanted the Lindford to be yours, how hard you worked toward that goal."

Francesca stared into her glass. "I can't say Mother's decision came as a total surprise. We all knew how she felt about the famous Lindford Tradition. I just didn't expect it to happen so quickly, though. Or so dramatically."

Randall shook his head. "I don't understand Margaret sometime. She is a shrewd woman. Can't she see that Travis doesn't give a damn about that child? That the only reason he's suing is because winning the custody suit will get him the hotel a little sooner?"

"I'm sure she does. But her desire to have a grandchild is far more important to her than Travis's distorted motives."

"A few months from now, when the hotel no longer belongs to the family but to a couple of million stockholders, she'll wish she had never made that decision. Of course, by then it will be too late."

Francesca nodded, remembering the day Travis had approached their parents with his idea of taking the hotel public.

"We could make millions of dollars from the sale,"

he had told them, showing them facts and figures he and his broker had worked out. "And with the money we could build another Lindford. And another one after that. I know this Saudi sheik who's willing to invest—"

Charles had cut him short. "As long as I live," he had thundered, "the hotel will *never* go public."

Although Travis had never brought up the subject again, and had sworn to Margaret he would always respect his father's wishes, Francesca knew that the idea was still stewing in his head.

She was silent the rest of the night, barely touching the dinner Meg, their housekeeper, had earlier prepared for them. At nine o'clock, after she and Randall had stacked the dishes into the dishwasher, Francesca told her husband she was going to bed.

Concern filled his eyes. "Are you all right? You're not coming down with something, are you?"

Smiling, Francesca kissed him lightly on the lips. Sweet, wonderful Randall. How would she have faced tonight's ordeal without him? "No. I'm just tired, that's all. I have a big day ahead of me tomorrow."

"Let me make you some hot chocolate to take with you."

She shook her head. "Not tonight, darling." She kissed him again, gazing deep into his eyes. "And stop worrying about me. I'll be fine. Really."

One shoulder against the door jamb, he watched her walk away, his heart tearing at the sight of the forlorn figure disappearing down the hall. No one understood parental favoritism better than he. Perhaps because he had experienced it himself years ago. He was a grown man now, and happier than he had ever been in his life, but the scars were still there. And at times, they still hurt.

He closed his eyes, not wanting to remember. But

the images, triggered by tonight's events, were already there, vivid and painful.

He had been born in Billings, Montana, the younger of two children. Because he was frail and hopelessly shy, it was easy for his brother, Jimmy, to pick on him day after day, humiliating him at home and in front of his classmates.

When Randall complained to his parents, their reaction was always the same. They laughed.

"Your brother is just playing with you, Randall. He means no harm."

It was no secret that Jimmy was their favorite. Although he wasn't too bright, he was big and strong and a first-rate athlete, like their dad, who always took Jimmy on bike rides and to football games. When Randall asked his father why he never took him along, Bill Atkins always replied, "Because you wouldn't have any fun."

It wasn't until years later, when Randall was thirteen and Jimmy sixteen, that tragedy struck, ending any hope Randall had ever had of being accepted by his parents.

He was in the barn of their Montana farm, repairing a ladder, when Jimmy and his girlfriend came in. Jimmy, eager to show off, ordered Randall to leave, but Randall, who had been punished a week earlier for not doing his chores, refused.

"In that case, dumb head," Jimmy said, grabbing Randall by his shirt collar, "I guess I'll have to throw you out."

But this was one time Randall wasn't going to be intimidated. Not in front of a girl. Before Jimmy could anticipate his brother's intention, Randall threw the first punch, catching the bigger boy off guard.

In spite of his size, Jimmy lost his footing and fell

hard, hitting his back on the heavy disk harrow his father used to work the soil before planting.

He had survived, but the fall had severed his spinal cord and he was never able to walk again. Randall spent the next five years trying to redeem himself. He went to church with his parents on Sundays, waited on Jimmy hand and foot, and made the honor roll year after year. Artistically gifted, he even won a blue ribbon one year with a painting he had entered in a competition.

Nothing he did was ever enough. His parents, who hadn't cared very much about him in the first place, now treated him like a stranger, hardly ever speaking to him and avoiding any kind of eye contact.

When he approached them, after his graduation from high school, and told them he wanted to go to art school, they showed no interest—and no willingness to pay his tuition.

"Maybe I should move out of the house," he told them one night after a particularly depressing weekend.

If anyone heard him, they gave no indication of it.

One week after his eighteenth birthday, with seven hundred dollars in his pocket and dreams of becoming the next van Gogh in his heart, he was on a bus to San Francisco.

Two years later when the *San Francisco Examiner* had done a feature on several of the city's promising young artists, and mentioned Randall's name, he had sent a copy of the article to his parents.

To this day, he had no idea if they had received it.

The mantel clock struck the hour. Pulling himself from the doorway, Randall walked over to the fireplace and checked the glowing ashes with the tip of a poker before closing the glass doors.

Fortunately, Francesca's family situation wasn't as

dismal as his had been. Although it was obvious Margaret favored Travis, she loved Francesca very much and would never deny her anything.

Except the hotel.

8

In the several days following his meeting with Travis, Kane had learned a great deal about Diana Wells. Most of the information had been supplied by Ron Ackerman, a private investigator Kane called upon regularly when working on a case.

Ron was thirty-five, a handsome Afro-American whose good looks and ability to play any role had greatly contributed to his success.

He had come to deliver his latest report in person and sat in Kane's office, his right ankle propped on his left knee. "You'll find a couple of newspaper articles that appeared in the *Globe*," he said, pointing at the file Kane was reading. "And a tape of an interview that was aired the day of her grand opening."

Kane nodded and kept reading. The Diana Wells who was emerging in front of his eyes didn't bear much resemblance to the woman Travis had described.

The daughter of two school teachers, she had given up her dream of becoming a doctor to care for her ailing mother and had later enrolled at the prestigious California Cooking Institute. In 1982 she had started her own catering service before finally opening Harbor View two weeks ago.

Although the article said she was the mother of a young boy, it made no mention of his being adopted.

The file also included information on an older brother who had done time for armed robbery in 1976, but apparently Diane had severed all ties with him long ago.

Kane looked up from Ron's report. "How is she handling working and taking care of the boy?"

"Her schedule is hectic, but she manages it quite well. She sees her son off to school every morning, goes to the restaurant for a few hours, and is back home before he gets back from school at three. She takes him to soccer practice or to his cub scout meeting, then has dinner with him. At six a baby-sitter takes over, and Diana goes back to the restaurant where she stays until closing. Harbor View is closed on Sundays."

"Any sign she is neglecting the kid?"

"Not from what I can see. Some of her neighbors, including the college girl who baby-sits Zachary, call her Super Mom and wish they had half her energy. From what I've been able to observe, the kid adores her."

Kane nodded and closed the file. "Good job, Ron." He smiled. "Just out of curiosity, how did you find out so much in so little time?"

Ron grinned. "You'd be surprised how loose people's tongues get when they think you're a Hollywood producer scouting for a possible movie location."

Kane chuckled. In past years, Ron had transformed himself into a telephone repairman, a street sweeper, a masseur, a newspaper reporter, and a priest. The movie producer was a new role.

"I'd keep that one in your repertoire if I were you."

"I intend to." Ron stood up. "Anything else you need me to do?"

"Not right now."

When the private investigator was gone, Kane picked up Diana's file again, studying the photograph that had been taken by a *Globe* photographer. Pretty. Interesting eyes, although he couldn't tell their color in the black-and-white shot. There was no affectation about her, nothing phony, just an easy kind of charm that made one feel totally at ease.

Still, appearances could be deceiving, especially when they involved a beautiful woman. He ought to know. It wasn't so long ago that he had let himself fall under the spell of a beautiful woman only to realize too late that she had the heart of a killer shark.

Maybe he ought to take a look at Diana Wells himself, talk to her if he could, find out what she was all about. It never hurt to know what sort of opponent he'd be meeting in the courtroom.

On impulse he buzzed his secretary. "Jackie," he said, still looking at Diana Wells's picture. "Are you doing anything special for lunch?"

"Not unless you call low-fat yogurt special."

"How would you feel about trying out a new restaurant?"

"I'm game. As long as it's not sushi."

"No sushi. It's called Harbor View, and it's down at the Marina. Make us a lunch reservation, will you, Jackie? Today if possible."

Harbor View was located on the western end of the Marina District, on a site that had been almost entirely destroyed in the 1989 earthquake and later rebuilt.

Kane and Jackie sat at a window table overlooking the Golden Gate Bridge. Beyond it, the rugged hills of Marin County stretched for miles, their peaks already shrouded in fog.

They had just finished their Dover sole when Diana Wells came out of the kitchen and began circulating around the dining room. Smiling and shaking hands, she chatted pleasantly with each customer, graciously accepting compliments.

The newspaper picture hadn't done her justice, Kane thought. The eyes, which at first he had expected to be brown, were actually a smoky shade of green. Her dark auburn hair was chin-length and reminded him of the wavy style Marilyn Monroe had made famous years ago. She was shorter than he had expected, five four at the most, but perfectly proportioned. She wore fashionable wide-legged silk pants in a rich hunter green, a matching blouse, and no jewelry.

"She's lovely," Jackie murmured, taking a sip of her club soda and watching Diana above the rim of her glass.

Kane didn't reply. As Diana neared his table, he found himself watching her with more interest than was reasonably needed. Her laughter was warm and infectious, her lips soft, inviting. If the news of the custody suit had caused her any distress, it didn't show.

"Hello. I'm Diana Wells." She smiled at him and Jackie, then glanced discreetly at the remains on their plates. "I trust the sole was satisfactory?"

Kane returned the smile. "Very good."

"It was superb," Jackie said enthusiastically. "Did you prepare it?"

"Not this time. But I'll make sure to relay the compliment to the chef." Her eyes drifted toward Kane. "I'm glad you're pleased. Come back and see us soon." She held his gaze for a second more before moving to the next table.

Jackie slowly lowered her glass. "She's charming."

"On the surface, yes."

"You still think there's a bitch hidden underneath?"

"Travis seems to think so."

"I've never known you to give much credibility to what Travis Lindford says."

Kane laughed. "That's true, which is exactly why we're here."

Jackie dabbed her mouth with a crisp, pink napkin and stood up. "In that case, why don't I let you do your job and I'll go do mine?"

"Are you sure you don't want dessert?" he asked as he stood up and held her chair. "I saw tiramisu on the menu."

Her gaze was full of mock reproach. "You sure know how to hurt a girl, boss. Lucky for me, I'm made of steel."

Kane laughed as he handed her his keys. "In that case, take my car. I'll catch a cab."

He waited until she was gone, before signaling his waiter. "I wonder if I could have a word with Miss Wells in private," he asked as he included a generous tip to his credit card slip.

The waiter, a good-looking young man who had given him impeccable service, bowed his head. "I'll see if she's available, Mr. Sanders. May I tell her what you wish to see her about?"

Kane scrawled his signature on the slip, looked up, and smiled. "It's personal."

"Very well."

Moments later, the waiter was back. "Miss Wells is in her office," he said, pointing to a hallway at the back of the dining room. "Second room on the left."

Kane followed his instruction and found himself in front of a door simply marked OFFICE. He gave two short knocks.

"Come in."

Diana Wells sat at her desk, surrounded by a mountain of cookbooks, menus, and catalogs. On her right was a MacIntosh, and behind her a bookcase filled with more books. French doors opened on a charming garden planted with flowers and herbs. As she leaned forward, a stream of sunlight fell over her hair, making it look as if it were on fire.

She watched him as he approached. A friendly light danced in her eyes. "Are you and your wife having second thoughts about the sole?"

"Jackie is my secretary. And no, we're not having second thoughts about anything. The food was perfect. And so was the service."

With a pleased smile she indicated a chair across her desk. "Then what can I do for you, Mr. Sanders?" She tilted her head to the side. "You're not a competitor, are you?" she asked in a playful tone. "If you are, I must warn you. My recipes are not for sale."

The light, friendly chatter was unexpected. And pleasant. There was something exciting about her, an energy, an undercurrent he found both startling and seductive. Foolishly, he found himself wishing he weren't here on business. "You have nothing to fear from me in that department," he said, watching her hair shimmer in the sunlight. "My culinary talents are limited to peanut butter and jelly sandwiches and soup from a can."

Her mouth curved into an understanding smile, and he decided that now was as good a time as any to level with her. "Actually, I'm an attorney."

The change in her was instantaneous. The green eyes chilled, seemed to grow darker. "Whose attorney?"

"I represent Travis Lindford."

This time her expression turned stony. "Kane Sanders. Of course. The name was familiar, but I didn't make the connection."

"I thought we could—"

"Shouldn't you be talking to my lawyer instead of me, Mr. Sanders?"

"I didn't come here as the enemy, Miss Wells, but rather as a mediator."

"Why? Is Travis getting cold feet? Did he finally realize he had no chance whatsoever of winning this battle?"

He held her cool gaze. "On the contrary. He's more determined than ever to take the case to court. I'm the one who's reluctant to do so."

"Does he know you're here?"

"No. But I'm confident that if I go back to him with a decent offer on your part, he'll drop the suit."

"If by decent offer, you mean my allowing Travis and his family to play a role in my son's upbringing, then you came for nothing, Mr. Sanders. It's just not going to happen."

It was to the point. In a few succinct words she had told him he was not only wasting his time, but hers as well. Maybe he needed a different, softer approach. "Won't you at least hear me out?" he asked gently. "In exchange, I promise not to preach, to judge, or to take sides. Fair enough?"

Diana sat back and studied the attorney for a moment. Although Mitch had told her Kane Sanders was an old friend of the Lindfords, he wasn't the kind of lawyer she had expected Travis to hire. There was a forthrightness and a credibility about him she wouldn't have associated with anyone in Travis's entourage. In his mid-to-late thirties, he gave an impression of latent strength and had a face that was lean and strong, almost too angular to be considered handsome. Yet, there was something compelling about his looks, a masculinity that had made her instantly aware of him in the dining room.

She would hear him out, she decided at last, for no

other reason than to satisfy her curiosity. "All right." She glanced at her watch. "I suppose I can spare you a few minutes."

His mouth curved into a smile. "Thank you." He leaned back in his chair. "First of all, let me say that I understand your frustration. Zachary is your son. You've raised him and loved him. And now, out of nowhere, his father reappears, demanding to become a vital part of the boy's life."

Her gaze remained cool. "Demands he had no right to make."

"Laws have changed, Miss Wells. Today, fathers have more rights than ever."

"Some fathers, maybe. But not those who walk away from their pregnant girlfriends never to be heard from again. "Conscious of his eyes studying her with open interest, she tried to ignore her heightened awareness of him. "That's what your client did, Mr. Sanders. Or did he conveniently forget to tell you that?"

His penetrating eyes held hers. "I know that's what you claim he did. And I don't dispute your sincerity. But isn't it possible that Nadine Snyder lied to you?"

Her eyes flickered defensively. "No. She had no reason to lie."

"What reason would Travis have?"

"I stopped trying to figure him out long ago. But I can tell you this—Travis knew about the baby. He was the first person Nadine went to after finding out she was pregnant."

"Were they still seeing each other at the time?"

"Yes. But his reaction was not at all what she had expected. He was angry. He told her she should have been more careful, that he wasn't ready to be a father. He even accused her of trying to trap him into marriage."

"Was she?"

"Of course not! Nadine had too much self-respect for that."

She stood up and went to stand by the French doors. A bluejay was perched on the birdbath, a watchful eye surveying the surroundings before it bent down to take a drink. "She was hopelessly in love with him," she said with her back to Kane. "I knew that from the moment she brought him to the house to meet me."

"And you? How did you feel about him?"

"I didn't like him. I thought he was arrogant and self-centered, too conscious of who he was. Nadine was a simple girl, devoid of any affectation. She believed he loved her, wanted to marry her. I tried to tell her she was reading him wrong, but she didn't believe me." An old, familiar ache stirred deep inside her. "After he found out she was pregnant, he gave her five hundred dollars and told her to get an abortion. Then he walked away, and next thing we knew, he had left for Europe. Nadine was in shock, inconsolable. For a while, I thought she was going to die of a broken heart."

She turned back to face him. Her eyes were filled with tears. If that was an act, Kane thought with an odd pinch in his heart, then she was one hell of an actress. "Your version is quite different from the one I was told."

She gave a sarcastic laugh. "I don't doubt it. But what you were told, counselor, is a pack of lies. Travis Lindford has no more desire to be a father to my son than I have to fly to the moon."

"Then why would he go to such extent to have him?"

"I don't know. Why don't you ask him? Or better yet, ask his mother."

"Margaret?"

"Yes, Margaret. Something tells me she's the one behind this custody suit. I never met her until she came to see me a week ago, but from the moment she stepped into my house, I had her pegged for what she was."

"And what's that?" he asked, curious to hear what she thought of Margaret.

"Margaret Lindford is obsessed with the idea of continuing the Lindford name. Now that she found out Zachary is her flesh and blood, she'll stop at nothing to lure him into her web, to ensure that he ends up where she thinks he belongs—with her." She held Kane's direct gaze. "How's that for a first impression, Mr. Sanders?"

It was harsh, but not totally inaccurate. "I take it you don't like her much."

"I don't like people who try to manipulate other people."

"Do you believe me when I say I have no wish to manipulate you?"

The soft, soothing sound of his voice almost convinced her. Annoyed she could be so easily influenced, she shrugged. "I don't know you well enough to form an opinion about you."

"Then let me reassure you. I'm not the manipulative type. And I don't play games. But I wouldn't be doing my job if I didn't at least *attempt* to reach some sort of compromise with you."

She came to lean against the side of her desk and folded her arms, admiring his persistence. "I appreciate your candor, Mr. Sanders. Now allow *me* to be candid. There will be no compromise. I have no intention of handing over my son to Travis Lindford for one weekend, one day, or even one minute. You can tell him that."

"Don't you think you're being unreasonable?"

"I thought you weren't going to be judgmental."

He smiled faintly. "Sorry." Her eyes connected with his, and for a moment the impact of her gaze had him fumbling for words.

You're behaving like a damn teenager, Sanders. Cut it out.

He stood up. "Thanks for your time, Miss Wells. I'm sorry my visit didn't turn out as I had hoped."

"It was nothing personal."

Her gaze, direct and self-confident, gave him another jolt. "I'd better go back to my office before my secretary sends out a search party for me."

And before I make a total fool of myself.

As she walked with him to the door, the silky fabric of her slacks rustled with every step, stirring his senses. Suddenly, he was aware of her nearness, and of her scent, which reminded him of wildflowers.

He pulled a pen and a business card from his breast pocket. "Call me if you change your mind about reaching an agreement." He wrote down his home phone number before handing it to her. "Day or night."

The look in her eyes told him she wouldn't be changing her mind. "Goodbye, Miss Wells."

"Goodbye, Mr. Sanders."

9

Perched on a stool in Diana's kitchen, Kat sipped coffee as she listened to her friend's account of Kane Sanders's visit the day before.

When Diana was finished, Kat leaned forward, her expression eager. "So what do you think of him?"

Diana dipped her finger into the pound cake batter she had just whipped and licked it. Satisfied it tasted as it should, she poured it into a loaf pan. "I don't think anything of him. So get that silly grin off your face."

Kat pretended not to have heard that last remark. "Mitch says he's very good-looking. Is that true?"

Diana slid the cake pan into the hot oven and set the timer for thirty-five minutes. "I suppose you could say that."

"Sexy?"

"You're asking the wrong girl."

"Oh, come on," Kat teased. "It hasn't been that long, has it? You still know a sexy man when you see one."

"For heaven's sake, Kat! Must you measure every male/female encounter on a sexual level?"

Kat laughed. "Of course. I'm an artist, remember? I deal with emotions, reactions, feelings."

"Well, don't expect inspiration from me. With this custody hearing getting closer every day, believe me, my mind isn't on romance. And even if it were, I wouldn't be so stupid as to fall for Travis's attorney."

Reaching into the cookie jar Diana always kept filled, Kat helped herself to a chocolate-chip cookie and dunked it in her coffee. "Oh, I don't know. From what you told me about Kane Sanders, and from what I know of him, you could do a lot worse."

"That's where you're wrong. For all his charm, Kane Sanders could turn out to be a formidable enemy."

"What makes you say that?"

"After he left the restaurant, I called John McKay and found out a few things about Travis's attorney that made me wonder about his true motive for taking the case."

"You know what his motive is. He's a close friend of the Lindfords."

"He's also a divorced man."

Kat shrugged. "So are millions of other men. What's your point?"

"When he filed for divorce four years ago, he also filed for custody of his five-year-old son."

Kat lowered her cup. "I didn't know that. I wasn't even aware he had a child."

"He keeps his personal life very private. But John, as you know, is a thorough man. He had heard a rumor or two about Sanders, so he checked him out. Custody of the child went to his wife, a former fashion model, who, according to witnesses, wasn't a very good mother. Two months later, she and her boyfriend went to Southhampton for the weekend and left the child in the care of a baby-sitter." Diana removed her apron and tossed it on a chair. "He fell into the back-yard pool of their North Jersey home and drowned."

Kat gasped. "How horrible."

"There was an article in a New York newspaper

about the tragedy, and Kane Sanders was quoted as saying that if it hadn't been for the unfairness of a justice system that almost always ruled in favor of mothers regardless of their character, the accident would have never happened."

Kat's eyes narrowed. "Wait a minute, kiddo. If you're implying Kane took the case as some kind of vendetta for what happened to him, you're way off base. Mitch doesn't know an awful lot about him, but he knows one thing—when it comes to integrity, the man is faultless."

"He's also human."

They were interrupted by the sound of the doorbell. Glancing out the kitchen window, which overlooked the street, Diana saw her brother's battered Oldsmobile parked along the curb. "Oh, God," she moaned. "Not him. Not now." As Kat glanced over her shoulder, Diana opened the window. "Go away, Nick."

The only answer was a second, more insistent ring. In the house across the street, a window curtain moved. Diana cursed under her breath. "I'd better let him in before Mrs. Carmichael starts wondering who he is."

Kat followed her to the front door. "Do you want me to stay?"

Touched by her friend's concern, Diana squeezed her hand. "Thanks, Kat. But that won't be necessary. He's not staying long."

As Diana opened the door, her brother came striding in, a tall, slender man with shoulder-length brown hair held in a ponytail, their mother's green eyes, and a smile that had conned more than one gullible woman out of her life savings. He was unshaven and looked grungy in a pair of faded jeans, a sweatshirt with a frayed collar, and a stained suede jacket.

He flashed a white smile in Kat's direction. "Hey, kid, what's happening?"

Kat, not one to conceal her feelings, gave him a scathing look. "Diana is much too nice," she said, her voice dripping with contempt. "If you were *my* brother, I would have already cut you in pieces and fed you to the sharks."

Nick watched her storm off. "What the hell is the matter with *her?*"

Diana closed the door. "My guess is she can't stand the sight of you."

"Yeah? Well, tell her the feeling is mutual." Before she could stop him, Nick walked past her and into the kitchen. "Mmmm, smells good in here. What are you baking?"

"I thought I told you to never come here again," she snapped as she followed him.

"I had to talk to you."

"You could have called."

"I tried. Your line was busy." He sat at the kitchen table and stretched his long legs on another chair. "Unless, of course, you took your phone off the hook."

That's exactly what she had done. Ever since Travis had announced to the press that he had a son, the phone, both here and at the restaurant, had been ringing night and day, leaving her no recourse but to unplug it.

With the back of her hand she pushed his feet off the chair and tucked it back under the table. "What do you want, Nick?"

"I heard about the custody suit that jerk filed against you." His tone was filled with feigned sympathy. "That's a real bummer, Sis. I would have come sooner, but I was out of town."

"Since when do you care about my problems?"

"I've always cared. Regardless of what you think of me, we're family, Di. Your welfare means a lot to me. Zack's, too, for that matter." He gave her a reproachful look. "Even though you've never allowed me to meet him."

"Is that what you came to say?"

"No. I came because I want to help you."

This time she laughed. *"You?* Help *me?* You've got to be kidding."

"Yes, me. I've got connections, people who can get you and Zack new passports, a new identity."

She gave him a disbelieving stare. "Are you suggesting that I run away? Have you lost your mind?"

"You're the one who's lost her mind if you think you can win against a guy like Travis Lindford. The man has a lot of clout in this town."

"He's nothing but a playboy!"

"So what? You think the judge is going to give a damn about that?" He shook his head. "Not a chance, Sis. Not with what the Lindfords have done for this town over the years. If you don't believe me, read the papers. Not one day passes by without the old lady being mentioned in some publication or another. Saint Margaret gives away enough dough each year to support a third-world country for the next hundred years."

"And for that I should run away like a common thief?"

"You got a better idea?"

He would never change, she thought. At forty-one, he was still thinking with the brain of a sixteen-year-old. "Just out of curiosity, Nick, are you offering your services on a pro bono basis? Or is there a price tag attached to this sudden bout of brotherly love?"

He had the grace to blush. "The latter. After all, a man has to eat, don't he?"

"And we know what a big appetite you have."

He ignored the sarcasm. "Thirty thousand ought to do it," he said without batting an eyelash. "I know you're low on cash at the moment, with the restaurant and all. But if you took an equity loan on the house, you'd have enough to pay me my fee and start a new life far away from here."

She didn't bother to tell him she had already re-mortgaged her house and couldn't raise a thousand dollars, much less thirty. "I see you've thought of everything."

"Somebody has to." His eyes bored into hers. "So what do you say, Sis? We have a deal?"

She shook her head, slowly, wondering once again how such a con artist could be related to her. Or to her parents. "Where do you get the gall, Nick? Just tell me that."

"What are you talking about?"

"I'm talking about how you involved me in your dirty little dealings four months ago. Anyone else would be too ashamed to face me, much less ask me for money. But not you. You waltz in here as if nothing had happened and expect me to hand you thirty thousand dollars just like that."

"Awh, come on, Sis. You still aren't sore at me over that little incident with Eddy's bodyguards, are you? I told you I was sorry about that. If I had known those bastards would come looking for the money here, I would have looked for another hiding place. I swear it."

It took every ounce of willpower she had to keep from losing her temper. He wasn't worth her anger. Not anymore. "I'm not interested in your offer, Nick," she said calmly. "So please get out of my house. Zack is due home any minute, and I don't want him to find you here."

Although her rejection didn't seem to faze him, he stood up. "You're making a big mistake, Diana."

"I guess I'll just have to live with it." She followed him to the door and waited until his Oldsmobile had coughed its way up the hill, before letting out a sigh of relief.

Back in the kitchen, she sat down and pushed her fingers through her hair. If it weren't for the promise she had made to her mother on her deathbed to be patient with Nick and look after him, she would have turned him in to the police four months ago and made sure he paid dearly for the "little incident" to which he had so casually referred.

It had begun innocently enough, with one of his unwelcome visits. But rather than ask to borrow money as he usually did, he had handed her five thousand dollars in cash and asked her to keep it for him so he wouldn't be tempted to blow it on a poker game.

Thinking he was finally turning a new leaf, she had tucked the bundle in her safe, unaware the money belonged to a loan shark.

Two nights later, while she and Zack were having dinner with Kat and Mitch, someone had broken into her house, forced the safe open, and taken the five thousand dollars.

Although nothing else was disturbed, the unsigned note she found in the safe the following morning told her the whole story.

"Dear Miss Wells, This time, my men only took what was mine. Next time, they won't be so nice."

Frantic, she had called Nick, demanding an explanation, and when he had reluctantly admitted owing that money to a loan shark by the name of Eddy, her first impulse had been to forget about her promise to her mother and call the police. But in the time it took her to reach the phone, she had changed her mind. If she called the police, there would be questions, an investigation, and the news would be out that she had a brother with a police record.

Unwilling to expose her son to such negative publicity, she had thrown Nick out of her house and told him to never come back. For a while, he had complied. But today's visit worried her. Now was not the time for anyone to find out about Nick's shady past and his even shadier connections.

The timer went off, jarring her out of her thoughts. When she went to take the cake out of the oven, her hands were trembling.

Considered one of the most beautiful estates in the Bay Area, the Lindfords' nine-acre ranch in prestigious Seacliff stood on a bluff overlooking the Pacific Ocean. Beyond the swimming pool and two tennis courts lay acres of paddocks and green pastures that were home to some of the finest Arabians in the area.

Sunday dinner at the ranch was a tradition the family had observed since Charles and Margaret had bought the property twenty-two years before. No invitation was ever extended to Travis or Francesca. It was simply expected of them, and now Randall, to be there.

On this Halloween Sunday, dinner had been uneventful, with most of the conversation centered on matters regarding the hotel, certain improvements Margaret was considering, and a series of monthly events the Lindford would be sponsoring in coming months.

Although Francesca hadn't completely recovered from her disappointment, she did her best to cover it up, and when Margaret asked if she would accompany her to the stables after dinner, she complied immediately.

Rather than stay alone with his brother-in-law, Randall stood up to leave, but Travis, who had been itching to pick a fight all afternoon, stopped him.

"So, Rembrandt," he said, using the nickname he only spoke in private. "Have you adjusted to the blow yet?" He tossed his Sunday paper on the chair his mother had just vacated.

Although Randall could easily have walked way, he sat down again. He wasn't particularly interested in listening to Travis brag about his good fortune, but this was his chance to throw a few shots of his own without upsetting Francesca. "What blow?"

"I'm referring to the fact that I'll soon be taking over as chairman of the Lindford Hotel, of course."

Randall squelched the urge to smash his face. "I wouldn't count my chickens too soon, if I were you, Travis. Zachary isn't yours yet."

"He will be in a few weeks."

Randall shook his head. "So that's what you've sunk to these days? Using an innocent child as a bargaining chip. That's pretty pathetic if you ask me."

A dangerous glint flashed in Travis's eyes. "You're a fine one to talk about pathetic. Have you taken a good look in the mirror lately? Or at that crap of yours you call art?"

Although Travis had touched a nerve, Randall kept calm. "That crap is selling in one of the best galleries in town."

"Only because my sister is backing you, and because Morales is selling you cheap." The blue eyes turned cruel. "Tell me, Randall, aren't you even the slightest bit ashamed of living off my sister the way you do? Without ever being able to reciprocate?"

This time, the harsh words struck like blows. "I reciprocate, in ways you could never understand."

Travis laughed. *"Au contraire, mon ami.* I understand perfectly." He gave him a lewd wink. "You repay her in the sack. Like a well-trained gigolo. How clever."

Although concealing his emotions was something Randall had mastered long ago, he did so now with great difficulty. "I don't know why you find the thought so surprising. After all, isn't that what *you* will be doing once your mother finds you a bride? Screwing on command?"

Travis stifled a yawn. "You know something, Randall? You're not even funny." He stood up. "For the life of me, I'll never know what my sister sees in you."

Then, with a pitying shake of his head, he strode across the deck and went into the library.

His mouth set in a tight line, Randall stared toward the ocean where the surf came crashing against the black, ragged cliffs. That no good son of a bitch. There had to be something he could do to bring him down a peg or two. Or better yet, expose him for what he was—a back-stabbing creep who would sell his own mother. Or in this case, the family hotel.

Randall remained where he was for a long time, looking in the distance, tossing ideas around in his head and rejecting them just as quickly as they came—until one began to emerge as a possibility.

By the time Margaret and Francesca returned from the stables, Randall's spirits had lifted considerably.

10

No matter how often Kane came to Sonoma County, he never failed to be astounded by the sheer beauty of it. Only an hour from San Francisco, the famous wine country was a vision of rugged canyons and lush, hillside vineyards that stretched from the shores of the Pacific Ocean to the Mayacamas Mountains.

Now that the harvest was over, the vines were a riot of fall color and the sweet, intoxicating smell of crushed grapes seemed to be everywhere.

As he left Highway 12 and turned west onto Madrone Road, Sanders Estates, which his aunt had owned for nearly half a century, came into view.

Some of the finest wines in the country were being produced there—prize-winning cabernets, merlots, and a chardonnay Aunt Beckie claimed was unequalled anywhere in the world.

Kane had spent the best years of his childhood in Sonoma, learning the rich history of the California wine country from his aunt, trout fishing in the nearby creek, and hiking the Mayacamas Mountains with his father.

After her father's death, Beckie, only twenty-nine at the time, had taken over the family's business, devoting every bit of her time and energy to Sanders Estates and its wines. A few skeptics hadn't thought her capable of continuing the long-running tradition Reuben

Sanders had begun at the turn of the century, but Beckie had proved them wrong.

With the help of her talented cellar master, Mel Adler, she had turned her father's legacy into one of the top-producing wineries in the county.

In spite of his busy schedule, Kane made it a point to visit Beckie often, especially when he felt the need for some serious soul searching, as he did now.

He brought his black BMW to a stop in front of the winery, next to Aunt Beckie's ancient but reliable Land Rover. As always, Tricia, a pretty blonde who acted as secretary, PR person, and tour guide, was at her desk.

Kane flashed her a smile. "Is the Queen Bee in?"

Tricia returned the smile, picking up her phone just as it rang. "Your aunt is in her office with Mel, Mr. Sanders."

Kane thanked her and walked toward a pair of heavily carved oak doors that opened into a vast room filled with enormous oak barrels. The smell of wine was pungent, impregnated in the walls and the clothing of the men and women who worked here.

His aunt's office was at the end of the room, up a short flight of stairs. Through the open door, he could see Mel and her poring over a computer printout.

At the sound of his light knock, she turned around, her eyes brightening instantly. "Kane! What a pleasant surprise."

"How are you, beautiful?" he asked, kissing her cheek.

Rebecca Sanders was a tall, solidly built woman with sharp, intelligent hazel eyes and gray hair that was cut in a short, no-nonsense style. She wore what she referred to as her uniform—baggy khaki pants, a loose matching shirt with the sleeves rolled up, and a slouchy fedora that had become her trademark.

At seventy-five she had the vitality of a woman half her age and enough brains and guts to have survived in an industry that was largely dominated by men.

"I'm fine," she replied in answer to his question. Then, as Kane shook Mel's hand, she gave him a critical, up-and-down glance. "I'm not sure I can say the same about you. Have you lost weight since the last time I saw you?" She turned toward her longtime associate. "Mel, don't you think he looks thin?"

Mel, a stocky man in his early seventies with thick white hair and a luxuriant white mustache, laughed softly as he perched one hip on Beckie's desk. "He looks as strong and fit now as he did two weeks ago." He winked at Kane. "Of course, you know where she's going with that tired old line, don't you?"

"Hmmm. Let's see." Kane pretended to be searching his memory. "Would she be trying to get me to move to Glen Ellen and start a nice, quiet practice here by any chance?"

"So she can keep an eye on you, feed you properly, see that you get plenty of fresh air . . ."

"Stop it, you two," Beckie said in an admonishing tone. "You make it sound like it's a crime to want the best for the ones you love." She shook a finger at Kane. "And don't tell me that hectic life of yours is good for your health. Profitable perhaps, but healthy? I doubt it."

Then, linking her arm with his, she walked out of her office with him. "Now tell me. What brings you to Glen Ellen in the middle of the week?"

"Hunger."

"In that case, you're in luck. Thelma made her famous Irish stew today. And I believe there's fresh apple pie for dessert."

Kane closed his eyes in mock ecstasy. "Aunt Beckie,

one of these days, when you're not looking, I'm going to steal Thelma from you.''

Beckie shook her head. "She'd never adapt to the hustle and bustle of the city. You, on the other hand, were practically raised in this valley and would have no problem feeling right at home."

As he opened the BMW passenger door for her, she settled into the plush leather seat and waited until he was behind the wheel before adding, "As a matter of fact, old Ted Grant is retiring at the end of the year, and Glen Ellen could use a talented young attorney to take his place."

Kane smiled as he steered the car onto the wide, rocky dirt road that connected the winery to the main house. Ever since he could remember, his aunt had tried to get him to move to Sonoma, partly because she honestly believed the quality of life was better out here, and partly because she loved him and wanted him near her.

He patted her hand. "And it won't have any trouble finding one, I'm sure."

Because she knew him so well, she sensed a change in him, a restlessness she hadn't noticed the last time he was here. She turned her sharp gaze on him. "Is something bothering you, Kane?"

"Sort of." He told her about his meeting with Travis and his decision to represent him in the custody battle.

Beckie slanted him a sharp, disapproving glance. "Did Margaret railroad you into taking the case?"

"I wouldn't call it railroading."

"But you did it out of loyalty to her."

"That had something to do with my decision, yes."

Beckie was silent as she studied her nephew's handsome profile. She had a deep affection for her brother's only child. Unmarried and childless herself, she had always considered Kane the son she never had. When her brother, Ray, had died, she had asked Claire and Kane to move to Glen Ellen with her. But Margaret Lindford had beat her to the punch and offered Claire a job at the hotel. Shortly after that, Kane had enrolled at New York University, but even with three thousand miles separating them, he had managed to come to Sonoma a couple of times a year.

"Is there another reason you took the case?" she asked softly. When Kane didn't answer, she lay a callused hand on his arm. "Is it because of what happened with Sean?"

As he turned a bend, a redwood farmhouse set on a knoll came into view. Farther beyond, toward the east, the outline of the Mayacamas Mountains stretched along the horizon, their dark slopes blanketed with oaks and giant redwoods.

He parked his car next to Thelma's Ford station wagon, stepped out, and came around to help his aunt. Arm in arm, they walked slowly toward the house. "Yes," he said at last. "Sean was a major force in my decision. At least he was at first."

"And now?"

"I don't know. I'm not sure I want to take this case at all."

Beckie pursed her lips. It wasn't like Kane to be so indecisive. "Have you met this Diana Wells?"

"I went to see her yesterday."

"And?"

His gaze followed the flight of a turkey buzzard as it dipped between two canyons. "She didn't remind me of Jamie, if that's what you're asking. Diana Wells is a good mother, devoted, hard working." He paused. "Tough."

"Jamie was tough."

"Yes. But in a different way. I guess a better description of Diana Wells would be that she is a survivor."

Something about the softening of his voice as he said those words made her smile. "Do you feel anything for this young woman?"

Kane chuckled. For a woman who had never had children, she was gifted with an uncanny intuition. "I admire her," he said, reluctant to admit anything else.

Beckie's eyes twinkled. "Is she pretty?"

He laughed and wrapped an arm around her shoulders. "You're still a romantic at heart, aren't you, Aunt Beckie?"

"And *you* are still a master at evading questions you don't want to answer."

"I tell you what," he said, kissing her forehead. "I'll answer all your questions about Diana Wells after lunch. Right now, I'm famished. Think Thelma will let me have a sample to tide me over?"

Beckie patted his solid back. "Oh, if I know Thelma, she'll sit you at the kitchen table the moment you walk in and forget about the rest of us."

Watching Travis charm his way out of a delicate situation had always been an education for Kane. In all the years he had known him, he had never seen a single maneuver backfire. Today was no exception.

"Absolutely not, Mrs. Barclay," Travis said, winking at Kane and pointing to a chair. "I assure you that since that regrettable incident last month, every employee on our staff has been subjected to a rigorous investigation, and those who did not meet our criteria were given notice immediately."

He waited for the woman's reply before adding, "I'm glad you feel this way, Mrs. Barclay. And to show you how much I appreciate your giving us a second chance, I'd like you and your husband to be my guest this weekend." His voice dropped to a conspiratorial level. "Pavarotti is in town as you know, and although his concert has been sold out for months, I have two tickets in my hand, with your name on them." He laughed. "I thought you'd like that. It's all settled then. I'll see you on Friday. Have a good day, Mrs. Barclay, and please give my regards to Mr. Barclay."

Travis hung up and let out an audible sigh. "Dumb bitch," he muttered under his breath. Then, turning on the charm again, he looked squarely at Kane. "What's up, old buddy?"

Although Kane had known before going to Glen Ellen that he was disenchanted with his decision to represent Travis in the custody case, the short time he had spent in that soothing, pastoral setting had cleared his mind. He saw no reason to beat around the bush. "You're not going to like what I came to tell you."

The affable smile grew weary. "Don't tell me they've changed the date of the custody hearing."

"No. You're still scheduled for December sixth." He paused a beat. "I'm withdrawing from the case, Travis."

Travis slapped the palms of his hands on his desk. "You're *what?*"

"It was wrong of me to—"

But Travis wasn't listening. His face an angry red, he rose from behind his desk. "Why? What happened to make you change your mind?"

"I realized I took this case for all the wrong reasons. I let personal feelings interfere with my judgment."

"Dammit, Kane. This isn't professional at all. I was counting on you. *Mother* was counting on you." He raked his fingers through his impeccably styled hair, and it immediately fell back in place, looking better than before. "You can't do this to us."

"I'm not doing it to foul things up for you, Travis.

Please believe that. In fact, I still think you'll be better off with a lawyer who specializes in family law. A man like Dave Panocek, for example.''

"Mother isn't going to like it, Kane. She's going to feel betrayed.''

"Margaret will understand.''

"Don't count on it. She wants that boy every bit as much as I do.''

"There are other ways for you to be a part of Zack's life if you really want to. You'll just have to use a less aggressive approach.''

"You talked to her, didn't you?" Travis said, his eyes narrowing into slits. "You went to see Diana and let her fill your head with lies about me.''

"Yes, I went to see her," Kane replied evenly. "But what she told me had no bearing on my decision.''

"Then what did?''

"The fact that she is a good mother—loving, stable, reliable.''

Travis's gaze turned mean. "So what are you all of a sudden? Her goddamn fan club?''

Kane, who had no intention of arguing with Travis when he was in that kind of mood, stood up. "I'll talk to you when you've calmed down.''

As Kane moved toward the door, Travis followed him. "How can you be so ungrateful after all my family's done for you, Kane? How can you turn your back on us when we need you the most?''

"Goodbye, Travis.''

"How do you think my father would feel if he knew . . .''

Travis was still ranting when Kane closed the door behind him.

Rather than take the elevator from Travis's second-floor office to the lobby, Kane walked down the wide, curving staircase, with its gilded banister and white marble steps. At the mezzanine level, where the tea shop, now empty, was located, he stopped, not sure why, and went to stand by the wrought iron railing to gaze at the activity below.

As always at this time of day, the lobby was busy—guests checking in, bellboys pushing luggage racks, people standing in small groups, talking and laughing.

It was a scene that had always fascinated him. As a child he had played what he called the guessing game. Who were those elegant, attractive people? Where did they live? What did they do behind closed door? It was in that very lobby, during an American Bar Association convention, that he had first dreamed of becoming a lawyer.

Then, quite unexpectedly, tragedy had struck, shattering all of their lives. In March of 1972, an IRS audit had revealed a discrepancy in the hotel books. Upon closer examination, a special agent had found that two million dollars had been embezzled from the hotel over a three-year period.

Kane's father, Ray, who was the Lindfords' comptroller at the time, was interrogated for days. But no matter how many times the police questioned him, he couldn't come up with an explanation for the disappearance of the two million dollars.

A week later, Ray Sanders shot himself with a hunting rifle he had been cleaning.

Although his wife, Claire, swore it was an accident, the public was quick to conclude that Ray Sanders had chosen to kill himself rather than face imminent arrest.

Three days after the fatal shooting, the two million dollars were traced to a bogus company by the name of Maddox Linen Service to whom Ray, as comptroller, had been making regular payments from the hotel account. By the time state and federal investigators were able to inspect Maddox's bank account, it had been closed and the money was gone. All that was left in the records was a bank signature card in the name of William Maddox, President.

Upon being shown the card, Kane's mother burst into tears. The handwriting was unmistakably that of her husband. "He's been framed," she told the authorities over and over. "My husband never stole a dime in his life. Someone forged his signature and framed him."

The Lindfords, who didn't want to believe a man they had trusted for fifteen years was an embezzler, hired a private investigator to look into the matter. Unfortunately, he wasn't able to clear Ray Sanders's name as Claire and Kane had hoped, and the investigation was eventually dropped.

Feeling sorry for Claire and especially for Kane, of whom she was very fond, Margaret offered Ray's widow a secretarial job in the hotel, a position that enabled her to support herself and Kane, if not in the manner they were accustomed to, at least in a comfortable, dignified way.

A few months before Kane graduated from high school, Margaret came to him and offered to pay for his college education.

Kane had turned her down. In his young, proud heart it had sounded too much like charity. For the next four years, while attending New York University, he worked his way through college by waiting tables, and later put himself through law school by working as a clerk in a Manhattan law firm.

His mother never got a chance to see him graduate from Columbia Law School. Two days before her forty-eighth birthday, she died of a pulmonary infection. Rather than return to San Francisco as Margaret had hoped he would, Kane had accepted a position with a prestigious criminal law firm in New York and stayed there for six years before going into private practice.

When Kane had come to San Francisco for Charles Lindford's funeral two years ago, Francesca had approached him about moving back home.

"Mother would be so happy if you did," she had told him as they strolled through the ranch together. "And maybe the change would be good for you, too. It can't be easy being reminded of the child you lost every day of your life."

She was right about that. Leaving New York City was something Kane had been considering on and off since Sean's death, but never seriously. It wasn't until Margaret's heart attack two days after Charles's funeral that he realized the grieving was over, and that it was time to make a fresh start.

"Hello, my dear."

At the sound of the familiar voice and the light touch on his arm, Kane turned around. Margaret stood just behind him, looking very elegant in a long, flowing brown skirt, and a white silk blouse.

Her blue eyes studied him. "You're looking very serious."

"I was indulging in a moment of nostalgia." He gazed around him. "This hotel holds a lot of memories for me."

"More good than bad, I hope."

He waited a beat before nodding.

"Good." She smiled, tilting her head to the side. "Did you come to see me, or Travis?"

"Travis." As much as he disliked upsetting her, he would have to tell her about withdrawing from the case before she heard Travis's version. "I came to tell him I would not be representing him after all."

Her eyes registered instant shock. And panic. "Why? What happened between you two?"

"Nothing." He told her what he had told Travis, and although she showed much more compassion and understanding than her son had, she was deeply disappointed.

"Kane, won't you please reconsider?" she pleaded. "We'll go to the penthouse and talk—"

He stopped her by taking her hand and holding it. "No, Margaret. My decision is made." Gently, he kissed her cheek. "Try not to look at this as a betrayal. Even if Travis tries to convince you that it is."

Before she could answer, he squeezed her hand and walked away, down the wide, curving staircase.

11

He couldn't get Diana out of his mind.

Standing under the hot, powerful shower spray, Kane poured a capful of shampoo into the palm of his hand, then rubbed it vigorously onto his head. He had been trying to concentrate on an arson case he was considering taking, but his mind kept straying in another direction.

Ever since his visit to Harbor View three days ago, he had been behaving like an absolute idiot, going as far as dialing Diana Wells's number and then hanging up after the first ring.

Lifting his face to the spray, he closed his eyes and let the water run over his broad shoulders and down his back. As the steam enveloped him, he tried to shut her out of his mind, but only succeeded in bringing her into sharper focus.

Without effort, he remembered how she had looked in her office, beautiful and indignant, and how she had smelled when she had come to stand close to him. It wasn't difficult to imagine how she would feel in his arms, all soft curves and silky skin.

Combing his fingers through his hair, he pushed the wet strands from his face. What the hell was he doing? Had he been sleeping alone so long he was now having erotic thoughts about a woman he hardly knew?

Was that all it was then? Lust?

Rather than answer the question, he shut off the water and stepped out of the shower. Half muttering to himself, he dried off, tucked the towel around his waist, and padded to the galley-size kitchen of his Presidio Heights condo. The red light on the Braun espresso machine told him the coffee was ready.

Taking a mug from the cupboard, he set it under the filter and pressed a button, inhaling the rich French roast aroma as the coffee dripped into the cup. He was about to take it back into the bathroom when the phone rang.

He picked it up on the first ring. "Hello."

"Kane, this is Ron," the private investigator said. "Have you read the papers?"

"I just got out of the shower. Why?"

"Travis Lindford has a new attorney. And it ain't Dave Panacek."

"Who did he hire?"

"Sam Barnes."

"Sam Barnes! The man is a snake."

"It makes you wonder what kind of court battle Travis has in mind, doesn't it?"

After thanking Ron for the information, Kane hung up. Samuel Barnes, who had practiced matrimonial law for more than two decades, was known in local courtrooms for his low-handed tactics and total lack of scruples. He would make mincemeat out of Diana Wells.

Not that Kane didn't have confidence in the talents of Diana's attorney. John McKay was a fine lawyer, one of the best in his field. But he was no match for Barnes's wizardry.

He wondered if Diana was aware of what she was up against.

Coffee cup in hand, he went back to the bathroom

to shave. Once he was dressed, he flipped through his pocket agenda and looked up Diana's address, which he had copied from Ron's report.

He would stop by her house on the way to the office and tell her about Barnes, just in case McKay hadn't had a chance to. Considering she had been so patient with him the other day, it was the least he could do.

Who the hell are you kidding? he thought, watching his face in the mirror as he knotted a gray-and-blue silk tie. You're itching to see her. Admit it.

With a low chuckle, he picked up his keys from a wooden tray on his nightstand, his money clip, a couple of phone messages he hadn't had time to answer, and shoved everything in his pocket.

If he hurried, he might catch her home, before she left for the restaurant.

It was almost five o'clock when Diana returned from her lawyer's office that day. Those long afternoon sessions with John McKay left her emotionally drained. As he paced and drank gallons of coffee, he questioned her about everything—her work, how much time she spent away from home and who cared for her son when she wasn't there. He also asked about her love life, which, thank God, was nonexistent, her financial status, whether or not she believed in corporal punishment when disciplining a child, and if she had ever stayed out all night.

"Are those questions necessary?" she had asked him. "You already know the answers."

"I want to make sure *you* know them and don't hesitate when the judge questions you."

Now, willing herself not to think about the hearing, Diana walked into her kitchen and wrapped an apron around her waist. Billy Cramden's mother would soon be bringing Zack back from soccer practice, and she needed to get dinner started.

She was pulling a prepared meatloaf mixture from the refrigerator when the doorbell rang.

When she went to answer it, she found herself face-to-face with Kane Sanders. Her heart skipped a beat, but she ignored it. "You again."

Undaunted by her less than cordial reception, Kane smiled. "Am I interrupting something?"

"As a matter of fact you are."

"I stopped by this morning, but you were already gone." When she made no comment, he added, "I promise I won't be long."

She hesitated. Ever since finding out he had withdrawn from the custody case, she had been curious to know why. She stepped aside. "Come in."

As he followed her inside, Kane had a glimpse of a small, charming living room with a slightly cluttered look to it. The kitchen, equipped with state-of-the-art appliances, was a chef's dream. Bright red counters contrasted brightly with the white cabinets, and an impressive collection of copper pots hung on a rack above the butcher-block island. To the left, framed in a large bay window, was a round oak table and four chairs. Cups and saucers were drying in a wooden rack next to the sink.

In spite of her chilly reception, Kane felt right at home.

"You don't mind if I finish what I was doing while you talk, do you?" Diana asked.

"Not at all." He watched her unwrap a ground meat mixture, admiring her quick, precise movements. Under the white apron, she wore a knit wool skirt, warm cranberry in color, and a matching turtleneck. Her dark auburn hair was held back from her face with two small barrettes, and except for lipstick, she wore no makeup.

He spotted a plate of chocolate brownies on another counter and smiled, remembering how he had looked forward to those special treats in his childhood. "It must be heaven for a small child to have a master cook for a mother."

She laughed without breaking stride with what she was doing. "I've had no complaints." She glanced over her shoulder. "You didn't come here to discuss the four food groups, did you?"

"No." He perched a hip on a shiny red stool. "I came to tell you that I'm no longer representing Travis Lindford in the custody case."

She transferred the meat loaf into a pan and put it in the preheated oven before turning to look at him. There was a look of quiet strength about him, about the way he talked, the way he looked at her with those calm, dark eyes. "John told me."

"Did he also tell you that the attorney who replaced me is a man by the name of Sam Barnes?"

She nodded as she wiped her hands on a dish towel.

"Do you know anything about him?"

"Only that he's tough and doesn't always follow standard procedures." She took four potatoes from an old-fashioned wooden bin on the floor, brought them to the island, and began to peel them. "Does that describe him accurately?"

"More or less."

She gave him a guarded look. "What would you add?"

"Besides his less than admirable qualities, he's known as a very thorough investigator."

"Should that worry me?"

Kane shrugged. "It depends."

"On what?"

He thought of the police file Ron had uncovered on her brother. That was exactly the kind of ammunition Sam Barnes thrived on. "On whether or not you have anything to hide. If you do, Sam Barnes will find it. And use it against you."

Turning her back to him, she filled a pan with cold water, hoping he wouldn't notice her hands were trembling. "I have nothing to hide."

"I didn't mean to imply that you had. I just thought you'd want to know whom you're up against."

When she turned around again, cool green eyes studied him. "You came to warn me about Sam Barnes?"

He nodded.

"Why?"

Their stare locked and held. "I didn't stop to analyze my motives. I just did it."

Her lips twitched. "I wouldn't have taken you for a man who gave in to impulses."

"Oh? And what did you take me for?"

It had been a long time since a handsome man had flirted with her. Under different circumstances, she might have enjoyed it, might even have responded with a little flirting of her own. But regardless of how unthreatening Kane Sanders seemed at the moment, he was still a close friend of the Lindfords. And that made him the enemy.

"A bully," she replied in answer to his question.

His mouth curved into a lopsided smile. "I suppose lawyers can be a bit overbearing at times." He continued to watch her, his gaze warm and playful. "I hope your opinion of me has improved."

"I wouldn't count on it. You know what they say about first impressions. They last forever."

"Then let me prove to you that sayings aren't always true. Have dinner with me."

"I can't. I always have dinner with my son."

"Lunch?"

She shook her head. "I work right through the lunch hour." Before he could make a third suggestion, she added, "And I don't eat breakfast."

"You make it tough for a guy to redeem himself."

She set the pan of potatoes on the stove and turned the burner to medium high. "Oh, I don't know. There might be something you can do for me."

His gaze skimmed her face. "Name it."

"John doesn't believe Travis can win. What's *your* opinion?"

"It's bad luck for a lawyer to make predictions."

"I'm not superstitious."

He gave a short bow of his head. "All right. Honestly? I'd say Travis's chances of winning are poor to fair."

"Somehow I don't find that reassuring. Why fair?"

"Because he is the biological father." He hesitated, wondering if she was up to hearing his other reason, the one the Lindfords were banking on. He decided she was. "And because he is a Lindford."

All playfulness on her part had vanished. "Won't his lifestyle and my claim that he knew about Nadine's pregnancy and walked away count for anything?"

"Of course they will. But Sam Barnes will underplay that and overplay Travis's claim that he was lied to and cheated out of his son's first eight—"

Before he could finish his sentence, a door slammed followed by racing footsteps. Within moments, a young boy burst into the room. He wore jeans with grass-stained knees, a blue windbreaker over a red sweatshirt, and black Reeboks, tied halfway to the top.

"Hi, Mom." He dropped the soccer ball he held under his arm and kicked it under the kitchen table. "Can I go out?"

"You just came in."

She caught his school bag just as he started to throw it on the island. Mesmerized, Kane watched the transformation in her. Gone was the controlled, aloof woman he had been talking to a moment ago. The coolness had evaporated, replaced by a warmth that radiated from everywhere—her eyes, her smile, even the way she pulled the boy to her, curbing his youthful impatience.

"Zack, this is Mr. Sanders."

"Hi."

His resemblance to Travis was uncanny. But there were some subtle differences too—the directness of his intelligent blue gaze, the wide, genuine smile. Pain stabbed through him as he was reminded of Sean. He would have been about Zack's age.

"I'm glad to meet you, Zack. I've heard a lot about you."

The handsome face scrunched up. "Are you another of my relatives?"

Kane laughed. "No, I'm not. Although I do know your grandmother."

"Mr. Sanders is an attorney," Diana said.

He turned to look at her. "I thought Mr. McKay was your attorney."

"He is." Before she could explain in greater detail, he had spotted the brownies and made a beeline for them.

"Hold it!"

He froze, his hand poised over the plate.

"Only one."

"Aw, Mom, they're small."

She walked over to the counter, took one brownie from the plate, and handed it to him. "Good try." She smiled as he took a healthy bite. "Any homework?"

"Just some dates I have to remember for my history class."

"Then why don't you go over there," she said, pointing to the kitchen table, "and get started. I'll quiz you before dinner."

It was Kane's cue to leave, and he did so without any further prompting. "So long, Zack."

The boy, already settled in front of a school book, waved. "Bye."

At the door, he paused. "Cute kid."

"Yes, he is." She glanced toward the kitchen. "I don't know what I would do without him."

Too late, she remembered his own loss. She started to apologize, then thought better of it. Some things were best left unsaid. Besides, she didn't want him to know that she had discussed his private life with John McKay.

On impulse, she extended her hand. "Thanks for stopping by Mr. Sanders."

"Kane. Please."

As he kept her hand in his a little longer than necessary, a tingle rushed up her arm and down her spine. She couldn't remember any man's touch ever affecting her that way.

She took a head-clearing breath and withdrew her hand. "Kane it is." It didn't matter what she called him anyway. She wouldn't be seeing him again.

She watched him walk down the driveway and when he reached his car and started to turn around, she closed the door before he could see her looking at him.

She didn't like the way Kane Sanders was affecting her. It was distracting. *He* was distracting.

She would do well to stay away from him.

12

It had taken Travis a couple of weeks to adjust to the idea of marrying Dunbar Dewitt. But after his mother had pointed out the many advantages of such a union, he had agreed that the Lindford Hotel was worth the sacrifice.

"First of all, she's been in love with you since her debut thirteen years ago," Margaret had told him the night of his first date with the brainy heiress. "Which will almost guarantee a yes to your marriage proposal a few weeks from now. Second, she is a member of the Junior League, sits on the board of three charities, and is currently involved in a program that will provide free school breakfasts for underprivileged children."

"And that qualifies her to be my wife?"

"That," Margaret had replied with a knowing look, "will qualify her to be the mother of your child. Which is exactly what we want the judge to feel."

Good old Margaret. She never did things halfway. With the consummate attention of a professional social planner, she had arranged for him and Dunbar to be seen everywhere—gallery openings, restaurants, the symphony, and of course, charity balls.

When a rather daring reporter had asked him point blank if his courtship of Dunbar was meant to gain him points at the custody hearing, he had replied, "Not at all. Dunbar is a woman I've admired from afar for a long time. Unfortunately, I never had the guts to ask her for a date until two weeks ago.''

Although the candid comment had been well rehearsed, it was too early to make predictions on how it would affect the judge. But one thing was certain. The publicity wouldn't hurt.

Now, as he was getting ready to leave for the office, his housekeeper knocked at his bedroom door and told him his attorney was here to see him.

"Show him into the living room, Ava. I'll be right down."

Moments later, Travis was greeting Sam Barnes in his usual affable manner. "How are you, Sam?" he asked, crossing the room with his hand extended.

In his mid-fifties and always dressed in expensive western attire, Sam Barnes was a tall, powerfully built man with slicked-back gray hair, shrewd brown eyes, and a Texas accent some said was as phony as his politician's smile.

Travis had liked him instantly. Barnes was resourceful and greedy—a combination that made them perfect for each other. "I hope you're the bearer of good news."

Barnes tossed his black cowboy hat on a chair and took the seat that was offered to him. "My investigator located the physician who attended Nadine Snyder after her boating accident."

"Splendid. Where is he?"

"Chicago General. He's the chief of staff there." Barnes met Travis's expectant gaze without flinching. "He told me on the phone Nadine was *not* under the influence of pain killers, or any other drugs, when she signed those adoption papers. She wanted to be in complete control of her faculties."

"Damm." Travis was thoughtful for a moment.

"Any chance we might persuade the good doctor to bend the truth a little?"

"That would surprise me. From what I could gather after my conversation with Dr. Nader, the man is as straight as the proverbial arrow. I'm flying to Chicago in the morning to talk to him in person." He shook his head. "But I'm almost certain the trip will be a waste of time. If I were you, I'd start thinking of some alternatives."

Travis sat down. He had counted on a favorable testimony to help him prove that Diana had applied undue influence on Nadine during her hospitalization and forced her to sign the adoption papers. But without the doctor's statement to that effect, the judge would disregard Travis's claim. "Do you have any ideas?"

Barnes studied the tip of a perfectly polished black alligator boot. "One. And we wouldn't have to look very far."

"What do you mean?"

"Diana. She could be the weak link we've been looking for."

"But you checked her out yourself. According to you, she's beyond reproach." He narrowed his eyes. "Unless you're thinking of using that brother of hers—the ex-con?"

Barnes shook his head. "That, too, would be a waste of time. She can't be held responsible for her brother's actions. Even if he were an ax murderer, as long as she's not involved with him, and we know she's not, it wouldn't affect her reputation."

Travis held back a sigh of exasperation. "Then how can she help my case?"

Barnes leaned back in his chair. "I checked into her finances and found out that besides remortgaging her house to finance her restaurant, she also used all her savings.''

''So?''

''So, if Harbor View should fail, she would lose not only her restaurant, but her home as well.''

''Would that affect the judge's decision?''

''It very well could.''

Travis narrowed his eyes. ''Why would Harbor View fail when it's doing so well?''

Barnes shrugged. ''Who knows? So many things can go wrong in the restaurant business—food poisoning, violation of health codes, bad reviews . . .'' He threw Travis a shrewd look. ''You have a restaurant in your hotel. Just ask yourself, what would do it the most harm?''

Long after the attorney had left, Travis sat in his living room, going over their conversation. Barnes's suggestion made sense. If Diana lost her restaurant through some sort of negligence on her part, her reputation as a restaurateur, or even a caterer, would be destroyed. She would have to find some other job. And leave Zack to the care of a full-time baby-sitter.

How would a judge feel about that?

He was thoughtful as he rode the elevator to his office on the second floor. He liked Sam's idea a lot, but he was still faced with one major problem. How to bring about the demise of Diana Wells?

Food poisoning was out. It was too dangerous. And anyway, he didn't know anyone who would dare risk the lives of dozens of people, even for big money. Health code violations, on the other hand, were too tame. In a week's time, all of San Francisco would have forgotten about it.

It had to be something else. Something subtle, safe, yet effective.

Slowly, an idea began to take shape in his head. He

sat up. Holden Nash. Of course. Why hadn't he thought of him sooner? The man was perfect for the job.

The question was, would Holden agree to help him? Would he put his reputation on the line for the sake of friendship?

Travis smiled. Maybe not friendship alone. But he would do it if the reward were substantial enough.

"Randall!" Joe O'Keefe opened the door to his office and smiled broadly. "This is quite a surprise. Come in. Make yourself comfortable."

The Lindford's former chief of security, a big man with bright red hair, golden eyes, and a jovial smile, removed a stack of files from a chair and put them on top of a wooden cabinet. "You have to excuse the mess. I'm in the middle of moving from one floor to another and things are a bit hectic."

Randall glanced at the attractive surroundings, the plush blue carpet, the large teak desk stacked high with more files. He was glad to see that things were going well for his friend. No one deserved it more. "I take it business is booming."

"Couldn't be better." O'Keefe circled his desk and sat down. "And I owe it all to you, Randall. If you and Francesca hadn't been there for me two years ago, God knows what I'd be doing right now."

"All we did was give you a head start. You did the rest all by yourself."

It was true. Joe had been celebrating his tenth year as chief of security at the Lindford when Travis had fired him for a minor infraction regarding one of his men. It had been a bum rap, a show of authority on Travis's part. And a way to pay Joe back for turning him in years earlier when Travis, then the hotel's purchasing agent, had been caught taking kickbacks from various hotel suppliers. Although Travis had been only mildly reprimanded, he had never forgiven the detective for humiliating him in front of his parents.

Randall liked Joe. He was the first hotel employee to come forward and congratulate Francesca and him on their marriage. From that moment on, the two men had made it a point to meet for coffee every now and then. When Joe was fired, Randall had asked Francesca to lend him the money to open his own private investigating agency.

Joe had never forgotten their generosity.

"If there's ever anything I can do for you or your lady," he had told Randall, "you just let me know, you hear?"

Now that he was actually here, ready to take him up on his offer, Randall was filled with a wave of apprehension. He had never done anything as bold as this before. What if Travis found out what he was up to? Or Margaret? Or even Francesca?

No, he thought, shaking the anxieties away. He shouldn't think about that. It would be all right. Joe was a good detective. And more important, he could be trusted.

"So." Joe leaned back in his chair. "Tell me what I can do for you, my friend."

Randall drew a breath and then let it out. "I want my brother-in-law put under surveillance."

A slow, satisfied smile spread across the big man's face. "What has that little skunk done now?"

"You've heard he has a son, haven't you?"

Joe nodded.

Without going into unnecessary details, Randall told him about Margaret's decision to name Travis as her successor after the custody hearing.

Joe crossed his hands over his vast stomach. "That's

a damn shame. Everyone knows Francesca would make a much better chairman."

"Margaret doesn't seem to think so."

"She always did have a blind spot big as the moon when it came to Travis." When Randall didn't answer, he added, "What exactly are you looking for, Randall?"

"A couple of years ago, Travis wanted to take the hotel public. He even had an investor lined up—a wealthy Arab sheik. Needless to say, Charles and Margaret turned him down flat, and Travis never brought up the subject again. He even has Margaret believing he's put the matter to rest. Permanently."

"But you don't think he has."

"I'm positive he hasn't. The sheik has been a frequent guest at the hotel since Charles died. Travis claims the man is just happy with the service, but I'm not convinced—and neither is Francesca."

"Have you discussed this with Margaret?"

"It wouldn't do any good. Without proof she won't listen to us. She'll think we're just being poor sports."

"So you want to get proof by wiring Travis's penthouse."

"And his office. And you might as well wiretap his phone, too, in case he talks to the sheik long distance. If I can show Margaret he's plotting behind her back to take the Lindford public, it will be the end of him, at least as far as the hotel is concerned."

When Joe didn't immediately answer, Randall leaned forward. "Look, Joe, I know wiretapping is illegal, and risky as hell. So if you'd rather not do it, tell me. Because I sure wouldn't want you to lose your license over this."

Joe shook his head. "Don't worry about me. Everything will be fine." He brought his chair to an upright position and flipped through the pages of a desk calendar. "When do you want me to start?"

"As soon as possible."

"Do you have a set of keys I can use?"

"I know where Francesca keeps the master set. I'll get it for you."

"Good. I'll also need Travis to be out of his penthouse for a couple of hours while I wire the premises. Can you arrange it?"

Randall nodded. "The family meets at the ranch every Sunday afternoon for dinner. Travis usually arrives at three, leaves at seven."

"Perfect. I'll try to do his office at the same time. If for some reason there's activity on the executive floor, I'll have to wait until later that night." Joe wrote a time in his calendar, but no name. "About my reports. I usually have them hand delivered by a special messenger on a daily basis. In your case, a tape of Travis's conversations would be included. Is that all right?"

"That will be fine. But tell your messenger not to come to my apartment before nine A.M. I don't want Francesca to know about this. Not yet anyway."

"I understand." As Randall stood up, Joe did the same. "Everything will be in place and ready to roll when Travis comes back from the ranch on Sunday, so don't worry about a thing."

"Thanks, Joe."

"I'm glad I'm finally in a position to do something for you," Joe replied, shaking Randall's hand. His mouth pulled in a crooked grin. "Besides, I've been waiting a long time to get back at that son of a bitch."

13

If there was one thing Travis had learned working side by side with his father all these years, it was to never sleep on a good idea.

"Too much thinking deteriorates the mind," Charles Lindford was fond of saying. "If something feels right to you, do it. There's a lot to be said for the gut instinct."

Acting on that gut instinct, early Wednesday morning, he had called the *Globe* where Holden Nash worked.

"I'll be delighted to have lunch with you," the columnist had replied eagerly. "As a matter of fact, there's this little restaurant I've been meaning to try . . ."

The parking lot of La Trattoria, in neighboring Sausalito, was only half filled when Travis arrived there shortly before noon that same day. In a great mood, he hummed softly as he glanced in the rearview mirror of his red Ferrari Spider to check his hair. Then, satisfied he looked his best, he stepped out of his car and walked briskly toward the restaurant.

Holden Nash was a huge man. Over six feet tall, he tipped the scales at close to three hundred pounds, a great portion of which was distributed around his middle. He had hazel eyes that all but disappeared under layers of fat, a moonlike face, and a gray beard that made him look like an obese professor.

Although the eating habits of millions of Americans had changed dramatically over the last few years, his never had, for food was Holden Nash's passion as well as his livelihood.

As one of the most respected restaurant critics in California, his reputation as a connoisseur of fine food had made him a household name. Few were the chefs and restaurateurs who didn't fear a visit from what many called "The Great One."

Travis had met him four years before, following a rather unflattering review of the Lindford premiere restaurant, Déjà Vu. Because he knew better than to challenge the man's opinion, Travis had swallowed his pride, sent Nash a box of his favorite Havana cigars, and thanked him for pointing out to him Déjà Vu's weak points.

A few months later, with a new chef at the helm, Travis had invited the critic for a return visit. This time, Déjà Vu was awarded four stars and given a glowing review.

Travis hadn't bothered to find out if the praise was deserved, or if the many amenities extended to Holden Nash and his family, which had included unlimited stays at Travis's plush winter cabin in Utah, had anything to do with it. The results were what mattered.

Now, as the two men sat across from each other, Travis glanced at the huge mound of fettuccine Alfredo on the critic's plate and smiled. "I take it you're hungry."

"Famished." Holden Nash rolled his fork around the creamy noodles, brought them to his mouth, and closed his eyes as he chewed. "Exquisite," he said with the look of a man on the edge of ecstasy. "There's a hint of aquavit in the cream sauce, and the cheese is Asiago, aged to perfection." Reopening his eyes, he motioned to his plate with his fork. "Feel free to try some."

Travis, who didn't know Asiago from a cheese ball, held back a shudder of distaste. Eating from someone's plate was a habit he despised, and he wasn't about to make an exception now, not even for Holden Nash. "No, thanks. It would interfere with my salmon."

He took a sip of his Pinot Grigio, letting the wine roll on his tongue before swallowing it. As always, Holden's choice of wine was excellent. "I appreciate your meeting me on such short notice. I know how busy you are."

"Never too busy for you, Travis. You know that."

Travis took a bite of his salmon. "How's the restaurant critic business these days? Challenging enough for you?"

Holden shrugged. "As challenging as one can make it after twenty-five years."

It was no secret to Travis that Nash was tired of his job. After a quarter of a century with the *Globe,* he was ready to do something else, explore new horizons. Unfortunately, offers for a man who had just celebrated the big six-o weren't exactly falling out of the sky.

Until now.

"Have you ever wondered if your talents were wasted at the *Globe?*"

"Many times. But what's the use of complaining when you can't do anything about it?"

Travis toyed with his snow peas, perfectly sauteed in a light olive oil. "What if I told you I had a proposition for you? Something exciting and right up your alley?"

Holden continued to eat, but more slowly. "I'd say tell me more."

Travis put his fork down and leaned forward. "You know that local television station my father left me?"

"KLBY. Yeah, I know it." He looked up. "Didn't you tell me once you were thinking of selling it because it wasn't profitable enough?"

"That's right. Unfortunately, there've been no buyers."

"Bad economy." Holden dipped a chunk of sourdough bread into the rich sauce and let it soak.

"Exactly. Which is why I decided to keep KLBY and turn it around." He leaned closer. "And *you* are going to help me."

This time Holden gave him his full attention. "Me?"

"I'm going to make some drastic changes in the operation of the station, Holden. I want to attract a new, richer breed of advertisers. In order to do that, I've got to offer the kind of programming sophisticated listeners will appreciate."

"What did you have in mind?"

"A new series featuring some of today's most popular topics—home decorating, travel, beauty, and, of course, food."

"Food?" The tiny eyes shone with a new light.

"You know . . . new trends in cuisine, who eats what, where, interviews with bright new chefs here and abroad."

His fettuccine forgotten, Holden listened with rapt attention. "You mean something on the order of *Lifestyles of the Rich and Famous,* but with a food theme."

"Exactly. And to carry it off, I'll need a personable host who's already known to millions of people." He grinned. "I want you to be that host, Holden. In exchange for your immense talent, I'm willing to pay you a competitive salary, plus expenses, of course."

As the words slowly sank in, Holden leaned back in his chair. "I don't know what to say, Travis. I'm too stunned for words."

Travis smiled. It was just the kind of reaction he had hoped for. "Does that mean you'll say yes?"

"Hell yes, I'll say yes! How often does a mere mortal get an offer like that?"

His big, beefy hand reached across the table and Travis shook it, glad he had thought of revamping the television station rather than selling it. It would take a big chunk of money to do all the changes he had in mind, more than he had at the moment. But in a few months, when the hotel went public, he'd be swimming in money.

"That calls for a celebration," Nash said. "A party. At my house." His left eye closed in a smug wink. "We'll invite everyone at the *Globe.*"

"Actually, I'd like our little arrangement to remain between us. At least until I get the necessary financing."

Some of Nash's excitement vanished. "Are you worried you might not get it?"

"Not at all. I just thought it'd be best if I waited until the hotel was actually mine before I approached the bank. But don't worry," he added with a small wave of his hand. "I've already had an informal talk with my banker, and he sees no problem at all." He laughed. "Hell, in another month, banks all over the city will be begging me to take their money." He took a sip of his wine. "Until then, feel free to put down your thoughts about the kind of program you want to do. Think of some of the chefs you'd like to interview, places you'd want to include in your travels."

His confidence restored, Holden nodded. "I'll do that. I've got great contacts, as you know."

"Good." Travis waited until the columnist had started to eat again before saying, "The offer, however, does not come without ties."

Holden seemed to have regained his sense of humor along with his appetite. "Let me guess. You want another star for Déjà Vu."

"No. Actually the favor I need from you concerns another restaurant. A place down at the marina called Harbor View."

"I've heard of it." Nash paused, his sleepy eyes suddenly alert. "Wait a minute. Isn't it run by Diana Wells—the woman you're suing for custody of your son?"

"That's right." Travis looked around him to make sure no one was eavesdropping. When he spoke again, his voice was barely above a whisper. "I want you to destroy that restaurant, Holden. I want you to give it the kind of review that will guarantee Diana Wells's downfall."

Dark clouds loomed on the northern horizon, casting a threatening shadow over the mountains of Marin County across the bay. In San Francisco, however, the sky was a deep blue with only a few clouds drifting out to sea.

Standing in front of her office window, Diana gazed at the changing sky pattern, her mood as somber as the distant clouds. The announcement she had just read in the *Chronicle*, kept playing in her head.

During last night's benefit hosted by The World Against Hunger Organization, Travis Lindford and Dunbar Dewitt put an end to weeks of rumors and speculation by announcing their wedding in March of next year. The bride-to-be, who is president of the organization, requested that donations be made to that charity in lieu of wedding presents.

Diana looked down at the newspaper still in her hand. Of all the dirty tricks Travis could have devised, this was the lowest. And so damned obvious. Surely the judge would see right through it.

Or would he?

Her gaze shifted to the photograph of the mildly attractive young woman, whose smile radiated happiness. How could anyone fail to be impressed by someone who had devoted the last six years of her life to children of all races and nationalities?

An insistent knock at the door pulled her out of her thoughts. It was Lilly, Harbor View's talented pastry chef.

"Come to the kitchen, quick!" she said, motioning from the door.

"What is it now?" Diana asked, hurrying after her. They had already had two minor mishaps in the kitchen this morning, and she prayed the old saying "trouble comes in threes" hadn't come true.

"Can't tell you. You have to see for yourself."

In the kitchen, Diana heaved a sigh of relief. Except for the entire kitchen staff's crowding around the door that separated the kitchen from the dining room, everything seemed to be in order.

"What in the world are you all gaping at?"

Lilly pushed her forward. "Take a look."

Diana approached the door and let her gaze drift across the room, then as it stopped at a table by the window, she gasped. "My God! That's Holden Nash!"

"In the flesh. *All* of it."

"What is he doing here?"

Lilly chuckled. "My guess is that he came for lunch."

"But how can that be? He never reviews a restaurant until it's been in business for at least six months. Some even have to wait a year for him to come."

From the stove where he had returned to stir a fragrant hunter sauce for the venison stew, her French chef, Maurice, spoke over his shoulder. "So, he made an exception for you. That is good news, no?"

"I guess." She laughed nervously as she watched Nash and his female companion study the menu, turning from time to time to question their waiter. Holden Nash was one of the foremost restaurant critics in the country. His reviews, which were accompanied with a rating ranging from one to four stars—never five— could make a restaurant soar to the top as easily as it could sink it into oblivion. Although some said he had outlived his usefulness, his influence on the San Francisco dining community was still too powerful to ignore.

When Nash's waiter finally came in, Diana and Lilly pulled him inside and spoke in unison. "What did he order?"

Jack grinned, taking his time as he read the order. "Let's see now . . . The lady ordered the lamb chops d'Artagnan and Nash the bouillabaisse. For appetizers, she wants the mushrooms fricassee and he, the ravioli."

Diana let out her breath. With the exception of the bouillabaisse, which was one of Maurice's specialties, the other three dishes were tried and true recipes she had made time and time again as a caterer. "You told him the bouillabaisse would take extra time?"

Jack picked up a cassoulet order from Maurice. "Yes. He said he had all the time in the world."

Without a word, Diana went into the back room,

took a clean apron from a shelf, and tied it around her waist. Then, looking at her expectant staff, she grinned. "All right, gang. Let's get to work."

Holden Nash's review appeared in the Friday edition of the *Globe*.

Standing in the kitchen in her robe and sleepers because she had been too excited to get dressed, Diana stared in disbelief at the single star below the restaurant's name.

It had to be a mistake. *One* star? Not four as she had expected? Or even three?

In a state of shock, she read the accompanying review.

A recent television interview referred to Diana Wells, proprietor of Harbor View restaurant, as "the new kid on the block." However, the interviewer failed to add that the kid was quite green, and that her cuisine lacked the excitement one might have expected after so many years in the business.

On a visit to Harbor View a few days ago, my wife and I shared an experience I will endeavor to forget as soon as this column is finished.

We began our meal with two appetizers the waiter assured us were excellent choices—a fricassee of mushrooms with truffles and a four-cheese ravioli in a light cream sauce. Although the ravioli was passable, I found the mushrooms soggy and the truffles practically nonexistent.

Because I'm fond of Mediterranean dishes, I ordered the bouillabaisse. The fish was fresh but carelessly selected for this particular dish. The result was a medley of bony fish that had me choking throughout the meal.

My wife's lamb d'Artagnan was equally disappointing. The meat was overdone, and the raspberry glaze tasted as if it had been spooned right out of a jar. The potatoes Anna, served as an accompaniment to the lamb, were acceptable, if a trifle salty. Dessert could have saved the day, but didn't. Harbor View was out of the first three choices, leaving only a rather starchy *tate Tatin* and a tiramisu so sweet and heavy, neither of us could eat it.

A less expensive restaurant might have been forgiven. At the staggering prices Harbor View charges, such carelessness is nothing less that highway robbery.

Diana sat down. She had prepared the lamb chops herself, cooking them to the medium doneness she knew Americans preferred. Mrs. Nash had eaten every morsel on her plate, and there had been no report from the dining room that anyone was choking.

In her eleven years as a caterer, she had been exposed to many reviews, from customers as well as from various periodicals. Most had been good. A few she preferred to forget. But she had never been attacked so harshly. Or so unfairly.

Fuming, she marched to the phone and called the *Globe*. "Is Holden Nash in?" she asked when a cheery female voice answered.

"No, ma'am. We expect him at about ten. May I take a message?"

"That won't be necessary. I'll deliver it in person."

It was a little after ten when Diana stepped inside the busy lobby of the *San Francisco Globe*. "Where can I find Holden Nash?" she asked a receptionist, not waiting for her to get off the phone.

The slender blonde covered the mouthpiece with her hand. "His office is in the newsroom on the third floor. But you can't go up there without an appointment . . ." The girl stood up. "Miss . . . Excuse me, miss, you can't—"

Diana was already out of earshot. Stepping inside the elevator, she pushed the appropriate button. When the doors hissed open on the third floor, she stepped out, went sailing past another receptionist, her green London Fog billowing behind her. Inside the newsroom more than a dozen reporters sat in front of computer terminals, typing feverishly and talking on the telephone at the same time.

"Holden Nash?" she asked the man nearest the door.

Without looking up, he pointed toward a cubicle at the far end of the room.

The glass door was open. Sitting behind a large desk, Holden Nash was on the phone, his massive chest shaking with laughter.

Diana came to stand in front of him and threw the newspaper with the review faceup. "Would you care to tell me what this is all about?"

After murmuring a quick apology into the receiver, Nash hung up and calmly looked at her. "What is what all about, miss . . . ?"

"Wells. As if you didn't know."

He glanced at the newspaper before returning his gaze to her. "I'm sorry if you're upset about the review, Miss Wells. But as you know, *should* know, I call it as I see it."

Her hands on his desk, Diana leaned forward, coming within inches of his pudgy face. "Well, you called this one wrong, Mr. Nash."

"That's a matter of opinion."

"No. It's a matter of telling the truth. Which you

didn't. Everything you said in that review is either false or grossly exaggerated."

"Miss Wells—"

"Carelessly selected fish, indeed. For your information, the varieties of fish selected for a true bouillabaisse are unavailable in this country. Talk to any chef you know, and he'll tell you that rockfish, sea bass, and cod are excellent substitutions. As for the lamb chops, I'm sorry your wife found them overdone, but it's my experience that American tastes differ greatly from those of the French when it comes to cooking meats. And for your information, I would *never* serve anything out of a jar in my restaurant—although I doubt you would know the difference."

The big man's face had turned red, and behind her she could hear people whispering. But she wasn't finished. Without moving an inch, she went on. "I suppose it's understandable that after so many years of excessive eating, your palate is no longer at peak performance, but that's no excuse for the hatchet job you did here." She straightened up. "I demand a retraction."

Cold hazel eyes looked up from beneath hooded lids. "That's out of the question, Miss Wells. I *always* stand by my reviews."

"That's not a review. It's an execution." She studied the expressionless face. "Why? What have I ever done to you?"

He smiled. "You haven't done anything to me, Miss Wells. I don't even know you. Now why don't you stop taking this review as a personal insult and look at it as constructive criticism instead? I'm sure that with a little effort, you could elevate that one star to . . . one and a half?"

She let the insult ride and gave him a scathing look. "What people are saying about you is true after all,

isn't it? You've lost your touch. It's high time you vacated the chair you've occupied all those years and let
a younger, more sophisticated critic take over. One
who will be more in touch with changing times."

Then, seeing his face blanch, she turned around
and strode off as the crowd of curious onlookers
parted in front of her.

By the time Diana arrived at Harbor View, the hostess had received two cancellations for lunch and six
for dinner.

"It's just the initial reaction," she told the kitchen
staff, who were already aware of the news. "Business
will pick up again, you'll see. Until then, it's work
as usual."

But by the end of the week, Harbor View had received more than two dozen cancellations, including
a large Christmas party Diana had been counting on
to offset her losses.

"It's a disaster," she told Kat one afternoon. "Even
people I thought didn't give a damn about reviews are
jumping ship."

"That rotten son of a bitch," Kat said unceremoni-
ously. "One of these days, someone will make sure he
does choke—and it won't be from some imaginary
piece of fish."

On Friday, November twelfth, one week after the
review had appeared, Diana glanced at the reservation
list for the next few days and knew she had to do
something drastic or risk losing the restaurant.

Back in her office, she sat in front of her MacIntosh
and started to punch a few keys. Her gross intake since
opening the restaurant was in excess of one hundred
and eighty thousand dollars. After expenses, salaries,
and loan payments, she had a little over seven thousand dollars left. Not a bad profit for a month's

work—but more important, it was just enough for what she had in mind.

Her eyes still on the screen, she dialed Kat's number. "I've just come up with an idea," she told her friend. "But I need your help. Can you come right away?"

Half an hour later, Kat walked into her office. She wore a red jogging suit and a matching wool cap. "What's up?"

Diana held a sheet of paper to her. "Take a look at this and tell me what you think."

As Kat read, a slow smile spread across her face. "This is good, kiddo." She pulled off her cap and tossed it onto a chair. "I guess what you need now is some graphic work to go with it, right? Something clever and eye-catching."

Diana nodded eagerly. "Got any ideas?"

Kat just grinned.

Sitting in the hotel coffee shop the following Sunday morning, Travis stared at the half-page ad Diana had taken in the *Sunday Examiner*.

At the upper left-hand corner was the caricature of an enormous man wearing the black costume of executioners in medieval times. He held a hatchet above his head and was getting ready to lower it on Harbor View Restaurant. The man in the sketch bore an amazing resemblance to Holden Nash.

Below the drawing was an open letter from Diana to the public.

On November 5th, a vicious and unfair review appeared in the *San Francisco Globe,* making it necessary for me to come to the defense of my restaurant. After a great deal of thought, I came to the conclusion that the best way to do that was to let

you, the San Francisco public, make up your own
mind about Harbor View.

On Saturday evening one hundred people will
be invited to Harbor View as my guests. The first
fifty diners will be served at the seven o'clock sitting and the second half at the nine o'clock sitting.
Reservations are necessary and will be accepted
on a first come, first served basis. Guests will be
able to order anything on the menu, as they always have.

I'll be available throughout both shifts and will
gladly answer all your questions. Until then, rest
assured that your pleasure, your comfort, and
your absolute satisfaction have always been, and
will continue to be, my most important priorities.

Diana Wells

Travis lowered the paper and muttered a short,
harsh oath. This couldn't be good news. Not for him
anyway. If readers reacted favorably to Diana's offer,
Harbor View would be more popular than ever. And
he'd be back at square one.

Impatiently, he snapped his fingers at a passing
waiter. "You there, bring me a phone."

"Right away, Mr. Lindford."

After the waiter had returned with a portable
phone, Travis dialed Holden Nash at home. "Have
you read the *Examiner*?" he asked, not bothering with
a greeting.

"I never read the competition. Why? What's in it?"

Travis read him Diana's letter and told him about
the cartoon.

Nash was silent for a moment, then made an audible sigh. "I must admit, it's clever."

"Will it work?"

"If you're asking will people respond favorably to

the offer of a free meal, the answer is yes. As to whether or not they'll continue to support her after that, we'll have to wait and see."

"Can you do anything to stop her?"

"Hell, no. Any attempt on my part to discredit her at this point would look damn suspicious." He paused. "And to tell you the truth, after that little scene at the *Globe* last week, I never want to get that woman pissed off at me again."

Travis hung up. He couldn't blame the guy. His end of the bargain had been fulfilled. He didn't need to do anything else.

With a sigh, he pushed the newspaper aside. Nash was right. All he could do at this point was wait and see.

14

Sitting in his office on Monday morning, Kane smiled as he read the ad Jackie had clipped from the *San Francisco Examiner* and left on his desk.

Holden Nash, whom he had met years ago, had never been one of his favorite people, and the thought that someone had finally struck back pleased him immensely.

Diana hadn't deserved that review in last week's *Globe*. When Jackie had pointed it out to him, he had been tempted to call Diana and tell her so. But he had stopped himself in time. She had made it clear during his visit to her house that she wasn't interested in seeing him. And maybe that was just as well. Although he no longer had any obligations toward the Lindfords, they were still his friends. And a relationship with Diana, on any level, would only jeopardize that long-standing friendship.

Then why the hell couldn't he forget her?

At first, he had tried to blame it on lust. On need. But he knew better. Oh, there was no denying the physical attraction was there. He had known that from the moment he had laid eyes on her. But if sex was all he wanted, why was he experiencing those sweet, tender feelings whenever he thought of her? That overwhelming need to help and protect her?

Reaching for the cup of coffee at his side, he took

a sip as he continued to look at the ad. Perhaps it was her complexity he found so fascinating, the way she could be playful one moment and aloof the next, ambitious and touchingly domestic, strong yet vulnerable.

What would it be like? he wondered, to love a woman like that?— to awaken the passion he felt simmering below that composed surface?

His thoughts were interrupted by the buzzer on his intercom. "Yes, Jackie?"

"Boss, what do you want to do about Lyle Remington's invitation on Tuesday? His secretary is on the phone."

"Ah yes, Lyle . . . Let's see, it should be right here. Somewhere." Shuffling through a pile of mail, he found the engraved invitation Jackie had handed him earlier this week. "To tell you the truth, I had forgotten all about it."

He glanced at the time on the card. Five o'clock. He often worked until late at night, but he could make an exception for one evening. He hadn't been socializing very much since moving back to San Francisco. He should change that. Maybe a preholiday party was just what he needed to put Diana Wells out of his mind.

"Tell Lyle's secretary I'll be there," he said.

To Diana's great relief, her gamble had paid off. Hundreds of calls poured in that Sunday morning, and while many customers had to be turned away, the event had been a tremendous success and the money well spent, judging from the number of people who were slowly returning to Harbor View.

Now, still dazzled by her recent tour de force, Diana stood in front of her closet, trying to decide what to wear at the cocktail party Mitch's law firm gave every year the Tuesday before Thanksgiving.

She normally didn't attend social gatherings, but

Kat had been insistent. "Surely the restaurant can spare you for an hour," she had told her. "Besides, you've been going nonstop since your grand opening, and unless you learn to relax a little, you're going to burn yourself out."

Kat was right. Between work, chauffeuring Zack to his various activities, and worrying about the custody hearing, relaxation had become a foreign word. She wasn't sure a noisy cocktail party was the answer, but if the event turned out to be a crashing bore, she could always leave.

After another minute of indecision, she selected a black suit with white embroidery on the lapels, added a pair of onyx earrings to finish the look, and spritzed herself with a mist of Fleurs de Rocailles.

Then, satisfied she looked festive enough for the occasion, she left.

The large conference room of Caldwell, Remington and Parker was filled to near capacity when Diana arrived. Standing on the threshold, she accepted a glass of white wine from a waiter, then, spotting Kat talking to an elderly couple, she made her way across the room.

The couple turned out to be a retired judge and his wife, who, upon learning that she owned a restaurant, felt obligated to tell her about their latest trip through the gastronomic capitals of Europe.

She had just managed to get away from them when a familiar voice behind her whispered in her ear.

"Hello again."

She turned around. Kane Sanders stood in front of her, his friendly grin in place. He wore dark gray slacks and a tweed jacket over a black turtleneck. In a roomful of Armani suits and two-hundred-dollar ties, he looked elegant and relaxed.

She felt the instant tug of attraction, but concealed it quickly with an easy smile. "I wasn't aware you knew Mitch."

"If you mean Mitch Parker, I don't. Lyle Remington invited me. He's an old friend." His lips twitched. "What about you? I didn't figure you for the office party type," he added, quoting her remark of a few days ago almost word for word.

"Mitch is married to my best friend." Struggling not to be drawn in by his warm smile, she added, "But you're right. Parties of any kind bore me. I came only because Kat insisted I needed some distraction."

The amused gleam in his eyes became more pronounced. "Do you?"

She took a sip of her wine. "Occasionally. A good book is usually enough. Or an old Bette Davis movie."

He raised his glass in salute. "At last. We have something in common."

"Bette Davis?"

"Old movies. Although I'm partial to Cary Grant and Ingrid Bergman myself."

"A romantic. How fascinating."

"I'll be glad to fascinate you further if you let me take you out for a cup of coffee."

Her first impulse was to say no. She was much too aware of his presence, of the way her pulse quickened whenever he was near, and of the stirrings she felt deep inside her when he looked at her with that warm light in his eyes. But she felt restless tonight. And she was enjoying his company.

"A cup of coffee sounds wonderful. But I won't be able to stay long. I have to be at the restaurant no later than seven."

"All right. Give me a minute to say goodbye to Lyle and I'll be right with you."

Turning around to do the same with Kat, she caught

her friend looking at her from across the room, a pleased expression in her eyes. "You rat," Diana hissed as she pulled her aside. "You planned this, didn't you? That's why you were so insistent that I stop by. You found out Kane was coming, and you arranged for me to be here as well."

As a waiter stopped to offer a tray of hors d'oeuvres, Kat helped herself to a shrimp canapé. "All right, I confess. But you have to admit, it was an inspired idea. And you two look great together."

"You know how I feel about matchmakers."

Kat pretended not to have heard and popped the canapé into her mouth as she watched Kane shake hands with a group of attorneys. "Where is he taking you?"

"The downstairs coffee shop." Diana put her glass down. "And wipe that silly grin off your face. Coffee and conversation is all we have on the agenda."

Then, as Kane made his way toward her, she kissed Kat on the cheek. "I'll talk to you tomorrow."

The Greenhouse coffee shop was crowded when they arrived, but Kane quickly spotted an empty table and took Diana's hand as he led the way toward it.

Following him, she was aware of several things—the way he moved, slowly, but with a coiled, controlled energy, how women stopped talking to look at him, and the tug of pleasure she experienced when their envious gaze drifted toward her.

You've been without a man too long, she thought as they reached their table. Get a grip on yourself.

A waitress brought them a menu, but Kane waved it aside. "Just coffee, please." He waited until Diana had slipped her coat off her shoulders before asking, "Do you have to be at the restaurant every night?"

"Yes. People enjoy having the owner on the premises, accessible and ready to answer their questions. It's a habit I picked up when I trained with a French chef years ago."

"It can't be easy, running a demanding business and raising a young boy all by yourself."

Although the remark was meant as a compliment, he saw her tense, and cursed himself for his poor choice of words.

"Zack and I are managing just fine. Besides, as soon as the restaurant is established, I'll be able to curtail my hours, spend more time at home."

He pulled back to let the waitress put two steaming cups of coffee in front of them, then said, "Does it get easier with time? Taking care of a boy, I mean."

Diana smiled. "You'd think so, wouldn't you? But no, it doesn't. The fact that he's growing up, wants to explore things I might not approve of, makes my job as a mother a daily challenge."

He found himself wondering why that daily challenge wasn't being shared by a husband. Surely a woman like Diana Wells didn't lack suitors.

Although wisdom told him not to pry, the words were out of his mouth before he could stop them. "How come you never married?"

The question didn't seem to offend her. "I came close to marrying once," she said, staring pensively into her cup. "Twice actually."

"What happened?"

"It didn't work out. The first man forgot to tell me he was already married. And the second one deeply resented Zack, felt threatened by him." She stirred a spoonful of sugar into her coffee. "From that moment on, I put marriage completely out of my mind. Zack and I are very happy together, and he'll always come first."

"He's a very lucky little guy to have a mother like you."

In the booth across from their table, a young mother was cutting a slice of apple pie in two, ignoring her two young sons' complaints that one half was larger than the other. As Kane's gaze settled on the younger boy, Diana remembered what John McKay had told her about Kane's own custody battle four years ago and the subsequent death of his son.

Unexpectedly, her eyes filled with tears.

After a moment, Kane returned his attention to her. "I had a son, too. Once."

"I know," she said in a faint whisper.

If he thought anything unusual in her answer, he didn't show it. "He would have been eight this past July."

Zack's age. "I'm sorry." She put her cup down. "How did you ever find the strength to go on?"

"It wasn't easy. But you learn how to cope. Somehow."

Whatever had seemed so threatening about him a few days ago, had vanished. Looking at him now, all she saw was an ordinary man, dealing with the same pains thousands of other people dealt with every day.

"But enough about me," he said, flashing a sudden smile. "I'd much rather talk about you." He added a few drops of milk to his coffee. "Is it true that you went storming into the *Globe*'s newsroom last week and reduced Holden Nash to a quivering mush of tapioca pudding?"

Diana laughed softly. "Who said that?"

"My secretary. You met her at the restaurant the day I came to see you."

"And how did your secretary find out about my confrontation with Holden Nash?"

"You may not realize it, but you're the talk of the

town. Rumor has it The Great One hasn't been himself since that day."

"Don't expect me to have any sympathy for him. The man is a pompous jerk. It was about time someone told him so."

"That's what my aunt said. She thinks you should be given a medal."

"Your aunt reads his column?" She asked, imagining an old, gray-haired lady in a rocker.

"She won't admit it, but yes, she does, even though she hates the man's guts." At her questioning look, he added, "My Aunt Beckie owns a winery in Sonoma. Twelve years ago, when she unveiled a Cabernet she was particularly proud of, he gave it a terrible review."

"Did it hurt her sales?"

"Initially, yes. But she recovered. And never spoke to Holden Nash again."

They fell into an easy conversation, he telling her about his aunt and the fun-filled summers he had spent in Sonoma, she confessing she had once wanted to become a doctor.

"When my mother became ill with cancer, I gave up the idea so I could stay close to her."

"Couldn't you have pursued medicine in San Francisco?"

"Yes. But the money that had been earmarked for my education had to be used to pay the bills, so I had no choice but to think of another career."

"It's quite a stretch from medicine to the restaurant business."

"I know." She told him how she had come to her decision, and how Nadine's death had almost put a stop to that second dream. "I was very reluctant to adopt Zack at first," she confessed in a faraway voice. "Not only did I feel I was not prepared to be a mother—certainly not as good a mother as Nadine was—but I also was terrified of what a child would do to my career."

"What made you change your mind?"

"Nadine. She had a way of stripping the veneer off people, exposing only what mattered."

"Which was?"

"In my case, it was my love for Zack. The thought of what might happen to him terrified me even more than becoming an instant mother."

He looked at her. Even in the harsh neon light of the coffee shop, she managed to look soft and glowing. His gaze drifted downward, toward the embroidered lapels, the creamy skin between them, and the little golden heart hanging from a chain and nestled in the hollow of her throat. "Well . . . You've done a terrific job."

"Thanks."

"How is Zack holding up under what's been happening?"

Her face clouded over. "He's trying to pretend everything is as it used to be, but things have changed dramatically. We now have to play games to avoid the press, and his schoolmates have been relentless in their questioning. Yesterday, his best friend, Billy, called him a rich man's bastard."

Kane experienced a quick burst of anger toward Travis and Margaret. If it weren't for them, for their determination to sue for custody, Zachary wouldn't have to be hurt by remarks like that. "How did he take it?"

"He was furious. I tried to tell him that Billy hadn't meant to hurt him, that it was something he had probably heard other kids say." She shook her head. "It didn't do any good. He says he hates Billy now, and he hates his school."

"He's young. And resilient. It'll pass."

"I know."

Their gaze met and held. Whatever decision he had made a few days ago not to get involved in Diana's private life seemed to melt away under the heat of that gaze.

With a self-conscious laugh, Diana glanced at her watch. "My, look at the time."

He didn't want to. He would have been perfectly happy to stay right where he was, talking to her and looking at her all night. Reluctantly, he stood up, dropping a five-dollar bill on the table. "I'll walk you to your car."

"I didn't drive."

"How did you get here?"

She smiled. "How else? The cable cars. It sure beats trying to find a parking space."

"In that case," he said, helping her with her coat, "I'll give you a ride."

Before she could protest, he had taken her arm and was guiding her toward the door.

The day had started with a rush of rain, but now that night had fallen, the rain had stopped and a heavy fog drifted in from the bay, enveloping the area in a damp mist. Straight ahead, the shimmering Transamerica Pyramid towered over the city, looking like a gigantic Christmas tree.

They quickly walked the short block to the parking garage, with Kane still holding her arm. He only released it to enter the elevator. Moments later, she was settled into the passenger seat of his BMW.

He drove the powerful car expertly, guiding it through the heavy downtown traffic as he talked. From time to time, she'd turn to look at him. She liked the way he sat behind the wheel, slightly laid back, like a man at ease with himself, with his body. She found herself thinking of his wife, wondering why a woman, any woman, would want to let go of a man like that.

Again, the direction of her thoughts startled her. It wasn't like her to think so intensely about a man. Or to wonder about his past loves.

The car slowed and came to a stop in the back alley behind the restaurant. "Thank you," she said as he turned toward her. "For the ride and the conversation. It took my mind off my problems for a while."

Her scent, a blend of jasmine and wildflowers, enveloped him. "Then I take it you no longer regard me as a threat?"

She pursed her lips, fighting off a smile. "I refuse to answer on the ground that it might incriminate me."

The warmth of her laughter filled the car, and his senses. Suddenly, he didn't want to let her go. Not unless he could see her again. On impulse, he asked, "What are you doing for Thanksgiving?"

The question seemed to take her off guard. "Zack and I will be spending it quietly at home. Why?"

"Just the two of you?"

"We normally have dinner with Kat and Mitch. But this is their fifth wedding anniversary, and they decided to treat themselves to a ski vacation in Steamboat Springs."

"Thanksgiving is no time to be alone. Why don't you and Zack come to Sonoma and spend the day with my aunt and me? She'll love it," he added, seeing she was about to turn him down. "If she knew you were alone, she would ask you herself."

"But I'm a stranger to her, and Thanksgiving is a time for families to be together—"

"And friends. Neighbors. People we care about." He grinned. "I promise after ten minutes in Aunt Beckie's company, you'll feel like one of the family. She has that effect on people."

"I don't know. I should discuss it with Zack . . ."

"It's beautiful out there at this time of year. Zack will love it. And Lady will love having someone to play with."

"Who's Lady?"

"Aunt Beckie's golden retriever. She's crazy about kids. At times, she even thinks she's one of them."

She felt herself weakening. Would it be so terrible to spend one day with him and his aunt? To pretend this was a Thanksgiving like all the others, peaceful and worry free?

"Say yes, Diana."

His smile was impossible to resist. She smiled back. "All right. You talked me into it."

"Great. I'll pick you up at nine on Thursday morning. Is that all right?"

"That will be fine."

She saw the change in his eyes, the way his gaze drifted to her mouth, lingered there for a moment before returning to her eyes. The effect was unnerving, as potent as if he had touched her. Turning away, she opened the door. "I'll see you on Thursday then."

Kane expelled a long breath and watched her disappear through the back door. His nerves were raw, aching with the need to touch her, hold her, kiss her. No woman had ever stirred him that way before. Not even Jamie.

After one last glance at the door through which Diana had disappeared, he put the BMW in reverse and backed out of the alley.

15

Sanders Estates, in the quaint hamlet of Glen Ellen, was an eight-hundred-acre vineyard Kane's grandfather had bought in the early 1900s when Sonoma County was a sleepy patch of green earth and home to more prune farmers than winegrowers.

The main house, designed after an old-fashioned farmhouse, was made of sturdy redwood and was visible for miles. The front door opened into a huge living area that combined dining room and family room. There were no divider walls, only big open spaces, wooden beams, and unfinished logs that gave the place a charming rustic look.

In the center of the room a broad redwood staircase, at the top of which was a loft, took center stage, creating an illusion of even more space. Comfortable early American furniture was scattered about in small groupings.

Aunt Beckie was as friendly and down to earth as Kane had described her, and not at all the old woman Diana had imagined. There was a ruggedness about her that was accentuated by the masculine clothes she wore. But underneath she was all softness and warmth. Especially when she talked to, or about, Kane.

Zack, who had been asked to make himself at home, had done just that, and established an instant rapport with Lady, the affectionate golden retriever Beckie had nurtured since puppyhood.

"Dinner will be served at three," Beckie told them after giving Diana and Zack a tour of the house. "So feel free to roam around the property, visit the winery or do whatever you want."

While Zack chose to play Frisbee with Lady, Diana agreed to let Kane show her the winery.

"The entire eight hundred acres are planted mostly to chardonnay, merlot, and cabernet grapes," he told her as they rode Beckie's Land Rover around the property. "Those are the only three wines Sanders Estates produces."

She slanted him an amused glance. "Are they any good?"

"Good? You mean you've never tasted Sanders wines?"

"I'm familiar with the label, but no," she shook her head, "I've never tasted them."

"Then you're in for a treat." He tossed her a quick grin before returning his gaze to the road. "By the time you leave here tonight, I guarantee you'll want to add our name to your wine list."

"So that's why you brought me here," she teased. "To sell me your wines."

She could tell by the way he talked about the vineyards that he was more of a country boy than she had realized. There was a passion in his voice as he told her how his grandfather, one of the pioneers in the wine industry, had traveled all the way to France and brought back enough cuttings to start his business, never dreaming he would one day produce some of the finest wines in the country.

He pointed straight ahead. "That white building over there, with the bell tower, is the winery."

"It's beautiful," Diana commented as Kane led her inside the missionlike structure.

"My grandfather wanted to build something people wouldn't easily forget. Some years later, the idea caught on and now, several wineries here and in Napa Valley are built to resemble missions."

Side by side, they walked into a warehouselike room filled with large steel tanks. "After the crush, the juice is conveyed into those tanks," Kane explained, "where it ferments for about two weeks. Then it's stored in wooden barrels for a number of years depending on the vintage. When the cellar master feels the wine is ready, it goes out to the bottling plant and eventually ends up on your table."

"Did you ever consider becoming a vintner?" she asked.

He laughed. "No. The truth is, I have deplorable taste in wine, in spite of my aunt's efforts to correct the problem. But I like the sense of camaraderie that exists here between winemakers and employees. People know each other by name, and are always there for you. It's like having an extended family."

"You seem to feel very much at home here."

"I do." He bent to pick up a steel funnel and laid it on a shelf next to a barrel. "But this area isn't for everyone. My ex-wife hated it."

He wasn't sure why he had said that. Perhaps because having Zack and Diana here reminded him of Jamie and Sean.

"Why is that?" Diana asked.

He shrugged. "She found the place too isolated, the people too 'coarse.' Whenever she came here, she was always bored."

"How about your son?"

"He loved it here. He liked riding around in the Land Rover, watching the grapes being crushed. And he loved Beckie's big, rambling house. She and Thelma spoiled him rotten every time he came."

They were back outside, and he stared at the mountains in the distance. He thought of all the things he and Sean would never do together, and how much he missed him. Even now after four years.

"I'm sorry," Diana said softly. "It must be painful for you, being here . . . on a holiday."

"He was going to learn how to swim that year," he said as if he hadn't heard her. "But the divorce threw everything out of whack. I tried to tell Jamie we should wait, try to make the marriage work. For Sean's sake. But she was in love with a fashion photographer who was going to resurrect her modeling career, and she wouldn't listen."

Diana felt an instant dislike for the woman. "Why didn't you get custody of Sean?"

"I tried. But halfway into the proceedings, Jamie said she would bring Sean in front of the judge if she had to." He kicked a twig out of the way and sent it flying. "I couldn't let her do that to him. I couldn't ask him to choose between his mother and his father."

"So you withdrew the suit."

He nodded. "Three months later, Sean was dead," he said quietly.

Although Diana had already known about the drowning, she felt a sharp stab of pain, and with a quick brush of her hand, had to wipe away a tear. "I wish there was something I could say. I feel so . . . helpless."

When he focused his eyes back on her, she was relieved to see that the anguish she had seen earlier was gone. "I've ruined your holiday, haven't I?"

She shook her head.

"Good. Because Beckie would slaughter me if I had."

When they arrived back at the house, Diana realized she and Zack weren't Beckie's only holiday guests. The cellar master and his wife were there along with a half dozen key employees, their wives, and children. They all sat together, twenty some people happily chatting about wine, restaurants, and a man by the name of Ted Grant, a local attorney, who would be retiring at the end of the year.

"I had a wonderful time," Diana told Beckie hours later when the two women took their coffee in front of the huge stone fireplace. The rest of the guests had left, and Zack, his head resting on Lady's comfortable stomach, lay on the floor, watching the Dallas–Miami football game on television. "Thank you so much for including us in your celebration."

"You're very welcome, and I'm delighted you could come." As Zack cheered, she smiled. "It isn't every day that I'm blessed with such lively company."

Beckie's friendly housekeeper came to refill their coffee cups, and Diana thanked her with a smile before turning to Beckie again. "Does Kane often bring strays home?"

"Not since the summer he turned eleven when he walked in with a wounded fawn in his arms. Together we nursed it back to health and then we set her free." She chuckled at the memory. "Kane was heartbroken for days after that. I couldn't bear to see him unhappy, so I went to the county fair and bought him a rabbit."

Diana's gaze drifted toward Kane, who sat next to Zack. She tried to imagine him as a young boy. "Did it help?"

"For a while. But after a couple of days he decided the rabbit was lonely, so I bought him a mate. The problem was, the mate was a she, and a short while later we had rabbits hopping all over the place."

Smiling, Diana picked up her cup and wrapped her hands around it. "You love him very much, don't you?"

Beckie's eyes softened. "Like a son. He's brought me much joy over the years. He's caring, honest, and loyal to a fault." She sighed. "Sometimes too loyal."

Diana pulled her gaze away from Kane. "Are you referring to Margaret Lindford?"

Beckie rolled her eyes upward. "The woman has been a thorn in my side ever since I can remember. But never more so than when she tried to manipulate him into taking that ridiculous custody case. Thank goodness, Kane came to his senses."

Diana thought about asking her why Margaret had such a strong hold on Kane, then thought better of it. She didn't want to put her hostess in an awkward position. And anyway, Kane's relationship with Margaret, or with any other woman for that matter, was none of her business.

But during the drive home, while Zack slept in the backseat, she couldn't resist bringing up the subject of Travis Lindford's strong-willed mother.

"Ah," Kane said, slanting an amused glance in her direction. "I see that you talked to my aunt."

Diana felt bound to come to Beckie's defense. "She only spoke of *her* feelings for Margaret, nothing else."

Kane glanced at the rearview mirror before merging onto Highway 101. "It hasn't been easy loving two women as stubborn and ill-willed toward each other as these two. Sometimes, I wonder how I've managed to do it and come out of it in one piece."

"One of the reasons might be that Beckie loves you very much." She couldn't bring herself to include Margaret in that statement.

"I know."

Although he had never discussed his relationship with the Lindfords with anyone but Beckie, the words came easily, the memory of the tragic events as vivid as if they had happened yesterday.

"I'm sorry," Diana murmured after he had finished telling her about his father's death.

"Aunt Beckie never shared my high regard for Margaret," he continued. "After my father died, she blamed Charles and Margaret for not pushing harder to prove his innocence."

"But you didn't share your aunt's opinion."

"No. The Lindfords did all they could. When the private investigator they hired couldn't come up with anything new, they thought it best to let the matter rest rather than perpetuate the scandal. Doing so would only have made matters worse—for all of us. And for the hotel."

The hotel. From the moment Diana had met Margaret, she had felt as if the Lindford meant more to her than the members of her own family.

Kane steered the car onto the Golden Gate Bridge. "I don't expect you to understand Margaret's motives. To a lot of people she seems like a self-serving, hard, even ruthless woman. But I know another side of her, a side she rarely allows anyone to see."

She understood perfectly. He was bound to her as strongly as if he were a Lindford himself.

"Your turn."

Startled, she turned to face him. "I beg your pardon?"

"It's your turn to tell all. One secret in exchange for another."

She stared at the glittering lights of San Francisco in the distance. "I don't have any secrets."

"Everyone has at least one secret." He glanced at

her, saddened at the way her eyes had cooled, at the sudden distance she had put between them. "You still don't trust me, do you?"

"It isn't a matter of trusting or not trusting. The fact is my life is an open book. A dull one at that."

He didn't press her. Maybe the reason she didn't talk about her brother was because they no longer saw each other and there was really nothing to talk about.

When he stopped the car in her driveway and switched off the engine, Zack stirred, but didn't wake up.

"I'll carry him up," Kane offered.

Moments later, Zack was in bed, his teddy bear snuggled up in his arms. "Would you care for some coffee?" Diana asked as they came down the stairs. "It will take only a minute to make it."

He shook his head. "It's late. I'd better let you get some sleep, too."

She walked him to the door. "Thanks for a wonderful day, Kane. And for insisting—"

She never had a chance to finish. His hands came up, quick and sure, folding around the back of her neck, drawing her to him.

She wasn't sure what startled her more, the kiss or the warmth of his mouth, the clever way he moved it, forcing hers open without seeming to force her at all.

It should have been easy enough for her to pull away. Instead, she found herself leaning into him, responding to his kiss while some distant part of her mind told her to end it before it went any further.

She ignored the order. Overwhelmed by sensations and longings she hadn't experienced in years, she shuddered, aware of a shifting, delicious ache deep within her.

As his fingers relaxed their hold at the back of her neck and moved along her throat, a moan escaped from her lips. Against his chest, her tightly clenched fists opened as she swayed closer.

He had kissed her on impulse, half expecting her to pull away. Her heated response took him by surprise, awakening his senses to a point that was dangerously high. Her lips were soft, pliant, and downright addictive.

Then, she pushed him away and the spell was broken.

"Diana—"

She shook her head. One hand over her breast, she waited a beat until the ground felt solid beneath her feet again. "That was a mistake."

His hands slid down her arms, gripping her wrists. "No, it wasn't. You wanted it as much as I did. Don't try to deny it."

She shook her head again, disengaging herself. She didn't like to lose control. Especially now. And especially with him. "Please go," she said in a whisper. She didn't trust herself to speak any louder, to even look at him, for fear he would see the truth—would see the need.

He took a step back, releasing her reluctantly. "All right." His eyes were still on her when he opened the door, but she kept her gaze focused on the wall behind him.

It wasn't until the door was safely shut that she leaned against it and closed her eyes.

It took her a long time to fall asleep that night. When she finally did, it was with visions of Kane dancing in her head.

16

Shafts of morning sun, swirling with dust motes, poured into the studio and onto the paintings scattered across the room.

Although Randall had loved Francesca's apartment on Telegraph Hill from the moment he had set foot in it, he felt most comfortable in this room, which he had decorated himself in the earthy, burnished colors that were reflected in his paintings.

A deep sofa covered in butterscotch velvet stood against one wall and was the only formal piece of furniture in the room. The rest consisted of wooden stools, stained with paint, a drawing table, an easel, and more than three dozen paintings in various stages of completion, stacked against the walls.

Wearing a pair of blue jeans and a sweatshirt, Randall sat on the sofa, reading the latest surveillance report Joe O'Keefe's messenger had delivered to him moments ago.

Like all the other reports before that, it contained nothing relevant, nothing he could use. According to the operative who was trailing Travis, his brother-in-law went out of the hotel only to meet his fiancée and take her to lunch or dinner. Sometimes both. As for the taped activities inside Travis's penthouse and office, they showed no irregularities whatsoever, no suspicious visitors, no telephone conversations with sheiks or other potential investors.

Either Travis had suddenly become as pure as the virgin snow, or the son of a bitch had more brains than Randall gave him credit for.

"Damn." Throwing the file on the cushion next to him, he stood up and went to stand by the bank of windows that looked out onto Treasure Island and the San Francisco–Oakland Bay Bridge. Could he have been mistaken about Travis? About him wanting to take the hotel public? Or was his brother-in-law just playing the waiting game.

His thoughts drifted to Francesca and what her reaction would be if she knew what he was doing. He had no doubt she would be furious, and would ask him to end the surveillance immediately. If there was one thing Francesca valued more than anything else, it was honesty.

"I fell in love with you because you were different from all the other men I've known," she had told him the first time they had made love. "You don't put on airs. You don't try to be someone you're not. And you don't lie. I like that in a man." Nibbling on his ear, she had whispered, "Honesty turns me on."

At the recollection of that day and all the wonderful days that had followed, his expression softened. He had met her in the spring of 1990 when he was still one of San Francisco's countless starving artists. A friend had given him an invitation to a gallery opening, and although such functions always left him depressed and a little envious, he had gone anyway.

As he stood in front of a large black painting with a single white dot in the center, someone behind him laughed softly. Turning around, he found himself staring at the most beautiful girl he had ever laid eyes on.

"What do you suppose the artist is trying to tell us?" she asked in a conspiratorial whisper.

He glanced back at the painting that had been titled "Universe." "I think," he replied, barely able to contain his own amusement, "he's trying to tell us that even though we've been told time and time again that nothing is ever black and white, apparently that assumption is wrong."

She laughed. "Should we believe him?"

"I never take phonies too seriously."

They had spent the rest of the evening in a nearby Chinese restaurant, getting to know each other. Although Francesca seemed fascinated by his being an artist, it took him two weeks to find the courage to show her his work. When he finally did, her reaction sent his hopes soaring.

"You must stop peddling your art in the street," she had told him as she walked around his studio in the Haight–Ashbury district, admiring the more than two dozen paintings he had completed. "And look into some of our downtown galleries like Levenberg or Hermitage."

It was she who had introduced him to Anthony Morales, insisting the gallery owner take a few of Randall's painting on consignment.

Three months later, Randall had sold his first painting for the staggering sum—at least to him—of four hundred dollars.

He had spent it all on a dozen roses for Francesca and a lavish dinner for two in one of San Francisco's most expensive restaurants.

It wasn't until Morales had sold two more paintings that Randall found the courage to ask Francesca to marry him.

A week later, they eloped to Las Vegas.

Facing the Lindford family afterward was like being

thrown into a den full of hungry lions. But Francesca had handled them all with a master's touch—even Travis, who had hated him on sight.

"He's the most exciting man I've met in years," she had told her brother during a private conversation Randall had overheard. "Totally devoid of pretense. After the phonies I've dated this year alone, that's quite refreshing."

And now here he was, betraying her trust in a way she could never imagine.

The phone on the drafting table rang, interrupting his thoughts, and he went to answer it. "Yes?" he said, his voice sharp with irritation. As soon as he realized it was Joe O'Keefe, he apologized.

"No need to apologize," the investigator replied. "I understand how frustrated you must feel. Which is why I called."

"You found out something?"

"I wish I had, Randall." Joe sighed. "I called because I need to know if you want me to continue with the surveillance. It's costing you a lot of money, and I'm not sure you're going to get the results you were hoping for."

Randall hesitated. Here was his chance to redeem himself, to drop the whole damn thing without Francesca ever knowing anything about it. She had accepted her mother's decision. Why couldn't he do the same and just concentrate on the two of them, on their happiness, on building the family they so badly wanted?

Then he remembered the dejected look on Francesca's face the night her mother had announced that Travis would become the next chairman. And her fears that Travis would take the hotel public. Nothing would ever be the same again after that, for Francesca, or for Margaret.

"Randall?" Joe said at the other end. "Do you want me to continue?"

Randall drew a breath. "Yes."

"Aw, come on, Eddy. Two more weeks is all I need. Surely you know me well enough by now—"

Eddy, a gaunt-looking man with a Mediterranean complexion and thin, chiseled features, gazed at Nick Wells with a look that sent a chill down Nick's spine. "You're not going to tell me I should trust you, are you? Not after the stunt you pulled a few months ago, stashing the money you owed me in your sister's house and forcing me to go there to get it."

In the cold, empty warehouse Eddy used as his meeting place, Nick shivered. "It was wrong of me to try to outsmart a guy like you, Eddy. But I was desperate. And desperation sometimes makes a man do stupid things." He licked his lips. "Believe me, I've regretted it ever since."

"Because Bulge and Curly *made* you regret it."

Nick didn't need to be reminded. The thought of the "workout" Eddy's two goons had given him the night they had come to his apartment made him wince.

He should have known better than to get tangled up with a guy like Eddy. But that latest venture with one of his co-workers at the loading dock had been too good to pass up.

"All we need is another partner with twenty thousand dollars and we're in business," Rocco had told him. "You'll double your investment with just the first boat load."

The deal had been deceptively simple. Thousands of Chinese refugees, eager to find a better life, left their homeland every week, all of them willing to pay up to three thousand dollars each for a safe passage to the United States.

A friend of Rocco, who had bought an old tanker from an oil company, would supply the ship and the crew in exchange for an investment of twenty thousand dollars per investor.

It had taken Nick several days to convince Eddy to lend him the money.

But the deal had gone sour. A television news station had gotten wind of the story and sent a crew to investigate. Realizing the scheme was about to blow wide open, Rocco had vanished without a trace.

With Nick's twenty grand.

Now the money, plus five thousand in interest, were due and he didn't have a dime to his name. "Look, Eddy," he said with all the humility he could muster. "I swear on my mother's grave, I'll pay back every cent."

Eddy took a pack of Marlboros from his breast pocket, pulled out a cigarette, and lit it. "Of course you will," he said after taking a puff. "Because if you don't, you're dead." His voice was soft, almost caressing. "Right boys?"

Behind Nick, Eddy's two bodyguards—each as big as a house—cracked their knuckles in perfect harmony.

Nick swallowed. "Jesus, don't do this to me, Eddy. I can get the money, I swear. All I need is a little more time."

"That's what you told me a week ago."

"And I meant it. But you know why I couldn't pay you. That bastard took all my money. He left me with nothing, Eddy. I don't even have enough dough to pay my rent."

Eddy threw a cloud of cigarette smoke toward the ceiling. "We all have our crosses to bear. Me, I've got a payroll to meet. And a daughter who wants to become Surgeon General of the United States. You know how much med school costs these days?"

Nick didn't give a damn about med school, but he kept his mouth shut. If Eddy felt like rambling, who was he to argue? "Okay, what about a week, Eddy? Is that better? I'll have the money to you by five o'clock next Friday."

Eddy pursed his lips as if he were giving the matter consideration.

Nick leaned over the table, his green eyes earnest. "Look, Eddy. You've always been good to me—generous, understanding—like a father."

Eddy took another puff of his cigarette. "That's because I like you, kid. You've got potential, initiative. I like that in a man." Behind the smoke, his eyes narrowed. "What makes you think you can get twenty-five grand in one week?"

Christ, he had no idea. He had exhausted all his contacts. Even other "lenders" had turned him down. The word was out that Nick Wells was a welsher. "My sister will lend it to me," he said, hoping his fake optimism sounded real enough.

"She's never helped you before."

He gave a short, nervous laugh. "I've never been in this kind of trouble before."

"True." Eddy leaned back in his chair. "I tell you what, kid. Seeing that I like you so much, I'll give you a break—"

"Thank you—"

"But it's going to cost you another five grand. That's the deal," he added when he saw Nick's eyes widen. "Take it or leave it."

Nick's shoulders sagged. It was a rotten deal. But at least he had bought himself a little time. "Okay. I'll take it."

His cigarette clamped between his teeth, Eddy

leaned toward Nick, his dark eyes glinting like two small chunks of coal. "And don't you try to skip on me, you hear? Because wherever you go, my boys will find you."

"I'd never do that to you, Eddy."

Eddy stood up and came around the table. "Good." He patted Nick's cheeks. "I'd hate to see that pretty face of yours squashed by a bulldozer." He pulled his black coat around his narrow shoulders. "I'll expect you here next Friday. With the money. Until then, Bulge and Curly want to leave you with a little ... incentive, shall we say?"

Then, without a back glance, he walked out of the warehouse, leaving the two grinning bodyguards behind.

The first blow hit Nick in the balls.

Kane sat across from Margaret and watched her as she poured tea into a cup so fine, he could almost see through it.

"Here you go." She smiled as she handed it to him. "Darjeeling. Hot and strong. Just the way you like it."

Although he never drank tea anymore, he took it anyway, aware that the four o'clock ritual was one Margaret had observed for more than fifty years, and she looked forward to it every day, more so when someone was there to share the moment with her.

"Thank you, Margaret." He took a sip before giving an appreciative nod of his head. "Excellent. As always." Then, putting the cup down, he added, "You know why I'm here, don't you?"

Because she knew how he despised playing games, she inclined her head. "You want me to use my influence on Travis and ask him to drop the custody suit against Diana Wells."

"That's right."

Margaret held out a small plate of ladyfingers to him, but he shook his head. "The problem is," she said, selecting a cookie for herself. "I don't want him to drop the suit. I have every right to that boy, Kane. He is my flesh and blood, our future heir—"

"He doesn't care about your money. He is perfectly happy as he is now, with a five-dollar weekly allowance and last year's toys."

"That's because he hasn't had a taste of the good life yet. He doesn't even know what a trust fund is and what it can do for him."

"Trust funds aren't the answer to everything. I grew up without one, and I didn't turn out so bad." The closed-up look on her face told him he was wasting his time. Still, he was determined to try. She was stubborn. And inflexible. But she had been known to change her mind—with the right approach.

"Can't you see what all this publicity is doing to Zachary? He's being chased by reporters. He can no longer take the bus to school like any normal child. There isn't a day that goes by without his name being mentioned on the six o'clock news or in some newspaper. Last week his best friend called him 'a rich man's bastard.' Can you imagine how things will be for him when the hearing begins?"

At the thought of what Zachary had had to endure, there was a quick pinch around her heart, but she didn't back down. "Diana is as much to blame for what's happening as I am. If she hadn't denied me access to my grandson, we wouldn't be facing a hearing right now."

"It's not too late to call it off. Drop the suit, Margaret. Then wait until the publicity has died down and contact Diana again. Tell her you're sorry about the way you approached her last month. Tell her how much it would mean to you to spend a few moments with your grandson once in a while. She won't refuse you. I'm certain of it."

Margaret's smile was sad as she held Kane's gaze. "A few moments with my grandson once in a while," she repeated. "Do you honestly think that's enough? Do you think that's *fair*?"

"It would be a beginning."

"If I were a younger woman, I could afford to wait until Diana decided to turn around. But I'm sixty-eight years old, Kane. Whatever years I have left, I want to spend them with my grandson. He and I have wasted enough time already." Then, her gaze turning suspicious, she added, "Why are you so adamant that we drop the suit anyway? What is Diana Wells to you?"

"She's someone I deeply respect. But I care about you, too. About what this hearing will do to you. I don't think you fully realize the effect it will have on your entire family. All of your lives will be exposed."

There was the slightest of hesitations. "The Lindfords have nothing to be ashamed of."

"Not you, perhaps. But what about Travis? He hasn't exactly led the life of a monk, as you well know."

"He has redeemed himself."

"Do you really think that announcing his marriage to Dunbar Dewitt will win the case for him?"

"Yes. And you do, too, otherwise you wouldn't be here."

Ten minutes later, feeling frustrated and angry, Kane had left the Lindford and was driving back toward Presidio Heights.

All around him Christmas decorations were going up—bright garlands, wreaths, stars, and giant snowflakes. A few days from now, the sound of joyous holiday music would be everywhere while inside a courtroom, the fate of a young boy and his mother would be decided.

He was filled with the sudden urge to see Diana, to let her know she wasn't alone. He glanced at the clock on the dashboard. Five o'clock. She would be home, getting dinner ready.

At the first left turn he could make, he spun the car around and headed toward Pacific Heights.

When Diana returned home after another meeting with John McKay, she found Nick sitting on her front porch.

Jumping out of the Cherokee, she hurried up the steps. "Are you out of your mind, sitting here in plain view of the neighbors?" she hissed, her hands trembling as she unlocked the door.

She saw him wince as he rose from the white wicker chair. "What's wrong with you?"

Holding his side, he moved slowly past her, into the house. "I'm in trouble, Sis. Big time."

She gave him a long, disgusted look. Everyone else she knew had normal brothers and sisters, cute little nieces and nephews running around, dropping by on Sundays, bringing Christmas presents they made in school. *She* had ended up with Nick.

For a moment, she considered slamming the door in his face. But after taking a closer look at him, at the way his arms were wrapped around his midriff, she couldn't do it. "What happened?"

"Eddy happened, that's what." Taking great pain not to make any sudden move, he lowered his body on the deacon bench, not bothering to go into the living room. "I owe him thirty thousand dollars. If I don't pay him by five o'clock on Friday, he'll kill me."

A chill settled in her stomach, and she leaned back

against the credenza. "I don't believe this. You borrowed from him *again?*"

"I had to, Diana. I needed the money for an investment, one that would have made me flush enough to live like a prince for the rest of my life. Eddy was the only one willing to lend me the twenty thousand dollars I needed."

"I thought you said you owed him thirty thousand."

"I borrowed twenty." He leaned his head against the wall. "Ten is the interest."

Diana pressed two fingers against the middle of her forehead where a fierce headache was beginning to throb.

"They've hurt me bad, Di. If I had any guts at all, I'd make a run for it. But they would find me. And kill me," he finished in a shaky voice.

"Why did you come to me? You know I don't have thirty thousand dollars."

"But you can get it. From Kat. She's loaded now that she's famous."

At the outrageous suggestion, her anger flared. "Forget it. I will not borrow money to help you repay a loan shark."

"It'll only be a loan, Sis. I'll pay it back in a little while."

"A little while? How long do you think it's going to take you to repay thirty thousand dollars?"

"I'll find a way . . ."

"Then find a way now. Because you're not getting the money from me. I have much more to lose than thirty thousand dollars, Nick. My son is on the line here. How do you think it would look in court if Travis Lindford's attorney found out that I was not only related to you, but that I had helped you pay off a loan shark? What kind of a mother would that make me?"

"How would he find out? I'm sure as hell not going to tell him."

"It's his job to find out such things. And it's his job to make me look bad."

"Help me, and you'll never see me again. I swear it on our mother's grave."

"No."

Nick's sweet-talking expression vanished. A mean gleam flashed across his eyes. "Goddamn you, Diana—"

She didn't back down. "I did what you asked. I listened to you. Now get out."

For a moment, she thought he was going to strike her. She knew he was capable of it. Years ago, before her mother had become ill and he had needed some extra cash for a ski trip, he had tried to take it from Mom by force. Diana had come home just as he was about to hit her.

At last, Nick pulled himself up. "You bitch," he hissed as he made his way to the door, still holding his side. "If I wasn't hurting so bad . . ."

Although the unfinished threat left her shaky, she raised her chin. "You don't scare me, Nick."

He opened the door just as a car pulled up at the curb, behind the Oldsmobile. She held back a groan as she recognized Kane's BMW.

The two men crossed paths in the driveway. Although Kane stopped and turned around to look at Diana's brother, Nick kept right on walking.

When the Oldsmobile was halfway up the street, Kane turned to Diana, who was holding the front door with both hands.

"Who the hell was that?"

17

Lying to him would have been stupid. And insulting. "My brother."

"I was wondering when you'd get around to telling me about him."

She let out a mirthless laugh. "Nick isn't exactly bragging material."

Hands in his pants pockets, he followed her into the kitchen. "What is he doing here?"

"Do you want some coffee?"

"No. And you're stalling."

"I know." Because she needed something to do with her hands, she picked up a sponge and started wiping the already immaculate red counter. "No one but Kat and Mitch know about Nick."

"What about Zack?"

She shook her head. "I never told him." She looked at Kane. "You knew about him, didn't you?"

"I knew you had a brother. And that he was a criminal."

"He's more of a con man than a hard-core criminal. He preys on innocent victims, using whatever trick will work at the time to extort money from them."

"He was arrested for armed robbery."

"That was a long time ago. He was just a teenager."

He leaned against the counter, close enough to

touch her, although he didn't. "What did he want?" he asked in a softer tone.

"The same thing he always wants. Money."

His eyes narrowed. "Is he blackmailing you? Threatening you in any way?"

She shook her head. "He just needed money to finance a new venture. When I told him I wouldn't give it to him, he got angry and left." She couldn't bring herself to tell him about the loan shark. Or about the break-in five months ago.

Although she willed herself to sound casual, something in her voice and in the way she averted her eyes must have given her away because, suddenly, his hands were on her shoulders and he was turning her around to face him. "Easy," he murmured.

Impulsively, she gripped his arms. It would have been so easy to let go, to lean her head against his broad chest and tell him everything. But in spite of the closeness they had shared on Thanksgiving, there was still a part of her that couldn't trust him all the way. In a few days, when the custody hearing was over, she would tell him the whole truth. Not before.

She let go of him. "I'm sorry. Nick's visits always leave me a little strung out."

"Then I'll see to it that he doesn't bother you anymore." He held her at arms' length. "Where does he live?"

His voice was mild, but there was a dangerous expression in his eyes. Alarmed, she shook her head. "No. You can't get involved in this."

"I'm already involved, Diana." His eyes bore into hers. "Don't you know by now how much I care about you? That everything that affects you, affects me?"

She wanted to tell him that she cared too, that she thought about him more than she should, more than she had ever thought about any man. "I—"

"Tell me where Nick lives," he repeated softly. "You know I'm going to find out one way or another, so you might as well save me time."

"What will you do to him?"

"I'm going to tell him to stay the hell away from you." He gave her shoulders a gentle squeeze. "I want him to know that he can't push his way in here any time he feels like it."

She nodded. Maybe a tough talk was just what Nick needed. Lord knows her warnings hadn't done any good. She gave him Nick's address in Oakland.

"Kane!"

At the sound of his name, Kane spun around and sixty pounds of hard flesh rushed into his arms. Shaken by the unexpected show of affection, Kane recovered quickly, catching Zack and swooping him up off the floor for a bear hug. "Hi there."

A knot formed in his throat, and he held Zack against him for a moment longer before releasing him and setting him down. "Where have you been?"

"Down the street at a Cub Scout meeting." Reaching into his pocket, he pulled out a folded sheet of yellow paper. "Want to see what I'm doing to earn my next badge?"

"Sure." Smiling at Diana, Kane took the paper from Zack's hand and unfolded it. It was a one-page, handwritten report of Zack's day at Sanders Estates on Thanksgiving and what he had learned about the growing of grapes, their care, and how the weather affected them. He had also mentioned a "lucky" coin he had found behind the winery—an old buffalo nickel blackened by age.

"This is excellent." He handed it to Diana. "We might make a vintner out of you yet."

Zack grinned. "My den mother wants me to make

a drawing to go with the reports—maybe the vineyards when the workers pick the grapes?"

"That's a great idea."

"Only thing is, I'm not too good at drawing." His expression turned sweet as pie. "So, I thought ... maybe ... you could help me?"

Kane grinned. "I'd love to. I might even get Aunt Beckie to give me some old photographs she has of earlier harvests."

"Cool." Zack sniffed the air and grinned at his mother. "Spaghetti?"

The interchange between Zack and Kane had brought tears to Diana's eyes. She had never realized until now how badly Zack had missed having a father figure, someone strong and kind to look up to. Not trusting her voice, she just nodded.

Zack glanced at Kane. "Are you eating with us?"

"Am I invited?"

"Sure." He looked at Diana, his blue eyes eager. "It's all right, isn't it, Mom?"

Diana smiled. It was hard enough keeping Kane at bay on her own, but with Zack going to bat for him, it was a lost cause. "Considering I made enough food for an army, sure. He can stay. And you"—she gave him a playful tap on the behind—"go upstairs and take a shower."

"Okay." He turned to Kane again. "And after dinner, we can play a game of gin rummy?"

"When did you learn to play gin rummy?" Diana asked.

"Aunt Beckie taught me."

Kane chuckled. "She didn't teach you any of her cheating tricks, I hope."

"Not yet. She said I was too young." The grin deepened. "Maybe next year."

He was still laughing as he dashed out of the kitchen and up the stairs.

Kane shook his head. "That's quite a kid you've got there."

Her earlier anxieties set aside for the moment, she threw him an amused glance. "I see he's got you wrapped around his little finger."

"Me?" He assumed a look of mock severity. "No way. I'm too tough, remember?"

"On the surface perhaps."

"Having second thoughts about me, Diana?"

Instead of answering him, she pointed to a cabinet next to him. "Why don't you make yourself useful while you're here and set the table? You'll find dishes and glasses in there, silverware in the drawer next to you. On spaghetti days, we have paper napkins. Big ones." She pointed to a pantry next to the refrigerator.

He gave her a two-finger salute. "Yes, ma'am."

As she stood at the stove, reheating the tomato sauce, she watched him move about the kitchen with an astounding familiarity, as if he had been here hundreds of times.

Her heart skipping a beat, she wondered what it would be like having a man like Kane Sanders around the house, waking up with him each morning, listening to him shower, smelling his aftershave in her closet, sitting across from him at the breakfast table . . .

The intimate thoughts sent a flush of color to her cheeks. What was she doing? She had a custody battle to fight. Foes to defeat. Foes who were his friends.

"How's that?" Kane turned so she could admire his handy work.

Her gaze skimmed the table, the three bright red napkins folded in triangles, the carton of milk he had found in the refrigerator. "Mmmm. Not bad—for a bachelor who eats nothing but Stouffers."

"How do you know that?"

"Your aunt told me."

"Really." He came to stand in front of her. "What other intimate secrets did she reveal about me?"

"I wasn't aware you had intimate secrets."

He braced his arms against the counter, trapping her between them. "I don't anymore."

His proximity made her dizzy. She saw him lean toward her, his eyes drifting toward her mouth. She held her breath, then expelled it slowly. "What are you doing?"

"Looking at you. Do you know that your eyes actually darken when you're troubled?"

It had been raining, and she could smell the dampness on his jacket mingling with the scent of his aftershave. "What would I be troubled about?"

His mouth curved into a smile. "You tell me."

The intensity in her eyes deepened, and there was a slight catch in her breath. Raising a hand to her throat, he felt her pulse beat wildly.

Emotions swarmed through him. Once again, that tightly held control he had perfected over the years threatened to slip. The need to touch, to taste, was so powerful, it nearly took his breath away. "Diana . . ."

His hand came up to frame her face, and this time she saw the kiss coming. But rather than pull away, she met him halfway, lips parted. Whatever had taken place prior to this moment was forgotten. Nothing mattered but the wet, delicious friction his lips created as they moved gently against hers.

In a featherlike touch, his fingers moved over her cheeks, her throat. When he gripped her shoulders and pulled her to him, the pressure of his mouth increased. But there was more than passion in his kiss. There was a gentleness, a tenderness that took away the tension and melted all her fears.

Oh, God, she needed this. She needed his hands pressing the small of her back, needed his mouth roaming over her face, murmuring her name. It had been years since a man had been close to losing control over her. She hadn't liked it all that much then, but she liked it now. She liked it from this man.

Slowly, reluctantly, she drew back. "Zack will be down soon."

He nodded, waited until he had regained his composure, then hooked a finger under her chin, forcing her to look at him. Her eyes had turned that smoky, sexy green again, and her cheeks were flushed.

She looked soft and vulnerable, and so damned desirable. Another time, another place, he wouldn't have let her go. "We're not finished, you know." His thumb brushed against her lower lip. "Not by a long shot."

18

The super at Mission Garden Apartments, where Diana's brother lived, had told Kane he would probably find Nick Wells at Rudy's Bar and Grill on Grand Street.

The place was nearly empty when Kane arrived. At one end of the counter two older men in cowboy hats sipped their beers while watching a *Cheers* rerun from a TV set above the bar. A few stools down, the man Kane had seen coming out of Diana's house sat staring dejectedly into a glass Kane guessed contained straight whiskey.

He took the empty stool next to his and ordered a club soda, waiting until the bartender had served him and left before turning his attention to Nick. "Do you remember me?"

Bloodshot green eyes that may at one time have been as attractive as Diana's focused on him. "Why the hell should I?"

"You and I crossed paths yesterday afternoon. I was coming into your sister's house, you were coming out."

The man's expression didn't mellow. "So?"

"So I'm here to tell you that was your last visit."

This time the man's face turned red, his tone belligerent. "What the fuck is that supposed to mean?"

Kane had met dozens of men like Nick Wells in the

course of his career—bullies who only understood one kind of language. Tough. "It means," he said in a voice that was low and charged with unspoken menace, "that from now on, you stay away from Diana. You don't come to her house, you don't call her on the phone, and you don't leave her any messages. In fact, I don't even want you within two miles of her house or her restaurant. Is that clear enough for you?"

Pivoting on his stool so he could face him, Nick let out a short, brittle laugh. "And just who the hell are you? And where do you get off telling me what to do?"

Ignoring the bartender, who was hovering nearby, polishing a glass, Kane leaned forward, trying not to wince at the stench of stale whiskey on the man's breath. More than ever, he was determined to keep this creep away from Diana. "My name is Kane Sanders. I'm and attorney, and believe me, you don't want to cross me, Nick. Ever."

"Oh, yeah?" For lack of better things to do, Nick bobbed his head a few times, his mouth twisted in a sarcastic snarl that was meant to look fearless.

"Yeah." Climbing down from his stool, Kane pulled three one-dollar bills from his pocket and tossed them on the dirty bar top, next to his untouched drink.

He waited a beat, just in case Diana's brother decided to challenge him. Then, satisfied he had gotten his point across, he walked out, aware that Nick's mean, resentful gaze followed him.

Closing the door to his mother's penthouse, Travis glanced around the drawing room. "Are you alone?"

"Margie's is in the kitchen, preparing dinner. Otherwise, yes, I'm alone." She frowned. "Why?"

"I've got bad news." Unable to sit still, he started

to pace the floor. "Judge Parson withdrew from the custody case."

"What?" Margaret stiffened. "Why? What happened?"

"Ethics. He told the assigning judge that because of his past friendship with Father, he wasn't qualified to hear this case."

Margaret's shoulders slumped as she fell back against the sofa. The assignment of Ted Parson to the case had been the reason she had felt so confident. "How did you find out?"

"Sam just called." Although Travis seldom drank in the middle of the day in his mother's presence, he walked to a liquor cabinet and splashed some scotch into a glass.

Watching him take a big gulp, Margaret sensed there was more bad news to come. "Have they assigned anyone else?"

"They sure have. Judge Arnette. Judge *Olivia* Arnette."

Margaret gasped. "A woman?"

"Not just any woman. Judge Arnette is divorced and the mother of a daughter she raised all by herself."

Margaret took a moment to digest the news. Although she knew nothing about Judge Arnette, she knew enough about the judicial system to realize that not even she could succeed in having the assignment changed. "It may not be as bad as you think," she said at last. "Having a woman judge doesn't mean she will automatically side with Diana."

"Like hell she won't! All those feminists stick together."

"That's not true. I'm certain Judge Arnette didn't get where she is today by being prejudiced."

"Are you telling me we have as good a chance of winning the suit as we did before her appointment?"

"I'm telling you that you'll have to work harder at impressing her, that's all."

"I'm marrying Dunbar Dewitt, Mother. What more do you want me to do?" He downed his drink in one gulp.

"I don't know. We'll have to think of something."

He set his empty glass on the coffee table. "Well, I'm fresh out of ideas."

"Maybe you could do something for that children's organization Dunbar sponsors. Host another benefit perhaps? Right here in the hotel? We could invite the press, gain tons of favorable publicity."

Travis held back an exasperated sigh. "Oh, Mother, that won't work. It's too tame. We need to do something bolder. Something a little more . . . devious."

"No!" Margaret's voice cut through the air like a blade. "You will do nothing of the sort. The Lindford name has always been synonymous with honesty and integrity, and as much as I want Zachary to be part of this family, I will not tolerate shady tactics."

"I don't want to lose my son, Mother."

"I don't want to lose him either. But if that's the judge's decision, then so be it." She sighed, knowing that if Travis lost the custody case, she might never see Zachary again unless Diana had a change of heart.

"And where does that leave me?"

At the sound of her son's whining tone, Margaret gave him a sharp look. "Is that all you can think about? How losing Zachary will affect you?"

Aware of his gaffe, Travis bit his lip. "Of course not. But I have to be practical. You made me a promise, Mother, and I would like to know if losing my son means I'll lose the hotel as well."

Margaret sighed. So she had been right after all. His real motive for wanting Zachary was the hotel, and not fatherly love as she had hoped. Well, it didn't matter. If Travis won the custody suit—and she still believed he could—she would take charge of the boy herself.

Sarcastically, she asked, "Since when have you ever known me to welsh on a promise?"

"Never, but—"

"Our deal was for me to relinquish my shares and give them to you at the birth of your first child. The fact that you already had a child accelerated things a bit for you. But if you should lose the custody case, then the original deal goes back into effect."

So the bottom line was still the same, Travis thought, swallowing his bitterness with another gulp of scotch. In order to have the hotel, he had to conceive a child. Great. Just great. Why the hell didn't she ask him to climb Mount Everest blindfolded? Considering he was now sterile, he would have a better chance of succeeding at that than he had of ever getting a woman pregnant.

Margaret laid a hand on her son's shoulder, already regretting her earlier outburst. It was true that he had weaknesses, many of which he would never get rid of completely. But marriage would change him. She was convinced of that. And once Zack was theirs, those fatherly feelings, so foreign to him now, would surface. She and Dunbar would see to that.

"I'm going to talk to Ted Parson and see what I can find out about Judge Arnette," she said. "In the meantime, why don't you talk to Dunbar about this benefit I mentioned, and see what she can do?"

"Should I tell her our reason?" he asked bitterly.

"Why not? I'm sure she'll have no objection, as long as everything is done in good taste."

"If you say so, Mother."

It was all he could do not to slam the door behind him as he left.

*   *   *

Standing in the kitchen of his garage apartment on Monte Vista Avenue, Nick Wells pulled a frozen dinner from the toaster oven and glared at it.

He was sick and tired of eating out of paper trays every day of the year. Until a few weeks ago, mealtimes with his unmarried buddies at Rudy's Bar and Grill had been fun. But now that he had to ration his money, frozen dinners were about all he could afford.

Don't complain, old boy. After Bulge and Curly are finished with you, you'll be eating all your meals out of a straw.

Provided they let him live.

He pulled off the foil lid and stared at the rubbery-looking chicken covered with brown gravy, the watery potatoes, and the spoonful of green peas next to it. Nestled between the peas and the potatoes, a crumbly mixture that vaguely resembled a cherry cobbler continued to bubble.

The sight of that unappetizing mush sent his stomach churning. He rubbed it gently, being careful to avoid his bruised belly where Bulge had hit him.

Bulge. Christ, that man had fists like bricks. And he wasn't shy about using them either. The thought of what he would do to him in a few days unless he came up with the money he owed Eddy sent another chill down his back.

Where the hell was he going to find thirty thousand dollars in less than five days?

Carrying his dinner into the living room, he set the tray on the coffee table and sat down. As he cut through the meat with the side of his fork, he glanced at a copy of the *San Francisco Examiner* next to him.

As usual, the upcoming custody hearing, which promised to be even more sensational than Roxanne Pulitzer's divorce trial, had made the front page. This time the headlines had focused on the withdrawal of

Judge Ted Parson and on his replacement, a woman judge by the name of Olivia Arnette.

As Nick studied the photograph of the severe-looking woman and read the accompanying article, he learned that Judge Arnette had heard more than three dozen child custody cases since moving to San Francisco a year ago, the majority of which had been ruled in favor of the mother.

He chuckled. "Well, Trav, my boy. I'm no expert, but at first glance, I'd say you're in deep shit. Old sour-face Arnette don't look to me as if she takes kindly to playboys like you. It would take a miracle for her to rule in your favor."

He ate slowly, thoughtfully, but his mind was no longer on the blandness of the food or the hopelessness of his own situation. It was on Travis Lindford. If the guy was serious about wanting his kid, then he might be willing to pay big bucks to anyone who could help him achieve that goal.

But what kind of help? What could a lowly dockworker like him do for a man like Travis Lindford? Tell him he was Diana's brother? He shook his head. The information in itself wasn't damaging enough. He needed something else. Something that would make Di look bad, really bad, in the eyes of that judge.

Halfway through the cherry cobbler, the thought came to him.

Of course! The solution had been here all along, right in front of his nose. He had just been too preoccupied to see it.

He put his fork down. All he had to do was give himself a little time to run the plan through his head a few times, and pray Travis Lindford would go for it. After that he'd be on easy street.

His appetite restored, he picked up his fork again

and shoved the rest of the cherry cobbler into his mouth.

The moment Nick set foot in the lobby of the Lindford Hotel, he felt as if he had stepped into another world. From the vaulted hand-painted ceiling to the gleaming mahogany reception desk and dripping crystal chandeliers, he was surrounded by a luxury he couldn't have imagined in his wildest dreams.

This is how I should live, he thought, watching an elegant couple come out of the penthouse elevator. Fancy hotels, beautiful women, gourmet food. It should all be mine. I deserve it. I paid my dues.

Keeping his fingers crossed that Travis would be as excited about his plan as he was, he stepped inside the plush penthouse elevator that said PH and pushed the button for the twenty-sixth floor.

It had taken three phone calls before a snotty secretary had finally put him through to Travis Lindford. The hotel heir hadn't been very friendly at first, but when Nick had told him he had a proposition that could change the outcome of the custody hearing, his attitude had changed considerably.

"Come on up to my apartment and we'll talk," he had told him. "Penthouse 2A on the twenty-sixth floor."

When the elevator stopped, Nick stepped out and walked toward Travis's door. Taking a deep breath, he pressed the bell.

Moments later, Travis opened the door. He wore beige gabardine pants, a brown V-neck with the collar of a white shirt showing, and comfortable loafers. In his hand was a snifter filled with what Nick guessed was cognac—very old, very expensive cognac.

"Mr. Wells I presume?"

Mr. Wells. He liked that. And he liked the man for saying it, for showing respect. "That's me."

Although Nick didn't want to stare at the opulent interior, he couldn't help it. Holy shit. So that's how the other half lived—ankle-deep carpet the color of butter, expensive antiques everywhere and enough art on the walls to rival any museum.

"Well then, Mr. Wells." Travis smiled, one of those rather haughty smiles the very rich had perfected. "I believe you said something about . . . a proposition?"

Nick would have liked a drink. His mouth was a little dry. And his nerves weren't quite as steady as they had been last night when he had thought of the idea. But Travis didn't offer. And Nick didn't ask. "That's right."

"I knew Diana had a brother, but I wasn't aware the two of you still had any contact with each other."

"She doesn't advertise it. We're not what you would call close."

"I see. And what do you do, Mr. Wells?"

"I'm an entrepreneur. A down-on-his-luck entrepreneur at the moment." Might as well set things straight from the start.

"And that's why you're here? You think I can change your luck?"

Nick didn't miss the contempt in the man's voice. Or in his eyes. He didn't mind. He was used to contempt. And anyway, he hadn't come here to win a popularity contest. "I could also change yours. From what I read in the paper yesterday, you could use a little luck yourself right about now."

The cool blue eyes grew a little cooler. "Why don't you tell me what you have in mind?"

Now that he had the man's attention, Nick felt more at ease. He glanced around the room, selected a brown leather chair with delicate bowed legs, and sat down, hoping it would hold him up. "What do you figure your chances of getting your kid are?"

If the question surprised him, Travis didn't show it. "Better than fifty-fifty. Why?"

"Even now? With that lady judge who has a reputation for favoring mothers?"

"*Natural* mothers. Diana is Zachary's adoptive mother."

"Oh, come on, Mr. Lindford. You know that's not going to make any difference. Not with your past history, and the women you've dated, and the fact that Diana is the boy's legal mother. An exemplary mother."

Travis took a sip of his Calvados and bit back a nasty reply. The guy's smug attitude was beginning to get on his nerves. But until he heard what he had to say, he would have to ignore it. "Just what is it you think you can do for me, Mr. Wells?"

"I can prove that my sister is providing an unsafe and dangerous environment for her child."

Travis's bad humor disappeared. "How? You said yourself that Diana was an exemplary mother."

Nick gave him a genial smile. "But she's human, like the rest of us."

Although the chair in which he sat was hard as a rock, Nick made a fairly good pretense of reclining into it and looking comfortable by propping one ankle over his knee. Then, his eyes fastened on Travis, he told him about the five thousand dollars he had tried to hide from Eddy five months ago.

"I had no idea they would go looking for it there," he added, glad that he had Travis's full attention at last. "I didn't even know Eddy was aware I had a sister." He laughed. "But I guess when you're in the money-lending business, it makes sense to investigate the borrowers."

"Did Diana call the police? Report the break-in?"

"No, sir, she didn't. She was afraid to. She didn't want Zack to find out what a louse he had for an uncle. She figured since nothing was disturbed or taken, other than the five grand, why make a fuss?" With his thumb and middle finger he flicked an imaginary piece of lint from his pants leg. "But boy, was she sore with me! She accused me of endangering her son's life as well as hers, and threw me out of her house. She also threatened to slap me with a restraining order if I ever came back."

"But she didn't."

"Nope." He thought about telling Travis she had sent her lawyer over to intimidate him, then changed his mind. It might scare Travis off, sour him against the deal. "She didn't do anything, even though I went back to see her several times."

"This is all very interesting, Mr. Wells. But I fail to see how it can help my situation."

Nick smiled. Those rich people were all the same. They had gobs of money, but zero brains. "What if that unpleasant little incident happened again? What if *I*, pretending to be those same two thugs, went to my sister's house one afternoon when no one is home, and ransacked the place? Really did a job on it this time. Do you think she would stay quiet and not report the break-in to the police?"

"You're her brother. You tell me."

"If her place was ransacked, she'd be so damned burning mad, she'd call the police faster than you could say 911. And the following morning, the story would be in all the papers."

"So?"

"Don't you see it, man? She would have to tell the cops who she suspected had done the job. Which means she would have to also tell them about the first break-in, about me and my involvement with a loan shark by the name of Eddy. How do you think the judge would feel once she found out that our respectable Diana had placed her son's life in jeopardy by not reporting that first break-in? Do you think she would allow the boy to stay with her?''

Travis didn't need a diagram to see where Nick Wells was leading to. No matter how biased Judge Arnette may be, she couldn't ignore the safety of a child.

But there were flaws in Nick Wells's plan. Too many for comfort.

"What about you?" he asked Nick. "The moment your sister reports the break-in, you'll be brought in for questioning. They'll want to know who the loan shark is. And the two thugs who broke into your sister's house. How will you handle that?''

Nick shrugged. "Like any good citizen should. By cooperating with the police."

"Are you telling me that you would be willing to give them a description of Eddy and his men?''

God, the guy was dense. "If I did, my life wouldn't be worth a plugged nickel. I could, however, give the cops a false description.''

"And if they show you mug shots?''

"I'll say I don't recognize anybody. Who's going to contradict me?'' He smiled confidently. "You see. I've got all the angles covered.''

"What if they want to trap Eddy and ask how you contact him?''

"Through a classified ad in the *Chronicle*.''

"Is that true?''

"No. But often that's how people in the public sector contact loan sharks, hired assassins, or other unsavory characters. The cops know that. It won't do them any good though, because that's not how Eddy operates. But they'll buy it.''

As the obstacles were removed one by one, Travis began to see hope again. By God, it *could* work. With the right publicity, the right slant, this incident could be blown to such proportions that Diana wouldn't stand a chance of keeping Zachary.

Twirling the brandy around in his glass, he took a few steps around the room until he stood in front of Nick again. "I take it you wouldn't be doing this out of the goodness of your heart."

Nick laughed. "Hardly."

"So what's the price for your ... uh ... services?"

"A quarter of a million dollars. Half payable in advance. The rest upon completion of the job."

"That's an awful lot of money, considering I have no guarantee your scheme will work."

"I have to make it worth my while, Mr. Lindford. I'm the one taking all the risks."

Travis was silent for a moment, lost in the contemplation of his drink. When he spoke again, his tone was no longer playful. "All right, Mr. Wells. You convinced me."

Nick beamed. "We have a deal?"

"With one minor alteration."

The handsome smile faded. "What kind of alteration?"

"The payout. I'll give you fifty thousand in advance instead of half."

"That's out of the question."

"Take it or leave it, Mr. Wells."

Nick raked his fingers through his hair, hoping the man wouldn't see the perspiration beads that were forming on his forehead. It wasn't the deal he had hoped for. But fifty thousand now was better than nothing. Nick inclined his head. "All right."

Travis put his glass down, but rather than offer his hand to seal their gentlemen's agreement with a handshake, he walked toward the door and opened it. "Come back here at the same time tomorrow evening. I'll have your money."

As Nick stepped into the penthouse elevator, the lyrics of an old song danced in his head.

Happy days are here again . . .

19

At ten o'clock on Monday morning, Nick parked his Oldsmobile at the top of the hill, one block from Diana's house, and waited inside the car until she had left. Then, acting nonchalant, he got out of the car.

Wearing a thick gray mustache and a mailman's uniform he had used successfully in a previous scam, he slung his leather satchel over one shoulder and walked down the hill, keeping his fingers crossed he wouldn't come face-to-face with a real mailman.

After making sure the nosy lady across the street wasn't peeking through her curtains, he circled Diana's house, already reaching into his bag for his burglar's kit—an assortment of picks, keys, and old credit cards he had accumulated over the years.

The back door was equipped with a dead bolt and not as easy to open as others. But he hadn't met a lock he couldn't spring yet, and this one was no exception.

In less than two minutes, he was inside the living room.

Reaching into his bag again, he pulled out a pair of black leather gloves, a face mask to protect himself from flying glass, and a stiletto knife.

Then, his face devoid of expression, he started on his rampage.

For the first time since Travis had come to the restaurant and dropped his bombshell, Diana's spirits were up. A couple of days ago, John McKay had called to tell her that Judge Parson had withdrawn from the custody hearing for ethical reasons, and another judge had been assigned in his place.

"Judge Arnette is one of the most impartial judges in the Bay Area," John had told her before hanging up. "So keep your fingers crossed, and I'll see you in court next week."

Now, as she drove home on this crisp Monday afternoon, she hummed softly, something she hadn't done in weeks. All around her, the sights and sounds of the holiday season were very much in evidence, especially on Sacramento Street where many houses, including theirs, were already decorated with miniature lights, beautiful wreaths, and an occasional Santa and his sleigh. Later today, when Zack came home from school, they would drive down to Riley's Farm and select a Christmas tree.

She was still humming when she unlocked her front door and stepped inside.

And then she saw the destruction.

The foyer, and what she could see of the living room, were in shambles. Before she could take a step, her instincts screamed at her to get out in case the burglar was still in the house.

She felt powerless to move, to react. Frozen in place, she listened for the sound of footsteps, the creaking of floorboards. There was nothing but an eerie silence. Whoever had done this was gone.

Slowly, like a robot, she moved toward the living room and gasped as glass crunched under her feet. The room was totally ransacked. Books, vases, and candle holders were scattered over the floor. Art work had been torn from their frames and from the walls.

Sofa and chair cushions were slashed open, their white stuffing sprouting from the gashes. The hand-painted cabinet she had bought in New Mexico years ago was tipped over, its drawers pulled out, the contents scattered. Knickknacks, lamps, and other mementos lay on the floor, broken or ripped apart.

Certain now that she was alone, she moved from room to room, her heart pounding, her emotions ranging from despair to rage as she saw the devastation throughout the house. Years of hard work and loving care had been reduced to a pile of trash. It couldn't have looked worse if an earthquake had rumbled through the area.

She bent to pick up the fragment of a vase that had belonged to her mother, holding it against her as tears burned her eyes.

In Zack's bedroom, where his Nintendo had been shattered, she stood in the doorway, her fists balled up against her mouth.

Eddy, she thought, remembering the warning note the loan shark had left in her bedroom five months ago. It had to be Eddy.

She drew a long, steadying breath. They wouldn't get away with this. Not this time.

Her mouth set, she moved toward the telephone, relieved that it hadn't been torn from the wall, and called the police.

They arrived within moments—two men in blue who shook their heads as they viewed the destruction.

The policeman who identified himself as Officer Kessler took a notebook from his shirt pocket and started to write. "Was anything taken, ma'am? Any valuables such as jewelry, furs, art work?"

"No. I have nothing of value in the house. Except things of a sentimental nature." Her gaze fell on the frame she held in her hands, one that had contained her favorite photo of Zack. Taken on his third birthday, the photograph was now in shreds, speared with fragments of glass.

"Do you have any idea who did this?"

She met his gaze unflinchingly. "Yes. A man by the name of Eddy."

"Eddy who?"

"I don't know. He's a loan shark my brother knows."

The officer stopped writing. "Did you say *loan shark?*"

"I've never met him, but I know about him." In a weary voice, she told him about Nick and about the previous break-in.

"What's your brother's address?"

Whatever family loyalty she had felt toward Nick before was gone. She had to take care of herself now. And Zack. Nick was on his own. She gave them the address.

The policeman closed his book. "All right. We'll report this and let a detective at the station take it from there. Meanwhile, don't touch anything until your insurance agent gets here." He slid the book back in his pocket. "Do you have a place to spend the night, ma'am? Parents? Friends?"

She nodded, thanked them, and walked them to the door. Anger had replaced the initial fear. Anger and despair. As a sob started to rise in her throat, she tried to hold it back, and couldn't.

Stepping over a broken lamp, she walked over to the telephone and called Kat. In a voice she struggled to keep neutral, she told her what had happened.

"Do you want me to come over?" Kat asked in a crisp, no-nonsense tone.

"No. But would you go and pick Zack up at school and take him back to your house?"

"Of course."

"Don't tell him anything," she cautioned. "I'll do that myself later." Then, after assuring her friend she was all right and would be over soon, she hung up.

Her eyes closed, she let herself slide slowly against the wall. She had never felt so alone in her life. Or so helpless. As hot tears ran down her cheeks, she thought of Kane, of his concern when she had told him about Nick last week, and of the way he had taken charge of the situation. That's what she needed right now—someone to take charge.

Her hand still shaking, she picked up the phone again and dialed Kane's office.

Jackie put her through immediately.

"I'm at the house. Please come over," was all she could manage to say before she burst into tears.

Her fears seemed to evaporate the moment Kane arrived. As he held her tightly against him, he took in the scene around him, his face livid, his expression grim. "What the hell happened here?"

"It's all my fault," she said, knowing there was no point in keeping the truth from him any longer. "If I had reported the previous break-in—"

"*Previous* break-in?" He relaxed his hold enough to glance at her. "You mean your house was trashed once before and you didn't report it?"

"It was different the last time." For the second time that afternoon, she repeated her story about Nick's connection with a loan shark and the five thousand dollars he had hid in her house.

"That son of a bitch," he hissed. "I guess he didn't take my warning seriously after all."

"On the contrary, I'm sure he did. Nick isn't very brave when it comes to confrontations with other men. Whatever he hid in my house this time, he must have done it before you talked to him."

Kane's gaze swept across the room. "Would he really be that stupid? Would he hide money in this house again knowing it would be the first place Eddy would search?"

"I don't know, Kane. I don't know how he thinks anymore. Or what motivates him."

"Diana, why didn't you tell me about Nick's connections with this Eddy character before?"

It was a rational question, one that deserved a truthful answer. "I wasn't ready to reveal so much about my private life. Some things are just too difficult to talk about."

"In other words, you didn't trust me."

"No. I mean, yes." Frustrated, she stood up. "I didn't know what to think. I was confused. My head was telling me one thing and my heart another."

She saw his eyes warm as he pulled her to him again. "All right. We can talk about that later. Right now, we have more urgent business to take care of. Like contacting your insurance adjuster, and finding you and Zack a safe place to stay."

"I've already made arrangements for Zack to stay with Kat." With a brave smile she disengaged herself and went to pick up her purse, which she had dropped on the floor earlier. "That way there will be someone with him all the time. Either Kat or myself can shuttle him to and from school." She searched through her wallet for the name and phone number of the Allstate representative.

"What about you?"

"Kat's house isn't big enough. I'll have to go to a hotel."

"No, you won't. You'll stay with me. My condo isn't big, but it has two bedrooms, two baths, and a twenty-four-hour security guard in the lobby."

She was too distraught to argue. And the thought

of spending several days, perhaps weeks, in a hotel wasn't particularly appealing. "All right. Thanks, Kane."

Her hands finally produced a business card with the name and telephone number of her insurance agent. "I'll only be a minute. Then I'll have to go to Kat's and tell Zack."

Kane nodded. "Okay. But I'm taking you there. From now on, I'm not letting you out of my sight."

Explaining to Zack about the mindless destruction of their house was a trying experience for her and an emotional one for Zack.

"Who would do something like that?" he asked, his face red with indignation.

Knowing he was bound to hear about Nick from someone at school, she told him about her brother herself, trying to be as truthful as possible without frightening him unnecessarily.

"Why don't you make *him* pay for all the damages?" Zack asked.

"I would. If he had any money."

"Is everything destroyed?"

She ran a hand through his hair, her heart breaking at the sight of tears welling up in his eyes. "Not everything, darling. What was broken, however, can be replaced. Every bit of it. In the meantime, I brought your clothes, and some of your favorite games." She pulled his stuffed teddy from her bag. "And Tiny."

His smiled warmed her heart. But it would take a long time before the horror of that afternoon would be erased from her own mind.

When Kat invited her and Kane to stay for dinner, Diana accepted gratefully. While they ate, she told Zack about their temporary arrangements and told him their house would be back in order very soon.

"Is it going to be the same house?" he asked unexpectedly, his big blue eyes full of doubt. "With the same furniture and stuff?"

Pulling him out of his chair, Diana held him close to her. "I can't guarantee we'll be able to find exactly the same sofa and chairs, or the same paintings for the walls. But other than that, yes, darling, it will be the same house. Within a couple of weeks, you won't even know anything was disturbed." She kissed the top of his head. "All I ask from you is a little patience. Okay?" She started to warn him to be cautious with strangers and stopped herself. She and Kat would see to his safety. There was no need to frighten him any more than he already was.

"Okay." He buried his head in her shoulder and in that instant, she hated her brother more than she ever had before.

"Dammit!" Nick screamed, slamming his hands on the policeman's desk. "You're not going to pin this thing on me, do you hear? I had nothing to do with that break-in."

Pleased with his performance so far, he ran a hand through his already disheveled hair and sat back in his chair, letting out an audible sigh. "I had nothing to do with it," he repeated.

A detective by the name of Manning leaned toward him. "Then tell us who did."

"I don't know!"

"Your sister told us you've had business dealings with a local loan shark by the name of Eddy. The same loan shark who broke into her house on June seventeenth of this year. Is that true?"

Affecting the look of one reluctant to cooperate, he nodded. "Yeah. I know Eddy."

"What's his last name?"

"He didn't tell me. And I didn't ask."

"You owe this Eddy thirty thousand dollars. Is that correct?"

"*Owed* him thirty thousand dollars," Nick lied. "I paid him back day before yesterday."

"Where did you get the money?"

"I called in a couple of favors." It was close enough to the truth. For five hundred dollars each, two of his friends at the loading dock had promised to back up his story.

"Tell me about Eddy. What does he look like?"

The interrogation lasted nearly an hour. By the time Nick was released, he had given Detective Manning the names and descriptions of three men he would never find, and the location of a warehouse five miles from where he always met Eddy.

Outside the police station, he pulled up the collar of his jacket and lit a cigarette, blowing the smoke in the air. He thought about the fifty thousand dollars he had already collected from Travis Lindford. And the two hundred thousand he'd be collecting in a couple of days.

Damn, it felt good to be flush again, to have money to burn. He had even been tempted to pay Eddy off before the Friday deadline. But he had reconsidered. Why the hell should he? He would make him sweat. The way Eddy had made him sweat.

He took another drag of the cigarette, then let it drop to the ground, crushing it with the tip of his shoe. Maybe he should call Travis, just to make sure everything was on schedule.

At the corner of Market and O'Farrell, he saw a phone booth and went in. Whistling to the tune of "We're in the Money," he dialed Travis's number.

"Mission accomplished," he said, his eyes following

a shapely blonde as she passed by. "When do I get the rest of my reward?"

"My broker said he'd have the rest of the money by three o'clock Friday afternoon."

Nick's smile faded. "That's a whole day later than you promised."

"You don't come up with that kind of money with a snap of the fingers, Wells. Friday is the best I could do."

Nick shrugged. What was he worried about? He'd get his money. "All right, Lindford. Three o'clock on Friday. I'll see you then."

Nick was grinning as he hung up. Wasn't life a peach?

20

Kane's condo in Presidio Heights was a typical bachelor's apartment—clean, functional, with comfortable furniture in a knubby, honey-colored fabric, and a giant-screen TV. On the walls hung framed posters from classic black-and-white films Diana loved—*The Maltese Falcon, Casablanca, Suspicion,* and one of her all-time favorites, *Gaslight.*

While Kane carried her bags into the guest room, she walked over to the large picture window. It was a dark, moonless night, but from where she stood, she could see the massive shadow of the Presidio, and further still, the twinkling lights of Golden Gate Bridge.

"I talked to the police."

At the sound of Kane's voice, she turned around.

"They picked up your brother and brought him in for questioning. He was very cooperative."

"That doesn't sound like Nick."

"Maybe he's feeling bad about what happened and wants to make it up to you." He shrugged. "I don't know. The fact is, the cops now have a description of the loan shark and the two men who work for him."

"How soon until they catch them?"

"That's hard to say. My guess is, if Eddy is responsible for the ransacking of your house, he and his men will be lying low for a while."

"What do you mean 'if?'"

"Nick doesn't think Eddy ordered the job. He claims he paid back the money on Monday, and therefore there would be no reason for Eddy to ransack your house."

Diana's eyes grew incredulous. "Are you telling me Nick was able to get his hands on thirty thousand dollars just like that? In two days?"

"That's what he says."

"He's lying! He's covering up for Eddy."

"Two guys at the dock swear Nick's telling the truth. But if it's any consolation, the cops aren't taking any chances."

"What do you mean?"

"They put an ad in the classified section of several local papers, hoping to trap Eddy into showing his face." He shook his head. "I wouldn't hold my breath, though. As I said, the man probably heard the heat is on and will remain in hiding until it's safe for him to come out."

She turned back toward the darkness outside. "What you're really saying is that they might never be caught."

"That's a possibility."

He waited a moment before giving her the rest of the bad news. "I tried to keep the story from being leaked to the press, but I was too late. A television reporter was at the police station when they brought Nick in."

"Terrific." Her arms folded around her chest, she walked over to the fireplace. Kane had lit a fire, and the room felt warm, cozy, safe. It felt good to be here. With him. "But I suppose I'm the one to blame. If I hadn't acted so impulsively. If I had called you before calling the police . . ."

His voice was a warm, soothing murmur. "You did what you had to."

"But it was the *wrong* thing to do," she said, her voice on the edge of tears. "And because of that, I could lose Zack."

His arms encircled her and held her protectively. "No, you won't."

Suddenly she wanted to believe that. Wanted to believe her life would soon return to normal, that today's nightmare would magically vanish. She let herself sag against him, her fingers curling inward, digging into the hard muscles of his chest.

Kane hooked a finger under her chin and tipped her head back. She responded to the gentle pressure, sighing softly as his mouth met hers. A shudder passed through her, and in that moment, all the horrors of the day and the fears of tomorrow were forgotten. She locked her arms behind his neck and instinctively arched her body into his, feeding the hunger with openmouthed kisses that left her gasping and wanting more.

He tugged her closer, sliding his hands down her back and cupping her buttocks, drawing her hard against him. Her breath caught as she felt his erection. Heat filled her, a heat that had nothing to do with the fire that burned hot and bright in the hearth.

With reckless fingers, she unbuttoned his shirt and slid her hands through the opening, moving them over the broad expanse of skin and chest hair. Boldly, she lowered her mouth to where his heart beat the strongest, and held it there for a moment before moving lower.

As she found his nipple and teased it gently with her tongue, a groan escaped Kane's throat. The touch had ignited a spark. Desire, too long ignored, stabbed through him, hot and potent.

He responded to it by lifting her up and carrying her into the bedroom. As he cradled her, he was aware of her breath in his hair, skimming his cheek, his throat. With no warning, love welled up in him, staggering in its intensity. It was unexpected, confusing as hell, but he didn't fight it. It would have been a losing battle anyway.

In the darkened bedroom he laid her gently against the pillows. "Are you sure?" he whispered against her mouth. "Is this what you want?"

"*You* are what I want," she whispered back.

She lay motionless as he ran his hands over the swell of her breasts, gently brushing his thumbs against her nipples. There was a quickening of her pulse, a mad scrambling of all her senses as she tried to absorb every touch, every sensation.

He undressed her slowly, unbuttoning her blouse and easing it off her shoulders, pressing his mouth to the soft hollow between shoulder and throat. She threw her head back, eyes closed, as she savored the moment, the searing sensation that rushed from the roots of her hair to the tips of her toes.

With infinite tenderness, he reached behind her and unfastened her black lace bra, removed it slowly, then tossed it on a chair.

A slice of moonlight found its way through the half-open drapes and fell on her breasts. They were small and round, perfectly shaped for her petite figure. Resisting the urge to devour, he bent to kiss one, tracing small wet circles around the already rigid pink bud before taking it into his mouth.

"Oh."

The single word, no louder than a whisper, reminded him of a child in a room full of treasures. There was a sweetness here, an innocence that was more powerful than the most potent of aphrodisiacs.

Struggling to keep his own desire under control, he continued to undress her, peeling the rest of her clothes layer by layer, her slacks, the knee-high stockings, the black silk panties. Then, stepping back, he shed his own clothes quickly, throwing them carelessly on the floor before returning to her waiting arms.

Her eyes on his erection, she pulled him to her, eager for them to be joined, for the aching need within her to be filled. But no matter how much she stretched and strained, he wouldn't let her go any further.

"We have all night," he murmured.

As his hands glided down the length of her naked body, he felt a tremor pass through her. Holding his breath, he let his hands trail lower, over the flatness of her stomach, the roundness of her hips, the softness of her thighs.

She was all heat and silky skin. Her body, powered by a passion he had never suspected, moved under his hands in an erotic dance, each sensual motion a demand for more. Her hands were all over him now, making it almost impossible for him to control his desire. "You're making it tough, lady."

Aroused by the deep, throaty sound of his voice, she wrapped a leg around his hip, thrusting herself forward and up, clutching his shoulders. She heard him suck in his breath. Beneath her roving hands, his skin had grown hot and damp.

He slipped into her, catching her gasp of pleasure in his mouth. For a moment, neither moved. Then, as the heat built and the need intensified, he gripped her legs and wrapped them around his hips.

She fell into his rhythm instantly, as if they had been making love forever. She had never been this close to a man before, never fully understood what it meant to be spiritually connected. She understood it now.

Heat coiled in her belly as they moved, slowly at

first, then with a deepening urgency. Sensations sharpened and the scent of passion rose, filling her senses. She could feel her muscles tensing, straining. Then, as reality faded and she cried out his name, he plunged deeper into her, pounding and thrusting until even her vision dimmed.

She fought to catch her breath, matching him stroke for stroke, clasping him deep within her. Her hands ran over his damp back in quick, eager strokes, pressing him to her.

The orgasm, more powerful than any she had ever known, slammed into her, leaving her stunned and fighting for air. But it was his pleasure, as his body lunged and the hot rush of his climax was released, that made her heart soar. When at last she felt him go limp, she cupped his face between her hands and captured his mouth in a long, passionate kiss.

A stream of sunlight squeezed through the heavy green draperies and came to rest on Diana's face. Eyes still closed, she stretched, smiling a little as she remembered last night.

"Good morning."

She turned to find Kane watching her, propped up on one elbow. She gave him a tentative smile. Then, because it had been ages since she had cared how she looked in the morning, she reached for her hair, arranging the wild tousle. "What are you doing?"

He grinned. "Committing your face to memory."

"Why? I'm not going anywhere."

"Good."

His fingers began to stroke her arm, awakening in her a desire she'd thought thoroughly satisfied the night before. Under any other circumstances, she would have loved nothing more than sliding under the sheets and finding out how much time it would take to arouse him again. But with morning had come reality and the reminder that the events of the day before still had to be dealt with. "What time is it?" she asked.

He glanced over her shoulder at the digital clock on the nightstand. "Ten after six." He brushed a dark red curl from her forehead. "Would you like some coffee?"

"Love some."

As he sat up, he saw that one impudent breast had peeked out from beneath the dark green cotton comforter, its pink nipple beckoning. Kane was tempted to suggest they forget about coffee, then stopped himself. She had told Zack she would take him to school this morning, and he knew that, short of a disaster, nothing would interfere with that promise.

Kicking off the covers, he got out of bed and slipped into a pair of jeans. "If you want to take a shower, there's a bathroom in there." He pointed to a door behind him. "And another down the hall. Your suitcase is in the guest room." He leaned over and gave her a long, lingering kiss. "You may want to bring it in here."

She looked deep into his eyes, stirred by the warmth she saw in them. "I will." Then, because she couldn't put it off any longer, she asked, "Do you get a paper?"

"The *Chronicle* and *L.A. Times.* They should be outside the door."

She took the robe he handed her, a thick terrycloth in a rich chocolate brown that smelled of his aftershave. "I'd like to see them," she said, slipping into the wrap. "I might as well find out how much damage I've done to myself."

*　　*　　*

It was worse than she had anticipated. News of the ransacking was in all the newspapers, on all the television broadcasts.

HOODLUMS TEAR APART THE HOME OF TRAVIS LINDFORD'S SON.

VIOLENT ATTACK ON ZACHARY WELLS'S HOUSE LEAVES HIM HOMELESS.

HOME OF THE LINDFORDS' NEWEST HEIR RANSACKED.

KYBC, the local television station Travis owned, had portrayed Diana in the worst possible light, exploiting the story for maximum impact.

In a show of fairness, one of KYBC's reporters had taken his microphone to the streets and interviewed people at random. While many San Franciscans admitted they had believed, days ago, that Diana would win the case, many were now undecided, and many more had changed their minds.

"The wife and I, we were on her side before," a cab driver said as he rested his arm over the taxi's open window. "But when we heard she was protecting her brother, an ex-con . . ." He shook his head. "She lost our vote. Blood is thicker than water and all that—but the safety of your kid should always come first."

And another, this time a mother of two. "I don't know. I feel sorry for her. She showed bad judgment, and it's going to cost her dearly. If I were her, I'd take my kid and run."

"That damn Travis," Diana cried, jumping from the kitchen chair. "He's taken the opinion of a handful of people and made it sound as if the whole city has turned against me. How can a judge remain impartial with an irresponsible newscast like that?"

Kane handed her a mug of strong black coffee. "Judge Arnette is too good a jurist to pay attention to media reports. And anyway, you'll get your chance to tell your side of the story on Monday."

When Kane offered to drive her to Kat's house a few moments later, she refused. "You can't protect me twenty-four hours a day," she said, lacing her fingers through his. "It would be impractical and nerve-wracking for both of us. Not to mention what it would do to your work schedule."

"I'm the boss. I can arrange my schedule any way I see fit."

She brought his fingers to her mouth and kissed them. "I'll be just fine. And I promise, you'll know where I am every minute of the day." She gave him a wicked smile. "And night."

Half an hour later, as she was driving Zack to school, the comment that woman had made on KYBC played in her head again and again. "If I were her, I'd take my kid and run."

What would it be like to be a fugitive from justice? To live underground under an assumed name and always have to look over your shoulder? She shook her head. She could never do anything like that. It might be the right solution for some. But not for her.

"Mom, look at that house!"

Following Zack's pointing finger, she saw a huge Santa and his sleigh propped up over the entire length of the roof. "Now that's what I call getting into the spirit of the season, huh?"

Zack fell back against the seat with a sigh. "Yeah."

At the dispirited sound of his voice, Diana's heart filled with a deep ache. Although he no longer believed in Santa Claus, Christmas still remained a magical time for him, a season he looked forward to with great anticipation year after year.

Reaching for his hand, she gave it a gentle squeeze. "I was doing some thinking earlier this morning."

Expectant blue eyes turned toward her.

"What would you say if I told you we can move back into our house within three or four days?"

He spun around in his seat. "But I thought you said it would take a long time to replace everything."

As a school bus coming from the opposite direction flashed its warning lights, she brought the Cherokee to a stop. "The sofa and chairs might take a while, but the rest—television sets, mattresses, dishes, they can be replaced in a day or two." She saved the best for last. "And when that's done, we could go get a tree—the biggest we can find."

Zack's happy grin was all the answer she needed.

After she dropped Zack off at school, Diana called the restaurant. "I guess you've seen the papers," she said when her hostess answered.

"Yes. Oh, Diana, I'm so sorry. We all are. If there's anything any of us can do, you'll let us know, won't you?"

Diana was touched by the sincerity in Elaine's voice. "I will. Thanks, Elaine."

"Will you be coming in today?"

"I don't think so. There's too much to do. You and the gang hold the fort, all right? Forsaking any complications, I should be in tomorrow."

At the house, where she had come to wait for the insurance adjuster, everything was as she had left it yesterday afternoon. Calmer now, she walked around the living room, assessing the damages, deciding what could be salvaged and what had to go.

The adjuster rang the bell promptly at nine, and by the time he left, a team of professional cleaners Kane had hired showed up at the door, ready to go to work.

While they scrubbed floors, shampooed carpets, and carried bags of debris to the curb, Diana and Kat made the rounds of department stores until she found one that could deliver what she needed before the end of the week.

They returned home at three-thirty and found Travis Lindford waiting in front of the house. Leaning against the hood of his red Ferrari, his arms folded, he gave her a nasty look. "Where the hell have you been?"

Diana slammed the Cherokee door shut. "Not that it's any of your business, but I'm trying to get my house back in order."

"On the contrary, it's very much my business. Zachary is my son, and his safety is my primary concern."

"Since when?"

"Since I found out he was my son."

Kat tugged at her arm. "Come on, Di. He's not worth—"

"Butt out," Travis snapped. Looking up and down the street, he asked. "Where is he?"

"If you mean Zack, Kane took him to soccer practice."

The answer seemed to take him aback for a moment. Then, moving away from the car, he came to stand directly in front of Diana. "You screwed up in a big way this time, didn't you, Diana? Cozying up with the mob, protecting that two-bit con at my son's expense." One corner of his mouth lifted, but the smile never reached his eyes. "My attorney is going to have a field day with that one."

"You bastard. Get out of my sight."

He was smiling now, clearly pleased with himself. "Enjoy Zachary while you can, Diana. Because as of next week, the boy will be where he belongs—with me."

Kat saw Diana's eyes darken with fury. At the same time, across the street, Mrs. Carmichael came out of her house and walked down her driveway, heading for her mailbox. Although she was pretending not to listen, Kat knew she was taking in every word. "Di, please, let's go inside. Mrs. Carmichael is watching."

But Diana wasn't listening. Her arms held rigidly at her sides, she walked toward Travis. "You'll never have him," she spat as Kat grabbed her arm and pulled her away. "Do you hear me? You'll never have my son. I'll kill you first!"

Across the street, Mrs. Carmichael stood clutching a stack of letters against her chest, a horrified expression on her face.

21

"I could have pulled his eyes out," Diana fumed later that evening as she prepared a mushroom omelet in Kane's kitchen. "The nerve of him, showing up at my door, accusing me of 'cozying up with the mob' and protecting my brother. Why can't he get it through his thick skull that I didn't report that first break-in because I wanted to protect Zack. Not Nick."

Kane, who had been listening attentively to Diana's recounting of her quarrel with Travis, smiled. "You mean the man is still walking around? Intact?"

"He has Kat to thank for that."

Kane watched as she sauteed mushrooms and sprinkled a dash of sherry in the pan. Neither had had anything to eat all day, and although he hadn't expected her to cook for him at such a late hour, she had insisted.

He liked her in his kitchen, pulling out pots and pans, whisking and stirring, a dish towel wrapped around her slender waist. Her body movements as she went about her chores brought back memories of last night, how she had felt in his arms, all heat and passion. He could get used to having her in his bed, too. Permanently.

"Here you go." She slid half of a perfect omelet onto his plate. "I hope it's all right. I'm afraid I wasn't concentrating."

"It looks great." He took a healthy bite, more hungry than he had realized. Diana, on the other hand, kept pushing her food from one side of the plate to the other, her mind clearly on other things.

Putting his fork down, Kane reached across the table and slipped his hand into hers. "Everything's going to be all right, darling."

Grateful for the contact, Diana linked her fingers with his. "I wish I could believe that. But too many things have been happening lately—incidents over which I have no control." Her tone turned rueful. "Except for today. I could have prevented that showdown with Travis by just walking away, and I didn't."

"I have a feeling the bastard set you up," Kane said, remembering how adept Travis was at pushing people to the edge. "He knew you'd be vulnerable so soon after the ransacking of your house, and he took advantage of it."

"Maybe. But that doesn't change the fact that my little public display is one more black mark against me—one Travis will make sure to bring up in court." She let out a small, mirthless laugh. "I can almost hear him now. 'I was worried about my son, your honor. I only came to make sure he was all right, and Diana Wells almost bit my head off.'"

Kane pushed his plate aside and took both her hands in his, holding them tight. "I'll talk to Travis. I'm going to ask him to drop this ridiculous suit. And by God, this time he's going to listen, even if I have to—"

Diana shook her head. "No, Kane. You've done enough. Another intervention on your part will turn the Lindfords against you, and I don't want that. I don't want to come between you and Margaret."

"What Margaret chooses to do is her own business.

Right now, my main concern, my *only* concern," he corrected, "is you."

She looked at him. Except for Kat, no one had ever defended her so vehemently. Somehow, it made everything easier. "I appreciate that, Kane. I really do. But the truth is, you love her very much. You said yourself she's been like a mother to you. How can you pretend losing her wouldn't hurt you? Wouldn't make you resent me?"

As she stood up and started to take her plate to the sink, he stopped her and pulled her to him, forcing her to sit on his lap. "I could never resent you. And it would hurt me more, much more, if I knew there was something I could have done for you and didn't."

She smiled. "Beating up Travis won't solve anything."

"Who said I was going to beat him up?"

She wrapped one arm around his neck and cocked her head to the side. "Are you denying you thought of it?"

"Mmmm. I'll have to plead the fifth on that one."

"You'll have to do more than that. You'll have to promise to stay away from him."

After a moment of silence, he nodded. She was right. Bullying Travis wasn't going to accomplish anything. It might even jeopardize her case, and that's the last thing he wanted.

"I promise." No longer hungry, he pushed an auburn curl aside and kissed her softly behind her ear. "Now . . . What do you say we leave the dishes until tomorrow morning and go to bed? It's been a long day."

Her lips curved into a slow smile. "I thought you'd never ask."

He watched her sleep. She lay curled up on one side, her hands tucked under her head, the scent of her skin drifting through his senses. In the moonlight, her features looked almost angelic. And so peaceful. It was hard to believe that only a few hours ago, she had been ready to pull a man's eyes out.

Smiling, he touched a finger to her cheek. At first, it had been sheer physical attraction, an overflow of hormones that had drawn him to her. But in the space of a few weeks, everything had changed. Hardly a moment went by without his thinking of her, of the way her hair looked in the sunlight, the habit she had of tilting her head to the side when she was puzzled, how her eyes glowed when she was happy.

He hadn't wanted to fall in love with her. He hadn't wanted to care about any woman ever again. But here he was, head over heels in love with a woman he wasn't even sure felt the same way.

Diana stirred and shifted, unconsciously fitting her body to his. A soft moan escaped her mouth as he slid one arm around her shoulders and pulled her close.

He wished he could tell her how he felt, how indispensable she had become, how badly he wanted to sit down with her and talk about their future. But it wouldn't be fair to do it now with all she had on her mind.

After the hearing, provided the ruling went the way they hoped, he would take her away for the weekend. Just the two of them. Until then, he would just have to be patient.

Randall thanked the messenger from O'Keefe Investigations and closed the door, anxious to be alone so he could play the tape that had just been delivered.

Half an hour earlier, the detective had called, barely able to contain his excitement. "I think we've got something this time, Randall."

"What?"

"I want you to hear it for yourself."

Now, placing the special tape player Joe had lent him on the drawing table, Randall inserted the long-playing cassette into the slot and pushed the PLAY button.

After a few static noises, he heard the ring of a doorbell and recognized Travis's voice as he greeted a man by the name of Wells—Diana's brother. The conversation that followed revealed a plot to ransack Diana's house in exchange for two hundred and fifty thousand dollars, fifty thousand of which would be paid in advance.

Moments later, Randall listened to a second, shorter conversation between the two men as Diana's brother returned to collect his advance.

Stunned, Randall switched off the machine. This was far more incriminating than anything he had hoped to uncover. Travis had conspired to commit a crime. One that would not only cost him the hotel, but could also send him to prison.

But how could he go to Margaret with this information? he thought, raking his fingers through his hair. She was a sick woman. That heart attack after Charles's death had nearly killed her; even now, although she was under excellent care and was probably exaggerating her symptoms, the shock could cause another heart attack. Or maybe even kill her.

He couldn't risk that.

He looked back at the tape player. How could he get that son of a bitch to pay for his sins without hurting anyone else?

When the solution finally came to him, he almost rejected it outright. He didn't have the stomach for blackmail. Travis would crush him like a bug after the first attempt.

But at the same time, something was telling him to

give the thought a try. There was nothing to fear. He had the upper hand now, not Travis. With a little effort, some careful rehearsing, he could pull it off. He *had* to pull it off. For Francesca.

Rewinding the machine, he played the tape again, listening to it with his eyes closed as he laid back against the swivel chair. When it was finished, he turned it off and called Joe O'Keefe. "Good work, Joe," he said when the investigator came on the line.

"Glad I could help, Randall. Anything more I can do for you?"

"Yes. You can remove the equipment now. I've got all I need."

"Are you all right, Di?"

Spooning a fragrant cassis glaze over wafer-thin slices of roasted duck, Diana nodded, aware she had been unusually silent since arriving at the restaurant this morning. "I'm fine, Lilly," she told the pastry chef as she handed the plate to a waiter. "A little distracted, that's all."

The last forty-eight hours had been a nightmare. Far from fading from the news, the story of the break-in had received more national publicity than any other local crime she could remember. Afraid she had ruined any chance she had of keeping Zack, she had called John McKay, coming straight to the point. "How bad is it, John?"

His sigh had filled her with dread. "I won't lie to you, Diana. It's not good. But it's not hopeless."

Not hopeless. Was that his way to say that it was? That, short of a miracle, she would lose her son?

She wasn't sure when she had arrived at her decision. She suspected it had been in her mind all along, and she just kept brushing it aside, unwilling to admit she was conceding. But as the morning had progressed, she had realized the time had come for her to act. Before it was too late.

After another moment of hesitation, she glanced at the clock and walked through a vestibule and into her office, closing the door behind her.

Pulling a small black book from her desk drawer, she looked up the number of the Lindford Hotel and dialed it.

"Mr. Lindford isn't in yet," his secretary informed her.

Rather than leave a message, Diana hung up and called Travis at home. After the fourth ring, an answering machine clicked on. Drumming impatient fingers on the desktop, she waited until the outgoing message was over before speaking.

"Travis, this is Diana. Please give me a—"

"Diana!" Travis exclaimed in a jovial tone as he took the call. "To what do I owe this honor?" He chuckled. "Or is it an honor?"

"I need to see you, Travis."

"What about?"

"I can't discuss it on the phone. Is today all right with you? After work?"

"No, it's not." There was a slight pause. "But I can give you a few minutes at four-thirty tomorrow afternoon."

"That'll be fine. Where do you want to meet?"

"My penthouse. Twenty-sixth floor—apartment 2A."

As she hung up, Diana let out a sigh of relief. Phase one had been relatively easy. Would she be equally lucky with phase two?

More than two hundred Gulf War veterans, in town for a second anniversary reunion, packed the lobby of the Lindford Hotel when Randall arrived there at four o'clock on Thursday afternoon.

He had debated whether or not to call his brother-in-law ahead of time, then, when he had overheard Francesca say Travis would be going home early to get ready for a movie premiere he would be attending with Margaret and Dunbar, he had opted for the element of surprise.

Pushing through the crowd of chatty, former servicemen, he quickly made his way toward the bank of elevators at the far end of the lobby and stepped into the one marked 26th.

Travis was fastening two-carat diamond studs into the cuffs of a formal white shirt when the bell rang. Remembering that Ava had already gone home, he went to open the door.

As Randall walked past him without waiting for an invitation, Travis didn't bother to conceal his irritation. "What the hell do you want?"

"I need to talk to you."

"You might have called." He let the door swing shut. "Or better yet, you could have waited until Sunday."

"This couldn't wait."

Travis's thick blond eyebrows went up. "What could *you* possibly have to tell me that's so urgent?"

Affecting a calmness he was far from feeling, Randall patted the briefcase in his hand. "I brought something I'd like you to hear." Ignoring Travis's sigh of exasperation, he set the briefcase on the coffee table, then opened it.

At the sight of the tape player, Travis shot Randall a sharp glance. "What the hell is this?"

Without a word, Randall pressed the PLAY button.

As the room filled with the sound of his and Nick

Wells's voices, Travis felt his blood turn cold. "Why you slimy, back-stabbing little worm. You bugged my house!"

Randall felt some of his nervousness ease off. "You never did give me enough credits for smarts, Travis." Then, seeing Travis's gaze sweep around the room, he chuckled. "It's gone. I had it removed last night while you were having dinner with your bride-to-be."

Taking advantage of Travis's shock, he went on. "I have been waiting a long time for you to make a mistake, Travis. And you finally made it—a big one."

"You son of a bitch."

"Call me all the names you want. But I'm the one sitting on the pot of gold now, dear brother-in-law. I'm the one calling the shots."

So that was it, Travis thought, trying to regain his composure. The slime wanted money.

For a moment, he was tempted to throw him out with nothing but a swift kick in the ass. Blackmail went against his grain. Partly because it was humiliating for a Lindford to find himself in such a position, and partly because he knew that blackmailers could never get enough. They always came back for more. Randall would be no different.

The thought of what could happen if the police got hold of that tape stopped him. "How much do you want?" he asked at last.

Randall smiled and pursed his lips. "How much do you think it's worth?"

"I don't have time to play twenty questions. Just name your price."

Feeling much more confident now, Randall focused his gaze on his brother-in-law. "I want you to tell Margaret that you've had a change of heart."

"A change of heart about what?"

"About the hotel. Tell her you don't want it, that she should give it to Francesca."

In the long silence that followed, Travis didn't react. In fact, his face was so totally devoid of expression that Randall thought the shock had put him in some kind of trance.

Then, like a dam breaking, Travis's voice exploded. "You want me to do *what*?"

A trickle of nervous perspiration ran down Randall's back. "I want you to give up the hotel."

"You're insane."

As he saw Travis's gaze dart toward the briefcase on the coffee table, Randall calmly turned off the player, removed the tape, and tucked it in his breast pocket. He didn't think Travis would be foolish enough to try something, but it wouldn't hurt to be careful. Especially since he had been in too much of a hurry to make a copy.

"On the contrary, Travis, I've never been more sane." He saw a flicker of fear in the handsome blue eyes. Pleased at the reaction, Randall smiled. "Well, Travis? Made up your mind yet?"

Travis glared at him. "You've been sniffing too many tubes of paint if you think I'm going to go along with a crazy deal like that."

"In that case I'll give the tape to the police." He waited a beat before asking, "What do you think conspiracy to breaking and entering, and destruction of property will get you? A couple of years in prison? More? Of course, with a clever lawyer you might get off with a lighter sentence. But you'd be finished with Margaret. Either way, you lose the hotel. The question is, *how* do you want to lose it? Quietly? Or publicly?"

"You wouldn't dare go to the cops. Not when you know what the shock could do to my mother."

"Margaret has survived many shocks in her lifetime," Randall replied with all the cold determination he could muster. "She'll survive this one. And if she doesn't . . ." He shrugged. "That's not my concern. After all, *you're* the one who screwed up. I, on the other hand, only discovered the truth." He smiled. "Who knows? I might even be hailed as a hero. Wouldn't that be a blast?"

Curling his fingers until his nails dug into his skin, Travis kept his rage under check. "I'll give you a million dollars. That's a lot of money, Randall, even by today's standards. You'll finally be able to take care of my sister in style without having to worry where the next dollar will come from."

"But money isn't what I want. The hotel is." Then, because he had been waiting a long time to bring Travis to his knees, he added, "You were never cut out to run such an operation anyway. Your father knew it. And I suspect Margaret does, too. She loves you too much to admit it. With this, however . . ." He gave his breast pocket a couple of taps. "She'll have no choice but to boot you out."

The fury exploded. His face white, Travis sprang forward, closing the distance between him and Randall in two quick steps. "Why you little scum ball," he hissed, his hands reaching for Randall's throat. "If you think for one minute I'm going to let you blackmail me—"

"Let me go!" In panic, Randall grabbed Travis's fingers and tried to pry them loose. "You're choking me, you maniac!"

"I'll do a lot more than choke you if you don't hand over that damned tape."

"Not until you . . . talk to Margaret."

Although Randall was equal to Travis in size, he was no match for his strength. He knew that if he didn't do something, in another few seconds, he would be unconscious.

As his legs began to buckle, he caught sight of a pair of bookends on the coffee table. They were stone replicas of the two lions that flanked the steps to the New York Public Library. All he had to do was pick one up and tap Travis on the head just hard enough to make him release his hold.

Gasping for breath, Randall extended his hand and wrapped his fingers around the heavy base, praying he wouldn't pass out too soon.

As Travis's right hand let go of Randall's throat and went into his pocket, Randall lifted the bookend off the table.

"I've got it!" Travis cried in triumph, letting go of Randall. "You stupid, incompetent asshole. You can't even—"

The blow caught him at the base of the skull.

For a fraction of a second, Travis's eyes, although glazed by the shock, grew wide with disbelief. Then they rolled upward, crossing slightly as if he were hopelessly trying to focus. His legs folded under him, making him look like a disjointed puppet. Then, still holding the tape, he crumpled in a heap at Randall's feet.

Taking big gulps of air and still holding the bookend, Randall stared at the inert figure, at the gaping wound in the back of Travis's head, and at the blood that flowed out of it like a stream.

He wasn't sure how long he waited until he was able to move. Or when the full implication of what he had done dawned on him. When he did, he lowered his arm. "Travis?" The faint whisper seemed to bounce off the walls.

There was no answer. He swallowed. "Say something, Travis, please."

The bookend slid from his fingers and fell on the carpet with a solid thud. He knelt by his brother-in-law's side and timidly touched his shoulder. "Travis?" He shook him gently, and as he did, the body, which had been lying on its side, rolled on its back.

Lifeless blue eyes stared at him.

Panic swam through Randall's head, making it spin. He had killed Travis. Inside his stomach, bile rose, almost choking him.

He hadn't meant to do it. He had only wanted to get away from him, to keep him from getting the tape.

It seemed like an eternity before he finally found the strength to stand up. As he did, he remembered that Travis had a cleaning lady who came in every day. What if she was still here?

He waited for the sound of hurried footsteps, but there was nothing. Nothing but the silence. And the sweet, sickly smell of blood filling the air.

Although his instincts told him to run, another side of him knew he had to get a hold of himself. There were things to do, details to attend to.

After picking up the tape from Travis's hand and putting it back in his pocket, he looked around him.

Fingerprints.

Pulling a handkerchief from his pants pocket, he proceeded to wipe everything he had touched, or thought he had touched—the coffee table, the back of the Louis XVI chair, and of course the bookend.

He thought of putting it back on the table, then changed his mind. The police would know it was the murder weapon anyway.

His breathing a little less labored now, Randall walked back to the coffee table and closed his brief-case. Then, studiously ignoring the motionless body, he walked across the living room. At the door, he wiped off the brass knob, held his handkerchief over it as he twisted it open, and peered out to the landing.

It was empty.

To make sure he hadn't overlooked anything, he gave one last glance inside the room, quickly averting his gaze when it fell on the body. Then, still using his handkerchief, he closed the door behind him and wiped off the doorbell. He took the same precautions with the elevator.

His eyes closed, he leaned against the mahogany back panel as he was whisked soundlessly down twenty-six floors.

Downstairs, one of the Desert Storm veterans, a big man with a shock of red hair and a glass of liquor in his hand, pointed a thick finger at Randall just as he stepped out of the elevator.

"Hey, aren't you Corporal Alan Blyden of the 101st Airborne?" he asked, slurring his words as he wrapped a big beefy arm around Randall's shoulders.

Resisting the impulse to run, Randall shook his head. "No. I'm afraid you've got me mistaken for someone else."

The man, whose stick-on name tag identified him as Master Sergeant Joseph Foster, let out a big booming laugh and tightened his hold. "Then who the hell are you, little buddy? And why aren't you having any fun?"

"I'm not with the reunion." Smiling congenially, Randall held his lapel. "See? No name tag."

"Well in that case ..." With a flourish, Sergeant Foster removed his name tag from his civilian jacket and stuck it on Randall's lapel. "There you are, my young friend. Now you have one." Pleased with himself, he laughed again. "You go to the bar and have a drink on me and I'll catch up with you later, okay?" Then, spotting someone he knew, he gave Randall a pat on the back that had him stumbling for balance, and staggered away.

Randall leaned against the wall, waiting for his legs to stop shaking. It was all right. The man was drunk as a skunk. He'd never remember him.

Removing his glasses, he wiped the sweat off his forehead with his sleeve. He was about to put the glasses back on when a young woman coming around the corner bumped into him. She glanced up, murmured a quick apology, then hurried toward the same penthouse elevator he had used moments before.

Frozen in place, he watched her as the doors closed.

Diana Wells.

Her photograph had been in so many newspapers lately, he would have recognized her anywhere.

What was she doing here? Whose penthouse was she heading for? Travis's or Margaret's?

Dear God, what if she discovered the body and started screaming? Sliding his glasses back in place, he looked around him. He had to get out of here before that happened—before someone called the police or decided to seal all exits from the hotel.

Shouldering his way through the crowd of ex-infantrymen, which had now doubled, he made it to the door and out of the hotel without being noticed.

Once inside his car, the temptation to lean his head against the steering wheel was overwhelming. But he fought it. He had to go home, get rid of the tape he no longer needed.

And he had to pull himself together.

After the third attempt, he was finally able to turn on the ignition.

22

As the elevator reached the twenty-sixth floor and stopped, Diana glanced at her watch, 4:25. If all went as she hoped, she would be out of here in ten minutes. Maybe less. If she failed . . .

She didn't want to think about that. Even though she hadn't discussed her decision to talk to Travis with John McKay, she knew her offer wasn't one Travis would turn down lightly. After much soul searching, she had decided she would let him have Zack two weekends a month and four weeks in the summer. In exchange, he would drop the custody suit.

Outside the penthouse, she took a deep breath, said a quick prayer, and rang the bell. After a moment, she rang again. When that, too, produced no answer, she knocked, discreetly at first, then louder as a sick feeling washed over her. What if Travis had changed his mind and left before she arrived?

She hesitated, but only for a moment. She hadn't come this far to give up now. Gripping the knob, she turned it, praying the door wasn't locked. It wasn't.

"Travis?" She opened the door just enough to allow her to poke her head inside. "Travis, it's Diana."

Total silence greeted her.

Pushing the door wider, she stepped in, closing it behind her. The lack of noise puzzled her, and made her feel uneasy. Could he have gone out?

She called his name again, waited, then, thinking it best to wait for him on the landing, she started to turn around.

It was then that she saw him.

For a moment she could only stare. Her body seemed to have gone numb. Even her throat had constricted, blocking the instinctive scream.

Travis lay in a pool of blood. He was on his back, his face a pasty white. His eyes were open and staring at the ceiling.

"Travis." It was only a strangled sound, but a sound just the same. With the return of her voice, Diana found out she could move. Her breath shallow, she took a step forward, then another until she stood by Travis's side.

As her reflexes took over, she knelt and pressed two fingers to his throat, searching for a pulse. There was none.

Horrified, she stared at the lifeless eyes, the chalk white skin, the still chest. as she looked around, her gaze fell on an object on the floor, and she picked it up. It was a small stone statue in the shape of a lion. Near the base of it was a thin streak of blood.

With a cry, she let the statue drop from her hand. Travis hadn't fallen down and hit his head as she had first thought. He had been killed. Murdered.

A spark of fear leapt in her breast. She stood up and backed away, her legs watery, her heart pounding. She should do something. Call the police. Or hotel security.

As a dozen thoughts scrambled through her head, a picture, as vivid as if she were viewing it on a screen, flashed in front of her. She saw herself standing outside her house two days ago, screaming at Travis. "You'll never have my son! I'll kill you first!"

The police will think I did it.

But she hadn't. She had come here at Travis's invitation. She had come to make him an offer, to discuss their son's custody in a calm, logical manner.

They'll never believe me.

They had to. She was innocent.

They would question witnesses—people like Mrs. Carmichael.

"She threatened to kill him, officer. I heard it with my own ears."

Reacting on sheer instinct, Diana ran.

She drove slowly, steering the Jeep through the rush-hour traffic. Her entire body shook, and her mind raced in a million directions as the scene inside the penthouse played in her head over and over.

After a couple of blocks, she relaxed her hold on the steering wheel. It would be all right. As soon as she got home, she would call Kane. He was a criminal attorney. The best. He would know what to do.

Then, almost instantly, she rejected the thought. She couldn't involve him. As an attorney, he would insist she turn herself in. She would be arrested, thrown in jail. She couldn't let that happen. Zack needed her.

At the intersection of Bush and Hyde streets, the light turned red, and she jammed on the brakes, jolting the Jeep to a teeth-jarring stop. *Jail.* The word sounded incongruous, the outcome too terrifying to imagine.

Stop it! The police didn't put innocent people in jail. Not unless they had evidence. And except for the fact that she had been in Travis's penthouse . . .

A chill ran down her spine.

The bookend!

Her fingerprints were on the murder weapon.

She ran her hand through her hair. How could she

have been so stupid? Why hadn't she left that damned bookend alone? Or left the penthouse after the second ring instead of letting herself in?

From somewhere inside her mind came a woman's voice. *"If it were me, I'd take my kid and run."*

She shook her head. It was an insane thought. She had nowhere to go. And she hadn't committed any crime.

Behind her, an impatient horn sounded. The light had turned green. With the automatic gestures of a robot, she lifted her foot off the brake and pressed the accelerator, amazed that she could drive at all, that she could still think and respond to various brain commands.

It was a few minutes after five when she pulled up in front of her house. She sat behind the wheel for another minute, aware that from across the street, Mrs. Carmichael was watching her.

Lowering her head against the steering wheel, she closed her eyes. She had never felt so frightened in her entire life, or so incapable of making a decision.

If it were me, I'd take my kid and run.

The voice was louder now, the words more convincing.

Slowly, she raised her head and reached for the door handle.

Sitting at her vanity table, Margaret leaned toward the mirror, narrowing her eyes in concentration as she fastened the Van Cleef and Arpels ruby necklace around her neck. Of all the many disadvantages of old age, deteriorating eyesight was one of the most frustrating.

She hadn't planned to attend the movie premiere of *Murder on the Bay*. Although several scenes of the movie had been shot at the Lindford, political thrillers bored her. But Travis had insisted.

"While Diana Wells's credibility as a mother is being chipped away piece by piece," he had told her, "ours as a strong, loving family keeps on getting stronger."

At last, she was able to fasten the catch and leaned back to admire the effect. Against the black taffeta of her Bill Blass gown, the rubies looked spectacular.

On the nightstand behind her the phone rang. Gathering the folds of her gown into her hands, she went to answer it.

"Hello?"

"Margaret, it's Dunbar."

Margaret's face lit up. "How are you, my dear?"

"Actually, I'm a little concerned. Have you and Travis been delayed for some reason?"

"Delayed? Why no. It's only . . ." Margaret turned to glance at the clock on her bedside table. "Oh, dear, it's almost six o'clock!"

"And Travis said he would pick me up no later than five-thirty. I tried to call him on his car phone, thinking the two of you were caught in traffic, but obviously you haven't left yet."

"I hadn't realized it was so late. I assume you tried the penthouse?"

"Yes. There's no answer."

At the concerned tone in Dunbar's voice, Margaret smiled. Travis was just like his father when it came to being late. It was a deplorable habit, but one Dunbar would have to get used to. Just as she had.

"He may have stepped out for a moment. I'll go find out what's keeping him and call you right back."

Margaret hung up and hurried out of the penthouse.

In the empty, silent house, Diana sat on her bed

and tried to clear her mind of all unnecessary thoughts.

The banks were closed, so withdrawing a large amount of money was out of the question. Fortunately, since this was Thursday, she hadn't deposited the restaurant weekly cash receipts yet.

Standing up, she went to the closet, pulled out a canvas pouch from the safe and counted the money. Because most of her customers paid with credit cards, the cash amount was low—thirty-eight hundred dollars—but it would have to do until she figured out a way to get more.

She stuffed the bills into her purse, then from the back of the safe, she retrieved a folder with her and Zack's passports, immunization records, and Zack's adoption papers. One glance satisfied her that everything was in order.

Because of its proximity and its language, she had chosen Canada as her destination. Once settled there, she would find a job—tutoring, waiting tables, working as a cook. She wasn't fussy, as long as she found an employer willing to pay her under the table.

In control now, she picked up the phone and called several airlines until she found a flight leaving for Boston with a connection to Montreal in the morning.

After she had given the United Airlines reservationist her name and credit card information, she hung up and immediately dialed Kat's house.

"Hi, kiddo. What's up?"

Diana tried desperately to match Kat's cheery tone. "Pretty good actually. I've decided to take Zack on a ski trip. To Mount Shasta."

"Really? When?"

"Tonight."

There was a short pause before Kat asked, "Wouldn't you be better off leaving tomorrow morning?"

"Can't," Diana replied lightly. "All the flights to Redding were booked. I was lucky to get those two seats."

Kat didn't sound convinced. "All right, but . . . what about the Christmas tree? Zack was so excited about it. That's all he talked about since he came home from school."

"We'll do that when we get back." She ran a trembling hand through her hair. She wasn't handling this well at all. "Look, Kat . . . If you could just get him ready for me? I'll be there in a little while."

"Sure." There was another pause, then in a much lower voice, Kat asked, "Diana, is everything all right?"

Diana pressed two fingers against her eyelids. She had never been very good at fooling people. Least of all, Kat. "Of course. Why do you ask?"

"I don't know. You don't sound like yourself."

Diana wished she could tell Kat the truth. But it wouldn't be fair to drag her into this mess, to force her to lie to the police. And to Mitch. It was better this way.

"I'm a little strung out because of the hearing on Monday," she offered as an excuse. "That's why I decided to take the trip. I know it's a last-minute decision, but it might just be what I need right now."

"I agree." Kat's good humor had returned. "But you don't know what you're missing. I've outdone myself in the kitchen today. The chicken paprika is simply scrumptious."

Diana forced a chuckle. "Save some for me then. And freeze it."

"I'll do that. Oh, one more thing. Kane called not too long ago. He sounded worried about you."

Diana closed her eyes. "I'll give him a call. Thanks, Kat." She paused. "For everything."

Before Kat had a chance to answer, Diana hung up.

The phone was ringing when Kane walked into his condo. Hoping it was Diana, whom he had been trying to locate for over an hour, he crossed the room in a few quick strides to answer.

It was only a salesman. After a curt "I'm not interested," Kane slammed the phone down, then went into the kitchen to get himself a beer.

It wasn't like him to worry. But he couldn't help it. According to Lilly at the restaurant, Diana hadn't returned for the dinner shift. Kat, who was keeping Zack with her one more night before Diana moved back into the house, hadn't heard from her either.

Standing in the middle of his living room, sipping a Samuel Adams from the bottle, Kane glanced at his watch. Seven-fifteen. Maybe Kat had heard from her by now. Still holding his beer, he walked over to the phone.

It rang only once. "Hello?"

"Kat, this is Kane again. Have you heard from Diana?"

"She called a few minutes ago. She . . . She's going on a trip, Kane. A ski trip with Zack."

"What?"

She gave a nervous laugh. "I'm not sure I understand it myself, but that's what she said. She's leaving tonight and won't be back until sometime Sunday I guess."

"She didn't tell me about any ski trip. When did she decide that?"

"It was a last-minute decision. She said she needed this time with Zack before the hearing on Monday."

He frowned. Diana wasn't the impulsive type—and she would never take Zack out of school to go on a ski trip.

She's running away, he thought as fear coiled in his stomach.

His mouth suddenly dry, he asked, "Where did she call from?"

"I don't know. She just said she would be by shortly to pick up Zack."

"I'm on my way. If she gets there before I do, don't let her leave."

"Why? What's going on?"

"I'll explain when I get there. Until then, tell her to stay put."

"All right."

Without wasting another moment, he grabbed the jacket he had tossed on a chair earlier and ran for the door.

"Good evening, Wayne," Margaret said to a worker as she came out of her penthouse. "Have they got you on overtime again?"

From the top of his ladder, the hotel maintenance man, who had been with the Lindford for more than thirty years, looked down and smiled. "Just replacing a light bulb, Mrs. Lindford. I'll be done in a minute."

"All right," Margaret said, walking around the ladder to get to Travis's door. "Good night then, Wayne."

"Good night, Mrs. Lindford."

He had just finished screwing the globe back in place when he heard her screams.

23

The wait was killing him. Standing in his living room in front of the gleaming glass and mahogany bar, Randall considered pouring himself a stiff drink to steady his nerves, then changed his mind. He wasn't much of a drinker, and in the state he was in, the alcohol would probably make him sick.

He glanced at his watch, something he had been doing every few minutes—six-fifteen. It had been more than two hours since he had left Travis's penthouse, and there had been no calls, no word of his death, nothing.

He started to pace. What the hell was going on? Why hadn't anyone called? If Travis had been on his way to a movie premiere with Margaret and Dunbar, someone should be wondering where he was by now.

A sudden, terrifying thought made his stomach contract with a new fear. What if he wasn't dead? What if he had come to, crawled to the phone, and called for help?

He gripped the bar top with both hands. Impossible. Travis was dead. He was sure of that. If he wasn't, he would have heard.

Looking up, he caught his reflection in the wall mirror. He looked aghast. He had to get hold of himself. He couldn't let anyone see him like this.

The sudden, strident ring of the phone at the end

of the counter made him jump. For a moment he could only stare at it. When it rang again, he went to pick it up, drawing a steadying breath before lifting the receiver. Easy. There could be no anxiety in his voice, no fear.

"Hello?"

It was Francesca. She was hysterical, talking and crying at the same time.

"Darling, slow down," he soothed. "I can't understand a word you're saying. What happened? Is it your mother?"

"No! It's Travis . . . He's dead!" she sobbed.

"What?"

"He was killed. Right here . . . in his penthouse."

"I'm on my way."

A uniformed policeman stood outside Travis's penthouse when Randall came out of the elevator.

"You can't go in, sir," he said as Randall approached.

"It's all right. I'm Travis Lindford's brother-in-law. My wife just called . . ."

The door opened, and a heavyset man in a rumpled brown suit came out of the apartment. He had gray hair cut in a military crew, a strong, square jaw, and watchful gray eyes. A gold shield was clipped on his breast pocket.

"I'm Sergeant Kosak, homicide. Did I hear you say you were the victim's brother-in-law?"

Randall's gut clutched reflexively. He nodded. "Randall Atkins. Francesca Atkins's husband."

Kosak nodded. "I sent your wife and her mother to the other penthouse." He gestured toward Margaret's door. When Randall started to turn around, the policeman stopped him. "Before you go, I'd like to ask you a few questions."

Sweat trickled down Randall's back. "Me?"

The sergeant pulled a small notebook from his pocket and flipped it open with a snap of the wrist. "Do you know if your brother- in-law was expecting a visitor this afternoon?"

"All I know is that he and my mother-in-law were supposed to go to the movie premiere of *Murder on the Bay* together."

"Did you know him to have any enemies? Anyone who would want to kill him?"

Relax, Randall thought. The man's only doing his job. "I couldn't really say, Sergeant. I suppose it's conceivable for a man in his position to have an enemy or two."

"What about you?"

Randall resisted the impulse to swallow. "I beg your pardon?"

Kosak watched him from under gray, bushy eyebrows. "How did you feel about him?"

Lying would have been senseless. And dangerous. Too many people knew how they felt about each other. He met Sergeant Kosak's gaze and held it. "I didn't like him. But I wouldn't want him dead. And I certainly wouldn't kill him."

"Why didn't you like him?"

"It was a mutual dislike. He thought I married his sister for her money." He paused. "May I go now? My wife needs me."

"Just one more question. When was the last time you saw Mr. Lindford alive?"

Randall pretended to be searching his memory. "We had dinner together last Sunday at Margaret's ranch. Then on Monday morning, we all met for breakfast right here in the hotel. We do that occasionally."

Kosak closed his notebook with a snap. "Thank you, Mr. Atkins. You can go now."

Hurriedly, Randall walked over to Margaret's door, aware that Sergeant Kosak was still watching him.

"Oh, Randall!" The moment Margaret's maid let him in, Francesca fell in his arms.

"Shhh." He held her tight, his heart breaking at the sight of her pain. "It's all right, baby. I'm here now."

Clinging to him, she cried softly as he stroked her hair. When the sobs began to subside, she pulled him inside, motioning toward the living room. "I'm worried about Mother . . . She should see a doctor."

Randall glanced at Margaret, who sat on the sofa. Her back was spear straight, her eyes empty as they stared into the distance. "Did you call Dr. Phillips?"

Francesca pressed a handkerchief to her eyes. "She won't let me."

Randall moved swiftly across the room, sat down beside his mother-in-law, and took her hands. They were cold and unyielding. "Margaret, listen to me. You've had a great shock, and we're worried about you. Please let us call Dr. Phillips."

She shook her head.

"Why not?"

She turned around to look at him. "Because that old kook will give me a sedative and send me to bed."

"Which is exactly where you should be. Tomorrow we can—"

"Get me Kosak."

"What?"

"Are you hard of hearing, Randall? I said, get me Sergeant Kosak. I have something to tell him."

Randall glanced uncertainly at Francesca, who nodded. "I'll get him. You stay with Mother."

A few moments later, she was back with Sergeant Kosak.

"You wanted to see me, Mrs. Lindford?"

Margaret inclined her head. "Earlier, you asked me if I had any thoughts on who may have killed my son."

"You said you didn't."

She ran a hand over her short white curls as if to make sure every hair was in place. "I was too overwrought at the time to think clearly."

"You remember something now?"

She fixed him with her cold blue gaze. "I know who killed my son."

The policeman's eyes narrowed. "Who?"

"Diana Wells!"

24

December 1993

The hour following Diana's arrest was like a scene from a bad movie. Afraid she wouldn't be able to contact Kane, she used her one allowed phone call for Kat.

"I don't have time to go into details," she told her best friend when she answered the phone. "But please don't show any reaction to what I'm about to tell you. And don't let anyone know you're talking to me."

"All right," Kat said in a guarded voice.

"Travis Lindford is dead, and I've been arrested for his murder."

There was a slight pause. "I see."

"I need you to contact Kane right away."

"Of course."

A loud drunk in a raincoat and nothing else was being escorted to a desk by two police officers. To shut out the noise, Diana turned away from the scene, shielding the mouthpiece with her hand. "Don't tell Zack anything," she continued. "And don't let him talk to anyone—in person or on the phone."

"What about . . . ?" Kat's voice started to break, but she recovered quickly. "The other arrangements?"

"You mean school?"

"That's right."

"Keep him home for the time being. And turn off the TV. Hopefully, I won't have to stay here long."

"All right."

After the phone call, Diana was taken to a room with gray walls and a small, barred window high on the wall. In the center was a long wooden table and four chairs.

Sergeant Kosak, who looked more like someone's favorite uncle than a policeman, brought her a cup of bitter, lukewarm coffee, and sat across from her. The other detective, a younger man by the name of Berkowitz, stood beside him, one foot on a chair, an unlit cigarette in his mouth.

"Now then, Miss Wells," Kosak said. "Do you understand your rights as I read them to you earlier?"

"Yes."

"Do you want to wait for your attorney, or are you willing to answer a few routine questions now?"

Refusing to answer questions until Kane arrived would only make her look more suspicious. "I'll answer your questions. I have nothing to hide."

"Very well." He leaned back in his chair, looking very unthreatening. "What were you doing at the Lindford this afternoon? And before you deny being there, I must warn you we have a statement from a desk clerk who saw you run out of the hotel at 4:45."

"And according to the coroner," Berkowitz put in. "Travis Lindford died between four and five p.m."

"I'm not denying being there. I came to see Travis. We were going to discuss my son's custody."

"How did that go?"

"I never had a chance to talk to him. Travis was dead when I arrived." She tried not to flinch under Kosak's penetrating stare. "I know you think I killed him. But I didn't. I swear it."

"Tell us what happened."

She glanced at Detective Berkowitz, who had sat down and was taking notes, then back at Kosak. "I found him there . . . like that."

Kosak's face showed no reaction, no emotion. "From the beginning, please."

She did, omitting nothing. From time to time, she took small sips of coffee as she tried to recollect some important detail. Or what she perceived as important.

After she was finished, there were more questions. Why did she let herself in the penthouse? Why hadn't she called the police upon finding the body? And then the question she had dreaded.

"Where were you going when we rang your doorbell, Miss Wells?"

During the course of the interrogation, she had decided that she would tell him the whole truth no matter how incriminating, and hope he would understand. But it was clear to her now that despite Sergeant Kosak's mild manners, he thought her guilty and would use any information she gave him to strengthen his case. She had no choice but tell him what she had told Kat.

"My son and I were on our way to Mount Shasta for a short ski vacation."

"Are you in the habit of taking your passports with you when you travel within the state?"

"Sometimes," she lied. "As a form of identification."

His expression didn't change. "Did you kill Travis Lindford?"

"No!"

"Did you ever want to?"

"No."

"Come now, Miss Wells. He was trying to take your son away from you. Surely you hated him for that."

"Yes. But—"

"And when you went to his penthouse to make a

deal with him and he turned you down, you became furious. You saw your last chance slip through your fingers. The bookend was right there. You picked it up, hit Travis Lindford on the back of the head, waited to make sure he was dead, and then you ran."

"No! You're making all this up. I told you the truth. I went there to discuss the custody, to make him an offer, and I found him dead!"

He leaned across the table, unfazed by her outburst. "You never had any intention of going on a trip until that very moment, did you, Miss Wells? And you weren't on your way to Mount Shasta. So where were you going? Canada? Europe? Mexico?"

Too late, she realized how wrong she had been in not waiting for Kane. The rapid-fire questioning was meant to confuse and intimidate her. If she allowed him to continue, he would trap her.

Folding her arms, she leaned back in her chair, putting some distance between them. "I won't answer any more questions until my lawyer gets here."

Kosak stared at her for a moment, his expression as unreadable as before. Then, rising, he turned to his partner. "Book her."

As if in a dream, she followed a uniformed policewoman into another room where she was photographed and fingerprinted the way she had seen it done in movies dozens of times.

It wasn't until she was led to a cell to await her bail hearing that she fully realized she had been charged with second-degree murder. Kosak hadn't believed a word she had told him. He only cared about two things—that she was at the Lindford when Travis was killed, and that she had a motive for killing him. Motive and opportunity—two favorite words in police language.

As the barred metal door clanged shut behind her, Diana looked around the cell, afraid to take another step. Against one wall was a cot with a folded army blanket on top. To her right was a gray, cracked sink and a toilet bowl with no lid.

She tried to ignore the stench and walked stiffly toward a wooden chair, pulled it away from the dingy wall, and sat down.

How long would she have to stay in here? she wondered, realizing she had lost track of time. Where was Kane? What if she didn't make bail? What if she never got out of this place?

Somewhere down the hall, a woman let out a string of obscenities. A man yelled at her to shut up, but the racket only got louder. Diana closed her eyes. After a moment, she felt herself doze off and jerked her head back, only to let go again a few minutes later.

"Diana!"

Startled, she opened her eyes and snapped her head up, suddenly wide awake. A guard was unlocking the cell. She jumped out of her chair. "Kane!"

He rushed to her, enveloping her in his arms.

She fell against his chest. "I thought you'd never get here." She clung to him, taking in his scent, fighting not to cry. She had tried so hard to hang on to whatever strength she had left, she couldn't break now. After a few seconds, she pulled back. "They think I did it, Kane. They think I killed Travis."

"I know. We'll talk about it later. Right now, let's get you out of here."

"The bail . . ."

"It's been taken care of. That's why I was so late in getting here."

"You paid my bail?"

"Yes. Now let's go."

She stopped walking. "How much was it, Kane?"

"Two hundred thousand." Seeing the look of disbelief on her face, he wrapped an arm around her shoulder and led her down the long, dismal hallway. "We'll get it back when you're cleared, so don't worry about it." He turned to her, his eyes glowing with humor. "Just don't jump bail, okay?"

Her eyes filled with tears as she tried to smile back. Until this very moment, she hadn't realized how much she had come to rely on him. It was an odd feeling, one she wasn't accustomed to, for she had always been able to take care of herself, to fight her own battles.

I'm falling in love with him.

No longer alarmed at the thought as she had been before, the admission brought her a sense of relief. She had said it at last. Not to him, because now was not the time, but to herself, which was just as important.

As they reached the door, half a dozen reporters rushed toward them. Holding her arm in a firm grip, Kane raised a hand. "Miss Wells has nothing to say at this time."

A stubborn reporter pushed his way to the front of the line. "Isn't this a little awkward for you, Mr. Sanders? Defending the woman accused of killing Travis Lindford and being such a close friend of the victim's family?"

"There's nothing awkward about it. I'm a defense attorney. I'm just doing my job. Now, if you'll excuse us." Still holding Diana, he cut through the crowd. "It's been a long day, and my client needs to rest."

Moments later, Diana was outside, breathing the cool night air. A light rain was falling, spreading a sheen on the road and the passing cars. She had never thought of freedom as a look, a smell. She did now.

"I have to talk to Zack," she said as they walked

toward Kane's car, parked half a block down the street.

Kane nodded. "I'll take you there. But you realize he can't stay at Kat's house a minute longer."

"Why not?"

"Because the press isn't going to be satisfied with the morsel I've handed them. By morning, they'll be at Kat's doorstep, trying to get a statement from anyone who goes in or out. Including Zack."

He opened the passenger door, then waited until she was tucked in before coming around to slide behind the wheel. "I talked to Beckie. She said he can stay with her. For as long as necessary. He'll be safe there."

"What about school, his activities . . ."

He looked behind him before pulling away from the curb. "There's a perfectly fine elementary school in Glen Ellen. He can transfer there until the trial is over."

The ordeal had made her nerves raw. But beneath her despair, she could see the wisdom of Kane's suggestion. Above all, she wanted Zack to be safe. She nodded. "That's very kind of Beckie. And of you, for thinking of it. Thanks, Kane."

Then, pressing her head against the back cushion, she let out a deep sigh. "Oh, Kane, I was so stupid. If only I had taken time to think before I went to see Travis, I wouldn't be in this mess right now."

"Why did you go there, Diana?"

She closed her eyes. "To talk. To beg. Whatever it would have taken, I would have done it." Tears pricked her eyes, but this time she made no attempt to stop them. "I didn't kill him," she said, turning to look at him.

"I believe you." He took her hand and squeezed it. "We'll get you out of this mess, darling. I promise."

"What will happen to me?"

"There will be a preliminary hearing. That's to determine whether there is cause, *probable* cause, to prosecute you. Then, either the charges will be dropped or the case will go to trial. You can expect the hearing to take place within a week. A trial, on the other hand, might not be scheduled for months."

"I could go to prison."

At the stricken look in her eyes, he wrapped an arm around her shoulders and pulled her to him. "No, you won't. I won't let it happen."

She wanted desperately to believe him.

It was ten o'clock when they arrived at Kat's house. Although it was well past Zack's bedtime, Kat had kept him up. The moment he saw Diana, he stood up from the floor where he had been playing checkers with Mitch, and ran to her. "Mom! Where were you? I thought we were going to pick out a tree tonight."

As Kane, Mitch, and Kat moved discreetly out of sight, Diana sat down on a chair and pulled him to her. "I was at the police station."

He frowned and tilted his head to the side. "How come?"

She squared her shoulders, as if the simple gesture would give her the strength she needed. "There's been an accident, Zack. Your ... Travis was killed today."

Choosing her words carefully, skimming over the parts he didn't need to know, she told him what had happened, and about the police coming to arrest her.

Zack's eyes filled with horror. "You mean, they put you in *jail*?"

"Only for a little while. Until Kane came to get me."

He wrapped a protective arm around her neck.

"But you couldn't have killed Travis. 'Cause you're not a killer. Didn't you tell the police that?"

"I did. Several times. But they don't believe me."

"Will you have to go to jail again?" Although he was making a desperate effort to be brave, the tremor in his voice betrayed his fear.

"No." She drew him closer, and when she felt him tremble against her, she laid a comforting hand on his head. "That's all you need to know now, darling. I promise you everything is going to be all right. In the meantime, I don't want you to worry about what you hear on television, or from your friends. If you have any questions, you come to me. Okay?"

His head moved against her breast in a nod. "Is Kane going to be your lawyer?"

"Yes."

He looked up. The fear had vanished. "Then you'll be all right."

She smiled—and prayed his prediction would come true.

Nick had just settled in front of the television set with a can of Budweiser and a bag of Doritos when a movie he had been watching was interrupted for a special bulletin.

"Travis Lindford, general manager of the Lindford Hotel, was found murdered in his penthouse earlier today. Diana Wells, against whom the hotel heir had filed a child custody suit, was arrested and charged with second-degree murder. Details at ten."

"No!" Nick slammed the beer can on the table. It couldn't be. Travis couldn't be dead. The bastard still owed him two hundred grand.

Frantic, he picked up the remote and started switching channels in search of another broadcast. Only CNN's *Newsnight* confirmed what he had just heard.

Travis Lindford had been killed, and Diana had been charged with his murder.

"Damn you, Di!" he screamed at the TV. "Why the hell did you have to go and fuck up everything for me?"

With a groan, he leaned back against the sofa. He had done the job he had been contracted to do, taken all the risks, and all he had to show for his hard work was a measly fifty thousand dollars. Thirty of which belonged to Eddy.

Dammit, no. He stood up. He wasn't going to get screwed again. Not after all the plans he had made, all the dreams he had envisioned. He'd take the fifty thousand dollars and split, salvage what he could out of a deal that had gone sour. It wasn't what Eddy would call a healthy move, but with fifty thousand dollars, he could start a new life in some other city, where no one knew him, where no one would find him.

He glanced at the clock—nine-thirty. He might still be able to catch a bus out of town. He would have to leave his car behind, but what the hell? He'd buy a new one when he arrived at his destination—wherever that was.

His heart racing now, he ran to his bedroom, pulled an old Samsonite suitcase from under the bed, and started to throw clothes into it. When he was finished, he went to his dresser, reached for a manila envelope he had taped to the bottom of a drawer, and removed a handful of bills from it, stuffing them into his pants pocket. Then he tucked the envelope with the rest of Travis's money between two shirts and closed the suitcase.

Maybe he should go to Reno. He had an old girlfriend there, a dancer he hadn't seen in a couple of years. With her help he would lay low for a while, and

when he was sure Eddy had called off his dogs, he
would move on.

Or he could stay in Nevada. If Monique was still the
looker she was a few years back, he wouldn't mind
making the arrangement a permanent one.

Running away on Eddy was the scariest thing he
had ever done. If Bulge and Curly found him, they
wouldn't be satisfied with a few blows. They'd wrap
him around a cement block and drop him into the
bay.

He would have to outsmart them.

Pulling the collar of his suede jacket around his
neck, he let himself out of his apartment, glancing in
both directions before walking toward the parking lot.

By the time Eddy realized he was gone, he'd be two
hundred miles away.

25

It was daylight when Diana woke up the following morning. Opening one eye, then the other, she peered from beneath the green comforter, realizing she was in Kane's room.

At first, she couldn't remember anything about the previous night, except for Kane gently leading her here, the comfort of the cool white sheets, the way he had held her, waiting for her to fall asleep.

Then, with a jolt that brought her to a sitting position, she remembered the rest of the day, Travis's murder, her arrest, the drive to Sonoma, where Zack would be staying for an indefinite period.

"Oh, no."

She rested her forehead on top of her drawn-up knees. The two Excedrins Kane had given her before going to bed last night had removed that dull ache at the back of her head, but done little for the cold fear inside her stomach.

She had been charged with murder.

Even in the clear morning light, the words sounded unreal. How could this have happened to her? One moment she was a successful restaurateur with nowhere to go but up, and the next she was being called a murderess.

"Feeling better?"

At the sound of Kane's voice, she raised her head.

His smiling face poked through the half-open door. She attempted a smile, but couldn't quite manage it. "A little." She raked her hair back with both hands. "I feel so . . . disoriented."

"That's a normal reaction. We'll take it slow, okay? One step at a time." He sat down on the side of the bed and took her hand in his. "First of all, Kat called to say not to worry about delivery of the items you bought earlier this week. She'll go to your house and wait for them."

Good old Kat. She could always be counted on to be one step ahead of everyone else. "I had forgotten about that."

"After breakfast, we'll drive to Glen Ellen to register Zack at his new school. All you need to do is call the school here and ask them to have his file ready for you to pick up. You'll need it."

She nodded, glad that somebody was thinking clearly.

"Do you feel like talking now? About what happened yesterday?"

He saw her relax as she leaned against the headboard. "Yes."

"Good." The strap of her nightgown slipped from her shoulder, distracting him for a moment. He reached out and pulled it back in place. "Tell me what happened. Just as you remember it."

Much calmer than she had been last night, she went over the events in chronological order, her decision to reach some sort of compromise with Travis, her phone conversation with him, the discovery of the body, her panic. She didn't tell Kane she had been about to leave the country. Not because she didn't trust him, but because she didn't want to hurt him, or to jeopardize his career by telling him something she had withheld from the police.

"Why the sudden decision to go skiing?" he asked. His tone was a little sharper now, his eyes more watchful.

Meeting his gaze was difficult, but she managed it. "I don't know. I thought that if I was away when Travis's body was found, the police wouldn't think of me as a suspect . . ."

"You never thought that it might incriminate you? Make you look more guilty?"

"I'm afraid I wasn't thinking very clearly at the time. I was very scared." That much was true.

Because he didn't want to put her on the defensive, he didn't question her further about the trip even though he was certain she hadn't been on her way to Mount Shasta. She was here now. That's all that mattered. "I wish you had called me first," he said simply.

She nodded without looking at him. "Me too."

His hand skimmed up and down her arm, in a comforting fashion. "Tell me what happened once you got to the hotel. Did you see anyone either on your way up or down?"

"There were a lot of people in the lobby. A convention of military men, I think. Some were in uniforms, others in civilian clothes. I remember I had to walk around a large display board with photographs tacked to it."

"Did you notice anyone who might have looked suspicious?"

She shook her head. "It was too crowded. I didn't pay much attention to anything except getting through the crowd. Both times." Her eyes narrowed at a sudden recollection.

"What is it?"

"I remember someone—a man I bumped into on my way to Travis's penthouse. He was standing in front of the elevator."

"Can you describe him?"

She bit her bottom lip, concentrating. "Not really. I was too preoccupied, in too much of a hurry."

"Try. Anything you can remember could be helpful."

"He wore a sports jacket—navy I think—and one of those stick-on name tags on the lapel."

"Then he was one of the men attending the convention."

"I suppose so."

Kane felt a flicker of hope. "Do you remember the name on the tag?"

She continued to frown. "John? James? I'm not sure."

"Last name?"

She shook her head. "That part is a total blank."

The pressure of his hand increased. "Would you recognize the man if you saw him again?"

"I don't know. Maybe." She sighed. "Probably not."

"It's all right. Don't push it. It'll come back to you later. Meanwhile, I'll talk to Francesca and find out who those people were."

The glimmer of hope she had glimpsed earlier grew a little brighter. "Do you think that man could have . . ."

"It's a remote possibility, but a possibility just the same, therefore it's worth checking into." His hand was gentle as it touched her cheek. "In the meantime, what do you say to a little breakfast? We can talk again later."

She covered his hand with hers and held it there. "I thought you couldn't cook."

"I can make coffee, pop bread in the toaster, butter the bread, spoon some marmalade on top of the butter."

"Mmmmm. You're making my mouth water."

He tilted her head back and kissed her. "Smart ass."

Joe O'Keefe learned about Travis's death on Friday morning, as Gladys, his wife of thirty-one years, poured him a second cup of coffee.

"Jesus Christ almighty!"

Gladys, a thin, dark-haired woman with sharp brown eyes, held the percolator to the side and tilted her head so she could see what her husband was reading. "What is it, Joey?"

"Travis Lindford was murdered yesterday. Right in his penthouse."

Gladys sat down, a hand over her breast. "My Lord! Do they know who did it?"

"Looks that way. They arrested Diana Wells."

"The woman he was suing for custody of his son?"

Joe nodded. "I guess he won't be suing her anymore."

"Well, if you ask me," Gladys said, her voice brimming with disapproval, "the man asked for it. Trying to take a child from his mother. Why, that's downright criminal."

Half listening, Joe heaved a small sigh of relief. Now that Travis was dead, Randall wouldn't have to confront him with that tape. Joe had been worried about his young friend. In spite of the tough image he sometimes tried to project, he wasn't the type to take on a sleek bastard like Travis Lindford. Whatever plan he had had in mind would have backfired. And Joe liked Randall too much to see that happen.

With Travis dead, he wouldn't have to do a thing. Thank God for that.

It was nine o'clock on Friday morning when Kane rang Margaret's doorbell. He had called the night before while Diana slept, and Randall had told him Margaret had gone to bed and was resting comfortably.

"She finally agreed to see Dr. Phillips," he had added. "And he said she was fine. Why don't you stop by tomorrow morning, Kane? I'm sure she'll be glad to see you."

He dreaded the ordeal. Margaret had adored Travis. Of her two children, he had always been her favorite, the one with whom she had felt the closest. There was no doubt that his death would affect her deeply—emotionally as well as physically.

Randall opened the door himself. He was dressed casually in dark blue jeans and a white shirt. Although there were circles under his eyes, he seemed alert and in total control of the situation, which was rather unusual, considering Randall had never been the take-charge type.

"How is she?" Kane asked after the two men shook hands.

"Devastated, but stoic. You know Margaret," he added with a shrug. "She won't allow anything to break her. Not even a tragedy."

"And Francesca?"

Randall's face clouded over. "She took her brother's death very hard. She's still asleep upstairs. We spent the night here, so I insisted she let Dr. Phillips give her a sedative."

"Who's running the hotel?"

Randall's tone turned brisk and businesslike. "I've already gone down to talk to Conrad. He was Travis's right-hand man, as you know. He'll be assuming the duties of general manager until Margaret decides what she wants to do."

Once again, Kane was struck by Randall's assertiveness. He would have never thought him capable of dealing with anything more complicated than choosing from a menu.

Kane gave him a friendly pat on the shoulder. "Good work, Randall. Now, if you'll excuse me, I'll go see Margaret."

"Certainly. If you need me, I'll be in the library."

Margaret was waiting for him in the drawing room. On the coffee table in front of her was a tray with her morning breakfast, black coffee and orange juice. During Charles's lifetime, the first meal of the day had been an elaborate affair, always served in the dining room. But now that she lived alone, she preferred to take all her meals in the drawing room.

"Hello, Margaret." In a few strides he had crossed the large room. "I'm so sorry," he said, closing his arms around her.

He felt her shudder, and for a moment he thought she would burst into tears. But she didn't. After a few seconds she pulled away. "Thank you, dear." She caught a lone tear with her middle finger. "How did you find out? Francesca tried to call you last night, but you were nowhere to be found."

He held her gaze. "I was at the police station, arranging for Diana's bail."

Slowly, she withdrew her hand from his. "Does that mean you intend to defend her?"

"Yes."

"Even though she killed my son."

"That's for a jury to decide."

Her eyes flashed. "I don't need a jury to tell me what I already know. She was in his penthouse. And she was seen running out of the hotel, looking half crazed."

"I'm aware of all that."

"But you still believe her."

He searched her eyes for a sign of understanding,

a hint of the warm, compassionate woman he knew existed under the hard veneer. All he saw was anger—and hatred. "Yes, I believe her."

"Then you're a bigger fool than I thought."

God, she was tough. "I remember a time when you told me to always trust my instincts, that they would never fail me."

"Instincts can sometimes be wrong."

"If I'm wrong about Diana, I'll be the first one to admit it. Until then, I have to follow my instincts and find the real killer."

Without flinching, Margaret held his gaze. He had his father's wisdom. And his mother's tenacity. She had always admired that in him. She had even wished some of it had rubbed off on Travis. Her voice mellowing a degree, she asked, "How do you plan to do that?"

He shrugged. "The same way I always do. By investigating."

She stared to tell him that the police had already done that, with excellent results, then thought better of it. He hadn't become a brilliant criminal attorney by taking the word of others at face value. "Investigate what?"

"I need to go through Travis's things. I need to find out whom he was acquainted with, what business deals he had pending, whom he was seeing."

"He had very few friends. You know that."

"A friend didn't do this to him, Margaret."

Briefly, as if to shut out the picture she couldn't seem to erase from her mind, she closed her eyes.

Claiming her hand again, Kane looked at the long, elegant fingers, stiffened by age, and remembered how quickly they had moved along piano keys once, enchanting him and his parents with classics she would never play again. "As the attorney for the defense," he continued in a gentle tone so as not to offend her, "I have the right to inspect the scene of the crime. I don't even need a warrant since the house is empty. But I'd rather do it with your permission. And your cooperation."

"Will you tell me what you're looking for?"

"I don't know what I'm looking for. A name, a clue, anything that might help unravel the mystery."

"Aren't you better off leaving that kind of work to Sergeant Kosak?"

"Sergeant Kosak has his way of conducting investigations. I have mine." He gave her hand a gentle tap. "So, Margaret. Do I have your permission?"

She sighed. He was going to do it whether she agreed to it or not, so why create bad feelings between them? "Very well."

Standing up, she walked over to one of the twin antique mahogany bureaus that flanked the fireplace, pulled a drawer, and retrieved a set of keys.

She came back to where Kane stood and handed them to him. "Those belong to Travis. I don't know what's what, other than the penthouse and office keys right here, but I imagine Francesca will be able to help you."

"Thank you. I'll check with the police to make sure it's all right to go in." He put the keys in his pocket. "Would you like me to help you with the funeral arrangements?"

At the thought of the ordeal still to come, she swayed slightly and he caught her arm, forcing her to sit down again. "Randall already took care of all the details. There will be a private church service, for friends and family only, at nine-thirty on Monday morning. I would appreciate it if you rode to the church with us."

"Of course." Kane hesitated, not wanting to leave

her alone. Then, remembering that Randall was there, he kissed her cheek and left, closing the door softly behind him.

After thirty years on the force and two citations, Sergeant William Kosak was looking forward to retirement.

Not that he didn't love the force. On the contrary, being a cop was something he had dreamed of doing since he was a little kid, and he would miss it, miss the camaraderie around the station, the challenge of a new case, no matter how complex.

Flipping through the file on his desk, he sighed. That's what the Lindford case was missing. Challenge. Everything was too damned pat. Oh, sure the evidence was there, all of it pointing to Diana Wells, but his gut feeling told him it wasn't enough. Or maybe it was too much.

"What's going on inside that ugly puss of yours?" Berkowitz, back from the coffee machine, handed him a steaming cup of coffee, then sat at his own desk, which faced Kosak's. "The Lindford case?"

Kosak blew on the coffee before taking a noisy sip. "The pieces are fitting just a little too snugly."

Berkowitz shook his head. "I knew it. That woman got to you, didn't she? You always were a sucker for a pretty face."

"She has nothing to do with it. I just don't like the way the evidence is stacked against her."

"Dammit, man, you're three months from retirement. Why do you want to go and borrow trouble at a time like this? The woman is guilty as sin. I know it. The D.A. knows it. Why can't you accept it?"

Kosak stood up. "Because I'm a hard ass, that's why." Then, unhooking his jacket from a rack next to his desk, he threw it over his shoulder. "Hold the fort, will you, Tom? I'll be back in—"

The phone on his desk rang. It was the desk clerk at Mount Shasta Lodge where Diana Wells claimed to have had reservations. After listening for a moment, he thanked the caller and hung up.

"Damn."

"What now?" Berkowitz asked.

"That was the desk clerk at Mount Shasta Lodge returning my call. He says there's no one by the name of Diana Wells or Zachary Wells registered with them."

"Of course there isn't. She wasn't heading for the mountains, Bill. She was fleeing the country. I'd bet my pension on it."

Kosak pursed his lips. Although he hated to admit it, Berkowitz was probably right. As for where exactly she had been going, there was only one way to find out.

With a sigh of regret Kosak picked up the phone again and called the airport.

"Oh, come on, Julie!" Kane exploded as he stood in the office of San Francisco district attorney, Julie Archer. "You can't possibly hope to make that charge stick."

Julie Archer, an attractive woman in her late forties, leaned back in her swivel chair, not the least bit bothered by Kane's outburst. Handling outraged defense lawyers was one of her specialties. And although she had never won a case against Kane Sanders, she was looking forward to winning this one. There was nothing like getting a conviction in a sensational murder case to instantly establish the reputation of a prosecutor.

"Not only do I intend to make it stick," she replied, watching Kane through narrowed eyes. "But I'm going to make certain Diana Wells gets the maximum sentence under the law for her crime."

"Why? Because you think she's guilty or because you see this case as some sort of cause célèbre?"

Archer picked up a pencil from her desk and tapped it gently and rhythmically on the edge of her desk. "I could throw you out of my office for a remark like that."

"You won't. You're enjoying this too much." Kane sat down. "Now, why don't you tell me why you think you have a case."

"With pleasure." She glanced at the open file on her desk. "First of all, your client herself admits being in Travis Lindford's penthouse at the time of the murder."

"She only admits arriving there at four-thirty, discovering the body, and leaving a few minutes later."

"Her time of arrival cannot be verified since the hotel clerk only saw her leave, which means she could have had ample time to kill Travis Lindford." She cocked a thin eyebrow. "And then, there is the matter of her fingerprints on the murder weapon."

"What else?"

"Forty-eight hours prior to the murder, she was heard to threaten the victim outside her house. She told him he would never have her son, that she would kill him first."

Already aware that Diana's neighbor, a Mrs. Carmichael, had come forward with that information, Kane nodded. "Is that all?"

"That's enough for a conviction as far as I'm concerned." Holding Kane's gaze, she added, "Unless of course, you'd like to make a deal. All your client would have to do is confess to the murder."

"She's not going to confess, Julie. She didn't do it."

"That's what they all say." Her lips pulled into a

smug smile as she reached inside her desk drawer and retrieved an envelope. "I was saving the best for last." She threw the envelope across her desk. "Go ahead. Take a look at what's inside."

Without a word Kane picked up the envelope and pulled out its contents. He raised an eyebrow. "An airline ticket?"

Julie nodded. "It belongs to your client." She waved her hand. "Go ahead. Check it out. You'll see that it's a ticket, two tickets actually, to Montreal, Canada. One is for her and one is for her son. *One-way* tickets."

Kane gave her a sharp look. "Did she give you this?"

"No. Sergeant Kosak called the lodge where Diana was supposed to be staying in Mount Shasta, and learned she wasn't registered there. Nor was she on the manifest of any flight to Redding, the closest airport to Mount Shasta. So, being the thorough cop he is, he started checking with various airlines for other destinations. That's how he found out she had booked two flights to Canada. The tickets were waiting for her at the airport."

She leaned back in her chair, obviously enjoying his confusion. "Diana Wells was fleeing the country, Counselor. Looks like we stopped her just in the nick of time." She smiled. "How's that for proof of guilt?"

26

Knowing that Zack was tucked away in Sonoma, away from the press and the tons of publicity the murder had generated, had taken a great weight off Diana's shoulders. It allowed her to think with a clear mind without having to fear for his safety.

As promised, the department store had delivered her purchases on time and, although she no longer had the same enthusiasm about putting her house in order, she had gone through the motions anyway.

Kane hadn't approved of her moving back into her house so soon. "That doesn't make sense," he had told her as they drove back from Glen Ellen Elementary earlier in the morning. "Why don't you wait until the men who broke into your house are caught?"

"Because that could take forever. And anyway, I'm afraid if I stay here much longer, the press will find out where I am, and I just as soon not have to explain our relationship to them. For the time being at least."

Rather than stay home and mope around, she had decided to go to work. She knew from past experience that staying busy kept her mind off her problems. She had been right. Being at the restaurant helped, as did Lilly's chatter. The dozen or so reporters who had been waiting for her earlier had been a mild inconvenience, but when Maurice had threatened them with his meat cleaver, they had made a hasty retreat.

"Di, did you hear me?"

Startled, Diana put her knife down, gathered the handful of mushrooms she had just finished chopping and tossed them into a colander. "I'm sorry, Lilly. What did you say?"

"My tickets arrived yesterday."

"What tickets?"

"To Jamaica. It's my Christmas present to Dennis, remember? Seven glorious days in the Caribbean with nothing around us but sun, sand, and surf." She rolled her eyes upward in mock ecstasy. "And sex. Lots of it."

No longer listening, Diana gripped the table.

The tickets!

She had never picked them up. They were still at the airport. With all the things she'd had on her mind, she had forgotten all about them.

"Di, are you all right? You're white as a ghost."

She untied her apron. "I'm fine. I just remembered something I have to do." She tossed the apron on a chair. "I should be back in a couple of hours."

She was reaching for the Cherokee's door handle when a hand, coming from behind her, clamped over her wrist. "Going somewhere, Diana?"

At the sound of Kane's voice, she spun around. There was a strange look in his eyes—a mixture of disappointment and anger. "What ... What are you doing here? I thought you had an appointment with the district attorney."

"I finished early. You didn't answer my question."

Why was he looking at her that way? "I have a few errands to run."

"Let me drive you."

She smiled, trying to keep the panic from her voice. "There's no need for you to do that. I'm just going to see one of my suppliers. I don't know how long I'll be." She hated lying to him, but she had no choice. He would never understand why she had tried to leave the United States. Why she had been willing to forsake everything she cared about, including him.

"Why are you lying to me, Diana?"

"What are you talking about?"

"I'm talking about that phony ski trip to Mount Shasta. And I'm talking about two one-way tickets to Canada that were waiting for you at the airport. Is that where you were going now, Diana? Did you suddenly remember they were still there, and you had to pick them up before someone notified the police?"

The look in his eyes was so chilling, she took a step back. "How did you—"

"The D.A. told me. That's right," he added when he saw the blood drain from her face. "She knows. Kosak called the airport. And guess what he found out?"

Grabbing her arms with both hands, he shook her. "Dammit, Diana, what were you thinking of? That the police wouldn't find out? That because you had been charged, you were safe from further investigation?"

Tears welled up in her eyes, but she said nothing.

"Why didn't you tell me the truth this morning?"

"Because I didn't want to hurt you. And because I knew you wouldn't understand my motives."

"Do you think I'm that insensitive?"

"I just—"

"How could you have made a decision like that without talking to me first?" he continued, staring hard into her eyes. "I thought we meant something to each other. I thought you . . ." He couldn't say it. He felt so damned frustrated, he couldn't bear to find out if she loved him or if he were just a passing fancy.

He felt her rigid body slacken. Her shoulders

sagged as she raised stricken eyes toward him. "You mean everything to me, Kane. If you believe only one thing I've said so far, believe that."

"Then why were you planning to run away without even saying goodbye? Without giving me a chance to help you? To see this thing through with you?"

"I panicked."

"Yet you carried out every phase of your plan with a cool, level head. Right down to your final destination. You even stood in your living room while I talked to you on the answering machine, didn't you? You had to be there if the police arrested you at seven o'clock. And yet you let the phone ring."

"You'll never know how hard it was for me to do that."

His grip on her arms tightened. Afraid to hurt her, he released her, his movement so abrupt she staggered back against the Jeep. From somewhere deep in his mind, the same voice he had heard thousands of times before, when he was married to Jamie, told him to walk away. No woman on earth was worth that kind of pain.

He couldn't do it. He could no more walk away from her now than he could stop breathing.

With a groan, he took her in his arms and crushed her against him.

To avoid turning Travis's funeral into a circus, Margaret had ordered a simple service with only friends and family present. But it was still an ordeal.

Thank God, Randall was here. Not only had he handled the funeral arrangements exactly as she would have, but he had been a continuing source of strength for her and Francesca. Looking at him now as he greeted mourners who had come to pay their respects, no one would have guessed there had been so much bad blood between him and Travis.

After the services the small gathering had driven to Seacliff where Travis was laid to rest next to his father, in the family mausoleum overlooking the Pacific Ocean.

As Margaret led the way back to the house where Margie had prepared a light buffet, Kane saw Dunbar Dewitt. She stood by one of the French windows, looking out toward the ocean. She was a tall, slender, moderately attractive young woman with light brown hair tucked under a small black hat, and soft brown eyes.

Although Kane had met her a year ago when he had attended one of her many fund-raisers, this was the first opportunity he'd had to talk to her since her engagement to Travis.

He went to her as soon as he was able to get away from Margaret and Francesca. "Hello, Dunbar."

Her eyes, red from crying, were full of resentment as she turned to him. "How dare you even show your face in this house?" she asked in a trembling voice. "And how dare you do this to Travis?"

"If you're referring to me defending Diana Wells—"

"Don't you see what you're doing to this family by taking that woman's side? To Margaret?"

"Diana Wells didn't kill Travis, Dunbar. And even if she did, she's entitled to a defense."

"Then let someone else defend her."

"You know I can't do that."

"Why? Because you're sleeping with her?"

He ignored the sarcastic remark, which sounded more like something Travis would have said. "Because I believe I'm the best man for the job."

"What makes you so qualified?"

"I knew Travis, knew how he thought, the kind of man he was."

"The kind of man he was," she repeated. "What does that mean?"

"He had enemies. One of them decided to take his grudge one step too far."

"Yes." Her eyes flashed. "And she was behind bars before you bailed her out."

"Or . . . the real killer is still at large." When she didn't answer, he added, "Wouldn't you like to see that person apprehended, Dunbar? And brought to justice?"

She started to move away, but he stopped her. He hadn't planned to question her until next week, but since the opportunity had presented itself, now was as good a time as any. "Did he confide in you about any of the people he was seeing? Things he was doing?"

She lifted a fine, aristocratic eyebrow. "You mean you expect *me* to help you clear Travis's murderer?" Before he could answer, she shook her head. "Forget it, Kane. As far as I'm concerned, the killer's been caught. And the sooner she's convicted and put away, the safer I'll feel."

Then, without another word, she pushed past him and walked away.

Kane watched her go, cursing under his breath. He should have waited until her grief had eased off before approaching her. The problem was, time wasn't a luxury he could afford. The preliminary hearing was only a few days away, and he was no closer to the truth than he'd been the day Travis was killed.

"Hello, Counselor."

Kane turned around. Sergeant Kosak, who had come to the funeral as an observer, stood in front of him. Dressed in a dark suit, he almost looked like one of the mourners. The only thing that differentiated him from all the others was his watchful gaze as it swept across the room. "What's up, Sergeant?"

The policeman took a roll of Tums from his pocket and popped one into his mouth. "My ulcer is acting up, my cat is missing, and funerals give me the willies. Besides that, I'm fine." He slanted him an amused glance. "But that's not what you wanted to hear, is it?"

Kane laughed. He liked Kosak. He had worked with him on a couple of murder cases, and knew him to be a tough and thorough investigator. The fact that he was here confirmed that. "I'm sorry about the ulcer. And I hope you find your cat. But you're right. I was hoping to hear something more from you. Like you found another suspect."

Kosak's gaze followed Francesca as she accompanied an elderly couple to the door. "Can't say that I have." He turned toward Kane again. "But if it's any consolation, you're free to search Travis Lindford's penthouse. We're done in there." Before Kane could thank him, he nodded. "Just let me know if you find anything we missed, okay?"

"You bet." He thought of telling him about the Desert Storm reunion at the hotel and the man Diana had bumped into on her way to the penthouse, then thought better of it. Francesca had contacted the officer in charge of the gathering and asked if she could borrow the photographs that had been displayed in the lobby and he had agreed. Most of them were snapshots, men in fatigues whose features were hidden by hats and dark sunglasses. But until Diana had had a chance to look at them, it was best to keep the details of his investigation to himself.

Ten minutes later, Kane was back in his car, heading east toward the Lindford Hotel.

Because Travis's penthouse seemed like the most

likely place to begin his search, that's where Kane went first. Except for the absence of the Aubusson rug, which had been sent to the cleaner, and the bookend, which had been taken as evidence, the place looked the same as the last time Kane saw it—luxurious and cold. Even when Travis had lived here, the penthouse had looked more like a museum than someone's home.

His mind focused on the task ahead, he started his search in the bedroom, going through Travis's closet, the wall-to-wall bookcase, and the antique ormulu desk by the window. He found nothing. Even the two nightstands produced nothing more than a racing form, a handful of chips left over from a recent jaunt to Las Vegas, a copy of Robert Ludlum's latest paperback thriller, and a half dozen condoms.

Back in the living room Kane looked around. The two pieces of furniture that dominated the room were a curio cabinet filled with rare jade figurines, and another desk, similar to the one in the bedroom.

The single desk drawer was locked, and after a few attempts, Kane found the appropriate key from the ring Margaret had given him, and opened it. The contents revealed a small black address book with the names and phone numbers of more than a dozen women, and a black Filofax that had never been used. He put the address book in his pocket.

In the back of the drawer were a checkbook, deposit slips, bank statements, and a letter from Travis's stockbroker. It was dated November 29, and signed Earl J. Morris.

"Dear Travis," Kane read. "Per our telephone conversation of November 26, enclosed is a copy of your sale order for twenty-one hundred shares of your ITT stock for a total price of $202,125.

As requested, $200,000 in cash will be delivered to

you on Friday, December 3. Let me know if I can be of further help. Sincerely, Earl.''

Kane let out a thin whistle. Two hundred thousand dollars. That was a lot of pocket money for a man who almost never used cash.

Opening Travis's checkbook, he flipped through it, checking each entry until he was confronted with another puzzle. On November 27, Travis had withdrawn $50,000 from his account. In the description column, he had simply written "cash."

Why would Travis need two hundred and fifty thousand dollars in cash?

Blackmail?

Kane was thoughtful for a moment as he looked around for a clue. He hadn't found the fifty thousand dollars, which meant it had been paid out to someone, provided the blackmail theory was correct. As for the two hundred thousand that would have been delivered this past Friday, Earl Morris had probably canceled the arrangement after learning of Travis's death.

Making a mental note to talk to Travis's stockbroker, Kane let himself out of the penthouse and headed for Travis's office. He didn't think he would find the answer to the puzzle there, but it was worth a try.

Travis's office, which had been Charles's before that, was a large, brightly lit room furnished with the same expensive antiques Travis had always favored.

A quick inspection of the desk revealed nothing of interest, and neither did the files in the large ebony cabinet.

A connecting door led to another room that Kane recognized as Travis's former office, the one he had occupied until his father's death two years before. It had been transformed into an attractive sitting room, complete with a leather sofa and chairs, a bookcase crammed with old books, and a massive Spanish credenza that had belonged to Charles.

The credenza was locked, and it took Kane a few moments to locate the right key. When he was finally able to unlock the heavy carved door, he saw that the interior was comprised of three drawers, each filled with more files, some dating back twenty years.

He was about to close the last drawer when his fingers brushed against something cold and hard. Lowering his head, he saw what looked like a gray metal box tucked behind the last file. When he tried to pull the box out, it wouldn't budge.

Quickly, he removed the files, stacking them on the floor, pulled out the drawer, and set it on the coffee table. The box—a small safe, actually—was bolted down and secured with a combination lock.

"Damn."

For the next fifteen minutes Kane tried every combination he could think of, starting with Travis's birthday, Travis's high school and college graduations, his parents' anniversary.

It was no use. Short of blowing up the damn thing, it wasn't going to open.

Without getting up from his sitting position on the floor, he reached for the telephone on the end table. "How good are you at opening safes?" he asked when his private investigator answered.

"No good at all. But I know someone who is."

"Is he in or out of prison?"

Ron laughed. "Out. And he'd like to keep it that way."

"Don't worry. This is legit. How fast can you get hold of him?"

"I have no idea. Where are you?"

"Travis's office at the Lindford." He gave him the

phone number. "And tell your friend I'll make it worth his while.

As soon as he hung up, Kane went to the bank, withdrew a thousand dollars, and returned to Travis's office.

The reformed safecracker, who answered to the nickname of Picks, showed up an hour later, an eager expression on his face. "Show me the way," he said with an ear-to-ear grin as he cracked long, slender fingers.

Within ten minutes, Picks had the safe open. Kane gave him the thousand dollars and closed the door behind him before going back to the safe.

To his disappointment, it contained nothing other than a white business card with the words "Saar International Bank" inscribed on one side. Below the Swiss address and phone number, was the name of the bank's vice-president, Hantz Fielder. Kane turned the card over. A twelve digit number was handwritten on the blank side.

"I'll be damned."

A Swiss bank account. A *numbered* account, which indicated Travis had requested anonymity and confidentiality. Although numbered Swiss accounts were no longer limited to tax evaders, many still used the system for that exact reason. Knowing Travis as he did, Kane had no doubt as to his own motive.

The question was, how much money had he siphoned into the account? And was Margaret aware her son was cheating the government?

Probably not. But someone else could have known about it. And blackmailed him in exchange for his or her silence.

Dunbar? Impossible. The young woman's grief was too genuine, and his conversation with her had cleared any doubt he may have had about her loyalty to Travis.

A former girlfriend then? Someone angry at the prospect of losing him? That made more sense, but Travis wouldn't be stupid enough to share such dangerous information with a passing fling.

Francesca? As distasteful as that possibility seemed, it was a consideration. With Travis out of the way, her lifelong dream of someday owning the hotel would have been realized. She could have tried to blackmail him into giving up ownership of the hotel in her favor.

But was she capable of murder?

Shaking his head, Kane tucked Mr. Fielder's business card in his wallet and closed the safe. Within moments he had everything back in place and was gnawing at his bottom lip in concentration.

One of the many friends he had left behind in New York worked for Chase Manhattan, in the international division. He would give him a call and see if he could find out anything about that Swiss account.

Picking up the phone again, he called Jackie at the office and asked her to look up the number of Dan Chancellor.

"How are you, you old shyster?" Dan said with his usual good humor when his secretary put Kane through. "Still behaving yourself?"

Kane laughed. "It's easy when I don't have someone like you leading me astray."

After a few more pleasantries, Kane told him what he needed to know.

"I'll see what I can do," Dan said after Kane was finished. "But you have to understand that those Swiss bankers are very tight-lipped. One of their greatest selling points is the privacy they offer their clients. Few of them, if any, are willing to breach that vow.

The fact that Saar Bank is a private bank makes it even more difficult. Are you in a hurry?"

"Yes. I'm defending a murder case and the information could be vital."

"I'll do my best, Kane. In the meantime, you may want to warn Margaret Lindford. Tax evasion is a serious charge. Even if she wasn't involved in the fraud, she could be affected by the outcome. There isn't much she can do until we find out for sure, but she should be made aware of the situation."

"I'll talk to her. Thanks, Dan. And give my love to Betty."

27

Although Margaret's face was pale and drawn, she was in control of her emotions when Kane returned to Seacliff that evening.

The drawing room, which had been full of mourners a few hours earlier, was now quiet and empty, except for Margaret. A bright, cheery fire crackled in the fireplace, contrasting sharply with the somber mood that still prevailed throughout the house.

Margaret motioned him to a chair. "I didn't expect to see you again so soon." She raised an eyebrow. "Did you find what you were looking for?"

"I found something. Whether it has anything to do with the murder or not is still in question."

He told her about the letter from the stockbroker, the fifty thousand dollars Travis had withdrawn from the bank, and the business card he had found in the hidden safe. "I think Travis may have been blackmailed, Margaret. I think someone found out he was putting money away in Switzerland, and confronted him with it."

Under the light makeup, Margaret's cheeks turned white. Her hands went to her throat. "Dear God." Her hands were trembling when she finally lowered them back to her lap. "Are you sure that's what he was doing?"

"No. But I have a friend in New York who will confirm it within a couple of days." He studied her face. "I take it you didn't know."

She looked away. "No." Then, meeting his gaze at last, she added, "You must stop this investigation at once."

Kane stiffened. "I can't. It could help solve Travis's murder, clear Diana."

"To hell with Diana! What about us? Do you realize the scandal this family will have to face if the press gets hold of this story?" Her voice cracked. "Our name would be tarnished forever."

Kane drew away from her, his eyes flashing in anger. "For God's sake, Margaret, we're talking about a woman's life here. And you're worried about your name being tarnished?"

Kane's outburst took her aback. In all the years she had known him, he had never talked to her in that tone of voice. It's that woman, she thought, watching him as his anger hung between them like an invisible wall. He's in love with her. And love, as she well knew, was a powerful emotion, capable of transforming even the most loyal of men into an enemy. She didn't want that. Not with Kane.

"I'm sorry if I sounded callous. This . . . discovery of yours took me by surprise. Of course you must do what you have to." She waited for some of the anger to fade from his eyes before continuing. "How will you be able to prove that Travis was defrauding the government? I thought Swiss bankers were sworn to secrecy about such matters?"

"If there is proof of fraud, they'll have to cooperate." His voice softened. "I wasn't going to tell you until I was absolutely sure, but my friend thought you should know, should be prepared."

After Kane left, Margaret stood up and walked slowly over to the fireplace. Above the heavy oak mantel hung a portrait of Charles taken on his sixtieth birthday. No longer trying to conceal her fear or hold back her tears, she gazed into the smiling brown eyes.

"Oh, Charles," she whispered as a sob rose to her throat. "What are we going to do now?"

Because Margaret and Francesca were the only beneficiaries of a will Travis had written shortly after his father's death, the two women were the only ones present in the law offices of Burgess and Mills, a law firm in San Francisco's financial district.

Oscar Mills, who had handled Charles and Margaret's legal matters for more than thirty years, read the document, which held no surprises. Travis had left everything to his mother, with the exception of his television station, which he felt Francesca would be better equipped to run.

"KYBC has been losing money for years," Oscar Mills told her as he removed his glasses. "Travis was planning to revamp it, but frankly, I'm not sure that's a good idea, considering what it would cost. If you want to sell the station, Francesca, I'll be glad to take care of it for you."

Francesca shook her head. "I don't know what I want to do yet, Oscar. Let me think about it for a while. I'll let you know what I've decided in a few days."

Kane couldn't remember a more frustrating case. Logically, Diana was the ideal suspect. She had motive and opportunity. And she had been caught fleeing the country. Or about to. She had lied to the police and she had lied to him. She also had a quick temper, a detail the prosecution would be sure to bring up at the pretrial hearing, unless Diana kept that flaw well concealed.

So far, he was the only one who believed Diana was innocent. The problem was, he couldn't come up with any other suspects. The blackmail theory was a hopeful one, but so far Dan Chancellor, although he was making progress, hadn't found out anything. The chance that he would uncover some sort of evidence by the time the hearing began on Wednesday morning was getting smaller by the hour.

Kane's interrogation of Wayne, the maintenance man who had been changing a bulb on the landing when Margaret had discovered the body, hadn't helped. Except for Margaret, Wayne hadn't seen anyone. Questioning of Travis's stockbroker, Francesca, and the chief of security Travis had fired two years ago, had produced nothing other than what he already knew. As for the men who had attended the Desert Storm reunion last week, Diana hadn't been able to recognize anyone in the snapshots Francesca had provided.

What would a military man, or ex-military man, want with Travis anyway?

Kane tipped his chair back and allowed his mind to follow another trend of thought. If he looked at motives, the only other person who had a valid one, other than Diana, was still Francesca.

And maybe Randall. It was perfectly conceivable that after taking his brother-in-law's put-downs for more than three years, he had finally had enough.

But unlike Diana, no one had ever seen Randall lose his temper. Or even raise his voice.

His eyes fixed on the ceiling fan, Kane continued to think of Randall. The change in him still baffled him, although he didn't know why. What could be more natural in time of tragedy than a family member looking over the rest of the family, taking charge, comforting them? Maybe he should talk to Randall, catch him off-guard, try to guess what was beneath that friendly, boy-next-door exterior.

On impulse, he picked up the phone and dialed Francesca's apartment. A maid answered. "This is Kane Sanders," he said. "May I speak to Mr. Atkins please?"

Randall's voice was curt when he came to the phone. "What can I do for you, Kane?"

"I wonder if I could stop by for a few minutes?"

Kane thought he heard a sigh of exasperation. "What for?"

"I need to ask you a few questions about Travis's murder. It won't take long."

"I'm afraid you're going to have to wait, Kane. Travis's death set me back in my work, and I'm trying to make up for lost time."

"How about tomorrow evening?"

"I want to spend the next few evenings with Francesca and Margaret. I'm sure you understand."

"Of course." Scaring him off wouldn't accomplish anything. "When will you have some spare time?"

"Oh . . ." There was a pause. "What about the latter part of next week? Thursday? Or Friday?"

It would have to do. "Fine. I'll call you back after I find out if the preliminary hearing has to go into a second day."

He was probably wasting his time, Kane thought as he hung up. But the way he was progressing, he couldn't afford to overlook even the smallest possibility.

The last three days before the hearing were devoted entirely to the rehearsal of Diana's court testimony.

Kane was relentless. He made her repeat her story so many times, she could recite it from memory. Playing the part of the defense attorney as well as the prosecutor, he put her through a merciless drill that left her exhausted and sometime angry.

Together they went over the events of December second. As he listened to the testimony she would be giving in court, he instructed her to remove words like furious, rage, and hate from her speech and replace them with milder ones.

Pacing her living room, he told her how to act on the witness stand, reminding her to always look the D.A., and the judge, in the eye, not to cross and uncross her hands, not to change the tone of her voice or express fear or panic in any way.

"No matter what the prosecutor accuses you of, don't look afraid. Concerned, yes. Afraid no. Remember that her role is to confuse you, to make you look nervous. And guilty."

And when they were done, he would start all over again.

Once, when the rehearsal had been so real and his cross-examination so harsh, she had lashed out at him. He had lashed right back.

"Don't *ever* do that on the witness stand," he had warned, pointing his finger at her. "There is no room for anger in a courtroom. Angry people lose control."

Sometimes he stayed over, and while she slept, he stayed up, studying the evidence against her, poring over autopsy and police reports, preparing his case as carefully and thoroughly as if his own life were on the line.

In the middle of the night, she would get out of bed, walk downstairs, and wrap her arms around his broad shoulders. "Come on, Kane. It's time to go to bed."

Once in a while he would give in. But most of the time he would send her back to bed without him. He should have been exhausted, irritable, and discouraged that his investigation was leading him nowhere. But if he was, he wouldn't let her see it. And he wouldn't let her lose hope.

They spent the weekend before the hearing in Glen Ellen with Beckie and Zack.

It had been a wonderful two days, filled with long walks, pleasant conversation, and even laughter. Now, with dusk, an unexpected chill had fallen over the valley, turning the air cold and wintry. The scent of crushed grapes had been replaced by that of burning firewood and roasted chestnuts, which Thelma served every night in a big earthenware bowl.

"Mel let me help in the winery this morning," Zack told Diana while Thelma cleared the dishes from the dining-room table. Proudly, he pulled a neatly folded roll of one-dollar bills from his pocket. "Look how much money I made. Fifteen dollars."

Diana smiled as she and Beckie exchanged an amused look. "Does that mean you're thinking about becoming a winemaker instead of an astronaut?"

He thought about the question for a moment, then, grinning, he shook his head. "Nah. I'd still rather be an astronaut."

Diana was glad to see how well he had adapted to his new surroundings, although occasionally, she caught him watching her, a worried expression in his blue eyes.

"What's bothering you, darling?" she asked him as Kane loaded their suitcases into the BMW later that night.

He came to sit at her feet, folding his legs, lotus style. "I'm scared about tomorrow, about what the judge will do to you."

The anxiety she heard in his voice tore her heart. "The worst he can do is decide there should be a trial," she said in a voice she hoped sounded reassuring. "But even if he does, that doesn't mean a jury will find me guilty."

"Kane told me he was going to find who really killed Travis."

She smiled. "That's right."

"You think he can do it?"

"Yes." She squeezed his hand. "If anybody can do it, it's Kane."

His head bowed, Zack nodded. "I wish everything was like it used to be. I wish we were back in our own house, doing all the things we used to do."

She hugged him. Holding back tears had never been so difficult. "We will, darling. I promise we'll have our life back."

A few moments later, when it was time for her and Kane to go, Zack walked with her to the car, his hand wrapped tightly around hers. His eyes were brighter than usual as he tried desperately to be brave.

As she kissed him goodbye, he put something in her hands.

"What's that?"

"The lucky coin I found behind the winery on Thanksgiving. I want you to have it," he whispered. "For luck."

28

A mob of reporters was waiting outside the courthouse when Kane pulled his car in front of the building on Monday morning. He and Jackie got out quickly, each taking a position at Diana's side as they escorted her up the stairs.

Immediately, more than a half-dozen microphones were pushed in front of her face.

"Miss Wells, do you feel confident there won't be a trial?"

"Will you change your plea if you're bound over for trial?"

"Did you kill Travis Lindford?"

As cameras flashed and questions were hurled at her, Diana kept walking. Following Kane's instruction, she looked straight ahead and didn't acknowledge the reporters' questions, not even with the perfunctory "no comment."

Hours of rehearsing had finally produced the desired results. On the outside, she appeared calm and poised. Inside, however, her stomach churned with doubt and apprehension. Would the judge believe her? Would the nightmare finally be over?

The courtroom was jammed. Holding her arm, Kane led her toward the defense table. As she walked, she was aware of countless eyes watching her, of people whispering to each other, some pointing.

She ignored them all. Except one. As she passed the second row and saw Margaret Lindford, she turned her head and met her cold blue stare.

Her legs turned rubbery. If it hadn't be for Kane's firm grip, she would have stumbled.

"Don't look at her," he whispered in her ear. "Don't look at anyone but Jackie and me."

As she took her seat, she felt a hand press her shoulder. "Di."

The gentle, familiar voice brought a surge of last-minute courage. She turned to smile at Kat and Mitch, who sat right behind her.

"All rise!"

At the bailiff's command, the courtroom rose to its feet, and the judge, a skinny, rather severe-looking man with wispy gray hair and a goatee, strode in and took his place behind the bench. Although less intimidating, the district attorney was nonetheless impressive. Attractive and impeccably dressed, Julie Archer projected a picture of competence and self-confidence. In a voice that was feminine yet strong, she introduced each piece of evidence, autopsy, fingerprints, the murder weapon, and police photographs.

One by one, experts in their fields took the stand—the uniformed officer who had been the first at the scene of the crime, Sergeant Kosak, who had arrived shortly afterward, and the medical examiner.

Kane's hand covered hers. "This is just routine, Diana. Don't worry about it."

The next person the prosecutor called as her witness was Diana's neighbor from across the street. A diminutive woman in her seventies, Mrs. Carmichael wore a prim gray suit and had had her white hair done for the occasion.

At the D.A.'s request to state what she had witnessed outside Diana's house on the afternoon of November thirtieth, the older woman, feeling important, squared her shoulders.

"I had just come down to get my mail when Miss Wells and her friend—that's her over there," she added, pointing at Kat, "pulled up behind a fancy red car parked in front of Miss Wells's house. A man was outside the car, waiting for them."

"And who was that man, Mrs. Carmichael?"

"Travis Lindford. I recognized him right away because his pictures had been in the papers and on television so many times over the last few weeks."

"What happened when Miss Wells came out of her car?"

"She and Mr. Lindford started arguing right away. I couldn't clearly hear what they were saying at first, but it was plain they were both very angry. Especially Miss Wells."

Julie Archer smiled encouragingly. "Do you remember what Miss Wells said to him just before she went into her house?"

"Oh, indeed, I do." She pulled herself erect. "She said to him: 'You'll never have my son. I'll kill you first.'"

A murmur arose from the courtroom.

"Objection, your honor," Kane said, rising to his feet. "The witness has already testified she couldn't clearly hear what was being said."

"My witness can explain how she was able to hear those words, your honor."

"Very well." The judge inclined his head toward Mrs. Carmichael. "Go ahead."

"I had just turned up my hearing aid so I could hear better," Mrs. Carmichael said without the least bit of embarrassment. "But even if I hadn't, I would have heard her anyway, because she was talking very loudly."

"Is there any doubt in your mind that Miss Wells meant those words?"

"None whatsoever. I've never seen anyone so angry."

Before Kane could object, Julie Archer flashed the judge a smile. "No more questions, your honor."

The judge looked at Kane. "Do you wish to redirect, Mr. Sanders?"

"Yes." Kane stood up, paced the floor for a moment, appearing to be lost in thought, then he came back to stand by the defense table. "Mrs. Carmichael," he said in a voice level that was several degrees above normal. "Have you ever experienced problems with your hearing aid? Such as a malfunction, fading out, or shutting off altogether?"

Frowning, Mrs. Carmichael leaned forward, touching her ear. "What did you say?"

"Didn't you hear me?" he said, moving closer to her.

"Not very well. You were too far."

Another murmur floated across the courtroom. "I was twenty feet away, Mrs. Carmichael. The distance between Miss Wells's driveway and your mailbox is almost twice the distance. How do you explain that you could hear her and not hear me?"

"She was shouting. That's how I can explain it."

Kane smiled. "No more questions, your honor."

The next person to be called was Kat, who walked toward the stand briskly, waited to be sworn in, then sat down.

Julie Archer smiled at Kat. Kat smiled back. "You don't wear a hearing aid, do you, Mrs. Parker?"

"No, I don't."

"Then you must have heard what Miss Wells said to Travis Lindford just before the two of you went inside."

Kat's smile was apologetic. "I'm afraid they were just words to me. You see," she added, turning toward the judge. "Travis Lindford was very close to losing control and at that moment I was concerned about only one thing—getting Diana away from him." She turned back to the district attorney. "So if you ask me, where they arguing? The answer is yes. But as to the exact words that were exchanged ..." She shrugged helplessly. "I couldn't tell you what they were."

If her reply upset the D.A., she didn't show it. "Did Diana Wells call you on the evening of December second?"

"Yes."

"For what reason?"

"She wanted to pick up her son, who was staying with my husband and me at the time."

"Why did she want to do that?"

"She was taking him on a ski trip."

"Wasn't that a bit unusual for her to leave so suddenly?"

"Objection, your honor," Kane said. "Calls for conclusion on the part of the witness."

"Sustained."

Archer paced slowly in front of Kat, forcing her gaze to follow her. "Where did she tell you she was going?"

"Mount Shasta."

"But she lied to you, didn't she? According to Sergeant Kosak's testimony, and the airline tickets he introduced as evidence, Miss Wells and her son were on their way to Canada." She paused. "Now why would she do that, Mrs. Parker? Why would she lie to her best friend?"

Kat smiled sweetly. "Are you asking for a conclusion on my part?"

Laughter rippled through the courtroom. A few moments later, when the prosecutor returned to her seat, she was clearly frustrated.

Kane, knowing Kat was on his side, was much more relaxed. "How long have you known Diana Wells, Mrs. Parker?"

"Fifteen years. Diana and I met when we were both college freshmen."

"Have you ever known her to be violent? To strike anyone?"

"Never."

"Do you believe her capable of murder?"

"Absolutely not. Diana wouldn't hurt a fly, and her regard for human life is higher than that of anyone I know. To imply that she could commit a crime, any crime, much less a murder, is totally ludicrous."

By the time the district attorney had jumped to her feet to object, Kane was finished.

When court recessed for the lunch hour, Diana followed Kane and Jackie into a private room, but was unable to eat or drink anything. Instead, she walked over to the window and gazed at the sunny courtyard already filled with federal employees on their lunch break.

Kane came up behind her and gripped her shoulders. "Hang in there, baby. Just a little while longer."

When court reconvened at two o'clock and Kane called Diana to the stand, she rose, aware that in spite of the hours of rehearsing, she was doing everything wrong. Her back was too stiff, her head held too high, her self-confidence level at near zero.

Kane waited until she was sworn in before approaching the witness box. "Miss Wells, did you telephone Mr. Lindford on the morning of December first?"

"Yes."

"For what reason?"

"I wanted to ask him to drop the custody suit he had filed against me."

"Did you tell him that over the phone?"

"No. But I'm certain he knew the reason for my call. The hearing was only five days away."

"And did he agree to see you?"

"Yes. He said he could see me the following afternoon at four-thirty."

"Did you go there feeling optimistic?"

"Hopeful would be a better word."

"Did you fear the meeting might turn violent?"

"No. I had no reason to think that."

"Did you think that if he turned you down, you might kill him?"

"Of course not. I could never kill anyone."

"Tell us what happened when you arrived at Travis Lindford's penthouse on December second."

A hush of expectation fell over the courtroom. Diana's palms grew damp, but she resisted the impulse to rub them against her skirt. "I arrived there at four-thirty, rang the bell—twice. But there was no answer, so I knocked, waited, and then knocked again. When there was still no answer, I tried the knob. The door was unlocked, so I went in."

"And then what?"

"I called Travis's name and walked into the living room. And that's when I saw him. I mean ... his body."

"Would you describe what you saw, Miss Wells?"

She looked at her hands, folded on her lap. The spectators seemed to have vanished. All she saw now was Travis's body. The image was so vivid that her heart began to race. "Travis lay on the rug, in a pool of blood. His eyes were open."

"What did you think had happened?"

"Nothing at first. I mean . . . I couldn't think. I just stood there, staring at him. I couldn't believe what I was seeing. It all seemed so unreal."

"Did you realize he was dead?"

She nodded. "I ran to him and searched for a pulse. There wasn't any."

"Did you realize he had been murdered?"

"I don't know. Maybe . . . in my subconscious. And then I saw the bookend lying next to him. There was a smear of blood on the base. I realized then someone must have . . . hit him with it."

"Then what did you do?"

She closed her eyes. How many times had she relived that moment, wished she could take it back? "I did something very stupid. I picked up the bookend. I don't know how long I held it. All I remember is dropping it, and then . . ." She faltered, looked down at her hands again. They were trembling.

"And then what, Miss Wells?"

"I panicked and ran." She turned toward the judge, who was watching her, his face unreadable. "I know it was wrong. I wasn't thinking clearly. And I was scared. But I didn't kill him, your honor. I swear I didn't."

"I have no more questions, your honor."

The district attorney was less gentle.

"How did you feel about Mr. Lindford, Miss Wells?"

"I don't understand—"

"Didn't you have every reason to hate him?"

"I resented what he was trying to do. But I didn't hate—"

"Oh come now, Miss Wells. Here was a man who threatened to take your dearest possession—your child. And you only *resented* him?"

"Yes."

"Yet, less than forty-eight hours earlier, you had threatened to kill him."

In spite of Kane's clever maneuver with Mrs. Carmichael and Kat's convenient loss of memory, she had known Julie Archer would eventually come around to that question. "Those were only words spoken in frustration. I never meant them."

"Frustration. Resentment. Those are mild words considering what you had at stake."

Remembering Kane's warning not to answer anything that wasn't a direct question, Diana remained silent.

"Isn't it true that you were very angry that afternoon, Miss Wells? And even more angry when Travis Lindford turned down your offer on December second?"

"No! I never had a chance to even talk to him."

Archer didn't seem to have heard her. "You realized you could lose your child. The two of you began to argue. You saw the bookend, lost control—"

Kane was already on his feet, but Diana was quicker. She sprung from her seat, every fiber of her being shaking with indignation. Her fist hit the railing. "That's not how it happened! I told you Travis was already dead when I got there. Why won't you believe me?"

As the gavel came down and the judge instructed Diana to sit down, pandemonium broke out in the courtroom. Reporters were already scrambling from their seats. It took a full minute for the judge to restore order.

When at last the silence returned, Julie Archer was smiling. "You have quite a temper, don't you, Miss Wells?" Then, because she hadn't expected an answer, she gave a short bow of her head. "I'm finished, your honor."

Diana walked stiffly back to her chair and bumped into the defense table, like a drunken woman. Kane held her as she sat down again. "I was awful. I'm sorry. I . . ."

"Shhhh. You were fine."

Through a fog, she heard the judge's voice. "On the basis of the evidence heard in this court, the defendant will be bound over for trial. Trial date May 1, 1994."

29

Diana had no recollection of the drive home from the courthouse. Like an obedient child, she allowed Kane to escort her back to the car, up her driveway, and into her living room.

She was aware of the fading sunlight, of the phone ringing, of Kane pressing a glass into her hand. "What . . . ?"

"Scotch. Drink it." He sat next to her on the sofa, waited until she had taken a sip. "I'm sorry."

"It's not your fault. You did all you could." She took another sip of scotch, then put the glass down. "I'm the one who ruined everything by doing exactly what you warned me not to do. I lost my temper."

"She pushed you pretty hard." He took her hands in his. "I want you to forget about today. It's behind us now. We'll concentrate on the trial."

"What can you do that you haven't done already?"

"Plenty." He told her about the Swiss bank account, his theory that Travis may have been blackmailed. "It's a small lead, but a lead just the same."

"But if Travis had intended to pay off the blackmailer, why would the blackmailer want to kill him?"

"That's what I have to find out."

When she looked at him again, her eyes were wide and weary. The strain of the last few days was beginning to take its toll on her. "In the event the trial

doesn't . . . turn out the way we hope, if I should have
to go to—''

"You won't." He cupped her face between his
hands and although his touch was tender, his voice
had turned rough. "I'll move heaven and earth if I
have to, but I'll find the killer. All I ask is that you
don't lose faith in me."

"I'll never lose faith in you, Kane." Tears burned
her eyes as she pulled his mouth down to hers. All at
once the tension and fear of the last few days was
released in that one fiery kiss. Hunger and need
poured out of her as she pushed his jacket off his
shoulders and tugged at his shirt, nipping at his bottom lip.

Matching her frenzy, Kane undressed her quickly,
dragging her skirt over her hips. It wasn't the way he
had intended to make love to her, but he understood
the need, the despair and the passion as they blended
into one.

Responding to it, he leaned into her and sank his
fingers into her hair. His kiss was hard, his tongue
thrusting, demanding. He had been prepared to offer
tenderness and comfort, but she wouldn't let him.

"Make love to me, Kane."

The first rays of sunset flooded the room as he entered her. Her face was flushed, her breath hot on his
skin, her eyes bright with a light he had never seen
before. As she raised her hips, he pushed deeper, gri-
macing at the excruciating pleasure.

Diana closed her eyes, surrendering to the outpour
of sensations, to the heat, to the mindlessness of hot,
frantic sex. She climaxed quickly, as she knew she
would. When the orgasm struck, she held his face between her hands and fastened her mouth to his. "I
love you. God, how I love you."

His breath ragged, he laid his head on her breast

and closed his eyes. That's all he had ever wanted to hear.

"How are you, Kane?"

Although Kane's visit filled him with a new anxiety, Randall greeted the lawyer with a smile and a firm handshake before leading him into the living room. "Can I get you anything? Coffee? Soda? Something stronger?"

"Nothing thanks." Kane watched as Randall walked over to the bar and opened a bottle of mineral water. The self-confidence he had glimpsed after Travis's death was still there. If anything, he looked even more relaxed. "I assume Francesca told you I've been questioning the hotel staff."

"She told me you were looking for clues." He turned around, his expression open.

"I'm also checking alibis."

Uneasiness crept into Randall's stomach. "Alibis?"

"It's the easiest way I know to eliminate suspects."

"Am *I* a suspect?"

Kane smiled. "At this point, everybody is a suspect." Randall brought the bottle to his lips and took a sip. He knew he didn't have to answer Kane's questions. But if he didn't, he would look suspicious. "What do you want to know?"

"Where were you between four and five p.m. on December second?"

"Right here. Working. Which is what I do every day."

"Can anyone corroborate that? A maid? A delivery person?"

"I'm afraid not. We have a cleaning lady who comes in daily, but she leaves at three."

"How did you feel when you found out Travis was dead?"

Randall shrugged. "It's no secret Travis and I didn't get along. But if you're asking am I happy that he's dead, the answer is no. I would have done anything to spare Francesca and Margaret the pain they're going through right now. Even if that meant putting up with Travis's insufferable attitude for the next four decades."

Years in the courtroom, questioning nervous witnesses, had taught Kane how to detect the slightest rise in tension. He felt it now, a subtle change in the atmosphere, a flicker of the eye, a darting of the tongue over dry lips. "You've never wished him dead?"

"Certainly not. Dear God, Kane, what do you take me for?"

"A mere mortal. And a man in love."

"What does that have to do with anything?"

"Weren't you upset at the thought that Travis would soon be taking control of the hotel? That your wife would be working under him, when everybody knew she was so much more qualified than he was to be chairman?"

"Of course, I was upset. But does that make me a murderer?"

Kane shook his head. "I guess not." He stood up. "One more question. Do you have any idea who would want to kill Travis?"

"The police have already asked me that, and I'm afraid the answer is still no. I'd like to help you, Kane, but the truth is Travis and I just didn't confide in each other, as you well know. I have no idea who his friends were—or his enemies for that matter." He took another unhurried sip. "Sorry."

Whatever nervousness Randall had experienced a moment before was gone. Had it been his imagination? Kane wondered. Or was Randall better at covering up his feelings than he realized? Either way, his questioning was finished—for now.

He stood up. "Thanks for your cooperation, Randall. If you think of anything that might be important, give me a call. You know where to reach me."

"Sure thing."

Randall closed the door and went back into the living room. For all his brilliance, Kane Sanders didn't have an ounce of proof to substantiate whatever suspicions he may have. He was just a desperate man grasping at straws.

Tilting the bottle to his mouth, he drank thirstily. There was nothing for him to be concerned about as long as he kept a firm grip on his nerves. Especially in front of Kane Sanders.

Standing in the bright morning sunlight that poured through his studio windows, Randall took a step back to look at his finished work.

Through a clever mix of colors, mostly rose, gold, and brown hues, he had achieved the perfect ochre for his rendering of *La Purisima Concepcion*, one of the many California missions Father Junipero Serra had founded in the late 1700s.

Rather than show the Lompoc mission as Californians knew it now, he had painted it as it had been two centuries ago, with herds of livestock roaming in the fields, and Indians and padres living in happy harmony.

A few days ago, halfway through the painting, he had realized that something extraordinary was happening. This was clearly the best work he'd ever done. Afraid to trust his judgment, he had asked Anthony Morales, the owner of the art gallery where his paintings were held on consignment, to come and take a look.

Anthony, a small, wiry man with an eye for talent, had reacted with an enthusiasm that had surpassed Randall's wildest expectations.

"Oh, my," the gallery owner had said, his dark Latin eyes roaming over the canvas. "This is excellent work, Randall. It has energy, power; and with those colors, you have created the perfect early California atmosphere."

Then, his Salvador Dali mustache quivering with excitement, he had added those magic words Randall had waited all his life to hear. "We must do a one-man show. In fact we'll do two of them, one in February, provided you can deliver ten more similar paintings. And another one in the fall. We'll call the collection Early California Missions." He had grasped Randall's hand in an ironlike handshake. "This is going to make you a star, my boy. A star."

Randall had been working like a madman ever since. Now, as he bent forward to add a few strokes to the leaves of an ancient oak with the tip of his brush, he hummed softly.

"Well, aren't you chipper this morning?"

At the sound of Francesca's voice, Randall turned around. "What are you doing home at this hour?" Dropping his brush in a glass filled with turpentine, he picked up a rag and started to wipe his fingers.

"I forgot my briefcase and thought I'd sneak in here for one more goodbye kiss."

Randall smiled and opened his arms. Now that her eyes had lost that mournful expression, she looked more beautiful than ever. There was a lift in her voice and a new spring in her step that reminded him of the old Francesca, the one he had fallen in love with. It felt good to know *he* was responsible for the change. "Come here."

He kissed her slowly, deeply, the way she liked it.

When they finally pulled apart, he took her hand. "Come. I want to show you something." He stopped in front of the easel. "It's finished," he announced proudly.

At the sight of the painting Randall had so mysteriously kept from her all those days, Francesca let out a gasp. The work in front of her was that of an early California mission bathed in a misty gold light that gave the stucco structure an almost spiritual quality. The colors were subtle yet vibrant, the strokes strong and masterful.

Her eyes filled with tears of joy and pride. "Oh, Randall, it's beautiful. The best you've ever done." Wrapping an arm around his waist, she asked, "Has Anthony seen this?"

"He came on Monday. He was ecstatic. He wants to do a one-man show."

"A one-man show." The words hardly seemed real. Not less than three months before, Randall had been ready to give up his art, convinced he would never achieve the greatness of other contemporary artists. "Why didn't you tell me sooner?"

"I wanted to wait until the painting was finished. Until you could see it."

She couldn't take her eyes off the canvas. "I always knew you were talented. Now you finally believe me."

"I owe it all to you, Francesca."

"No. The talent was always there, darling. You just had to find a way to express it."

"But you're the one who believed in me, who stood by me." He grinned. "What do you say we celebrate?"

"All right. I'll come home early, and we'll have champagne."

"I have a better idea. Let's fly away somewhere. A long weekend in Acapulco perhaps. Or Hawaii."

Her shoulders sagged. "I can't. I still have to sort

through the stack of correspondence on Travis's desk. And I promised Kane I'd help him with his investigation of the elusive soldier.''

Randall laughed. "What elusive soldier?"

"I guess I've been so busy, I didn't get a chance to tell you about it. Diana Wells remembers bumping into a man on her way to Travis's penthouse the day of the murder—apparently one of the Desert Storm men who were attending the reunion that week. She can't describe him, but Kane thinks she might be able to recognize him if she saw a picture of him. Lieutenant Morrell, who organized the event, was nice enough to let me borrow the snapshots displayed in the lobby, so Diana could take a look at them.

Slowly, Randall released his hold around her waist. Like a film in slow motion, pictures unrolled in front of his eyes—Diana coming around the corner, bumping into him, her distracted glance, her quick apology. "Was she able to identify anyone?"

"No. The reunion is over now, but I've been in touch with Lieutenant Morrell who has promised to send the photographs that were taken on Thursday and Friday. That's why I want to be available."

Forcing his voice to remain casual, Randall asked, "Does Kane think this man Diana bumped into is the killer?"

Picking up her purse from a chair, Francesca walked slowly toward the door, holding Randall's hand. "Not necessarily. But the fact that he was standing right in front of the penthouse elevator makes him suspicious. Or at the very least, an eyewitness."

"Eyewitness to what?"

"He may have seen someone coming out of the elevator. Maybe the killer."

A cold knot clutched his gut. "Are you telling me you think Diana is innocent?"

Francesca sighed. "I don't know what to think, Randall."

"Then look at the evidence. Everything points to her guilt."

"I know." She gave him a worried look. "But what if Kane is right? What if someone else killed Travis, and that someone else is still roaming the streets?"

"Let Kane worry about that. He's Diana's lawyer. Not you."

Francesca gave a stubborn shake of her head. "That wouldn't be right. If Diana is innocent, I owe it to her, and to Kane, to help her prove it. Especially since I'm in a position to do so."

Randall held back an exasperated sigh. Francesca had always been on the side of the underdog. It was one of her most endearing qualities.

"Your mother would be furious if she knew what you were up to." She was much too stubborn to let that remark stop her, but it was worth a shot.

"Mother will get over it."

"What about me? What if *I* asked you to keep out of Kane's investigation?"

She frowned and turned to look at him. "Why on earth would you do something like that?"

"A man has already been killed, Francesca. Don't you think I have a right to be a little fearful? What do we know about this killer? Or whom he'll strike next?"

She laughed. "Oh, Randall. Aren't you being a little melodramatic? I'm in no danger." She patted his cheek. "But I love you for worrying. It makes me feel so . . ." She smiled. "Loved."

He knew her too well to press the argument further. And anyway, what was he worried about? While Diana was occupied with all those photographs, she wouldn't be thinking of him.

He felt his body relax. He was safe.

As long as he stayed away from Diana Wells.

Back in Travis's office, where she was faced with a mountain of paper work, Francesca picked up the phone and called Oscar Mills, her mother's attorney.

"Oscar," she said when the lawyer answered, "I'm calling in reference to that television station Travis left me. I've decided not to sell it."

"Are you planning to go ahead with Travis's plans to revamp it then?"

"I'll be doing some reorganization to increase revenues, but those shows on food and home improvements Travis was working on are out of the question. They're much too costly." She shuffled through a file on her desk. "I see here that he had already hired a couple of people—informally I guess, since no salary was paid and no contract was signed."

"I wasn't aware of that. Who are they?"

"Some fashion guru who was axed from a big, national magazine, and Holden Nash of the *San Francisco Globe*."

"Isn't he the food and wine columnist who wrote that awful review of Diana Wells's restaurant last month?"

"That's the one. Why Travis would hire a pompous jerk like that totally baffles me."

After she hung up, Francesca buzzed her secretary. "Amy, would you call Holden Nash at the *Globe* and tell him I'd like to talk to him?"

"Do you want him to come here, Mrs. Atkins?"

"Yes." She glanced at her watch. "At noon if he can make it."

30

In all his sixty years, Holden Nash had never felt more outraged. The request from Francesca Atkins to come to her office had led him to believe that, as the new owner of KYBC, she was prepared to discuss the reorganization plans her brother had begun to put into motion before his death.

Excited at the prospect of dazzling her with his list of famous chefs who had agreed to be on the show, he had left the *Globe,* where he still worked, and hurried to the Lindford. But instead of the enthusiastic response he had expected, she had listened to every word, then had quietly informed him that she would not be needing his services.

Now, sitting across from her desk, he stared at her in disbelief. "I don't understand. Are you . . . firing me?"

"Correct me if I'm wrong, but you were never officially hired, were you?"

"No, but I was promised this job. Travis and I discussed our plans in length. I spent a great deal of time and effort on this project. If you don't believe me, ask the station manager. He'll tell you—"

Francesca smiled sweetly. "I believe you, Mr. Nash. But it doesn't change the fact that I can't afford such expenditures at the moment; therefore I have no choice but to cancel your arrangement with my brother.''

Although diplomacy had never been one of his virtues, Nash forced a smile to his lips. "I don't think you fully realize the situation, Mrs. Atkins—the impact that such a reorganization would have on the station—in terms of size and revenues. It would finally put KYBC in direct competition with some of the most successful stations in the area. Perhaps in the state.''

Francesca, who had despised the food columnist on sight, leaned back in her chair, thoroughly enjoying his disadvantage. "I'm all in favor of healthy competition, Mr. Nash, but not if it means pouring hundreds of thousands of dollars into a single project.'' She stood up to signal their meeting was over. "Now if you don't mind, I have another appointment.''

"Perhaps if we trimmed down on some of the expenses, cut the frills, we can bring the budget to a more suitable level. I could make some projections for you if you'd like.''

Francesca shook her head. "I don't think so.''

"Dammit, you can't dismiss me like yesterday's garbage.'' Bracing himself on the armrests, he lifted his great bulk off the chair. "Not after what I've done for your brother. For your family.'' The words, spoken in a rush of despair, were out before he could stop them.

Francesca tilted her head to one side. "What did you do for my brother, Mr. Nash?''

Was it his imagination or had her expression mellowed? Was that the way to win her over? By letting her know how loyal he had been to Travis? "Didn't he tell you?'' he asked in a guarded voice.

Francesca shook her head. "Why don't *you* tell me.''

He hesitated, still unsure. He knew nothing about her except that she and her brother had been close—which was a point in his favor. If she approved of what he had done, she might change her mind about the station—or show her gratitude in some other way.

On the other hand, if she didn't approve, he could be in deep trouble.

"Well, Mr. Nash?"

In the moment it took her to smile, he made up his mind. She was okay. Just a green kid flexing her muscles. Who could blame her? "This must remain between us," he said, assuming an air of confidentiality.

Francesca continued to smile, but said nothing.

Encouraged by that smile, Nash brushed away the last speck of doubt. "That review I wrote about Diana Wells's restaurant?" he puffed his chest a little. "I did it at your brother's request."

She frowned. "I don't understand."

"Travis wanted to destroy her financially so he would have a better chance to win custody of his son."

The revelation left her stunned. She knew Travis well enough to believe him capable of a lot of things. But not this. Not anything so cold-blooded, so ruthless. "I don't believe it."

"It's true. He called me about a month ago and invited me to lunch. He told me about the station, the plans he had for it. And for me. When I accepted his offer, he told me what he wanted in exchange." He let out a small sigh of regret. "A pity Miss Wells recovered so quickly. But who would have thought she'd come back with that rebuttal in the *Examiner*?"

Francesca thought back to the day Holden Nash's review had appeared, how thrilled Travis had been. The thought that *he* had engineered the deed made her feel sick. "Diana Wells didn't deserve that review?"

Nash shook his head, but thought it best not to incriminate himself any further.

"So, what you are telling me," Francesca said, not bothering to hide the contempt in her voice any longer, "is that you not only tried to destroy a woman's business, but you betrayed the trust that thousands of readers placed in you as well."

A chill washed over him. Everything about her had changed, the look in her eyes, the tone of her voice, even the way she held herself. Too late, he realized he had made a costly, irreparable mistake. "I did it for your brother, for your family—"

"You're a despicable man, Mr. Nash."

The insult, uttered in a voice that shook with wrath, cut through some vital cord in Nash's brain. He gripped the back of the chair he had occupied earlier as his jaw went slack. "You don't understand—"

"Get out of my office."

Nash, his face ashen, didn't move. "I did it for your brother," he repeated dully. "It was his idea."

"You did it for yourself, to satisfy your own greed. You never once thought of what it would mean for a hard-working woman like Diana Wells to lose her reputation, see years of hard work crumble."

"She recovered," he stammered.

"Yes. And for that I'm thankful. But you, Mr. Nash, are a disgrace to your profession. If I were half as ruthless as you, I would expose you for the fraud that you are." She walked around her desk and toward the door. "But I won't. I will, however, expect you to resign from your position at the *Globe*."

"*What?*"

"Feel free to stay there if you wish, but not in your present position. In fact, if I hear—and I will—that you tried to seek employment as a restaurant critic, in this city or anywhere else in the country, I'll go public with the story."

"If you do, you'll have to expose your brother as well."

She held his gaze without flinching. "I'll do whatever I have to."

"You sanctimonious little bitch," he spat. "You won't get away with that. I'll deny every word. I'll sue you for defamation of character—"

Francesca held the door open. "If you do, my lawyers will come down on you so hard, you'll wish you had never heard of me."

"They'll never be able to prove a thing."

"They will after I tell them how you chose to review Miss Wells's restaurant so soon after her grand opening when everyone knows that has never been your policy. And how you accepted a job offer from my brother days after that review appeared in the paper. And if that's not enough, I'll tell them about the many gifts you took from him over the years." She smiled. "Oh, yes, I know all about those—lavish dinners in our restaurant for you and your family, expensive cigars, weekend getaways to his ski chalet in Utah. Need I say more?"

She didn't. It was obvious from the hateful look in his eyes that she had made her point. After a few seconds, during which he just stood there, as if measuring her, he gave her a parting glare and then walked out.

Francesca closed the door and returned to her desk. Stopping in front of an ebony cabinet, her gaze fell on a photograph of her and Travis taken when they were children. She had been six, Travis eleven. She had idolized him, loved him, trusted him.

"That was low, Travis," she murmured, gazing at the picture. "Even for you."

*   *   *

Kane had just walked into his office, following a meeting with Sergeant Kosak when Dan Chancellor's call came through.

"I'm sorry it took so long getting back to you," the banker said. "But the information you wanted wasn't easy to get, as you can imagine."

"Did you find out something?"

"Yes. Although you might find the results disappointing as far as your murder case goes."

"Why?"

"Travis Lindford didn't open that account in Zurich."

"Then who did?"

"His father—Charles Lindford."

Kane took a moment to digest the startling information. "Are you sure?"

"Positive. The account was opened in 1969 and remained active until spring of 1972. After that the deposits stopped."

"You mean Charles closed the account?"

"Not at all. He just stopped depositing money into it. When he died two years ago, his widow was notified that she was the sole beneficiary of two million dollars plus interest accumulated over a period of twenty-four years. It comes to a little over thirteen millions dollars, but since Mrs. Lindford didn't do anything to collect that money, the account is still open and continues to accrue interest."

Kane fell back against his chair. "Are you saying that Margaret Lindford knew all along about the secret account?"

"That's hard to say. The account was in Charles's name only. And only his signature was on record."

Charles had been defrauding the government, not Travis. And Margaret had known about it. She must have. He remembered her reaction when he had told her about finding Hantz Fielder's business card, the panicked look in her eyes, the way she had ordered him to drop the investigation.

She hadn't been trying to protect the Lindford name. Or Travis. She had been protecting her husband.

Something else was nagging him, but he couldn't quite put his finger on it. "Do you know how the money was transferred to Switzerland, Dan? Did Charles just write checks—"

"The money didn't come from the hotel account, Kane. All the checks came from a company by the name of Maddox Linen Service."

31

Kane's whole body went numb. His mind, trained to react in an instant, refused to comprehend, to accept.

Maddox Linen Service was the bogus company that Kane's father had been accused of creating for the embezzlement of the two million dollars. And now, after twenty-one years, the mystery of how the money had disappeared and where it had gone was finally unraveling.

Charles Lindford and William Maddox had been one and the same. But when the embezzling was discovered and the investigators had pointed the finger at Ray Sanders, Charles had let his comptroller take the blame. He had done more than that. He had forged Ray's handwriting on the bank signature card so that in the event the embezzlement was discovered, Kane's father would be the prime suspect.

But why? Why did a man as wealthy as Charles Lindford need to embezzle funds from his own hotel? Was he in some kind of financial difficulty? Or was his motive pure and simple greed?

"That company mean something to you, Kane?"

When he was finally able to speak, Kane's voice was low and raspy. "You're damned right it does." He waited for his thoughts to unscramble before speaking again. "How were the deposits made? In person? By check? Wire?"

"By checks drawn on a third bank in Petaluma, California. Apparently this Maddox opened another corporate account there, withdrew the cash from the San Francisco bank and deposited it in the Petaluma bank before transferring it to Switzerland. The three-bank method is often used by embezzlers and money launderers to avoid detection."

Which explained why the Maddox account at the First Mercantile Bank in San Francisco had been empty when the police got to it. Petaluma was only an hour from here. It would have been easy enough for Charles to make weekly trips there, deposit the cash, and return home.

"When did you say the account became inactive?"

He heard Dan shuffle a few pages. "March 1972."

The month the IRS inspectors had come to audit the hotel. A week later, his father was dead.

"Kane, are you all right?"

"I'm fine." It was easier to pretend the rage wasn't there. "Thanks for all your help, Dan. I owe you one."

After hanging up, he sat for a long time, staring out the window. Images he thought he had forgotten flashed across his mind. Pictures of his father being escorted to the police station while the neighbors watched, the funeral a few days later, his mother crying softly, her hands covering her face, Charles and Margaret beside her, comforting her . . .

Margaret. At the thought that she, too, had betrayed him, his heart filled with a dull ache. Had she stood silent all those years knowing another man had paid for Charles's sins?

After a while he stood up. There was only one way for him to get the answer to his questions.

"Mrs. Lindford is resting right now, Mr. Sanders." Marcie, a plump Jamaican woman with short hair wrapped in a net, smiled at Kane as she let him in. "I'd be glad to bring you some coffee— "

"Wake her up, Marcie. It's important."

"That won't be necessary. I'm awake."

Kane turned around. Margaret stood just behind him, dressed in a straight midcalf black skirt and a black beaded sweater. Even in mourning, she managed to look stunning. "Hello, Margaret."

Too sharp to miss the sudden change in him, Margaret's eyes grew a little warier. But the smile remained. "Marcie, why don't you put another cup on the tray—"

"I won't be staying." He heard Marcie quickly retreat to the kitchen and waited until she had disappeared before saying, "My friend from Chase Manhattan called back."

Without a word, Margaret walked past him into the drawing room and sat down. She should have known he would eventually find out the truth.

"How long have you known?" His voice was harsh, unforgiving.

It took her a moment to collect her thoughts, to accept the fact that the moment she had dreaded for two long years had finally arrived. "I only found out after Charles's death," she whispered, raising imploring eyes toward him. "You must believe that."

He continued to look at her, waiting for her to continue, to fill in the blanks.

"I don't know how the Saar bank found out Charles had died. Through the newspapers I guess. A week or so after the funeral, a Mr. Ziebrandt called and told me I was the sole beneficiary of thirteen million dollars. At first, I thought there was some sort of mistake. Charles and I had no secrets—or so I thought at the time. I told Ziebrandt to send me a complete summary of the account."

She walked slowly back into the drawing room. "When I saw the various dates the deposits were made, I was able to put two and two together. You see, the hotel was experiencing huge losses in those days, and Charles was worried we wouldn't recover."

"And you never suspected he was embezzling funds and sending the money to Switzerland?"

"I had no idea, Kane. Not until Mr. Ziebrandt called. I understood everything then—Charles's reluctance to pursue the investigation after your father died although I kept insisting that we should, his hope that you and your mother would move to Glen Ellen with your Aunt Beckie."

"Why was that so important?"

"Guilt, I suppose. If you weren't around, he wouldn't be reminded of what he had done. When I told him we should offer Claire a job, he fought me. I couldn't understand why at the time. It took me three weeks to make him change his mind."

She stopped in the middle of the room, but didn't sit down. "I wanted to tell you so many times."

"Why didn't you?"

"What was the point? Your father was dead. So was your mother. And Charles. What could I have said or done that would have changed that?"

"Didn't it occur to you that I might want my father's name cleared?" Then realizing the stupidity of his question, he laughed. "Of course not. It was more important to keep the precious Lindford name clean. That's why you kept quiet, isn't it? To safeguard the family name. And the hotel. It didn't matter that I lost a father, that my entire life was turned upside down, that I was forever branded the son of an embezzler."

She bowed her head and said nothing.

"I trusted Charles as much as I trusted my father. I looked up to him. And to you.

She closed her eyes, knowing she had forever lost his trust—and, quite possibly, his love. "I'm sorry," she whispered. "So very sorry." She looked up, hoping to see a glimmer of understanding in his eyes. There was none.

Kane didn't reply. He had waited twenty-one years for this moment, for the chance to clear his father's name and bring the person who had framed him to justice. Unfortunately, that person was dead, and somehow, the thought of turning his widow in left a bitter taste in his mouth.

"And to think I was planning to speak to Diana on your behalf," he said, his tone bitter. "I felt so sorry for you, Margaret. Sorry that with Travis dead, Francesca so busy, and Zack lost to you, you'd give up on life. And I didn't want that. I thought that if I could convince Diana to let you see Zack once in a while, you'd get over Travis's death quicker."

Margaret bit her lip, realizing too late how much she had lost. "Will you ever be able to forgive me?"

"I doubt that very much." Then, without another word, he turned around and walked away.

Margaret stood watching the door for more than a minute. For the first time in her life, she was beginning to feel like an old lady—frail, sad, and so very alone.

Kane was right. She had kept Charles's secret to preserve the family name—without a single thought as to the consequences.

It was too late for regrets. But it wasn't too late to do something for Kane, something she should have done long ago. She dialed the new general manager. "Conrad," she said when Travis's former assistant came on the line. "I would like to make a statement to the press. If they want to know what it's about, tell them I want to clear an old matter, one that was highly publicized some years ago."

"Certainly, Mrs. Lindford. When would you like to schedule it?"

"This afternoon if possible."

Curled up on the blue-and-white striped sofa Kat had lent her until her new one arrived, Diana pored over a new batch of photographs Francesca had sent earlier, and heaved a deep sigh before handing them back to Kane. "No one here looks even remotely familiar," she said with a shake of her head.

Kane gathered the photographs and slid them back into a manila envelope. "That's all right. Francesca told me a few more pictures are on their way—the last of the batch. You might find something in there."

"It's very nice of her to go to all that trouble for me," Diana said, watching him tuck the envelope into his briefcase. "It can't be easy for her. Not when her mother disapproves of me so much."

"Francesca has always had a mind of her own."

"I think I'd like to meet her someday."

He smiled. "Warming up to the Lindfords, darling?"

"Mmmm. Just her. Maybe."

The name "Lindford" coming from the kitchen radio made them both turn around.

"What now?" Kane mumbled, walking into the other room to turn up the volume.

Knowing how devastated he had been to find out about Margaret and Charles's betrayal, Diana followed him, wrapping an arm around his waist as they listened to a special news broadcast together.

"We've just received word that Mrs. Margaret Lindford, owner of the Lindford hotel, and mother of the recently murdered Travis Lindford, is about to make an important statement. We now switch you to the grand ballroom of the Lindford Hotel.

A few seconds later, the buzzing of conversation died down and Margaret's clear, well-modulated voice filled the air waves.

"Good afternoon, ladies and gentlemen, and thank you for coming so promptly. The statement I'm about to make is short and painful, therefore, as you must already have been told, no questions will be taken afterward."

She waited for the murmur of disappointment to die down before continuing. "Twenty-one years ago, Ray Sanders, one of my most trusted employees, was unjustly accused of embezzling two million dollars from the Lindford Hotel. A few days later, he died a tragic death. Two years ago, after my husband died, I found out that he, not Ray Sanders, had embezzled the money and transferred it into a Swiss bank account."

The room exploded with questions, and it was a full minute before Margaret was able to continue. "I should have reported the felony then. But I didn't. Partly because I didn't think it would do any good, after all these years, and partly because . . . I didn't want to tarnish the Lindford name. It was a terrible thing for me to do, and I will regret it for the rest of my life. I will be taking steps to pay back the money owed to the Internal Revenue Service plus any fine and penalty. Whatever is left will be donated to various charities. I know that no amount of remorse or public apology can erase the harm that was done to Ray Sanders and his family. Ray was a wonderful and honest man, and although I have waited a long time to clear his name, I do so now with the utmost love and respect. May God forgive me. Thank you all for coming."

As the announcer came back on the air to comment about the staggering announcement Margaret had just made and the reaction from the people in the room, Diana turned off the radio and glanced at Kane, who hadn't said a word. "I can't believe she did that."

Kane didn't reply. Despite his anger and his unwillingness to forgive Margaret, he couldn't help being impressed. It had taken a lot of courage to face the world and admit what she had done. It didn't change the way he felt about her, but it reinforced his belief that when it came to guts, Margaret Lindford had tons to spare.

The phone was ringing when Kane walked into his office the following afternoon.

"Boss," Jackie said, "there's a man on the line who wants to talk to you, but won't say who he is or what he's calling about. Just that it's important and related to the Lindford case."

An anonymous caller, Kane thought. It could be nothing. And then again, it could be his first break. "Put him through."

The voice at the other end was low, with a faint Bronx accent. "I've got some information that could clear your client. Are you interested?"

Kane didn't even blink. In his line of work, tips of this kind were common. Some were worth pursuing, others were as phony as a three-dollar bill. "I might be. What have you got?"

The man laughed. "Come on, Counselor. You know better than to ask me a question like that. You want it, it's going to cost you. Ten thousand dollars."

It was an unusually low amount. Either the guy was in desperate need for some quick cash, or what he was selling was worthless. "Where do I find you?"

"Ghirardelli Square at five o'clock. I'll be the guy in the Santa suit standing by the Mermaid Fountain."

The line went dead.

32

Diana knew someone was in her house the moment she opened the door and smelled the cigarette smoke. This time, at the command to run, her brain reacted instantly. She spun around, not bothering to close the door behind her.

But before she could take a single step, a big, beefy arm shot out, wrapped around her waist, and lifted her off the floor.

Her limbs went numb as fear coursed through her body. Her first thoughts were that a rapist was attacking her and why hadn't she taken that self-defense course with Kat last summer?

"Put her down, Bulge."

At the softly spoken order that had come from the living room, the man obeyed and set her down. Then he closed the door and positioned himself in front of it, folding his arms across his massive chest. The dome of his bald head shone in the dark. Other than that, and his bulk, Diana couldn't see anything. It was too dark.

"Come in, Miss Wells," the voice said. "And don't be afraid. I won't harm you."

In spite of the man's reassurance, fear kept her rooted to the floor. The living room, like the foyer, was in shadows, although the light from the deck allowed her to see the outline of furniture. "Who are you? What do you want?"

"I don't like to carry on a conversation from twenty paces away. Now, you can come in here on your own, or my friend can carry you in. Your choice."

The thought of that big ape touching her again made her shudder. Knowing she had no choice but do as she was told, she stepped into the living room, her eyes slowly adjusting to the darkness.

The man sat by the fireplace, in one of the high-back chairs she had brought in from the dining room to fill in the empty spaces. All she could make out was a wide-brimmed hat and the glow of a cigarette.

"That's much better."

"Who are you?" she repeated, her voice a little steadier.

"My name is Eddy."

She took a quick breath, fighting the impulse to lunge at him. "You're the bastard who ransacked my house."

"No, I'm not." His voice had sharpened, sounding surprisingly sincere. "It's true that two of my men were here a few months ago, looking for the money your brother owed me. But this recent job, which I read about in the papers, is not my doing. I don't care if you believe me or not. That's not why I'm here."

The cold knot inside her stomach loosened slightly. "Why *are* you here?"

"I'm looking for your brother. He vanished, you see. He moved out of his apartment and split before settling his debt."

"He told the police he paid you back."

"He lied. And I'm not going to let him get away with it. I want my money."

Panic speared through her again. "I don't have it!"

"I know that." He took a puff of his cigarette, held

the smoke in his lungs for a moment, then released it in a long, thin stream. "But you might know where I can find your brother."

"I don't."

"Think, Miss Wells. Does he have friends who live out of town? A girlfriend perhaps? A foolish mother who would want to hide him?"

"Our parents died years ago, and I don't know anything about any of his girlfriends." That wasn't quite true, but as much as she despised Nick for causing her so much grief, she had no intention of handing him over to his executioner.

"You're lying."

"No, I'm not—"

"Bulge," the man said, his voice dangerously low, "show the lady what happens when people lie to me."

Once the site of a woolen mill, and later that of a trading center for chocolate and spices, Ghirardelli Square had emerged, after nearly a century of renovations, into a magnificent plaza, complete with shops, restaurants, art galleries, and beautifully landscaped terraces.

It was a little before five when Kane arrived at the crowded complex. The holiday spirit was everywhere, with the San Francisco Bach Choir entertaining the crowd and jolly Santas in padded suits and fake beards ringing their bells and collecting money for the Salvation Army.

Standing far enough from the Mermaid Fountain so he could have a better view of the people around it, Kane let his gaze move in all four directions, waiting for one of the Santas to approach him.

But after several donations and a few words with each man, it was obvious the one he had come to meet had changed his mind.

That, or . . .

The thought hit him with the force of a brick hammer. Guided by nothing but sheer reflex, he ran back toward the garage where he had parked the BMW, pushing through the crowd, mumbling apologies as he went.

He had fallen for the oldest trick in the book. Somebody had wanted him out of the way so they could get to Diana. It was the only logical explanation—one that made his stomach clench with deadly fear.

Why hadn't he realized that before embarking on this wild-goose chase? Had this case frustrated him to the point he couldn't even think straight anymore?

Moments later, he was in his car, speeding down the ramp toward the exit, where he handed the attendant a twenty-dollar bill. "Keep the change."

Once outside, he dialed Diana's house. "Come on," he muttered impatiently. "Answer."

After the line rang busy, he hung up and dialed Sergeant Kosak at police headquarters. "I don't have time to go into details," he said, maneuvering the car through the heavy traffic as he spoke. "But Diana may be in danger."

"What kind of danger?"

"I don't know. I got an anonymous phone call asking me to be at Ghirardelli Square at five o'clock. No one was there, and now Diana's line is busy. Or the phone is off the hook."

"She's not at the restaurant?"

"No. She went to Glen Ellen to see Zack earlier and was on her way back. I know because I talked to her on her car phone and told her I'd be a little late."

Kosak didn't ask any more questions. "Okay. I'm on my way."

"I'll meet you there. But please hurry."

Heading toward Pacific Heights, Kane floored the gas pedal.

Diana winced as Bulge's big hand took a handful of her hair. The other clamped over her mouth, smothering her scream.

"I'm a patient man, Miss Wells," Eddy said in that same low, dangerous voice. "But I have my limits." Getting up from the chair, he walked slowly toward her. "Now, for the last time, do you know where your brother is?" As he talked, he moved the glowing end of his cigarette toward her neck.

Cold with panic, she shook her head. "If I did, I would tell you."

"Or you may want to protect him."

"Why would I want to protect him after all he put me through?"

Eddy slowly pulled the cigarette away and brought it to his mouth. He took a long drag. "Very well. But if you should hear from him, please tell him this planet isn't big enough to hide him. Wherever he is, I'll find him. And when I do, he's going to be sorry he crossed me."

He walked past her, his shoulder brushing with hers. She caught a whiff of expensive cologne, and then he was gone.

The moment the door closed, she ran to the telephone, which had been taken off the hook, and called the police.

Sergeant Kosak and a uniformed officer were already at Diana's house when Kane arrived fifteen minutes later.

"Thank God, you're all right." No longer caring how his behavior would look to the police, he closed his arms around her. "That damn traffic. I thought I'd never get here."

For his benefit, Diana repeated the story she had already told Sergeant Kosak. When she mentioned Bulge using force on her, Kane's whole body went rigid. "That son of a bitch," he hissed between clenched teeth. "I'll kill him."

"Bulge isn't important." Diana looked from Kane to Sergeant Kosak. "What is important is that Eddy isn't responsible for ransacking my house. I'm sure he's not."

"Then who is?" Kane turned toward the policeman. "Why would anyone want to ransack her house?"

"Beats me. But I have a hunch Nick Wells will be able to shed some light on the subject."

"What makes you say that?" Diana asked.

"I read the statement he made to one of my detectives when he was brought in the other day, and in my opinion the man was a little too cooperative, too anxious to blame the incident on this Eddy."

"You're not suggesting *Nick* was involved?" She couldn't bring herself to think her brother might have done the job himself.

Kosak shrugged. "I'm not suggesting anything just yet. As I said, something about him is not sitting right." He paused before asking, "Do you have any idea where he might be?"

After a moment of indecision, Diana let out a resigned sigh. If Nick was guilty of ransacking her house, she wanted him punished. If he didn't, he would be safer in police custody than running around loose with Eddy and his men after him. "He's had an on-and-off relationship with a Reno dancer for years. Her name is Monique Marler, and the last I heard she was part of an all-girl revue at the Desert Fox Hotel and Casino.

It's possible Nick went to her place to hide. He's done that before.''

"You know her address?'

Diana shook her head.

"All right." Kosak and the officer headed toward the door. "I'll get a warrant for his arrest and see what he has to say about all this."

"How long until you have him in custody?" Diana asked.

Kosak shrugged. "If we find him in Reno, no more than a few hours. If not, we'll have to put an APB and start checking bus and train stations, airports. That might take some time."

"You'll let us know, won't you?" Kane asked.

"You bet."

Nick Wells, his face pale and his eyes bloodshot from lack of sleep, slumped in a chair across from a man who had identified himself as Sergeant Kosak, and pressed two fingers over his eyelids. The Reno cops with a warrant in their hands had showed up on Monique's doorstep in the middle of the night and brought him all the way back to San Francisco without a word of explanation.

"You're wanted for questioning," was all they had told him.

Questioning, hell. The chunky sergeant with the cheap suit and the sleepy eyes had put him through a fucking meat grinder, threatening to book him for every felony under the sun, including illegal possession of a .357 Magnum, unless he leveled with him.

Christ, he couldn't go to prison. Eddy had friends there, hard-core criminals who could turn his life into a nightmare. Maybe even kill him if Eddy gave the word.

He had to get out of here. He had to make some

kind of deal with that dumb cop and put as much distance between him and Eddy as possible.

"So, Wells. Are you ready to talk?"

Nick glanced at the other detective, a pasty-skinned guy with a notepad in front of him. "What's in it for me if I do?"

Kosak calmly unwrapped a roll of Tums. "I'll tell the D.A. what a good boy you were, cooperating with us and all, and I'll make sure the gun charge is dropped. That alone is ten years off your sentence."

"How do you know the D.A. will go for it?"

"Because it's my job to know those things." He popped the antacid into his mouth and leaned back in his chair, looking relaxed and confident. Nick threw a nervous glance at the clock on the wall. "Where the hell is my attorney?"

Kosak shrugged. "I guess he's been delayed. You know how those public defenders are. He might not even show up until tomorrow morning."

"I can't say anything until he gets here."

Kosak stood up. "Suit yourself. But the D.A. won't like it. She'll feel you need the protection of an attorney because you're hiding something."

Shit. They had him by the balls. He didn't even have money for bail. The Reno cops had taken him away without giving him a chance to get his suitcase. The fucking money was still at Monique's apartment.

With a sigh, he fell back against his chair. "All right. What do you want to know?"

Kosak's sleepy expression vanished. He sat down again and nodded at the younger detective. "Who ransacked your sister's house?"

"I did."

Kosak didn't show any surprise. "Why?"

"Because I needed money." He told him about calling Travis, their subsequent meeting. "It was the perfect arrangement," he said as he met the policeman's hard stare. "I needed money. Lindford needed the kid."

"What happened after you collected the fifty-thousand-dollar advance?"

"I completed my part of the bargain and waited for Travis to pay me the rest of the money. Except somebody punched his light out before I could collect," he added sourly.

"You never saw Travis Lindford alive again?"

"Nope. I heard about his death the same as everyone else in San Francisco—on the evening news."

Kosak ran his hand along his cheek, where a stubble of beard had begun to show. If the guy was lying, he was doing one hell of a job. "Why did you skip town?"

"When I realized I wouldn't be getting my two hundred thousand dollars, I started to do a little arithmetic. I owed thirty thousand to Eddy. If I paid him out of the fifty I already had, I'd be left with only twenty grand. A paltry sum, considering the risks I had taken. So ..." He shrugged. "I decided to keep it all for myself and make a run for it."

"Or maybe you were trying to escape a murder charge."

Nick sprang out of his chair, his face red with indignation. "You son of a bitch! Are you trying to pin a murder on me now? You conned me into telling you the truth, and now you want to hang me for something I didn't do?"

"It makes sense though, don't you think? You go to collect your two hundred thousand dollars, and on the way there, you decide that's not enough. So you ask for more. Travis Lindford gets angry, things get rough, and before you know it, the guy's dead." He bobbed his head. "Yeah, I'd say that makes a lot of sense."

"I don't give a shit how much sense you think it makes, it's not true! I didn't kill Lindford!" He banged an angry fist on the table. "And I'll be damned before I'll admit to that just so you can take the heat off my sister."

Kosak stared at him for a long time. But Nick didn't flinch. After a while the policeman stood up. "Let's go."

Nick gave him a wary look. "Where?"

"We're going to hold you until tomorrow. When your attorney shows up, we'll decide what to do with you."

"You believe me?"

"About not killing Lindford?" Kosak nodded. "Yeah. I believe you. But don't do an Irish jig just yet. You're still in a lot of trouble."

Heavy footsteps on a bare floor woke him up with a start. Running his fingers through his hair, Nick kicked off the army blanket and sat up on his cot.

"Rise and shine, Wells."

He stood up. "Where are you taking me?"

The guard unlocked the door. "Nowhere. You made bail."

Nick frowned. How could he have made bail when he hadn't been able to reach Monique and tell her about the money in the suitcase? "Who posted it?"

The guard shrugged. "Some woman."

Nick heaved a sigh of relief. Diana. She had come through after all. He chuckled. He always knew she had a soft spot for him. She was just like her mother.

Now all he had to do was go back to Reno for the money and take off before the cops realized he had jumped bail.

Mexico sounded good.

*　　*　　*

Once outside, he didn't linger, but hurried across the sidewalk, barely noticing the sleek black limousine inching its way along the curb.

"Yo, meathead."

At the sound of the familiar nickname and the dreaded voice, Nick froze in place. Bulge was grinning at him, one shoulder against the lamppost, ankles crossed. In his hands a switchblade glinted in the morning sun as he used the point to clean his fingernails.

"We haven't seen you around, pal. Been on a trip?"

Nick's legs turned to mush. He glanced toward the police station, trying to gauge the distance. He'd never make it. Bulge was too fast.

Calm down, he thought. He's not going to do anything crazy here. They were in front of a frigging police station for Christ's sake—with dozens of armed cops swarming all over the place. What could be safer than that?

But at the moment, there wasn't a cop in sight. Just him and Bulge.

Rivulets of sweat ran down Nick's back.

As if he had read his mind, Bulge's grin widened. He pulled away from the lamppost and moved toward him, gently tapping the blade against his palm.

It was then that Nick saw the limousine. It was moving slowly along the curb, getting closer to him. From inside, someone swung the back door open.

Bulge gave him a hard shove. "Get in."

In the plush interior of the limousine Eddy sat, looking at him.

He, too, was smiling.

33

That same night a homeless man found the body of Nick Wells as he rummaged through a dumpster at the north end of Fisherman's Wharf. Nick had been badly beaten before being shot with a single bullet to the head.

Standing outside the morgue, where she had come to identify the body, Diana leaned against a sterile-looking white wall, waiting for Kane to finish talking to Sergeant Kosak.

When she had learned that Nick, and not Eddy's men, had ransacked her house, she hadn't wanted to believe it. How could her brother, her own flesh and blood, have done something so vicious?

Because news of Nick's death had come so soon afterward, her anger had been short-lived, replaced by memories of a young boy with brown curly hair and a winning smile. Somewhere between then and now, something had gone dreadfully wrong.

She closed her eyes to chase away the pictures of the battered body the medical examiner had unveiled for her moments before. She hadn't meant for this to happen. If she had known that helping Sergeant Kosak locate Nick would have ended in this gruesome, brutal death, she would have never done it.

"I failed you, Mom."

"No, you didn't."

Unaware that she had spoken the words aloud, she opened her eyes. Kane was watching her with that tender, concerned expression that never failed to warm her heart. "Eavesdropping, Counselor?"

"Bad habits die hard." Wrapping his arm around her shoulders, he led her down the long corridor, toward the exit sign. "I don't want you to blame yourself for what happened to Nick."

"If I hadn't—"

"He was a ruthless man, Diana. A criminal who stopped at nothing. Look what he did to your house. You had a right to want him apprehended."

They stood outside, arms wrapped around each other. Night had fallen, bringing with it a dense fog. Everything looked so normal, she thought, taking a deep breath. So peaceful. "Do you think they'll find those men?" she asked.

"I don't know. You didn't give Kosak much to go on."

She turned on him, nerves raw. "How could I when I didn't *see* anything!" Almost immediately, she regretted the outburst. "I'm sorry. I shouldn't take my frustrations out on you."

"Yes, you should." They had reached the BMW, but before she went in, he took her chin between two fingers and forced her to look at him. "I love you, Diana—totally and unconditionally. That means I'll take the good with the bad." He smiled. "The loving and the shouting."

She managed a small smile. "I'll try to keep the shouting to a minimum." Then, unable to shake off her somber mood, she added, "What happens now, Kane? I know Kosak thought Nick was the killer. But he doesn't think that anymore. And neither do I. So where do we go from here?"

There was no point in lying to her, in pretending

they were making headway when they weren't. "Back to square one." He opened the passenger door. "And the last batch of photographs Francesca delivered today."

By the following morning, the story of Nick's death and Travis's involvement in the ransacking of Diana Wells's house was in all the papers.

Hoping she would intercept the news before her mother had a chance to read about it, Francesca had rushed to the Lindford while Randall slept. But it was too late. Margaret had not only read and heard every account of the incident, she had been fighting to keep the reporters at bay for the last hour.

"I'm here now, Mother," Francesca said, embracing her mother. "I'll make sure the press doesn't bother you anymore."

"We won't be able to avoid them forever. One of us will have to face them eventually."

"Then I'll do it—and that's not open for discussion. You had your say last week when you held that impromptu press conference regarding Dad's dealings, and although I admit you did a great job, I have no intention of seeing you raked over the coals because of another one of my brother's incomprehensible deeds."

Margaret smiled. Dear, sweet Francesca. When had she become so strong? So wise? And how could she find it in herself to be so kind to a mother who had treated her so unfairly?

Her first impulse was to reject the offer. As the owner of the Lindford, Travis, and the consequences of his actions, were her responsibility.

But she was tired. And getting more tired with each passing day. It was time to concede, to admit she was no longer the energetic, fearless woman she had been in her prime.

It was time to hand over the hotel to Francesca. If Francesca would have it. "All right," she said at last. "I'll be glad to let you take care of the press for me." Then, patting her daughter's hand, she added, "Thank you, my dear. I don't know what I would have done these past two weeks if you hadn't been here for me."

Francesca skimmed her mother's face and felt a tug in her heart at the sadness she saw in the beautiful blue eyes. "That's what families are for."

Margaret nodded, then, her gaze growing distant, she said, "I gave Travis life and yet ... I hardly knew him."

"None of us did."

"What he did to Diana, hiring Holden Nash to destroy her, and now this ..." Her voice broke. "I can't believe anyone would do something so despicable—much less a son of mine." Unexpectedly, she covered her face with her hands and cried softly. "I'm so ashamed."

Her heart breaking, Francesca circled her arms around her mother and drew her close, rocking her as she would a small, weeping child. "Shhh."

When Margaret's sobs subsided at last, Francesca gently pushed her away. "I know what would make you feel better."

Margaret took a white, lacy handkerchief she kept tucked inside the cuff of her blouse and pressed it to her eyes. "What?"

"Let's go see Diana Wells."

Startled blue eyes gazed at her. "What on earth for?"

"Because I feel the family owes her an apology. For all Travis put her through."

Margaret was silent for a moment, then shook her head. "I don't think so."

"Mother, I know you still believe she killed Travis, but I don't. She's not a killer, Mother. If you knew her, you would realize that."

"You don't know her either."

"But Kane does. And he believes she's innocent."

Margaret's expression remained stern. "I don't disagree that we owe Diana Wells an apology, but it's too soon for me to go there. I need more time. I need . . . a little more courage than I have now."

Courage had nothing to do with her refusal to go, Francesca thought, choosing not to press her. Pride did. "In that case you have no objection if *I* go to see her, do you?"

Margaret smiled. "Would it make any difference if I did?"

Francesca shook her head.

Her face grim, Diana studied the reservation list for the week of December thirteen. Ever since she had been bound over for trial, business had declined a little more each day. Only tourists, those who had somehow managed to escape the media blitz, called in for an occasional reservation. But the familiar faces, the repeat customers who were the backbone of every business, had vanished.

"I don't know how much longer I can stay open," she had told Kat this morning. "I barely make enough to cover salaries. Another week like this one, and I'll have to dip into what's left of my savings. Or close the restaurant."

With a sigh she pushed the list aside and picked up the invitation that had arrived in the mail a few days ago. *Les Dames d'Escoffier,* a twenty-year-old international educational group of women in food professions, would be holding its annual week-long "Salute to Women in Gastronomy" in New York City in mid-January, and had asked her to be part of Bloomingdale's showcase of women restaurateurs.

It was a unique opportunity, an event that would make it possible for her to not only promote her restaurant but also to rub elbows with famous chefs such as Julia Child, Madeleine Kamman, and of course, Pierre and Michel Escoffier, the founders of the organization.

She glanced at the date. January 16th through the 23rd. Three months before her trial. She would have to turn the offer down. Accused murderers on bail weren't permitted to leave the state. And even if she were allowed to go, how could she face a prestigious organization like that with a murder charge hanging over her head?

Maybe next year, kiddo.

She was saved from further self-pity by the ring of the telephone.

"Mom! Guess what!"

Her heart swelled with instant joy. Those daily conversations with Zack were her lifeline, one of the few holds she had on her sanity. "You scored a goal in today's game."

"Better than that!"

"You scored ten goals!"

He laughed, making her forget about her troubles. "No."

"Then I give up."

"I'm in the Christmas play. They're doing *A Christmas Carol* this year."

"Oh, Zack. That's wonderful. I'm so proud of you, darling. What part are you playing?"

"Tim Cratchitt. You know, the little sick boy who

gets well at the end? I don't have too many lines, but it's a lot of fun. I've never been in a play before."

"You'll be wonderful in it."

"You'll come won't you, Mom?"

"Are you kidding? Wild horses wouldn't keep me away."

His voice grew shrill with excitement. "That's what Aunt Beckie said. And Thelma. And Mel is coming, too. The whole winery is coming!"

She laughed, glad that he was so happy with his new school. "Does that mean you're going to start signing autographs? Like all the big stars do?"

"I don't think so." There was a scramble as he climbed down from the kitchen stool in Beckie's kitchen. "I've got to go. Pete Wilson's mom just brought him over to play. He's in my class, and I like him a lot. We're in the play together. I love you, Mom. 'Bye."

" 'Bye. I love you, too."

After she hung up, she sat at her desk, staring out the window. Although he had taken the news of her preliminary trial badly, he had rebounded with the spirit of the young. Even the incident with his friend Billy, which had devastated him at first, seemed forgotten. He hadn't even asked how Kane's investigation was coming along, something which, for a while, had preoccupied him a great deal.

And that's exactly how she wanted it.

Although Francesca had been apprehensive about meeting Diana, her doubts evaporated the moment she was shown into the young woman's office and shook her hand. She was everything Kane had said—unaffected, gracious, and very pretty.

"I wasn't sure you'd agree to see me."

The green eyes twinkled. "Really? Why?"

"Well, so far, the Lindfords haven't exactly endeared themselves to you."

"That's true." She pointed to a chair across her desk. "But you came highly recommended—by Kane."

Francesca felt herself relax. "Kane and I have a mutual admiration for each other. In fact, he's the one who encouraged me to come here."

"I'm glad you did." Diana leaned back in her chair and steepled her fingers. "But I'm curious. Why did you come? Kane was rather vague about that." She hoped it wasn't to make a pitch in Margaret's behalf. Although she no longer felt as strongly as she had in the past about allowing Zack to meet his new family, she had too much on her mind right now to engage in some sort of truce between her and the Lindford clan.

"First of all," Francesca said in answer to her question, "I came to apologize."

"For what?"

"For the nightmare my brother put you through." She paused as if searching for the right words. "I also wanted to tell you that although I was thrilled to know I had a little nephew, I never approved of Travis's decision to sue you for custody of Zachary." She stared at her hands. "He was a desperate man. I didn't realize how desperate until I found out about his conspiracy to vandalize your house."

She debated whether or not to tell her about Holden Nash. After a few seconds of reflection, she decided not to. Diana Wells was facing a long and difficult trial. She needed positive thoughts, the company of people who loved and supported her. Finding out Travis had tried to destroy her career would only depress her more. "My mother is equally devastated," she added as an afterthought.

"This must be a difficult time for her, trying to deal with her son's death and the press at the same time."

Francesca nodded. "I'm very worried about her. I've never seen her looking so tired. At times I find myself hating Travis for what he did to her. To us."

Diana knew the feeling. She had experienced it only yesterday when she had found out about Nick's death. She gave Francesca a long, thoughtful look, then, afraid that in spite of the young woman's kind words there might still be a seed of doubt in her mind, she said, "I didn't kill him, Francesca."

"I know that now. I saw you on the witness stand the afternoon you testified, and I realized that no matter how much you had rehearsed, no guilty person could talk with such conviction."

"Thank you. And thank you for sending all those pictures."

"I'm sorry they didn't help." As she spoke, her gaze fell on Zack's photograph and stayed there.

"That was taken last year," Diana said. "On his eighth birthday."

"He's a very handsome boy."

"My pride and joy." On impulse, she said, "Would you like to meet him sometime?"

Francesca's smile widened. "I'd like that very much."

"He's staying with Kane's aunt in Sonoma until after the trial, but I could bring him into the city one day. Or you could come to Glen Ellen."

"That would be wonderful. He could meet my husband. Randall is crazy about kids. We've been trying to have a baby ourselves for almost three years now, but . . ." She smiled. "Maybe next year."

She stood up. "Well, I guess I'd better let you get back to work." At the door she turned to face Diana.

"Would you like to have lunch one day this week? That is if you can spare the time."

Two weeks ago, Diana wouldn't have had time for a coffee break, much less lunch. Now, she was practically a lady of leisure. "I think I can. Wednesday would be good for me."

"Then Wednesday it is. Do you like Chinese?"

Diana rolled her eyes toward the ceiling. "One of my many weaknesses."

"Mine, too. Shall we meet in the lobby of the Lindford at twelve-fifteen? The restaurant I have in mind is an easy walk from there."

Before Francesca disappeared down the hall, Diana called her name, waiting for her to turn around. "Thank you," she said again.

34

Standing in her black and white marble bathroom, her two hands gripping the sink, Francesca waited for the nausea to pass before running cold water over her face.

Wow. This one had been a doozy. Touch and go there for a while. Pulling a black, lace-bordered towel from the rack near her, she blotted her face as she tried to get her breath back.

She was pregnant. Why else would she be retching so violently every morning for the past three days? At first she had thought it was something she ate. Or maybe she had caught that nasty stomach flu everybody seemed to be getting this year.

It wasn't until this morning, when another wave of nausea had sent her flying into the bathroom, that she had realized she could be pregnant.

A baby. The words danced in her head, making her forget about her previous discomfort. A baby. A tiny, precious little bundle for her to love and care for and watch grow.

Randall was going to be ecstatic. She couldn't wait to tell him. But not yet. Not until she was sure. She'd had false alerts before when she had been late with her period, and he had been terribly disappointed.

She would make an appointment with Doctor Geary right away, this morning. He was a busy obstetrician, but as an old friend of the family, she was sure he would squeeze her in—considering what a momentous occasion this was.

Through the rush of running water, she heard a knock at the door.

"Darling, are you all right?" Randall called. "I thought I heard you being sick."

She turned off the faucet, hung the towel back, and gave her cheeks a few quick pats to restore the color before opening the door. "I'm fine," she said, almost burning with joy at the thought of what they might be celebrating tonight. "My vitamin C went down the wrong pipe, that's all."

As he went to the kitchen to start the coffeemaker, she walked over to the telephone and called Dr. Geary at home.

Half an hour before Francesca was due to meet Diana for lunch, her secretary buzzed her on the intercom. "Mrs. Atkins," Amy said, unable to hold back a giggle. "There's a very handsome gentleman in my office who insists on taking you out to lunch, even though he has no appointment. Of course I told him you *never* have lunch with strangers but—"

Before she could finish, Randall's voice came through the intercom in his best Bogart imitation. "Look here, *schweetheart.* I've come a long way and I'm hungry. So don't even think of turning me down. *Capisce?*"

Francesca laughed. "Bogart never said *capisce.*"

A moment later, Randall was behind her, spinning her chair around and kissing her long and hard on the lips. "Mmmm," she murmured when he finally let her go. "And I bet Bogart never kissed Bacall that way either."

"Some people don't know how to have fun." He

sat on the edge of her desk, feeling happier than he had in weeks. "So, are we on for lunch?"

"Can't." Because she knew he wouldn't approve, she didn't tell him about her lunch date with Diana. "I have to meet with our wine distributor. But I'll make it up to you, I promise."

He heaved a resigned sigh. "When?"

"Tonight." Dr. Geary, who had examined her and taken all the necessary tests early this morning, had promised to call shortly after lunch with the results. "I'll leave work early and raid the hotel kitchen for some caviar and a bottle of our best champagne." If all went as she hoped, *she* would be drinking club soda.

"Champagne? Are we celebrating something?"

She tried not to look too mysterious. She wanted him to be totally surprised. "We're celebrating us."

Randall drew her to him and gazed into her deep brown eyes. God, how he loved this woman. Every day with her was a celebration. "Mmmm. I'm not sure I can wait that long." Then, letting her go, he added, "Sure you don't want to dump what's-his-name and have lunch with me instead? I've got some etchings I'd like to show you . . ."

Giggling like a school girl, she slipped out of his arms. "Stop tempting me, Casanova, and scat."

He spread his arms in a helpless gesture. "I can't. My car's in the garage for a tune-up, and I sent the cab away, thinking you wouldn't have the heart to turn me down."

Reaching for the keys on her desk, she threw them at him, admiring his dexterity as he caught them in midair. "Take the Jaguar. I'll come home in the limo."

"All right." He shook a finger at her. "But don't forget you promised to quit early."

"I won't forget."

After he was gone, she walked back to her desk, a slow, satisfied smile spreading across her face. "And you won't forget this day, Randall P. Atkins. I guarantee that."

It was a little after twelve o'clock when Diana arrived at the Lindford. Standing in the middle of the lobby, she paused and looked around her, aware that the three desk clerks behind the reservation counter had recognized her and were watching her. Fortunately, the young woman who had testified in court wasn't on duty, which made the moment a little less awkward.

Unbuttoning her green London Fog, she walked toward a grouping of chairs in front of the blazing fireplace. Settling into a gold velvet Queen Anne, she let her gaze roam around the crowded, elegant lobby.

People were streaming in at a steady pace, some walking directly toward the elevators, others lingering, greeting whomever they had come to meet.

She was about to pick up a copy of *San Francisco Focus* from the table in front of her when her gaze fell on a handsome, dark-haired man with glasses, walking briskly toward the reception desk.

Her heart did a somersault.

It was the man she had bumped into on her way to Travis's penthouse!

She stood up, her legs so shaky, she thought they wouldn't be able to support her. Could she be mistaken? There must be thousands of handsome, dark-haired men in San Francisco. What made this one different? And what about the glasses? She didn't remember them at all.

At the reception desk the stranger pulled a handful of bills from his pocket and handed them to the clerk as he pointed toward the street. Grinning, the girl nodded and took the money.

It was him. She was sure of it now. She hadn't thought she had looked at him long enough to recognize him, but she must have. That finely etched face, that dark, stylishly combed hair, those eyes. They had been buried into her subconscious so deeply that she hadn't been able to come up with a description.

Shaking herself into action, she hooked the strap of her purse around her shoulder and started across the lobby. The man had turned around and was heading toward the elevators. She had to talk to him, try to make him remember if he had seen someone coming out of the penthouse elevator.

Frantic, she ran after him, aware that one of the clerks was watching her. But the elevator's doors closed before she could reach it. He was going down, she realized. To the garage. She could still catch up with him.

She looked around her and caught the attention of a bellboy. "Are there stairs to the garage?"

"Sure thing, ma'am." He pointed to a door at the end of the hall before glancing at the lighted elevator panel. "Wouldn't you rather wait for the elevator to come back up? It'll be here in a minute—"

The rest of his sentence was lost to Diana as she ran toward the door marked STAIRS.

It was exactly twelve-fifteen when Francesca alighted from the elevator. Pausing in the middle of busy lobby, she glanced around, searching for Diana. After about five minutes, she walked over to the reception desk where the senior clerk, a pretty brunette with gray eyes, had just finished helping a guest.

"Vicki, I had an appointment with Miss Wells. Did you happen to see if she came in?"

"She did, Mrs. Atkins. A little before twelve. She sat over there." She pointed at the chairs in front of the fireplace.

"Do you know where she went?"

Vicki shrugged. "I have no idea. I didn't see her leave." She glanced toward the lounge. "Could she have gone to the ladies' room?"

"I'll go check. If you see her in the meantime, tell her to wait for me. I'll be right back."

"Yes, Mrs. Atkins."

As Francesca headed toward the ladies' room inside the cocktail lounge, Vicki chuckled as she bent to whisper into the ear of the other clerk. "Boy, is Mrs. A going to be surprised when she comes back from her lunch date."

The other girl, a slender blonde, looked up from her computer. "Why?"

"You know that Vietnamese woman at the corner of Mason, the one with the flower cart?"

"I know who you mean. What about her?"

"Mr. Atkins just gave me three hundred dollars, all he had in his wallet, and told me to give the money to the woman in exchange for all the flowers on her cart and have them delivered to Mrs. A's office before she returned from lunch."

The blond clerk rolled her eyes toward the ceiling. "Now that's what I call treating a lady right."

"Do you want to hear what the card says?"

The girl nodded eagerly.

Vicki pulled a card from her pocket. "It says: 'And what did what's-his-name give you?' "

"What does that mean?"

Vicki shrugged. "Beats me. But isn't he just about the most romantic guy you've ever known?"

"Yeah. Some women have all the luck."

*   *   *

Breathing hard from her race down the two flights, Diana pushed the heavy garage door open and looked around her. Except for a couple getting into a gray Town Car, the garage was deserted.

And the dark-haired man was nowhere in sight.

She started walking down the first aisle, glancing in both directions as she went. He had to be here. He couldn't have reached his car and driven away in the time it took her to run down the stairs.

The sound of footsteps echoing down the left aisle brought her to a stop. Retracing her steps, she rounded a corner and saw him, walking in a jaunty fashion and flipping his keys in the air and catching them.

"Sir!" She ran after him, her raincoat flying, the heels of her leather boots clicking against the concrete flooring. "Sir!"

Randall turned around. Eyes narrowed, he watched the woman run toward him, trying to distinguish her features. She looked familiar. "Are you talking to me?"

She nodded and slowed down, catching her purse just as it slipped off her shoulder. "Yes." She took a deep breath. "Thank God I caught you."

Randall blinked and shook his head. It couldn't be . . .

A few feet away, Diana stopped, smiling sheepishly, pressing a hand over her breast and taking long, deep breaths. "My name is Diana Wells, and I desperately need your help."

He told himself to relax. She didn't know who he was. All he had to do was get rid of her, and get the hell out of here. "I'm in a hurry," he mumbled, turning around.

"Please, don't go." Her voice had turned imploring. "You're my last hope." She walked toward him. "You and I were in this hotel on December second. I bumped into you. You must remember."

For a moment Randall remained perfectly still. Then, calmly, he said, "You must be mistaken, miss. I've never set foot in this hotel until today."

"Yes, you did. Two weeks ago. It was a Thursday afternoon, just a little before four-thirty. You stood just outside the penthouse elevator."

Nerves jangling, Randall gave his glasses a little shove. "That wasn't me, miss." He swallowed. "I'm sorry."

He doesn't want anyone to know he was at the Lindford, Diana thought with a sinking feeling in her stomach. He's married, probably having an affair, and he doesn't want his wife to find out.

How was that for rotten luck?

"I'm sure it was," she said stubbornly, coming closer to him. "I remember you perfectly." She decided to change tactics, to make herself sound as unthreatening as she could manage. "Look, I understand you may have reasons for not wanting to tell me the truth. But whatever they are, I swear to you that my reasons for wanting to know far outweigh yours. You see, I've been accused of mur—"

As Randall shook his head and turned toward a black Jaguar, her gaze fell on the name painted on the floor to designate the owner of the parking space.

F. Atkins.

F as in Francesca? She held her breath. This was Francesca's car?

Eyes wide with shock, she looked from the white painted lettering to the face of the man in front of her. "You're Francesca's husband! You're Randall Atkins!"

35

When Francesca's efforts to locate Diana remained unsuccessful, she returned to her office, totally puzzled over the young woman's strange behavior. Where could she have gone? Surely if she had had second thoughts about meeting her for lunch, she would have called—or left a message at the desk. But so far no one had heard from her. She seemed to have vanished into thin air.

After glancing at her watch one more time, she picked up the phone and dialed Kane's office.

As always during the lunch hour, Kane answered the phone himself. "Kane Sanders."

"Kane, it's Francesca. Have you heard from Diana by any chance?"

"Isn't she with you?"

"No. According to Vicki at the reception desk, Diana came in at about twelve, waited for a few minutes, and then disappeared without a trace."

Kane frowned. "She didn't leave a message with the desk? Or with your secretary?"

"No. I've been looking for her everywhere, except for the garage."

"She wouldn't have any reason to go to the garage."

"Didn't she drive?"

"No. She almost always takes the cable cars. A true San Franciscan at heart."

"Kane, this is a little odd. I don't know Diana very well, but she didn't strike me as the kind of person who would do something so rude. Especially since she seemed rather eager to have lunch with me."

"She was. That's all she talked about this morning." He stood up, suddenly restless. "Did you call Harbor View?"

"Yes. The dining-room hostess said Diana left at eleven-thirty and told her she'd be back no later than one-thirty."

Kane glanced at his watch. It was almost twelve-thirty. This wasn't like Diana at all. "All right. Let's not panic. Something must have come up, and she had to leave. I'll make a few calls and see if I can locate her."

"You'll call me back?"

"As soon as I find out something."

No sooner had he hung up than he was on the phone again, calling Kat.

Instinctively, Diana took a step back. The eyewitness she had been hunting for days was Randall Atkins.

For a moment her mind refused to accept the implications of that revelation. How could Francesca's husband have been at the Lindford at the time of Travis's death when he had told Kane, and the authorities, that he had spent the entire day at home, painting. And why would he lie about . . . ?

The truth hit her like a fist. "Oh, my God. It was you! *You* were in Travis's penthouse that afternoon. *You* killed him!"

Panic shot through him. His mind raced as he tried to think of a way out. But there was none. Not now that she had recognized him.

Relax, he thought. It was her word against his. No one would ever believe her.

Except Kane Sanders. The man was suspicious of him as it was. The moment Diana told him she had identified the mysterious man as Randall Atkins, he wouldn't let up until he had found someone in that hotel who could corroborate her story. Like that drunken sergeant.

He thought of Francesca, of all he had to lose if he went to prison. For the first time in his life, everything was falling into place. His career had taken a new turn, and he and Francesca were happier than ever. Even Margaret, who had never paid much attention to him, was relying on him more and more now that Travis was gone.

Diana Wells could end it all for him.

If he let her.

Without taking his eyes off her, Randall slowly closed the driver's door.

Still in a state of shock, Diana took another step backward. She didn't have to stay here and argue with him. She knew who he was now, knew where to find him. All she had to do was go back to the lobby and call Kane. He would do the rest.

But the man was too quick for her. As she started to run, he sprang forward, gripped her arm, and yanked her back. "Where do you think you're going?"

"Let me go!"

Moving quickly, he dragged her toward the Jaguar's passenger side, opened the door, and fumbled through the glove compartment. He let out a sigh of relief. It was there.

Her eyes wide with panic, Diana saw him pull a gun out of the glove compartment. "What . . . What are you doing?"

"Shut up." He slammed the passenger door shut and opened the back door. "Get in."

He was kidnapping her!

"Help!" She screamed as she fought to get free. "I'm being kidnapped! Somebody help!"

Before she could find out if anyone had heard her, thousands of lights exploded all around her, and pain ripped through her head. Then, she plunged into darkness.

Spotting Kane walking across the lobby, Francesca ran toward him. "What did you find out?"

"Nothing. Kat hasn't heard from her. And neither has Beckie—or the people at Harbor View." He scanned the busy lobby. "You?"

"One of the bellboys saw her earlier," she said hurriedly as she led him toward a door behind the front desk. "She wanted to know if there were stairs leading to the garage."

"The garage? But that doesn't make sense. Elaine at the restaurant told me the Cherokee was parked in the alley. Diana came here by cable car."

Francesca pushed the door open. "Why don't you question him yourself, Kane?"

The uniformed bellboy looked nervous when Kane and Francesca walked into the night manager's office. Francesca quickly made the introductions, then said, "Brad, please tell Mr. Sanders what you told me."

The bellboy nodded. "I was just coming back from delivering luggage to the seventh floor when Miss Wells—"

"How do you know it was Miss Wells?" Kane asked sharply.

"I recognized her from a newspaper picture. And from seeing her on the six o'clock news. She was wearing a green raincoat and black boots."

Kane nodded. "Go on."

"She was coming from the lobby and was apparently in a hurry to get to the garage. Someone was using the elevator, and she wanted to know where the stairs were. I told her the elevator would be up shortly, but she didn't want to wait."

"Did she say why she wanted to go to the garage?"

"No, sir."

"Did you see her after that? Did she come back up?"

Brad shook his head. "I had to take another load of luggage up to the sixteenth floor, sir, so I left." He glanced from Kane to Francesca. "I'm sorry."

There was a knock at the door, and Vicki came in, followed by one of the front-desk clerks, a perky looking brunette. "Mrs. Atkins, this is Beth," Vicki said. "She is the only one who saw Diana Wells leave the lobby."

Kane was instantly alert. "What happened?"

Beth turned to him. "Well, she was sitting in front of the fireplace, then all of a sudden, she stood up. She looked upset, strange, as if she had seen a ghost or something."

"Did she talk to anyone?"

"No. But after a few seconds, she started running . . . after someone." She looked away. "A man."

"Do you know who he was?" Kane asked.

Beth's face turned red, and she slanted a nervous glance in Francesca's direction. "I don't know if I should . . . I mean, I don't want to get anyone in trouble."

Francesca walked over to her and laid a gentle hand on the girl's shoulder. "It's all right, Beth. I know we insist on the utmost discretion here at the Lindford. But these are special circumstances. Miss Wells could be in serious danger."

Beth nodded, then drew a breath. "It was . . . Mr. Atkins."

"Randall?" Francesca's brows furrowed. "That's impossible. They don't even know each other."

Beth didn't say anything.

Kane's next question was directed at Francesca. "Was Randall here earlier?"

She nodded. "He came to take me out to lunch, but I told him I couldn't go." She frowned, trying to make sense out of what she had just heard.

"Did you tell him you were meeting Diana?"

"No."

"Where did he tell you he was going?"

"Home." The frown deepened. "He didn't have a car, so I told him to take mine."

"Where do you keep it?"

A knot formed in Francesca's stomach. "In my space in the garage." She gave a hard shake of her head. "But it couldn't be Randall, because he had no reason to go down to the lobby. He could have gone directly from my office to the garage."

"I think I can answer that," Vicki interjected. "Mr. Atkins came to my desk earlier and asked me to run an errand for him."

"What kind of errand?"

"He gave me money to buy all the flowers from that woman at the corner of Mason and asked that they be delivered to your office while you were out to lunch."

Kane glanced at Francesca, who nodded. "They arrived a little while ago."

Kane turned toward the three hotel employees. "Thank you all for your help. If you remember anything else, please let Mrs. Atkins know." Then, taking Francesca's arm, he said, "Show me where you park your car."

She ran to keep up with his long strides. "Kane, I

know what you're thinking. But believe me, there is no connection between Diana's disappearance and Randall. I'm sure of that."

"Then how do you explain that she took off after him?"

"Maybe Beth was mistaken. Maybe, she only *thought* she saw Diana run after Randall. Maybe she was running after someone else."

He shook his head. "I don't think one of your employees would make a mistake like that, do you, Francesca? They're trained to be not only efficient, but observant as well. Besides, she sounded quite positive, and since Randall *was* at the reception desk at just about that time, her claim is even more valid."

The elevator doors slid open, and they went in. Moments later, they stood in front of Francesca's parking space. As they had both suspected, the Jaguar was gone.

"Damn," Kane muttered under his breath. "Where the hell could he have taken her?"

Francesca's cheeks colored. "I don't like what you're implying, Kane. You're talking as if Randall had abducted Diana."

"You can't deny the whole thing looks strangely suspicious."

"It could be purely coincidental."

"Coincidental or not, I'm calling Sergeant Kosak."

His face grim, he walked up and down the parking space, looking for evidence that Diana had been here, hoping she might have left a clue. There was nothing. Just a dark, empty space.

And a feeling in his gut that Diana's life was hanging by a thread.

Heading west toward Seacliff, Randall kept his hands tightly gripped around the steering wheel.

Whenever a break in the traffic permitted it, he turned around to make sure Diana was still unconscious. Before leaving the garage, he had tied her hands and feet with two pieces of rope he had found in the trunk of the car and gagged her by stuffing his handkerchief into her mouth. Then he had laid her limp body on the floor in the back and covered it with newspapers.

What the hell was he going to do with her?

With a hand that was as damp as the rest of him, he wiped the perspiration off his forehead.

There was only one answer to that question.

He had to kill her.

But how? His gaze slanted toward the Beretta .32 automatic on the seat next to him. A year ago, when a doctor who lived in their building was attacked while waiting at a red light, Randall had insisted Francesca buy a gun and learn how to use it.

"I'm not going to let you drive home late at night unless you have some sort of protection with you," he had told her shortly after that brutal attack.

They had taken the lessons together and decided to keep the Beretta, fully loaded, in the glove compartment of her car.

Now he would have to use it—in cold blood—on another human being.

Could he do it? Was he capable of aiming a gun at a living person and pulling the trigger?

He had to. It was a mater of survival. It was either her or him.

He ran his tongue over dry lips. Oh, God, what had he gotten himself into?

Sitting in Francesca's rose-toned office, which at the moment was overpowered with the smell of hundreds of flowers, Sergeant Kosak listened quietly as Kane briefed him on the events that had just occurred. From time to time, he glanced at Francesca, but she kept staring out the window, her back to him. Other than hello, she hadn't said a word since he had arrived.

"Mrs. Atkins," he said at last when Kane was finished, "do you concur with everything Mr. Sanders said so far?"

She turned around slowly. "Everything except that crazy notion of his that my husband kidnapped Diana Wells."

"Have you tried to reach your husband?"

She looked away. "Yes. He isn't home yet."

"Do you have a phone in your car?"

"Yes."

He could see she wasn't going to make it easy for him. "And?"

"He doesn't answer. But that doesn't mean anything. He could be out of range. That happens frequently."

"Or," Kane remarked, "it could be that he doesn't want to answer."

She spun around to face him. "Why don't you just say what's on your mind, Kane? Instead of making all those ridiculous insinuations?"

"All right, then, I'll say it. I think Randall killed your brother. And I think Randall is the man Diana bumped into on her way to the penthouse that Thursday afternoon. She recognized him and that's why she ran after him."

"The man she bumped into wore a name tag! Which means he was attending the Desert Storm reunion."

"I don't have an explanation for that. But the fact is she didn't recognize any of the photographs we showed her. Which means she could have been mistaken about seeing a name tag.''

"What about what she told you about him not wearing glasses? Could she have been mistaken about that, too?''

"Possibly.''

She gave him a scathing look. "Possibly. Mistaken. With words like that, how can you call it a positive identification?''

Kosak stood up. "Regardless of whether or not she identified the right man, the fact remains that Diana followed your husband to the garage and never returned. And Mr. Atkins is nowhere to be found.''

The lost look in her eyes made him wish he could be wrong about her husband. She was a good kid. And she reminded him a lot of his daughter, loyal to a fault. "Do you have any idea where he may have gone?''

She shook her head.

"The ranch!'' Kane, who had been impatiently pacing the floor, came to a dead halt. "There's no one there during the week, except a deaf caretaker.''

"You're crazy,'' Francesca shot at him. "Why would he take her there . . .''

Kosak silenced them both with a wave of his hand. "Does your husband own a gun, Mrs. Atkins?''

"No, but I do. I bought it a year ago when—''

"Where do you keep it?''

The blood drained from her face. "In the glove compartment of my car.''

Kosak was already on the phone, calling for squad cars to be dispatched to the Lindford ranch. His last words, "The suspect is armed and possibly dangerous,'' sent a chill down Francesca's spine.

When the door slammed shut behind the two men, she stared at it for a long time. Her eyes were dry, but her hands shook as she clasped them in front of her mouth.

She hadn't wanted to believe them. How could Randall, so sweet and gentle, be a murderer? Yet, the evidence against him was building up by the minute. She remembered his reaction when she had told him about the man Diana had bumped into, how adamant he had been that she shouldn't get involved, shouldn't help Kane. Had he been afraid he and Diana would eventually meet? And that she would recognize him?

Beside her, the phone rang. In an automatic gesture, she extended her arm and picked it up. "Yes, Amy?"

"Dr. Geary's on the line."

She closed her eyes. "Put him through."

"Congratulations, my dear," the obstetrician said, not bothering with a hello. "Your intuition was right after all. You and that handsome husband of yours are about to become proud parents."

36

As Randall had expected, the Lindford ranch was deserted when he parked the Jaguar in front of the guest cottage. Luther, the deaf caretaker who watched the place on a year-round basis, spent most of his time inside his apartment above the garage, tinkering with his trains.

Randall felt safe here. Four miles away from its nearest neighbors, the ranch was accessible only through a private road no one but the Lindfords ever used.

Stepping out of the car, he opened the back door. Somehow, Diana had managed to sit up and was watching him, her green gaze so filled with hostility that if she hadn't been tied up he was sure she would have struck him.

Holding her by the waist, he pulled her out of the car and set her on the ground for a moment before hoisting her over his shoulder.

She fought him hard, writhing and kicking her legs, making it difficult for him to hang on to her. Fumbling in his pants pocket, he brought out a set of keys, selected one, and opened the door.

The cottage, hardly ever used anymore, was dark and musty, every blind drawn to shut out the light. With a grunt he dropped Diana on the living room sofa and turned on a table lamp.

He had to figure out what to do with her—and how

to dispose of the body afterward. His hands trembling, he lay the Beretta on the coffee table.

Christ, how did hard-core murderers do it? How did they think of everything?

Many don't. That's why they get caught.

He wouldn't get caught. He would take his time and plot everything very carefully, down to the smallest detail.

Ignoring Diana's hot, angry gaze as it followed him, he started to pace the width of the small living room. At the moment the safest plan of action was to shoot her and dump her in the ocean. That way there wouldn't be a body.

But that could be risky. What if she got caught on one of those rocks down below?

Maybe he could shoot her and bury her somewhere on the property. Since no one knew she was with him, the police would have no reason to come looking for her here.

On the sofa Diana was getting restless, kicking her legs and making incoherent sounds. Exasperated because the racket interfered with his thinking, he walked over to her and yanked the handkerchief from her mouth. "What the hell do you want?"

"I have to go to the bathroom."

"Tough." He circled around the room like a lion in a cage. "This is all your fault. I told you you had the wrong guy, but no, you couldn't leave it alone, could you? You had to go and be Dick Tracy."

She threw him a murderous look. "I was trying to save my life."

He didn't answer.

"Where are we?"

"At my mother-in-law's ranch."

"What are you going to do to me?" She already knew the answer to that, but drawing him into a conversation, making him talk about alternatives, might convince him to change his mind.

"I'm going to kill you."

So much for that.

"And if you think of trying anything, like screaming or escaping, forget it." He picked up the gun and waved it at her. "I won't hesitate to use this again if I have to."

Diana nodded obediently. The back of her head still throbbed from the first blow, and she had no intention of encouraging him to hit her again. Besides, she had to conserve her energy for more important things.

Like escaping.

But how was she going to accomplish that with her hands and feet tied and him holding a gun on her?

Would he really use it? she wondered. He hadn't had any qualms about hitting her on the head, but to actually shoot someone was quite different. She remembered Francesca's comment about Randall loving children. How bad could a man who loved children be?

Just as bad as the next guy if his life is threatened.

Opting for a different approach, she took a deep breath. "Whatever you plan to do with me, you can't do it here. People saw me while I was waiting for your wife. They'll—"

"What?"

"I said you can't—"

"You were waiting for my wife? What for?"

"She and I were supposed to have lunch together at twelve-fifteen. Didn't she tell you?"

Christ. Randall ran his fingers through his hair, remembering his earlier conversation with Francesca. Why hadn't she told him the truth instead of making up that story about the wine distributor? He wouldn't have gone down to the lobby if he had known Diana was there. And he wouldn't be in this mess right now.

"She *didn't* tell you."

"Shut up." He slumped in a chair, his head in his hands. This changed everything. Francesca would wonder where Diana was. She would question the staff, find out he had been in the lobby, talking to Vicki at the desk.

But so what? What did that prove?

"Why did you kill Travis?"

It wasn't what she said as much as how she said it that made him look up. There was a softness in her voice, a look in her eyes that reminded him of Francesca. He pulled his hands down, dragging them along his cheeks. "I didn't mean to do it. We were struggling. For a moment I thought he was going to strangle me. The bookend was right there. I only meant to . . ."

He shook his head. Why the hell was he confiding in her?

"Are you saying it was self-defense? That you didn't go there with the intention to kill him?"

"Of course I didn't go there with the intention to kill him! I'm not a cold-blooded murderer."

Diana fell back against the sofa. Thank God. There might be a way out of this nightmare, after all. "Then you have nothing to worry about."

"What the hell are you talking about? I killed a man."

"Yes, but it was self-defense—not premeditated murder. There's a big difference, Randall. With Kane as your attorney, you—"

The wail of police sirens pierced the air. Randall jumped from his chair, ran to the window, and peered through the blinds. Three squad cars, moving at high speed, were coming up the winding road, lights flashing. A quarter of a mile behind them, an unmarked car was gaining on them.

"Jesus Christ."

Feeling trapped, he picked up the gun from the table and looked around him. He couldn't stay here. They would surround the house in an instant. He had to be out in the open, where he could keep an eye on them. Make some sort of deal.

"Come on," he said, yanking Diana from the sofa.

"I can't!" she cried, stumbling. "I'm tied up, remember?"

Without letting go of the gun, he knelt down to untie her ankles. Then they were running out a back door and across a deck that jutted over the cliffs. Below, the ocean roared.

"Don't try anything," he said, shoving the gun barrel under her jaw.

"What are you—"

"Shut up." He opened a gate and forced her down a rocky path that wound is way through the cliffs. Where the wooden guard rail ended, he stopped.

With a muffled cry, Diana glanced down at the dark, ragged rocks below and the surf pounding against them. Her hands, tied behind her back, gripped the guard rail. It wasn't much, but that's all she had.

"Atkins!"

At the sound of his name, Randall turned around. Kane was the first one he saw, then Sergeant Kosak. Behind them, half a dozen uniformed policemen were already in position, their shotguns aimed.

"Let her go, Atkins, or so help me God I'll kill you with my bare hands."

"You're in no position to make demands, Kane." He had to shout to make himself heard above the sound of the surf. "You either, Sergeant. So call off your dogs. Go back to your cars and get the hell out of here. Unless you want to see her going over the edge.''

As he shifted his weight from one foot to the other, Diana bit her bottom lip to hold back a scream. One false move and they would both be going over the edge.

"Take it easy, Randall," Kosak shouted back. "All we want to do is talk."

"You want to put my ass in prison."

"I'm willing to cut you a deal if you cooperate. But you've got to let Diana go. Unharmed."

They were lying. Trying to trick him . . .

"Randall!"

He looked up at the same time Kane and Kosak whipped around. Francesca stood just behind them, her long hair flying in the wind, slapping against her face. She took a step forward before Kosak stretched his arm out to prevent her from going any farther.

Randall saw them argue. Francesca kept shaking her head. Then, at last, the policeman lowered his arm.

"Randall, I'm coming down," she called out. "Don't do anything foolish."

He didn't reply. His throat tight with emotion, he watched her come along the path. Her face was white as she held tightly onto the railing. She had always had a mortal fear of heights.

Five feet away, she stopped, unable to go any farther.

"You shouldn't have come," he said in a strangled voice.

"Wouldn't you have done the same if the situation had been reversed?'

"I didn't want you to see me like this."

"You're my husband, Randall. And I love you. Nothing can ever change that."

"I killed your brother."

"I know. But please don't make it worse by killing an innocent woman, too. Give yourself up, Randall. Let Kane help you."

Randall shook his head. "No."

"Randall, listen to me—"

"Tell them to leave, Francesca. Once they're gone, I'll keep Diana with me until I'm safe, and then I'll let her go."

"What about you? Where will you go?"

"I don't know . . . I'll let you know when I get there. I'll send for you."

"Is that the kind of life you want for us, Randall? For our child?"

Randall stared at her. "What did you say?"

"I'm pregnant, Randall. We're going to have a baby. That's why I came. I knew that once you found out you were going to be a father, you would do the right thing."

He shook his head, and Diana felt him sag against her. "Randall, please," she whispered, trying to sink her heels into the gravel. "I can't support both of us."

He didn't seem to hear her. "You can't be pregnant."

"It's the truth. Remember how sick I've been these past few mornings? And today? It was morning sickness, Randall. I suspected it, but didn't want to tell you for fear of disappointing you in case it was another false alert. So I went to see Dr. Geary before work."

"You really are . . . We're really going to have a baby?"

Tears streamed down her cheeks. "Dr. Geary confirmed it a little while ago."

The arm that had held Diana so tightly, slackened. The gun slipped out of his hand, ricocheting over the cliffs before being swallowed by the surf.

Quick as lightning, Diana tore away from him, aware that Kane was already running toward her, past Francesca. He caught her as she stumbled. Strong arms closed around her.

"Are you all right?"

"Yes."

He dragged her close and held her there. "Thank God."

Two policemen were already making their way down the path. As Kane untied Diana's wrists, she turned around. Francesca was in Randall's arms, sobbing helplessly.

"Come on," Kane said gently, leading Diana back toward the cottage. "You've seen enough for one day."

37

It was six o'clock by the time Francesca returned to the Lindford Hotel. She had declined Kane's offer to drive her back to Margaret's penthouse, and had gone there alone, her eyes red from too much crying and her heart heavy with a sorrow she was certain would never go away.

Now, sitting in a chair in her mother's drawing room, she leaned her head back and answered her questions quietly, fearful that any show of emotion would only upset her mother more.

"After listening to Randall's statement, the D.A. agreed to have the charge reduced to manslaughter, but he'll still have to answer to kidnapping charges and illegal possession of a gun."

"Will they grant him bail?"

"Kane says yes. The bail hearing is tomorrow at ten o'clock. He'll have to stay in jail until then."

"And you said Kane agreed to represent him?"

"Yes. He's been very helpful throughout this entire ordeal, Mother. Very kind—Diana, too."

"I'm glad." Margaret sat down in the chair across from Francesca, still trying to absorb all that her daughter had told her. A number of emotions, ranging from shock to a debilitating rage, had threatened to break that famous self-restraint of hers. But although it had taken a tremendous effort, she had kept it all under control. For Francesca's sake.

Her gaze drifted over the beautiful, tired features. "How are you holding up, darling?"

Francesca shrugged. "I don't know. I'm too numb to tell."

"Is there anything I can do?"

Francesca closed her eyes. "Make it all go away, Mother. Tell me it was all a horrible nightmare and it's all right to go back to sleep."

"I wish I could." She took her daughter's hand in hers and held it, gently stroking the smooth white skin with her thumbs. She, too, had felt numb at first, shocked that someone she had trusted so implicitly and loved like a son could have done this to her. "Why don't I ask Marcie to make you some soup? And perhaps some tea. It will—"

"I don't want anything."

"Francesca—"

"I'm pregnant, Mother."

The stroking stopped abruptly, and there was a short intake of breath, almost like a sigh. "Oh."

"I found out this morning," Francesca continued, opening her eyes at last. "That's why I went to the ranch to talk to Randall."

In a rare show of affection, Margaret hugged her. "Oh, Francesca. I . . . I don't know what to say."

"Say that you're happy for me. I am. I think a baby will give Randall the courage he needs to get through the next few months."

"Of course I'm happy for you. This is wonderful news." Then, a crease of worry forming between her brows, she asked, "Are you all right? Physically I mean. You didn't fall or anything."

"I'm fine. A little nauseated, nothing more."

"You'll spend the night here. And tomorrow, we'll

go to the bail hearing together. Whatever the bail is, I'll pay it." Her initial wish had been to see the bastard rot in jail, but there was Francesca to consider. And now, a child. That made all the difference in the world.

"There'll be reporters there, Mother—lots of them."

Margaret shrugged. "After all this family has gone through in the past couple of months, what's another two or three dozen reporters?"

A small smile tugged the corners of Francesca's mouth. "That's what Diana said."

Diana. Margaret sighed. That girl had gone through hell because of her. "How is she doing, Francesca?"

"Amazingly well, considering. She's a real trouper, Mother. A lot like you in that respect. I think you would enjoy knowing her."

Margaret was silent for a moment as she remembered the feisty young woman who had stood up to her. "As a matter of fact, I was planning to visit her in a day or two—if she'll see me, that is."

Francesca squeezed her hand. "She'll see you."

Margaret gazed at her daughter for a few seconds more. "What about you, Francesca? Will you ever be able to forgive me?"

"Forgive you for what?"

"For slighting you, for thinking that because you were a girl, you had to be denied the opportunity to run this hotel."

Francesca waved the remark away. "You did what you thought you had to do, Mother. All that is behind us now."

"But not over. In a few days, when you feel up to it, I would like to sit down with you and discuss your future. And the future of the Lindford."

Francesca held back a sarcastic chuckle. She had

waited so long for this moment, and now that it was here, it no longer meant anything. But she was a Lindford, born and bred, and therefore, she would do what was expected of her. "Yes, Mother, in a few days."

The Parkers, Kane, and Diana sat in Kat's living room, the remains of a pepperoni pizza on the table in front of them. Except for Mitch, who still claimed to be a growing boy, no one had eaten very much.

"What happens now?" Kat asked, filling up Diana's glass with iced tea. "I mean besides the charges against Diana being dropped."

One arm around Diana's shoulder, Kane leaned back against the sofa, pulling her back with him. "Randall made a full confession and will plead guilty, which means the state won't have to go through the expense of a long trial. The sentencing judge will most likely take that into consideration, plus the fact that Randall was acting in self-defense."

Mitch, a handsome man with brown hair and the physique of a linebacker, helped himself to one more slice of pizza. "Do you feel comfortable representing him, Kane? Considering what he did to Diana?"

Kane nodded. "Diana and I discussed it. Randall isn't a bad guy. He got off on the wrong track there for a while, but he doesn't have the instincts of a killer—or of a blackmailer for that matter. He even went to bat for Joe O'Keefe, the private investigator who bugged Travis's penthouse. Apparently, O'Keefe is an old friend of Randall's and he was afraid he'd get in trouble with the law."

"Bugging *is* illegal."

"I know. But since that tape O'Keefe made helped prove the conspiracy between Nick Wells and Travis,

thus making it possible to close that case, Kosak chose
to let O'Keefe off the hook."

"What about Margaret?" Kat asked. "Will she be
prosecuted for keeping silent about her husband's defrauding the government?"

"No. She didn't know about Charles's activities until
after his death and had no intention of benefitting
from the money. That plus the fact that she's given
so much money to charity over the last forty years had
a lot to do with the U.S. attorney's decision not to
prosecute. The most she can expect is a stiff fine.
What the scandal will do to the hotel, however, is another matter."

Her head resting against Kane's arm, Diana stared
at a spot on the ceiling. "The one I truly feel sorry
for is Francesca. She was trying to be so brave the
other day, but I know she's scared. I hate to think
what this ordeal will do to her and the baby."

"She'll be just fine," Kane said. "You and I will
make sure of that."

"What about you, kiddo?" Kat asked Diana. "Are
you excited about going back to work without that
damn trial hanging over your head?"

Diana sat up and took a sip of her iced tea, gently
twirling the ice in the glass. She thought of Zack, so
happy in Glen Ellen. Exciting things were happening
to him every day, and she hated the though of dis-
rupting his life once again. "I should be, but strangely
enough, I'm not."

"With all this publicity, business will probably be
booming by week's end."

"Probably."

"You're still in a state of shock over what happened.
It will pass," Kat assured her.

"Perhaps."

An hour later, Kane and Diana were driving toward

Glen Ellen to attend the Christmas play and witness Zack's big moment on the stage. As they came off the Golden Gate Bridge, Kane turned toward Diana. "Have you made any plans for Zack's birthday yet? It's in a few days, isn't it?"

She hadn't forgotten, but she loved him for remembering. "I have made tentative plans. Beckie, of course, wants to have a huge party for him with ponies and clowns, but I'm leaning more toward something small and intimate, with a few close friends and family."

"Sounds good to me."

"When I gave Beckie my list of prospective guests, she balked—at first."

He raised a questioning eyebrow. "Balked? That doesn't sound like Aunt Beckie."

"She didn't balk at the number of guests, but rather at one of the persons I want to invite."

"Who's that?"

"Margaret."

He shot her a quick look before returning his eyes to the road. "Are you serious?"

She nodded. "I think there's been enough bad blood between her and me, don't you think? And as much as I have been trying to forget it, she is Zack's grandmother."

When Kane didn't reply, she rested her hand on his thigh. "I know you still haven't come to terms with what she did. And I might never forget that she was the force behind the custody suit, that if it hadn't been for her, none of this would have happened."

"Then why do you feel sorry for her?"

"Because I think she's suffered enough. And because she's an old lady."

"She's a tough broad."

"Perhaps. But the truth is, it would be good for

Zack to have a grandmother. He liked her a lot, you know. Right from the start." When he didn't answer, she inched closer to him and laid her head on his shoulder. "Have you ever heard the saying 'Every cloud has a silver lining'?"

"What about it?"

"You were my silver lining," she said softly. "If it hadn't been for the Lindfords, I would have never met you." When he squeezed her hand, she added, "So what do you say, Counselor? We give Margaret another chance?"

Kane smiled. If he had learned one thing about Diana, it was that she possessed an incredible ability to forgive. "I might be swayed," he said, pretending to still be somewhat reluctant.

"Oh?" Catching the teasing light in his eyes, she snuggled even closer. "And just what is it going to take to sway you?"

"Well . . ." Without taking his eyes off the road, he bent his head to kiss her hair and inhaled deeply. Those wildflowers again. Driving him crazy. "Do you remember Ted Grant, that old man we talked about at Thanksgiving dinner? The lawyer who's retiring in a few days."

"I remember."

"Well . . . I've been thinking of taking over his practice."

She looked at him. "Really? You would move to Sonoma? Give up your career as a criminal lawyer and take on a *family* practice?"

"You don't think I would make a good family lawyer?"

"It isn't that . . ." She was taken aback, didn't know what to say. The distance between San Francisco and Sonoma, combined with their conflicting schedules, would definitely put a crimp in their relationship. A chill went through her. Or did he intend to end the relationship? "It's just that I'm surprised . . . I would have thought—"

"Don't you want to know what this has to do with my being swayed?"

"Sure." But her mind was no longer on the pleasant banter.

"Well, it has to do with the practice itself, you see. No self-respecting country lawyer would dare start a family practice without being a family man himself. Otherwise, what sort of example would he be setting in the community? And how could he relate to the myriad problems he'll inherit from his predecessor if he remains a bitter old bachelor?"

There was a thump in her chest, and it was a few seconds until she realized it was her heart. "Kane, what are you saying?"

He pulled to the side of the road and brought the car to a stop. "I'm saying that I can't live without you, Miss Wells. I'm saying that I want you with me until I'm old and feeble. I'm saying that I love you more than I thought I could ever love any woman. And I'm crazy about Zack, too, and can't wait to be a real father to him, not just a buddy . . ."

The words had her heart jumping into her throat. Until now, she hadn't realized how she had longed to hear them. "Kane, I—"

Worried she was trying to let him down gently, he laid a finger on her mouth, "I know this Sonoma idea is a little unexpected. But when I heard you tell Kat you weren't very excited about returning to work, I started thinking that maybe a change of scenery was exactly what you needed. You could sell Harbor View and start looking for another restaurant in Sonoma. Glen Ellen may not have the sophistication of San

Francisco, but you have to admit that it has a charm all its own. And Zack loves it out there—"

Laughing, she took his face between her hands. "Oh, darling," she said breathlessly, "will you please shut up so that I can accept your proposal?"

Relief made his knees go weak. For a moment all he wanted to do was take her in his arms and crush his mouth to hers. Unable to resist having a little fun, however, he held her back. "Proposal?" he dead-panned. "Who said anything about a proposal? All I want is a friendly woman, preferably a pretty one, to wash my socks, cook my meals, keep my house clean—"

The rest of his sentence was lost in a fiery kiss.

If you loved *Silver Lining* be sure
not to miss Christiane Heggan's equally
sensational *Passions* and *Betrayals*.

Passions

Passion's Promise

Paige Granger lives in a world of passions—
passions that possessed her, passions she inspires.
From the California gold coast, to the winding
canals of Venice, to the high-rises of Manhattan,
she pursues the most beautiful works of art
in the world.

Passion's Secret

But with passion comes peril as Paige is led from
a marriage of true love to an obsessive love
triangle . . . and discovers the greed and lust and
savage intrigue behind the seductive masks of
those in power . . . and those she trusts the most.

Passion's Price

As Paige finds herself torn between the ex-husband
she still loves and the husband-to-be she should love,
she is forced to heed the timeless needs of the heart
to decide which passions are worth what price. . . .

"A sophisticated, compelling tale of love,
emotions and manipulation. Finely crafted and
superbly written . . . first-rate entertainment."
—Lucianne Goldberg,
author of *Madame Cleo's Girls*

Betrayals

*In a world of glamorous passion, no one knows
Stephanie Farrell's secrets; no one knows of the
betrayals that have scarred her forever; and no
one knows of the danger in her past that is
threatening to destroy her....*

On the surface, Stephanie Farrell appears to have it
all, as one of television's most in-demand
actresses and the mother of a beautiful daughter.
But beneath her carefully constructed image is a
girl whose childhood was scarred by a tyrannical
father and whose one chance at happiness was
overturned by a shocking betrayal....

Miles away, in a small town, someone is plotting
revenge. Someone who is tied to Stephanie in a
way she cannot imagine, and who has been torn
from her by one man's greed and lust. As
Stephanie climbs to the highest heights of fame
and success, she must face the man she thinks
betrayed her long ago—the only man she
ever loved. But she must also face the one
person who knows her secrets—and who
threatens all she holds dear....

"CHRISTIANE HEGGAN IS RAPIDLY
BECOMING A VOICE
TO BE RECKONED WITH!"
—*Rave Reviews*

"A MAGNIFICENT WORK!"
—*Affaire de Coeur*